Max

Max

JUVAL AVIV

C

Century · London

Published by Century in 2006

1 3 5 7 9 10 8 6 4 2

Copyright © Juval Aviv 2006

Juval Aviv has asserted his right under the Copyright, Designs and
Patents Act, 1988 to be identified as the author of this work

First published in the United Kingdom in 2006 by Century
The Random House Group Limited
20 Vauxhall Bridge Road, London SW1V 2SA

Random House Australia (Pty) Limited
20 Alfred Street, Milsons Point, Sydney,
New South Wales 2061, Australia

Random House New Zealand Limited
18 Poland Road, Glenfield
Auckland 10, New Zealand

Random House South Africa (Pty) Limited
Isle of Houghton, Corner of Boundary Road & Carse O'Gowrie,
Houghton 2198, South Africa

The Random House Group Limited Reg. No. 954009

www.randomhouse.co.uk

A CIP catalogue record for this book is available
from the British Library

Papers used by Random House are
natural, recyclable products made from wood grown in
sustainable forests. The manufacturing processes conform to
the environmental regulations of the country of origin

ISBN 1 84413 875 5
ISBN-13 978 1 844 13875 3 (from Jan 2007)

Typeset by SX Composing DTP, Rayleigh, Essex
Printed and bound in Great Britain by
Mackays of Chatham plc, Chatham, Kent

While the character Max Robertson is based on Robert Maxwell and this novel deals with the various theories behind his death, all other characters in the book, his family and associates, are fictitious and are the product of the author's imagination. They are not in any way linked to any real person whether living or dead and, should there be any resemblance to actual persons, then it is entirely coincidental.

Juval Aviv is President and CEO of Interfor Inc., an international corporate intelligence and investigations firm. Before founding Interfor, Juval Aviv served as an officer in the Israel Defence Force leading an elite Commando/Intelligence Unit and was later selected by the Israeli Secret Service (Mossad) to participate in a number of intelligence and special operations in many countries in the late 1960s and 1970s. In 1984, a true account of one mission was published, entitled *Vengeance*, which inspired the major motion picture, *Munich*, directed by Steven Spielberg.

To Tsila, Atalya, Don, Todd, Zoé and Lula for their immeasurable love and support.

ACKNOWLEDGEMENTS

I wish to acknowledge the steadfast guidance of my publisher and editor, Mark Booth, whose patience and words of wisdom helped bring this book to fruition. Also, I would like to thank Matthew Lynn for his invaluable contribution.

Many thanks to Daniel Aharoni, Esq., my lawyer and best friend, for always keeping me out of harm's way.

I am indebted to my staff at Interfor Inc. for their endless support.

ONE

Sam could tell within seconds the woman wasn't going to buy anything. She paused to examine some of the treasures displayed within the crowded space: first an eighteenth-century German writing desk; then a nineteenth-century British carriage clock; next a gilt-edged mirror made in France. None of them detained her attention for more than a few seconds.

Whatever she wants, decided Sam, it's not an antique.

Genuine customers had a certain manner to them, one Sam had learned to recognise in the three years since he had opened up this business in among the strip of antique shops lining both sides of Pimlico Road. The shop was just one room measuring twelve feet by twenty, its walls painted a distressed white, and its floors polished wood. Sam kept it disorganised, putting piece next to piece to create the impression of chaos. It had been much neater when he started out, but he soon discovered it was better to let the shop look a bit of a mess. Most of the customers were collectors, and they had a masochistic streak to them: the harder you made it for them to find something, the happier they were.

Antique lovers were a well-defined breed. They all had their own interests and enthusiasms. As soon as they walked into the shop, they scanned it, hungrily seeking out their own passions. It might be pictures, rugs, furniture, glassware, whatever. They were only ever interested in one thing. Anyone examining desks, clocks and mirrors was a phoney.

'Mr Wolfman?' said the woman.

She ran her finger along the edge of the desk. It was an item Sam had bought on a trip to Frankfurt three months ago, and he was hoping to turn a good profit on it. A heavy, solid writing desk, twisted with ornaments set into its wooded surface, it had been polished until it gleamed. The desk had been made in a workshop in Gladbach where Jean-Henri Riesener had trained: Riesener went on to become the chief cabinetmaker to the court of Louis XVI. He completed the famous Bureau du Roi, considered by many the finest piece of furniture ever made, and now on display at the Louvre in Paris.

This desk was nothing like the Bureau du Roi: a simple piece of furniture, it had probably been made for a local businessman by a cabinetmaker who never even met Riesener. Still, for the right kind of collector, any connection to Riesener was worth paying for. The antiques trade wasn't so unlike the assassination trade he sometimes told himself. You just had to know your target, and close in on it.

'It was made in Gladbach,' said Sam, standing next to the woman. 'Eighteenth century.'

She looked at him and smiled. About thirty-five, Sam judged. The same age as his wife. Yet the woman in front of him had more swagger and verve about her. More time to look after herself, Sam thought. And probably more money as well. Her blonde hair was tied back into a ponytail, held in place with an emerald-green ribbon, and her cheekbones were delicate, sculpted as sharply as a pair of scissors. She was wearing blue jeans, with a Ralph Lauren label, and a black top. A string of pearls swung from her thin neck. Her lips were red and full, looking slightly out of place on the delicacy of the rest of her face, as if they had been put there by a surgeon.

'Where's that?' she said.

Her blue eyes were resting upon Sam's face for a fraction longer than necessary: she seemed to be appraising him, with perfect self-confidence, the same way a few seconds earlier she had been appraising the desk.

'Germany,' Sam said.

'I'm not interested in German desks,' she said. 'French.'

Sam could smell champagne on her breath as he walked back to his own chair. Yes, she's rich, he thought. Rents on the Pimlico Road were high, business sometimes slow, and even though he ran the shop as a cover, Mossad still expected the outfit at least to break even. His accounts were scrutinised by Adi Siegel, the chief accountant back in Tel Aviv.

The first year he'd run at such a loss, Siegel had refused to believe it: they'd accused him of stealing from the Supreme Institute for Intelligence and Special Assignments, to give the Israeli secret service its long and formal name, which was invariably shortened to Mossad, the Hebrew word for institute. 'Don't be ridiculous,' Sam had said angrily. 'I'm out there every day risking my life for this organisation. If I wanted to steal from it, there would be a lot smarter ways than running a few phoney invoices through an antiques business.'

'He doesn't mind being called a thief,' Siegel had said to Hanna, the ancient, crooked-backed old woman who helped maintain the ledger. 'It's being called an idiot he doesn't like.' He'd paused, looking back up at Sam. 'I think you might be both. I'll be watching you, Mr Wolfman.'

The allegation had stung. The second year, the loss was a bit smaller. This year, he should break even. Next year, a small profit maybe. Antiques were a natural business for an assassin trying to disguise his true profession: there was plenty of scope for travelling, most of the deals were completed in cash, and nobody thought it was suspicious if the shop was closed for several days at a time.

'French?' he said, looking back at the woman. 'Bureaux are, of course, a French speciality.' He smiled, trying to recognise the label of the champagne on her lips. Moët maybe. Or a Charles Heidsieck. Something expensive.

'A Gastou.'

Sam shook his head. 'A Gastou? I can't say I've heard of it.'

The woman rested her handbag on Sam's desk. A neat, black Chanel bag, it was open a fraction, and Sam could see a tube of lipstick and a bundle of fifty-pound notes inside. 'Hervé Gastou. He had a workshop in Senlis, about forty miles from Paris, in the 1850s and 60s. He made writing desks. Exquisite.' She paused. 'I'm hoping to find one somewhere.'

'I don't know of any pieces by Gastou for sale right now. At least not in London.'

The woman smiled. 'Ask around,' she said.

Reaching to the desk, she picked up her handbag, pushing aside the bundle of notes, and took out her wallet. She placed her card down on the desk. Sam glanced down. Selima Robertson. Of course. I thought I recognised her from the papers. Selima Robertson was the stepdaughter of Max Robertson, the billionaire publishing and newspaper tycoon who had died three months earlier, in November 1989 in mysterious circumstances. Robertson had married her Swiss-born mother in 1957 when Selima was two, but her mother had died in a car crash two years later, and Robertson had raised her as his own child. She looks better than her pictures, though, he decided. More vibrant. More lively. And more earthy. The pictures in the papers portrayed an immaculately groomed billionaire's stepdaughter, but standing here in front of him, you could easily believe it was her that had crawled her way up from nothing, not her stepfather.

'If you find one, call me,' she continued.

Sam tucked the card into the top drawer of the desk. 'I was sorry to hear about your stepfather.'

Selima laughed, the sound peeling across the room, as if she were making a point. 'Then you're the only person who was.' Then she looked straight at him. Sam almost took a step back, surprised by the intensity of her stare. Then his eye was caught by the single diamond encased within a white-gold necklace. An expensive rock, Sam noted. Ten, maybe even twenty thousand pounds worth of stone. The Robertson family can't be quite as broke as the papers have been saying over the last few months.

'May I talk to you in private?' she asked.

'We better go to the back room,' Sam said.

They walked in silence, Sam leading the way, to a small office at the back. Upstairs, Sam kept a one-room apartment for his own use. In addition, there were another two flats: one owned by a barrister who spent a few days a week in London and the rest of the time with his family in Devon; the other by a Saudi businessman who only ever spent a couple of nights a month there. Sam said hello to them on the staircase. Nothing more. *In this building, we keep our lives private.*

At the centre of the office there was a Louis XV '*chinoiserie secrétaire*', an eighteenth-century French bureau, made in a mock-Chinese style that was briefly popular during Louis XV's reign. It was made from black wood, ornately decorated with oriental images picked out in gold on the writing table and across the drawers. Sam had found it in a village outside Troyes, paid a few hundred francs for it and had it restored. He'd expected to sell it for a decent profit, but after two years, it was still just taking up space in the shop, so he'd moved it into the back room to use himself.

'Take a seat,' he said.

Selima sat down in front of him, crossing her legs as she did so. Sam followed the curve of her thigh disappearing into the tight suede miniskirt.

'What do you want?' he asked.

Selima hesitated. He could see her eyes furrowing. How much to tell me, and how much to conceal, that's what she's asking herself.

'I want to find out what happened to my stepfather.'

'Buy a paper.'

A flash of anger shot through Selima's eyes. 'I want you to find out what *really* happened to him.'

'I'm an antiques dealer.'

'Right. And I'm a grieving stepdaughter.'

She leaned forward, the back of her hand brushing against the top of his knee. 'I know who you really are, Mr Wolfman.'

He scrutinised her face. All the intensity had drained away. Her expression was as flawless and unemotional as the rock hanging from her neck.

'I'm an antiques dealer,' he repeated, his tone flat.

'Mossad cover,' said Selima. 'They set you up with a small business so that your stay in London looks legitimate.'

Her eyes glanced up to meet Sam's. 'In reality you are Sam Wolfman, the son of Yoram Wolfman, one of the most famous Israeli spies of the 1960s. You joined the Israeli Army, then fought with the commandos. On leaving, you joined Mossad. You worked in security for the Prime Minister. Then five years ago you were given this mission. You became a *kidon*. A Mossad assassin. With the task of systematically assassinating the Palestinian terrorists operating out of Europe.' She smiled demurely. 'But then you already know your own CV.'

'You know a lot about Mossad?'

'My stepfather taught me.'

Sam paused. He had read the rumour reported in one of the papers that Robertson worked for Mossad but had paid little attention to it at the time. It was just one of the dozens of rumours about the billionaire businessman that had circulated since his death. Maybe it was true, maybe it wasn't. Mossad kept connections throughout the world, and it kept them secret even from its own people. The connections were known as the *sayanim*, derived from the Hebrew word *lessayeah*, to help, and there were believed to be about 200,000 of them around the world: Jews sympathetic to the State of Israel, who would perform useful functions on behalf of Mossad. A *sayan* working for a car rental agency would provide a car off the books; another running a hotel would supply information on its guests. It was the job of every *katsa*, or local case officer, to recruit a dozen *sayanim* in every town they could. They were stored away, kept ready, for the day when they would prove useful. Robertson could well have been among them.

'You see,' she said. 'I know everything about you. Including what you will do next.'

'And what will I do next?'

'Find out what happened to my stepfather.'

'He fell off his boat.'

Selima shook her head. 'There is more to it than that.'

'What?'

'I don't know, but I want you to find out.'

Sam reached across the desk for a copy of the Yellow Pages. 'Look for a detective. There's plenty in the book.'

'A detective is no good.'

'Why not?'

'They'll never get to the heart of it.'

'Then neither will I.'

Selima folded her hands across her lap. 'You're the best man there is,' she said decisively. 'Mossad is the best intelligence agency in the world, everyone knows that. You are their best man. There is simply no one else. Only you can discover whether Max Robertson is alive or dead.'

The words caught Sam by surprise. Of course, from following the papers, he knew there was some mystery about Robertson's death. But if there was any doubt that he was really dead at all, this was the first that Sam had heard about it.

'I saw his funeral.'

Selima laughed: a laugh that was both brittle and knowing at the same time. 'A man such as yourself should know that just about anything can be forged. If you can fake a life, then why shouldn't a man fake a death?'

Sam shrugged. 'I've heard of wives looking for husbands who have vanished,' he said, 'but not stepdaughters looking for their fathers. If he's alive, I should imagine he'll be in touch soon enough.'

'Not Daddy,' said Selima with a shake of the head. 'He cared about no one but himself. I think he might be alive, and I want you to find him for me.'

Sam stood up from his desk. There had been a brief moment, he reflected, where he might have been interested. In some parallel universe, the mystery of what happened to Max Robertson might have tempted him. But not in this one. His mission was almost finished. *All I want right now is to get it over with and retire.*

'I can't help you,' he said, steering her towards the door that led back into the interior of the shop.

'You'll regret it.'

Sam smiled. 'It takes a lot of work to even get into the top twenty of my regrets.'

'Call me when you change your mind,' said Selima.

'I'm not going to change my mind.'

Selima glanced across at him, with sudden warmth. 'You seem very certain,' she said. 'But we'll see.'

Sam shook his head. 'I'll call you if I find the desk,' he said. 'Nothing else.'

'A Gastou, yes,' Selima said with a shrug. 'Call me if you find a Gastou. I'd appreciate that.'

TWO

A row of beech trees lined the entrance to the chateau. It was sited just south of Orleans, in the border region where central France turned into the Loire Valley. Sam pulled the rented Ford Sierra to a stop at the start of the driveway. The early eighteenth-century house was set in twelve acres of parkland. There was a lake to one side, its surface speckled with lilies just starting to flower now that spring was close, and beside it an apple orchard. Next to that, there was a rectangular garden, sprinkled with plants, few of them yet in bloom this early in the year. Beyond it, there was a long series of formal lawns, broken up by pathways built from fading, grey stone.

One last request for information, thought Sam. Then this is over.

He locked the door on the car, deciding to walk the rest of the way. The driveway stretched for three hundred yards. *Enough time for a man to think about what he is going to say.*

Hassim. Sam turned the name over in his mind. Of the twelve names they had been given by Mossad five years ago, eleven were now dead. Hassim was the one name left on the list.

If I could just get to Hassim, then this mission could finally be laid to rest.

His life and Papa's had become curiously intertwined in the five years he had been working undercover. At the time he had been plucked out of the bodyguard unit and told that he had been chosen to lead a five-man *kidon* unit, who would track down and assassinate the twelve most dangerous Palestinian terrorists operating in Europe, Sam had never heard of Papa. He had never even imagined that such a man existed. Sometimes, when he thought about it, he still couldn't.

The *kidon* units had started operating right after the Munich Olympics of 1972. Palestinian terrorists had massacred the Israeli Olympics team, and the government had decided it could no longer tolerate the attacks on its people. It would fight terror with terror. The *kidon* units had spread out across Europe and the Middle East, tracking down the terrorists, and eliminating them with the same cold ruthlessness that they eliminated Israelis. It was not just a matter of removing your enemies, although that was important. Nor was it just a matter of punishing them, although that was important as well. They had to experience the fear of imminent death. A *kidon* unit would prepare each death with immaculate precision. Notes would be sent to the families letting them know who was responsible for the deaths of their sons and husbands. Each victim would know who would be killing him before he died. Terror, Sam could recall his Mossad instructor Zvi Imer telling him one evening, was too important a weapon to be left to the terrorists.

That was the official story anyway, although in recent years Sam had started to wonder about it. In reality, the hands of Mossad had been dripping in blood since the first roots of the Institute had been put down in the 1920s. When the Haganah, the underground Jewish army of pre-war Palestine had been formed, it had recognised from the start that it needed intelligence on its enemies if it was to have the remotest chance of survival. It had fought with determination, ruthlessness and a cold-blooded will to survive ever since.

10

It was Sam's father who first put him in touch with the old Papa. Yoram Wolfman had been a hero during the Arab-Israeli wars of the 1960s. Sam knew that much about him, even when he was growing up. What he didn't know was that his father had gone on to work for Mossad, been captured, tortured and broken by the Egyptians, and eventually abandoned by his old employer. By the time Sam saw him again, he was a sick man, the strength all drained out of him, bitter and angry about the way he had been let down. They had given him an Itur Hagvura, the country's highest military honour, and then they left him to rot.

Sam could recall going to see his father a few days before he had left for London. The old man had written down a phone number on a piece of paper. 'If you are in real trouble, then call this number,' he said. 'Ask for Papa. Tell him I told you to call. But remember,' he added, 'it's a last resort. Only call him if everything else fails.'

A last resort, thought Sam with a rueful smile. He'd called Papa about three weeks into the mission. What else was he meant to do? He'd been dropped into Europe with four colleagues. Their task was to track down and assassinate twelve terrorists. He had names on a list. That's all. No addresses. No phone numbers. No contacts. The training had prepared him for many things. But it hadn't prepared him for this.

After he was plucked out of the commandos and readied for life inside Mossad, the training had taught him everything that was known about survival. He'd been dropped down on the outskirts of Glasgow and been told to make his way down to London with no money and no papers. He'd had to steal food, and travel on trains without a ticket. There was no purpose to the journey: it was just a way of teaching him that he could make it on his own, with no support, no back-up, nothing to rely on apart from his own wits. Next, they'd dropped him into Cyprus and told him to do the same thing, just to see if he could survive in a place where he didn't even speak the language. He'd been taken in by MI6 for three months, and given their training in survival. Despite their image in the UK as a bunch of public-school bumblers, Mossad had become close to British intelligence over the years, particularly when the IRA was getting most of its arms from Arab terrorists. It had learned that when it came to disguise, subterfuge and assassination, there were no better tutors than the British. He had been taught how to forge bank accounts, passports, credit cards, the works.

But nothing had trained him for this. How were you meant to locate and destroy twelve men who had dedicated their lives to disappearing into thin air?

So three weeks into the mission, he'd called Papa. And after that he'd never looked back.

A curved stone staircase led up to the house. There were three cars parked on the gravel: two Renaults and a Mercedes. Sam wondered how many people might be there today. Certainly Papa – so far as Sam knew he hardly ever left the house these days. Probably Michel, his cousin. Maybe one or other of the sons? You could never tell. With Papa life was always a mystery tour.

'Is Papa expecting you?' Jacques said.

Jacques was the elder of the two sons. A man in his early fifties, his hair was still jet black, and his eyes deep brown. He was wearing a dark blue suit, with a white cotton shirt open at the collar. Sam had only met him a couple of times before, and had taken an instant dislike to him. Jacques had inherited most of his father's brute strength, but none of his subtlety and charm.

'I sent him a message,' Sam replied. 'I said I'd come and see him today.'

'He's with the nurse. You'll have to wait.'

Sam took one of the seats in the hallway. The chateau had

three wings, built around a central courtyard. In the heart of the countryside, it was far removed from any of the main tourist routes. Sam had no idea what the history of the castle might be. Built by some rogue duke, who plundered a fortune through torture and destruction, he liked to think. That would be appropriate.

Papa probably picked it up for nothing after the war. *When everyone else was poor and he was rich.*

Sam glanced at some of the pictures that hung on three of the hallway's walls. To the few people who knew of his existence, the old man was a legend, one of the few criminal entrepreneurs of real genius left in Europe. Born in 1907, of Sicilian ancestry, Papa was past eighty now. His father had been a jobbing salesman in Paris, who had been killed at Verdun during the First World War, along with another half-million Frenchmen of that generation. His mother had been murdered soon afterwards – killed by one of the clients at the brothel she was working in. The boy was placed in an orphanage, but soon took to petty crime: theft, prostitution, drug running, he'd done it all by the time he was out of his teens. But it was during the Second World War that he started to flourish. During the Nazi occupation of Paris, he'd run the black market, dealing in food, clothes, drinks and drugs throughout those four dark years. The Germans had known and trusted him. Yet Papa had been running the Resistance as well. 'De Gaulle was nothing,' he would snort contemptuously in the rare moments when he could be persuaded to recollect those days. 'A nobody. A showman, sucking up to the English in London.' According to Papa, it was he and his men who ran the networks which smuggled explosives and weapons to the saboteurs arranging hits on the Nazis. And it was his men who were behind the Paris uprising of August 1944 which finally liberated the city. That had been his training in terrorism: as his snipers took up position on the roof of the Opéra, he had learned how just a few men could defeat even the most formidable of armies. *If you could terrorise people, you could achieve anything.*

What had started as the French underground Resistance had turned into Le Groupe, the most formidable criminal gang in Europe. It took all that it had learned during the occupation, and redeployed it during the peace. Drugs, prostitution and smuggling right across booming post-war Europe – all were controlled by Le Groupe. It had a network of informers that covered the Continent, and could better anything available to any of the official intelligence agencies. The disabled, or *mutilés*, were taken under the wing of Le Groupe, and positioned as beggars, flower sellers, baggage handlers at stations and airports, as newspaper vendors, hotel cleaners, anywhere they could keep a watch on the movement of people around Europe, and report back to Papa when necessary. Little escaped the watchful eye of the organisation.

Well, that's the legend anyway. Sam smiled to himself. The truth? Who knows? Only Papa knows, and he was too experienced a dealer in secrets to give any of them away without striking a hard bargain. Like all leaders, he knew that power thrived on myths.

Sam always hesitated before asking to see Papa. He would give you the information you needed, usually, but there was always a price attached. Sometimes it was money he wanted. Other times it was information. It was never quite spelt out, but Papa liked to joke that, apart from his own, Mossad was the one truly global intelligence network: there was an advantage in their cooperating, so long as it was on his terms.

When Sam had first called on him five years ago, they had struck up a rapport that was as intense as it was unexpected. 'We are the same, you and I,' Papa had told him after that meeting. 'Rocks fallen from the same stone.'

I hope to God that isn't true, Sam could remember thinking to himself. He dealt with Papa because he had to.

Yet he was fighting for a nation, an ideal. Papa was just fighting for himself. *I can trade with him, but I don't want to become him.*

Papa didn't just give you the information on where the man you needed could be found. He gave you the means to deliver the death as well. The principle of Mossad was that a man should, where possible, die by his own sword. If he gave instructions to murder people over the phone, then he should be killed while talking on the phone. If he blew up people using explosives, then he should be blown up himself. If he assassinated men with a gun or a knife, then the same weapon should terminate his own existence. It was an important principle, Sam thought. It meant they weren't just killers. It meant their business was vengeance.

Papa appreciated those subtleties. He knew it was not enough just to kill a man. Any thug could do that. It had to be done in the right way.

'Let him have a couple of minutes, then go in,' said the nurse, glancing back towards Sam as she passed through the hallway.

She was a severe woman, maybe fifty, dressed in black. Thick glasses obscured her eyes, making it impossible to judge her mood. Sam nodded back, and remained in his seat. He knew better than to interrupt Papa.

One minute, two minutes. Sam stood up, pushing open the door to the library. Papa liked to spend his mornings surrounded by his books, although as far as Sam knew he never read any of them. Three walls were lined with leather-bound volumes: Balzac, Rousseau, Zola, all the greats of French literature. The fourth wall was dominated by two long thin windows, each with a seat inside them, looking out on the formal grounds.

'Are you OK?'

Papa nodded. 'The nurse is nothing,' he replied, speaking in heavily accented English that sounded partly French and partly Italian. 'I have a slight cold. At my age, you take all the medicines you can persuade the doctors to give you.'

For a man of his age, Papa was fit and healthy. His skin was pitted with layer upon layer of wrinkles, until his face looked like a sea during a rough storm. His brown eyes were sunk deep into their sockets, the bone around them worn away by the tides of time, and his mouth sloped away from his nose, giving him a permanent air of detached amusement. But his torso and his arms were still bulging with muscles that rippled out through the slick creases of his formal white shirt. It was the build of a much younger man.

The genes of generations of Sicilian and French peasants are within him, thought Sam. Their bodies were always strong. *They had to be.*

'You wanted to see me.'

Sam glanced sideways. Pierre was sitting in the corner. The man was even older than Papa. He'd never asked his birth date, but he'd heard him referred to within the family as Papa's older cousin. That would place him in his mid-eighties at least. He was thin, but less well preserved. He was wearing a brown three-piece suit, with a crimson cravat tucked into his white shirt, and in his hands he was holding a black walking stick. His hands were covered with warts, the skin folding up on itself, and he seemed to be having trouble breathing. Yet his face looked relatively healthy: his long, thin nose arched out of the centre of his face, and his brown eyes were clear and alert, with no sign that he needed either glasses or contact lenses.

In fact, Sam noticed, he was the precise opposite of Papa: his head was keeping well, while his body was showing the wear and tear of the eight and more decades he had been using it. Whenever you met with the boss, he was always sitting in the corner, always listening, always nodding gently to himself, but never saying a word. He just sat there, making a mental note of everything that happened in the room.

Pierre's role in the family had been explained to Sam once, and he had never questioned it since. He was the computer. Papa didn't believe in taking notes. He didn't have ledgers, or invoices or accounts. Nor did the family take minutes, prepare plans or make lists. They just had Pierre. The man had a photographic memory. Whenever Papa had done something for Sam, whether it was betraying a Palestinian, supplying some arms or disposing of a body, he would just ask Pierre what the bill was next time they met, and the old man would reel off a number instantaneously. Two or three years later, you could ask him how much you'd been charged, and he would tell you precisely, down to the last penny or centime. Le Groupe controlled a million different pieces of information. Secrets were the one vital raw material of its trade. *And they were all safely locked up in Pierre's head.*

The written word can betray a man in a hundred different ways, Papa had explained once. But not the memorised word. Pierre would never betray us. *He's family.*

'I need to take down Hassim,' said Sam.

Papa smiled, revealing a set of glimmeringly white teeth. 'He will be in London for one week, in three days' time.'

It was as if he already knew what I was about to ask him.

Sam hesitated. In his dealings with Papa over the last five years he had learned never to question where the inform-ation he was fed came from, how it had been obtained, how accurate it was, or how much it would cost. That was another piece of advice his father had given him when he first put him in touch with the old man. *You don't ask Papa where he gets his information, the same way you don't ask a butcher where he gets his meat. Because you don't want to know.*

'Where?' asked Sam.

'We'll get to that,' said Papa sharply. 'First, I want to know what you are going to do with the information if I give it to you.'

Sam reached out for the bottle of Volvic mineral water standing on a folded card table in the centre of the library. Papa had never asked him that before, and as far as Sam knew there had never been any need to. It was already clear what he would do with the information.

'You already know. When you tell me where Hassim will be, I'll kill him.'

'Even though he'll be in Britain? In London?'

Sam hesitated again. He could see what Papa was driving at. During the five years the mission had lasted so far, the team had based itself in London. For a cell that needed to be able to spread itself throughout Europe, it was the natural place to be. It had a flourishing trade in secrets and money, and from Heathrow, you could be nearly anywhere on the Continent in less than two hours. That the British intelligence agencies had some idea they were operating from London, Sam had no doubt: they had one of the most sophisticated surveillance systems in the world, and they probably knew Hassim was there as well. There was a deal, unspoken perhaps, but no less powerful for that: the cell could base itself in London, but all its hits had to be completed in other countries. The British didn't want to see any blood spilt on the streets of their own capital. That kind of trouble, and the cell would find itself in jail. Or worse.

'I'm tired.'

'That's not a good reason.'

Sam walked across the room. The sun was streaming across the garden, shimmering off the water of the orna-mental lake. 'I've been working for five years,' he said. 'As you know, there were twelve men on our list. Eleven of them are now dead. Just one is left. Hassim. Eliminate him, and my work is finished.'

'A man's work is never finished. You're like me. You'll never lay down your gun.'

Sam flinched. If he was being honest with himself, Papa

had touched a nerve. But he wanted out from Mossad, and to join his wife Elena and his two children in the suburbs of Frankfurt, where they had been living while he'd been working undercover. That much was clear. The only question was how much did he want to reveal to Papa.

'I want to get back to Elena,' said Sam. 'It's not natural for a man to be apart from his family for so long. We only see each other twice a year, and that's only for a week at a time. We're not even allowed to contact each other. Most of the time, she doesn't even know if I'm alive or dead.'

'And what will you do with yourself?' said Papa. 'A man doesn't just need to see his family. He needs to support them as well.'

'I have the antiques business. I'm getting quite good at it. A free training from Mossad.'

'You won't be happy.'

Sam laughed. 'No more assassinations. No more hiding. No more visits to the widows of my friends after they've died on a mission, when I know in my heart it was my fault. I think I can . . . be happy.' He looked at Papa and shrugged.

'You're a bullet, my boy. And a gun is always going to find you.'

'Please tell me where Hassim will be,' Sam snapped.

Papa smiled. 'The truth bites.'

'The time and the place?' Sam persisted.

'Nine o'clock this coming Tuesday night,' said Papa, 'Hassim will be hosting a dinner at the Ghaban restaurant. A Lebanese place, just off the Edgware Road. A private room. He'll be there for a couple of hours at least.'

Sam's heart leapt. He's mine. I've got five days. *The last trap can be set.*

'Thank you, Papa. As usual, I don't know how I'm going to repay you.'

'I'll find something.'

As he was leaving the room, Sam caught Pierre's eye. 'How much is on the account?'

Pierre's face remained immobile, as if it were cast from iron. 'One hundred and seventy-two thousand francs already,' he said. 'And today's item adds another one hundred and thirty-three thousand. You can settle next time we summon you.'

Sam walked through the hallway and went upstairs. A room, as usual, had been prepared in the left wing of the chateau. It was always the same room, every time he came here: neat, but small, with a single bed, a writing desk and an oil painting of the battle of Austerlitz on the wall. Whether all Papa's customers stayed in the same room, Sam didn't know. If so, more assassins and terrorists must have slept in this bed than anywhere else in Europe.

Dinner, thought Sam, as he went back down again at seven thirty. There was always a dinner. It didn't matter how deadly the business was you had just transacted. It made no difference how much blood was about to be spilt, nor how many secrets had just been betrayed. Papa's stomach was always strong enough for a rich meal.

'Sausage,' said Papa. 'We start with the sausage and the wine.'

Sam took a sip of the burgundy. It was a 1971 red, and according to Papa the best burgundy vintage of that decade. Sam had tried it before and found it dry to the palate. The thick slice of sausage was as hard as rock, and oozing with pork fat. Sam bit hard on the meat, washing it down with the wine.

'Let me tell you a story,' said Papa, settling back into his chair. 'General André Devigny, have you ever heard of him.'

Sam shook his head.

'One of the great heroes of the French Resistance. A film was made about him, called *A Man Escaped*. He was locked up in Klaus Barbie's Gestapo prison in Lyon, Fort Montluc. One of the only men ever to get out. He made his way to North Africa, then to Britain, poor soul, from where he took part in the invasion of '44. That old fraud de Gaulle gave him the Cross of the Liberation, and gave him a job in military intelligence.'

Sam took another bite of the sausage and a sip of his wine. 'So?'

'We sprung him from Montluc. And you know why? Because Barbie was using Lyon to ship gold from occupied France into his bank accounts in Switzerland. Devigny knew all about it. The routes, the passwords, the account numbers, everything. And you know what we did with the information? Absolutely nothing. Because it was enough just to know which bank was sitting on all that Nazi gold. It's a useful thing to have a Swiss bank doing your bidding. Very useful. More than worth a man's life.' He laughed. 'We weren't pleased when Barbie was put on trial, though. A courtroom is a dangerous place. You never know what kind of secrets might be revealed.' Suddenly Papa tapped Sam on the side of his arm. He reached out across the table, and picked up a folder. Slowly he pulled out a picture, measuring six inches by twelve, full colour. It showed a man lying flat out on a pavement. Blood was seeping from the dagger that had sliced through the throat. In his eyes, there was the glazed look of fear that descended upon a man who had died slowly. 'I thought this was nicely executed,' he said. 'Did he squeal much?'

Sam recognised the picture at once. It had been taken three months ago, in Seville. His unit had executed Omar El-Fassi as he left a tapas bar in the centre of the city. He was number eleven on the list: a Moroccan, recruited into one of the extremist Palestinian groups, he had specialised in brutal knife work, which he used to torture anyone his paymasters needed information or cooperation from.

21

Intelligence officers, bankers, even a pair of Mossad agents, they had all broken under El-Fassi handiwork. Only with Papa's help had they been able to track him down and eliminate him; still, it came as a surprise to Sam that the old man had a picture of it.

'Like a pig,' said Sam. 'Torturers are all cowards.'

Papa sliced a fresh portion of sausage on to his plate. 'How will you kill Hassim?' he said, turning to Sam and arching his eyebrows.

Jacques was sitting opposite him, and next to him Henri, the younger of Papa's two sons. Both of them were married, and well into middle age, but Papa still treated them like children. They were nearly always in the family chateau, although both nominally had their own houses. And their father expected them to listen at length to his stories of the wartime resistance. They were as tied to him as any toddler.

'With a gun,' said Sam.

'Why?' said Jacques sourly.

'The way of Mossad,' said Sam. 'Hassim is an assassin. He's taken out at least a dozen of our people, always with a pistol.'

'You kill them the way they kill their victims,' said Jacques.

'And they know it's us,' said Sam. 'That's fundamental. A man who doesn't know why he is dying has been murdered. A man who knows why has been executed. It's an important distinction.'

'That's what I like to see, a man with a sense of himself,' said Papa, slipping his arm around Sam's shoulder as he spoke. 'One day you'll come and live here. And then my family will be complete.'

Sam laughed. 'Some day soon, I'll be retired, and running a small antiques shop in London. And then *my* family will be complete.'

THREE

Sam reckoned he could walk straight across Wembley Stadium in the middle of a big game and nobody would notice him. *I know how to become an invisible man.*

The trick was to measure yourself against your backdrop. If people were walking fast, you walked fast. When they went slow, you went slow. Your goal was to move just 10 per cent slower than the rest of the street: any human brain searching a street would latch on to averages, but if you were just below average, it was unlikely to focus on you. You didn't make any sudden movements. Your expression was neutral, grey, neither happy nor sad, just purposeful. Your eyes remained straight ahead of you. Combine that with wearing dull, respectable, unremarkable clothes, and your presence on the street was unlikely to be detected.

Sam hesitated just long enough to inspect the premises. He gave himself five seconds precisely: to dawdle any longer would be to draw attention to himself. The Ghaban had nothing to mark it out from a dozen different Lebanese restaurants sprinkled around this part of London. As Papa had said, it was just off the Edgware Road, the centre of London's Arab quarter, amid a sea of Middle Eastern restaurants, cafés and bookshops. It was the only place in London, Sam noticed, where a woman in a skirt was more noticeable than a woman in a burka. A yellow awning stretched out into the street. The menu was posted up on a board inside. The doors were glass, and there was a row of potted palms covering the windows. Nothing exceptional.

It was a three-storey building, with a basement. Even from a cursory glance, it was obvious the kitchens were downstairs, and the offices on the first floor. There was a side door, leading up to a second-floor flat. At either side, there were two more office buildings: an estate agency and an employment agency. Behind, a small yard, filled with rubbish, overlooked by two residential houses that had been turned into flats. My five seconds is done, Sam noted. Time to move on.

Stepping back across the pavement, he nodded to another unexceptional man on the other side of the street. Five minutes, he mouthed silently.

The man didn't respond. He didn't nod, nor wave or smile or blink. With his head down, he just kept walking along the street, at just a tiny percentage below average speed.

The coffee was hot and milky, the way Sam liked it. He took a sip pulling out a chair. Joe Kopel was just about to sit down. Michael Boaz was collecting his coffee from the bar.

'So,' said Sam, checking that there was no one else in the almost empty café who might hear what they were saying. 'What's the score?'

Joe stirred some sugar into his coffee, folding the paper wrapper neatly into quarters and dropping it in the ashtray. At just over forty, Joe was the oldest of their group. His black hair was starting to thin, and there were lines under his eyes, but he remained a handsome, forceful man: his nose was as straight as a ruler, his jaw looked as if it had been chiselled from stone, and his brown eyes tapered away gently from the centre of his face. To an outsider, the group would have looked like a bunch of businessmen sitting down to discuss their work.

'In the street,' said Joe. 'That's where we take him.'

Michael was sitting down next to him. He put down his copy of the *Evening Standard*, and took a sip on his coffee. Michael was just thirty-one, the baby of the team. His hair was thick and curly, dropping down over his ears in a way that would never have been allowed when he was still in the army. His face was puffy, prone to fat, but his body was strong and tall. Michael told jokes – it was his way of dealing with the stress and the tension. You could be walking away from a hit, the smell of blood still lingering on your hands, and Michael would start right into one of his gags. 'Did you hear the one about the rabbi and the . . .'

'Outside, definitely,' said Michael. 'The street is safe enough.'

There were five of us when we started, noted Sam. Five Mossad trained agents let loose in Europe, with a simple, uncomplicated mission. They worked completely alone, with no back-up or assistance from Mossad: they had money, and their brains, and that was it. Two of them had died already. Ron Bronstein had been blown up when the bomb they had planted to eliminate a Palestinian terrorist had been detonated accidentally. And Danny Netzer had been taken out by the opposition.

And who knows, maybe there will be more deaths before we're finished. There are no reinforcements in this unit. We kill them, or they kill us, until nobody is left standing. Those are the rules of engagement.

'Maybe, maybe not,' said Sam. 'First we review the options.'

Sam was never certain why he had been chosen to lead this mission. He had served for five years in the commandos, and was thinking of applying to train as a pilot, when the invitation to join Mossad had come. Only reluctantly had he followed in his father's footsteps: he'd seen how his family had been broken by the service, and he didn't want the same thing to happen to him. Initially, Sam had worked as a bodyguard, assigned in rotation to different ministers in the cabinet. Then this, the leadership of his own undercover unit. Why me? he'd asked his commander Zvi Imer at the time. I know nothing about assassinations. Imer had laughed at him. 'You think anyone does?' he'd snapped back. 'We've chosen you because we can't think of anyone else. Trust me, if we could, we would. But we can't, so you've got the job. Now go.'

Sam had thought about it often since, and slowly realised that wasn't quite true. Israel didn't have any assassins, that part of the explanation was true enough. It had soldiers, plenty of them, but that wasn't the same. Soldiers fought in packs. They had lines, orders, structure. Assassins had none of that. We work outside all the rules. *We rely on nobody except ourselves.*

They chose me, because I instinctively know that assassins are the painters and decorators of warfare; they understand that to get the job done, what really counts is the preparation. Any idiot could shoot a man. It was easy. You get a gun, walk up to the guy, pull the trigger. Bang, it's done. A monkey could do it. The difficult part was getting away with it. And that was the point of preparation. You covered every obstacle, examined every response, practised each step of the exit route. Not because it helped you make the hit. *But because it helped you get away with it.*

'OK,' said Joe. 'Can we get inside the restaurant, do it there?'

'I've eaten there the last two nights,' said Michael. 'They're starting to know me. It's never full, we'll get a table all right.'

Sam took another sip on his coffee. He was trying to play out the scenario in his mind. You go in, carrying a gun. Take a table. Eat your meal. Wait for the right moment. Head for the room where Hassim is eating, take out the piece, kill him, then get out.

A monkey could do it. *But how would you get away?*

'Hassim's going to have security,' said Joe. 'Plenty of it. A private room. We try to get in there we're going to be stopped.'

Michael nodded. 'How about as he goes in?'

'Any back entrances?' asked Sam.

'One, leading up from the basement, into a small yard,' said Joe.

'He's not coming in that way, it's full of rubbish,' said Michael. 'To get to the private room, he has to go through the main restaurant. We're sitting at a table. When he goes past we let him have it.'

Sam paused. Take your time, he warned himself. He discovered years ago that your first judgement was not always the best. You had to allow yourself the space to make the right decision. They had been planning to shoot Hassim, because that's how he had killed in Israel, but he was an explosives expert as well. 'How about a bomb?'

He glanced up at Joe as he spoke. When the team was put together by Imer, each man brought to it his own skills. Michael was the driver. If there was a getaway car needed, he was the man who handled it. Ron had been their munitions expert: when they were deciding what guns they needed, he was the man they turned to. Danny handled identities: passports, papers, safe houses, fake jobs, travel arrangements, he always had it covered. Since their colleagues' deaths, they'd had to split those jobs between them. Joe handled explosives: give him a hardware shop and some money, and he could knock together any bomb you needed from components available on any high street. And me? Sam sometimes wondered to himself. *I provide leadership, whatever that might be.*

'Sure, we could put a bomb in the private room,' said Joe. 'Put a remote control on it. Detonate it from wherever we want. We just have to make sure he's going to be in the room at the time.'

'Can we hide the bomb and be certain they won't find it?'

'You can't hide anything for sure,' said Joe. 'Anyone looks hard enough, they might find it.'

'And we can't guarantee he's going to be in the room at the time,' said Michael.

Sam nodded. It was three years ago now, but all of them had memories of the elimination of Omar Lahoud, a Syrian terrorist, and number five on their list. A bomb had been planted in his flat: he was a bomber, so it had to be an explosion that killed him. They waited for him to walk inside the Paris apartment building, then pulled the trigger. The flat blew apart creating a lot of dust but no casualties. Lahoud had walked away unhurt. It taught Sam a valuable lesson. You have to be certain your victim will be there to take the blast. Assume nothing. People take detours, visit neighbours, whistle to themselves on the stairs. Whatever. Unless you see them there, they aren't there.

'Have you seen the private room?' Sam asked Joe.

Joe nodded.

'Any windows?'

Joe shook his head.

'That rules out a bomb,' said Sam. 'Unless we can see him in there, we can't trigger the explosion.'

'That leaves the street, then,' said Michael. 'We hit him in the street.'

Sam pondered the issue. They had done three street hits in the five years they had been together. You could deliberate for hours about the best way to kill a man, but in the end, the conclusion was always the same. Simpler was better. One man had been taken out as he left his house in Hamburg one morning. Another as he left the Rome kiosk where he bought a morning paper. A third, on the pavement outside the café where he stopped for a drink in the evenings. Every time, the advantages were exactly the

same. You could see the victim. You got a clear shot and –
best of all – a clean getaway.

'When he goes in or out?' asked Sam.

'Out,' said Michael.

'Why?'

'Easy,' said Michael. 'We need to find a safe place to
watch from. Hassim is going to have at least a couple of
bodyguards touring the area beforehand. I don't think we
can just wait in a car until he shows up. They're going to
spot us. That means we watch and wait. By the time we see
his car draw up outside the restaurant, it's already too late.
So we see him go in. Then wait another couple of hours
before taking up our positions.' He smiled to himself. 'Take
him on the way out.'

'Where's the nearest police station?' asked Sam.

'On the Edgware Road,' said Joe. 'About a mile away.'

'Fire station?'

'Same road, another mile up.'

Sam nodded. That was good. You couldn't attempt a hit
on the street if there was a police station just around the
corner. Any kind of emergency services had to be at least a
mile away: that gave you some time to put distance between
yourself and assassination.

'Patrols?' said Sam.

'Along the Edgware Road,' said Joe. 'I've watched for
two nights. They travel in police cars, plus one foot patrol a
night. They don't go down the side streets. Even if they are
passing down the main road at the time we strike that still
gives us fifty yards to play with.'

'Regular times?'

Joe shook his head. 'These are the British police. They
aren't that stupid. The times are varied but on average once
every two hours.'

Sam smiled. Eleven hits in five years, but not one of them
had been on British soil. They had taken down terrorists in

29

France, Italy, Norway, Spain, Cyprus, and even one in Switzerland – Sam rated that as the most stomach-churning of them all, since the Swiss police were as efficient as they were ruthless – but never Britain. That was partly because the team had made London their base. But it was also because the Metropolitan Police had spent two decades fighting the IRA. They knew more about combating terrorism than any other force in the world. *Except Mossad.*

You could burgle your way through the city, and nobody minded very much. But assassinations were different. There was no harder city in which to kill a man. *Perhaps that was why it was the base for so many of the world's terrorists. They felt safe here.*

'So there could be a patrol just down the street?'

Joe gripped his hands together. 'We can station our car just on the junction, fifty yards from the restaurant. That will give us a chance to watch the road. Any police in the area, we abort.'

'And we will,' said Sam firmly. 'That clear?'

Completing a hit was like completing a deal: you had to be ready to walk away at any moment. It didn't matter how much hard work or good fortune had gone into preparing the assassination. Nor did it matter how long it might be before the chance presented itself again. If anything felt wrong you had to drop your weapons immediately. Without a thought. Without a backward glance.

You'd always get another shot. *But, botch this one, and no one would give you another life.*

'Hassim is the last one on the list,' said Joe. 'Finish him, and the mission is complete.' Sam could see how the stress had built up in Joe as the years went by. His face was more rugged, and the voice harsher. He had become crueller in the past five years, and that was the change that shocked Sam the most: this work had taken a gentle, quiet man, one without a trace of anger within him, and slowly roughened him, shortening his temper and making him quick to criticise, to snarl and to complain.

Like meat going through a grinder. You went in solid, and came out in shreds.

'That doesn't make any difference,' said Sam. 'The job feels wrong, we abort.'

A soldier was always at his most vulnerable when he thought he could go home soon. His mind was filled up with all the things he would do when the job was finished: the time he would spend with his wife, the presents he would buy for the kids. He stopped concentrating. He became sloppy.

Sam pushed away the remains of his coffee. 'We do it in the street, two days from now,' he said. 'Remember the rules. Think like your target, be him, until the moment when you pull the trigger.'

FOUR

Sam shifted his position, struggling to make himself comfortable. He had been sitting in the passenger seat of the BMW 3-Series for an hour now, and the leather of the seats was starting to dig into his skin. 'How much does this guy eat?' he said.

Joe shrugged. 'Too much is bad for the health.'

Sam glanced up and down the street. It was dark night, with just a light drizzle falling. It was Tuesday evening, just after ten, but as busy as mid-morning. Just like the cities it resembled in the Middle East, this part of London never slept. The cafés and bars were open until three or four.

The plan, so far, was unfolding just the way they had mapped it out. For the last two nights, they had researched the area until every last detail of the hit had been painted in. They had walked through the streets a hundred times, memorising the layout for half a mile in every direction: you never knew when you might have to escape on foot, you didn't want to start running down a dead-end alley. Each member of the unit was assigned his own patch to survey. Michael had rented a small flat two blocks down the street, but with a good view of the restaurant: none of them actually lived there, it was just for observation. They had waited there until they had a clear view of Hassim drawing up outside the building. He arrived in a black Toyota. So far as Sam could tell, this was bargain-basement terrorism. Hassim had just one man with him, doubling up as both a driver and bodyguard.

After he went into the restaurant, they waited two hours, then Sam and Joe walked down to the BMW they had already parked down the street. Michael left the flat, walking to a Volvo estate parked just off the Bayswater Road. Sam and Joe would do the hit, then escape in the BMW. They would ditch the car after a mile, and switch into the Volvo. They'd be out of Britain within an hour. It was virtually impossible that the London police would have any way of linking them with the hit, so there was little chance of their London flats being searched. If they were, the team wouldn't return from Europe.

Sam had used BMWs and Volvos for every hit the team had attempted. They were reliable cars that drew no attention to themselves. More importantly, each member of the team knew those vehicles backwards. You didn't want to be making a getaway and have to start searching around for a button to switch on the windscreen wiper.

'Looking forward to finishing?' said Sam.

Joe remained silent. Sam was aware he had broken one of the few unwritten rules of their tiny brotherhood. They never discussed what they would do afterwards. In the time they had been working together, they had all become good friends. Sam knew as much about these men as he did his own family. Probably more. When you worked undercover for year after year, he sometimes reflected, you'd become friends with the Devil himself. He knew their moods and tempers. Their strength and endurance. What made them laugh, what got them down. But of all the hundred different things they discussed, they never talked about what came next. It was a taboo. As if even mentioning the subject was assuming too much.

'Sure,' said Joe.

'Another tour?'

Joe paused. Sam could tell from his expression that he had posed a question that Joe regularly posed to himself. They all did. Mossad didn't talk about careers, that was not how the organisation worked. There were no hierarchies, no promotions, no ladders to climb, or pension schemes to look forward to. It modelled itself on a corporation in everything except its loyalty to its staff: you were expected to serve the institute loyally, and expect nothing apart from your salary in return.

'Of course.'

'Why of course?'

'Because there aren't many openings for a forty-year-old assassin,' said Joe. 'And because –' He stopped suddenly. 'There's movement.'

Sam looked up towards the restaurant. The door was opening, casting a shaft of light across the pavement. A man was standing in the doorway. About five eight, wearing a thick sheepskin coat. No, that's not Hassim. *We're still waiting.*

'And because?' continued Sam.

'Because there's still the cause, isn't there?' said Joe. 'These people are destroying our nation. People have always hit the Jews, and we're the first generation of Jews to fight back. That's something to be proud of.'

'You think we're winning?' said Sam.

Joe shrugged. 'I don't know. We sure as hell aren't losing as badly as we used to.'

Sam glanced back along the street. It was ten forty-five. Hassim has been there for nearly three hours. Whatever business he was conducting must be almost finished by now.

My gun, thought Sam with a stab of anxiety. He was carrying an Israeli-made Jericho 921 handgun, a pistol that was standard issue for both the Israeli Army and police force. It might not be the best gun in the world, but it was a sturdy, reliable firearm, and the one Sam had trained with. It was always the same. Whenever he was on a mission, he sat

34

around worrying about his gun. Have I loaded it? Is the safety catch off? Did I load the bullets? Was it a live round? Are all the mechanisms working?

Don't check, he told himself. That was all part of the training. It was natural to want to check your gun, in the same way a man on his way to the airport keeps checking his wallet to make sure he has his passport. But the instinct had to be ruthlessly suppressed. Why? Because if you started fiddling around with your gun, then you could be certain it wouldn't work when you needed it.

The odds are with you, Sam reminded himself. Otherwise you wouldn't be here.

'He's coming,' said Joe.

Sam turned the key, firing the BMW into life. He couldn't see Hassim yet, but up ahead he could see Hassim's driver start to pull away from the kerb, steering towards the front of the restaurant. Joe glanced across at Sam. His lips remained sealed but in his eyes there was a message. *Wish me luck.*

Sam nodded. 'Go,' he said, his voice barely more than a whisper.

Joe stepped from the car. As he did so, Sam looked around. No policemen in view. No passers-by. Perfect. Joe started walking down the road, at just below average pace. They had measured the fifty yards from the parking spot to the restaurant door, and calculated precisely the time Joe would need. Eighty-one seconds. Sam could see a shaft of light. A man was stepping on to the pavement. Not Hassim. The owner maybe. A friend. Sam held his breath. If Hassim wasn't standing outside the restaurant at the moment Joe passed, he would have to keep on walking. A pause would create suspicion. These men lived their whole lives in a permanent state of combat: they had learned to regard every shadow in every street as potential enemy. If he wasn't there, Joe would keep walking, then five minutes later double-back to the car. Sam would walk past next time they thought Hassim was emerging. The hit would be his.

It didn't matter how well you planned a job. *You were always dangling at the end of fate's thinnest thread.*

Thirty yards. Twenty . . .

He watched the door carefully, his eyes trained on the few square yards of pavement outside the restaurant. Checking the rear-view mirror, he could see one person walking behind the car, perhaps fifteen yards back. A woman. Her expression suggested she wasn't paying any attention to them, but you could never tell: if she was a professional, she'd mask her interest. She was wearing a black coat, with its collar wrapped up high around her neck. Her age was impossible to judge. About forty, maybe forty-five. Her pace was fast, moving at five miles an hour, but she wouldn't get close enough to interfere. Witness the execution from about thirty-five yards, yes, but she would just be a bystander. The police would ask her a lot of questions, but she would tell them nothing of consequence.

A figure.

Hassim.

Joe was ten yards from him now. He was walking steadily, his head bowed just a fraction. Another man on his way home from the pub, thought Sam. Nothing suspicious about him at all. *Only I can tell the difference.*

He pulled the BMW away from the kerb. The next twenty seconds had to be timed to precision. But they had practised it a thousand times, and they knew their moves the way a ballerina knows her steps.

Sam steered gently along the street. His right foot was putting gentle pressure on the accelerator, enough to up the speed of the car. A vehicle that is moving too slowly will attract attention, especially from a man trained to suspect assassins everywhere.

As soon as the bullet left the chamber of Joe's pistol, the BMW would slide up alongside him on the street. With the car still moving, Sam would fling the door open, and Joe would slip inside. Before anyone had time to react, they would have cleared the scene.

Joe slowed half a pace; his hand was dug into his left pocket. Sam saw he was about to pull the pistol from the pocket. Hassim spun round. For a moment, their eyes locked on to each other, two men staring into the moment of death. Sam could see Joe's lips moving. 'Mossad,' he was saying. 'Your time has come.'

It was the phrase the unit always used before dispatching another terrorist to his death. Just occasionally, Sam reflected, you could look straight into their eyes in the split second before the execution, and you could read the fear and dread in their expressions. *In that instant, you understood what it was like to die.*

Ahead, Sam could see Joe raising his gun. His hand was stretched out before him, and his legs were rooted to the ground, a yard apart. The classic firing position. Drawing level, Sam prepared to fling open the door.

Then ahead of him, on the other side of Joe and Hassim, he could see the door of Hassim's car opening. Something was emerging from the window. There was no time to see what it was.

But then he heard it. A sound that was etched into his memory from the first time he'd seen combat. The rapid, frenetic chatter of a machine gun.

A hail of bullets was ripping across the pavement. Within a fraction of a second they started to collide with Joe's body, peppering him with wounds. He staggered backwards. The gunfire was hitting him in the chest, sending tiny rivers of blood spurting on to the pavement. He was struggling to hold his balance. In his hand, the pistol fired once, but all contact between his brain and his hand had already been severed. The bullet smashed harmlessly into the brickwork of the building opposite.

Joe fell to the ground.

Sam jammed his foot on the accelerator. The engine roared. He could see Hassim standing on the pavement. The collar of his jacket was turned up high around his neck. Briefly, he looked towards Sam. A taunt was written into the stretched pupils of his dark brown eyes.

For a moment, Sam was about to steer the car on to the pavement and into Hassim. His mind was furiously calculating the odds. But Hassim's own car was blocking his route. It would be impossible to swerve off the road, crash into Hassim, then drag the car back on to the road. The only option would be to come straight in at a sharp angle. You'd kill the man, for sure, but then crash straight into the wall behind him.

This is not a suicide mission, he told himself. He was struggling to suppress his anger, to bring the desire of instantaneous vengeance under control. *You owe it to Elena to come out of this alive, if you can.*

Another flick of the wheel, and the decision was already made. The BMW steered out into the centre of the street. One check in the rear-view mirror showed Hassim calmly wrapping his coat around himself, and climbing into his car. He's not giving chase, Sam realised. He knows better than to start a running gun battle in central London.

He's happy enough to have killed one of us. He can come for the rest of us another day.

As Sam screeched around the corner, and on to the Edgware Road, he could hear the sound of a dozen cars honking wildly. And the sound of an insistent voice within his own head.

You should have killed him. You should have killed him. *You should have killed him.*

Even if it cost you your own life.

★

After dropping the BMW at the prearranged spot, Sam ran across the road to where Michael was waiting in the Volvo. If the plan had worked, it would be the three of them driving towards Heathrow. The mission would be completed.

But now this . . .

Sam climbed into the car and slammed the door. He glanced across at Michael, but he knew he didn't need to say anything. Sam getting into the Volvo alone. That could only mean one thing.

'And Hassim?' Michael said.

'He got away.'

Sam fell silent. His breathing was short and one word was playing through his mind. *Betrayal.*

'To Heathrow?'

Sam nodded. You stuck to the plan no matter what happened. You never deviated. The plan was to drive to the airport, get on the flight they had booked for Amsterdam, and then lie low there for a couple of days, while they assessed the situation. So long as you judged it was safe, you could slip quietly back into the country.

The Volvo slipped into the traffic along the Bayswater Road, then joined the M40 heading out of London towards the airport. The cars were thinning out at this time of night: flights out of Heathrow were sparse after eleven. Michael was driving at sixty-eight miles an hour, just below the speed limit. If he was in a hurry, no one would have guessed it.

'What happened?'

Sam looked at Michael. His hands were steady on the wheel, and his eyes gripped the road. There was not a flicker of emotion on his face. A professional, Sam noted. He never abandoned his composure. Not ever.

'He knew we were coming.'

A flicker. Sam could see Michael's lips tightening. He could see his hands holding hard on the wheel of the Volvo, as if he wanted to squeeze the life from the machine. The sentence was simple, but carried a weight of meaning.

'You sure?'

Sam nodded. It was one of the rules – his rules, not Mossad rules – he had laid down when the five of them had started on this mission half a decade ago. Say what you think. Always. Don't embellish, distort, exaggerate, or soften any observation. Keep it straight. *One day our lives will depend on it.*

'He was ready. I saw the whole thing, frame by frame. Joe walked towards him, and Hassim knew he was the bait, and didn't care. Just as Joe was approaching him, the window came down on the waiting car, and a burst of machine-gun fire spread out into the street. Joe didn't stand a chance.'

'They saw his gun?'

Sam shook his head. 'Joe hadn't drawn yet. They had no way of knowing he was an assassin. Unless they were expecting it.'

Michael steered the car into the turning that led to the airport. 'But who? Anyone back at base?'

'No,' said Sam firmly. 'Not possible. Nobody knows the details of any of our operation. The mission, yes. The details, no.'

'Then who?'

Sam remained silent. He could feel Michael's eyes bearing down on him.

'How did we know Hassim was there tonight?'

Sam said nothing.

'How the hell did we know, Sam?'

Still nothing.

'Was it Papa?'

A red light. Michael pulled the car slowly to a stop.

40

'Of course,' said Sam softly. 'Where the fuck do you think we get information like that.'

'Then he betrayed us,' said Michael bitterly.

'No, he wouldn't.'

'Fuck it, Sam,' said Michael, the anger ripping through his voice. 'He's been betraying the other side to us for years. It was only a matter of time before he delivered us to them.'

The lights changed. Michael drove hard away from the road, barging his way past two vehicles.

'He wouldn't,' Sam said. 'I'm family to Papa.'

FIVE

Sam ordered his second cup of coffee. He'd already spent twenty minutes at the pavement café, a tiny place in Amstelveen, one of the quiet, genteel suburbs of Amsterdam. It was his third day in the city, most of it spent by himself, touring art galleries and inspecting antique shops. With all their previous hits being outside Britain, they could always return to London to lie low while they waited for the dust to settle. Not this time. Not until they were certain the British police had no leads to connect the hit on Hassim with his unit.

That would depend on whether they could identify Joe as a member of Mossad or not. Every member of the unit had been supplied with a 'legend', a complete back story, explaining what they were doing in London. For ordinary purposes, it was good enough: they all had jobs, apartments, documents and credit cards. If the intelligence agencies got involved, however, they might be in trouble. There were few legends good enough for MI5 not to see through them.

Sam had picked up the British newspapers at a kiosk, but there had been nothing in them about Joe's murder. If the British police suspected it was anything more than a random murder, they were not telling the press. Maybe they didn't want a 'blow-back' operation to start. If anyone started wondering about Joe, the media would be full of stories about Middle Eastern terrorists bringing mayhem to London streets.

A dark-skinned man walked past, glancing twice at Sam as he did so. Sam could feel himself flinching inwardly. Since arriving in Amsterdam, he had been nervous and jumpy. Hassim is out there somewhere, thought Sam. He knows I tried to kill him. *And now it is my blood he'll want.*

He watched as another man walked down the street, paused to tie his shoelace, then looked across at Sam. He had pale, freckled skin, and his body looked twisted, as if all the bones had been taken out and replaced by rubber. It's always the same, reflected Sam. *The messenger boys are the runts of the litter.*

'You have something for me?' said Sam.

The man looked startled. He was thirty, maybe thirty-five. 'Yes,' he said. 'You could tell?'

'Don't worry about it, you're doing fine,' said Sam. 'I just have a good eye, that's all. I can tell the passers-by from messengers.'

Last night, Sam had called the offices of a shipping broker in Rotterdam. It was a respectable business, but the man who ran it was one of Mossad's many *sayanim*. He passed messages, and occasionally supplied boats. The message for Sam was to sit at this café at eleven o'clock the following morning.

The man remained silent. Then he opened the canvas bag he was carrying in his right hand. He took out a music box, measuring eight inches by six, and placed it down on the table. 'Here,' he said. 'For you.'

The man retreated, scuttling back along the street. Sam stood up, put some money down on the table, and returned to his hotel room. When he arrived, he put the box down on the desk in one corner of the room. The box was nothing special, certainly not an antique. There was a picture of some bears on the side, nicely painted in oil, but it was cheaply made. Sam punched the lever. *Hum, de hum, de hah, de hum.* Carefully, he noted down the series of notes. Next, he checked a ledger in his suitcase. Each note corresponded to a number. The number gave you a series of coordinates. From his case, Sam took a series of detailed European maps. Studying the coordinates, he translated the numbers into a place. Nieuwe Binnenweg. In Rotterdam.

He knew precisely what the instruction meant. The musical box was the standard way that Mossad headquarters in Tel Aviv contacted him. This was a summons. The first tune gave you the place. The second the time. There was no need to reply. You were just expected to be there.

He tapped the lever again on the music box. Another tune. *Dum diddy, dum dum dum, diddy diddy, dum dum dum.* Sam jotted down the notes on his pad, then, using another set of established formulas, translated them into numbers. Again, each note corresponded to a number. The time.

Eleven thirty. Next Tuesday morning. Four days from now.

In the five years he had been in the field, this was only the second time he had been called in for a meeting. The news, he sensed, was not going to be good. That was not the way the organisation worked. They didn't call you in for a pat on the back. There were no pep talks or bonuses. Nobody received praise or encouragement.

Perfection was just assumed. *The only time they called you in was to give your soul a roasting.*

With days to go Sam knew there was one job he had to do. He stood in the phone booth and glanced through the narrow Maastricht street, lined with the ornate old trading houses that dominated the town. The desire to travel around Europe had been one of the magnets that had drawn him towards Mossad in the first place. Crazy though it seemed to him now, at the time, Mossad had seemed the only route out of suburbia: an escape from a life spent inhabiting one of the boxy modern concrete houses that fanned out from the newly built suburbs of Tel Aviv and Haifa.

The decisions we make as young men. They seem increasingly inexplicable to us as we grow older. *What the hell was I thinking?*

This is one trip I won't miss. Each time you have to tell a wife she is never going to see her husband again, it rips a chunk out of your heart. This was the third time. A few more chunks, and there wouldn't be anything left.

Sam punched the number. His fingers felt cold. The phone rang for a while. Maybe she was out.

'Jessica,' he said as soon as the phone was answered.

'Yes?'

'It's Sam.'

'Oh, Sam.' She sounded pleased.

'Michael and I are about to come and see you. I just wanted to check you were in.'

'And Joe?'

'No,' he said flatly. 'Just Michael and me.'

A pause.

One second. Two, then five, then ten.

Fuck it, should I say something?

'I see. I'll get something ready for you both,' Jessica finally said, coldly.

Sam put down the phone. He walked back to where Michael was sitting in a rented Volvo. There were a few clouds drifting above them, but the sun was still bright, and the sky was a delicate pale blue. Just the kind of morning Joe had lived for, reflected Sam.

'She's home,' said Sam. 'Let's go.'

Michael put the car into gear, and headed for one of the roads out of town. Jessica was about six miles from Maastricht, living in one of the quiet, anonymous central European villages Mossad had arranged for the families of the five men chosen for the assassination unit to live while their mission was completed.

Places where they could be quietly forgotten.

'Hey,' said Michael, steering the car into a country lane, 'there was this rabbi opening his mail one morning. There was one that was just a single sheet of paper with the word "schmuck" on it. So at the next Friday-night service, the rabbi gets up and says, "I have known many people who have written letters and forgotten to sign their names, but this week I received a letter from someone who signed his name and forgot to write a letter."'

Sam smiled. It didn't matter that the jokes were never funny, he thought. We all have our own way of dealing with the pressure.

Sam and Michael slipped off their shoes and put them by the side of the door. Jessica took their coats, hanging them up next to her own on the rack in the hallway.

'Come through,' said Jessica.

The house was immaculate. A modern bungalow, maybe ten years old, it was modest but well looked after. There was a cream carpet leading through to a sitting room, and behind that a kitchen. There were just two bedrooms. One for Daniel, their little boy, now almost six. And one for his parents. 'I've made some sandwiches,' said Jessica. 'And some coffee. Or would you prefer tea?'

'Coffee is fine,' answered Sam.

He sat down on the sofa, with Michael at his side. He'd only met Jessica twice before. She was a thin, elegant woman, with dark hair that curled into the side of her neck. Joe had worshipped her, Sam knew that, but had also found her difficult: she was obsessive about keeping her house clean, about cooking, about keeping Daniel out of danger. In many ways, she reminded Sam of his own mother, another devoted, hard-working woman, who dedicated her life to her family, only to see first her husband and then her son devoured by Mossad.

'A sandwich?'

Sam nodded. There was a selection of cheese and tuna fish sandwiches, all cut into neat squares, on brown bread. He took one, chewing slowly. It tasted fine, but he wasn't hungry. He ate anyway. Jessica would be offended if he didn't eat at least three of the damned things. That's something else she has in common with my mother. Always ramming food down people's throats.

'Some cake as well,' said Jessica. 'I made some cakes.'

Looking flustered, she disappeared into the kitchen. Sam glanced across at Michael, but the look was not returned. He was eating his third sandwich as if he was genuinely hungry. Just like when we're on a hit, thought Sam. He builds a wall between himself and the events he is part of. *That's what makes him strong.*

'Here,' said Jessica, putting down a plate of cupcakes on the table. 'Take one. They're still warm from the oven.' Her face was reddening, and he could see the traces of moisture around her eyes. She knows. She knows that she can't flutter about with sandwiches and cakes much longer. She's going to have to ask us why we're here.

'It's about Joe,' said Sam.

His hand rested on one of the cakes as if he was about to take one. Then he put it back. 'He's dead.'

'I see,' said Jessica.

She didn't blink. Or hesitate. 'What happened?'

'There was a job,' said Sam. 'Something went wrong. They were expecting us. Joe was killed.'

He could see her bottom lip tightening. How much Joe had told her about his work, he couldn't be sure. Mossad rules stated quite clearly that wives should be told nothing about what their husbands were doing. They were simply to be told they were away on institute business, nothing more. Mostly that rule was ignored. Certainly Elena knew what he was doing, even though Sam never shared the details with her. Sam reckoned Jessica knew as well.

'Was it . . . was it painful?'

Sam shook his head quickly. The truth didn't matter in these situations – he had learned that long ago. You never told the bereaved the truth. What was the point? 'No,' said Sam. 'He died instantly.'

Jessica stood up, flattening out the crease in her skirt. 'You'll have to excuse me,' she said.

She went into her bedroom and shut the door behind her. Sam's eyes flickered up towards the door. He caught an echo of what sounded like a sob.

Michael leaned forward, put two of the cupcakes on his plate, and ate them with a slow, methodical purpose.

'Did you hear the one about the rabbi and the bishop . . .?'

'Please,' said Sam.

Twenty minutes ticked by, the time moving with excruciating slowness. Sam tried to think about other things. He needed to get in touch with Elena. Most of all, he needed to find out who might have betrayed them to Hassim.

Eventually Jessica returned from the bedroom. Her face showed evidence of fresh make-up. If she had been crying, she had hidden all traces of it. 'More coffee?' she said, looking across at Sam and Michael.

Sam shook his head.

'And Elena, how is she?'

'I wish I knew. I haven't seen her for six months.'

Jessica smiled with a trace of bitterness. 'You should try and get home more often.'

'Yes,' he answered flatly.

'And you, Michael? Have you settled down?'

Michael took another cupcake, stuffing it into his mouth. 'No.'

'My sister lives in Frankfurt now, she has all these nieces,' Jessica continued. 'I should put you in touch with her.'

A sheepish grin spread out across Michael's face. 'Do that.'

Sam stood up. 'I think we'd better be going,' he said. Reaching out, he held on to Jessica's hand. Her skin felt cold to his touch. 'I'm so sorry.'

Jessica nodded, following him to the door and handing him his coat. He took it from her, and started to walk back through the neatly manicured garden to where he had parked the car. 'Stop,' said Jessica.

Sam turned round. She was looking straight at him. He took a step back towards her, his eyes locking on to hers.

'Daniel is so young,' she said. 'On the twelfth of November 2005, he will be twenty-one. Will you come and see us and tell him about how his father died? And what sort of man he was?'

Sam nodded. 'It would be an honour,' he replied.

Sam stirred one sugar into his coffee. The Westerpaviljoen, on Nieuwe Binnenweg, was one of a row of ornate old cafés that stretched through the main shopping district in Rotterdam. At this time on a Tuesday morning, there were only a few people there. Some housewives, filling up the morning. The grandmothers who seemed to spend their lives eating cakes and sipping coffees across whole chunks of central Europe.

And me. A Mossad assassin who has had enough.

'We need to take a walk.'

It was eleven thirty, the time the music box had given him for the meeting. The man standing next to his table was just over five foot ten, thin, and wearing a thick black overcoat even though the weather was mild and sunny. His hair was greying and slicked back over his head. His brown eyes were set deep into his head, and his expression was fierce. Pleased to see me? *I don't think so.*

'Anywhere in particular?'

'Down towards the waterfront.'

Sam put some money on the table and stood up. Joseph

Rotanski had been the head of Mossad for three years. They had only met once since then, on the one occasion the team had been recalled to Tel Aviv, but enough of the man's reputation had filtered back into the field for Sam to be nervous of him. He had brushed into the institute demanding cost cuts and more efficiency. He regarded Mossad as a bloated, secretive organisation, spending money freely and delivering few results. Word had it that Rotanski was politically ambitious. His stint running Mossad was part of his career, not the end of it. Like other Mossad bosses, he planned to use the institute as a platform to take him into government. *Whatever the agents did in the field, it had to make Rotanski look good back home.*

Only one unit had so far been exempt from his economising. Assassins. They could spend what they wanted to. *So long as they kept sending home the corpses.*

'What the hell happened?' barked Rotanski, as soon as they were out of the main square, walking down one of the alleyways that led to the old port. The smart shops had given way to the bars and cheap clothing shops used by the sailors who made Rotterdam one of the busiest ports in Europe.

'In London?' said Sam.

'Of course in London. What the hell do you think?'

'It was a set-up,' said Sam. 'We were fed the time and place for a hit on Hassim. But it was us that was taking the hit.'

'Who?'

Sam paused. He had never told Mossad where his information came from, and before today they had never asked. Those were the rules of the game: the unit was let loose, and expected to get results. It didn't have to explain or justify anything it did. 'I can't say.'

'If you've been betrayed, then that person must be punished.'

'Don't even think about it,' snapped Sam.

Rotanski kept on walking. His arms were tapping against the side of his coat. 'In London,' he said. 'Who the hell said you could do a hit in London? It shouldn't have happened. One of our men got killed. And now the British are furious with us. They're threatening to kick out half of the staff of the Israeli Embassy. They don't want our feuds on their streets, and I don't blame them. I wouldn't want the bloody IRA blowing up Tel Aviv.' He paused, looking directly at Sam. 'I tell you, it shouldn't have happened.'

'We'd been tracking Hassim for five years,' said Sam. 'It was a good opportunity.'

Rotanski lit up a cigarette, holding it contemplatively between his fingers before he took his first puff. 'OK. I don't want excuses,' he said sourly. 'I want to know why you fucked up. And what you plan to do about it.'

'I plan to get out, that's what.'

Rotanski took the first long puff on his cigarette, blowing the smoke out into the breeze drifting in from the sea. It blew straight back into Sam's face. 'We all want out, Sam,' he said, a thin smile creasing up his lips. 'A nice house by the sea. Grow some olives. Play with the kids.' He paused, looking towards the sea as a wave crashed up against the wall. 'When Israel is safe from her enemies, then maybe we can think about getting out.'

Sam shook his head twice. 'No, I mean it,' he said firmly. 'I want out.'

'When I say so.'

Sam took a pace back. 'There were twelve men on the list we were given five years ago. Eleven of them are dead. Three of our team are dead. Fifteen men, and only three are left above ground. Hassim knows who we are, he knows we're on to him. He's coming after us now.'

'You don't understand. This job doesn't allow for resignations. Those are the rules.'

Sam turned away, walking along the edge of the seafront.

Looking out, he could see the waves hurling themselves against the faded, beaten stone of the dock. 'Then the rules have just changed,' he said.

Behind him, he could hear a voice. 'The only rule that matters is that you don't quit until you finish the mission,' said Rotanski. 'That rule never changes.'

Sam didn't turn round. There was, he reflected, nothing left to say.

SIX

The journey had been a long one. From Rotterdam, Sam had taken the train up to Frankfurt, via Brussels and then Cologne. His mind had been in turmoil. That he had been right to hand in his resignation he had no doubt. With Joe's death, he had lost the will. In battle, he told himself, without will-power you are nothing. *You are already beaten.*

The house was in the Hauptwache district, a prosperous suburb to the south of Frankfurt. As soon as the unit had been sent into action, the family had been moved here by Mossad, and a regular monthly allowance was paid into Elena's personal account. All ties were meant to be severed for the duration of the mission. It had to be that way. Sam was tasked with killing some of the most brutal men on the planet: if they could find a way of taking vengence on his family they would. *She had to be untraceable.*

There was nothing grand about the house: three bed-rooms, a kitchen and a sitting room, which Elena kept immaculately neat. Luke was seven now, and Samantha five, but the two of them had already gone to bed by the time Sam arrived. He crept into their rooms and knelt down by their beds. That's what you miss as an absent father. Just holding your children, and feeling their warm breath against your skin.

Elena had been thrilled to see him. He'd called her from the station, then taken a cab to the house. They ate, then he told her what he had done. At first, he could see the

53

excitement sparking up her eyes. He's coming home. He could tell that was what she was thinking. We'll all be together again. *A family.*

But then there was something else in her expression. Fear. Worry. She was already running the calculations in her head. What will we live on? How will Sam get another job? What will this new life be like? What will become of us now?

Like any mother, she was always worried about how the family was going to pull through.

'The thing is this,' said Sam.

'The thing is what?'

Sam hesitated, trying to form the sentence in his own mind. 'You need a lot of conviction to kill a man with an easy conscience. And I just don't have that kind of conviction any more.'

'Then that's your decision,' said Elena. 'You quit. We can go back to Israel. Home.'

Sam shook his head. 'I don't think so.'

He could see the surprise on her face. On the two or three visits home he'd managed to make every year, they had rarely discussed what they would do when the mission was finished. There had been too much life to pack into a few short days and, anyway, they never had any idea when it would be over. But they had always assumed they would go back to Israel. That was where they had grown up, where their families were, and where they expected the children to live.

'In Israel, Mossad will always be after me. There will always be another job they want done. I need to put all of that behind me. We both do.'

'Where shall we live, then? Here? We're not German.'

'In London,' said Sam. 'The antiques business is going OK. I know it was just set up as a cover, but I think if we can give it a couple of years, we can start making a decent profit out of it. And you'll like London. It's not small and provincial like Frankfurt. Anyone can live in London, because the whole world meets there. Apart from New York maybe, it is the most cosmopolitan city in the world.'

'I've never spent more than a day there . . .'

Sam reached for her hand. 'You'll like it,' he said.

'The weather . . .'

'That's just in the movies,' said Sam, attempting a smile. 'Most of the time, it's no worse than the German weather.'

'And we'll have enough money?' said Elena. 'I thought the antiques didn't make anything. I thought the accounts department was always criticising you for its losses.'

'It doesn't make money now, but it could do,' said Sam. 'I'm learning the trade. This year it should break even, which means by next year I should be making a profit. All my salary for the past five years has been paid into an account in Switzerland. There should be $150,000 in that account by now. That should be enough to keep us going.'

He looked at her, putting a protective arm around her waist. 'We'll be together, that's the main thing. You, me and the kids. Like a proper family at last.'

'Maybe . . .'

He could sense the deliberation in her voice. She wasn't the same fresh-faced teenager who had entranced him twenty years ago. The years of separation were etched into the lines around her eyes: there was a tiredness there that he hadn't seen before. She was still a beautiful woman: she had high cheekbones, eyes as soft as pillows, and thick black hair that framed her face as if it was encasing a picture. But the carefree amusement had drained out of her. *She was worried.*

'It'll be OK,' said Sam.

A noise. They listened.

'What's that?' said Elena.

Sam walked carefully towards the door. At first he thought it might just be a bird, or a distant car, but after a few seconds he recognised the dry rasp of a hammer. Stopping in the kitchen, he picked up a knife, checking it was sharp enough to kill a man, then advanced through the hallway. You picked the wrong house to burgle.

He paused. The sound had stopped. His ears were alert, tuning into the darkness to see if he could detect any sounds. Nothing. Slowly, he undid the latch. Again he hesitated. His hand gripped the knife, poised for action. He opened the door a fraction. Somewhere in the distance, he could hear a car driving away. He peered outside. The soft glow of a street lamp thirty yards away filled the quiet street. Sam scanned the front lawn. Nothing. He looked at the side of the house, then up along the gutters towards the roof. Nothing.

Maybe I imagined it.

Sam took a step forward, to the paving stone that crossed the small garden leading down to the street. The road was empty at this time of night. It was just after two in the morning. Sam looked left and right, scouring the area, before turning round. Then he saw the photograph.

It was pinned to the door. A picture of Samantha. Around her face, a circle had been drawn in black felt-tip pen, and through its centre there was a cross. As if you were looking at her through the cross-hairs of a rifle. *As if you were about to kill her.*

It took several seconds for the blood in Sam's veins to unfreeze. As it did so, he ripped the picture from the wall. He recognised it at once. It was a photograph he had taken himself, a year ago, and sent home to his father. Whoever did this knew everything about him. Where he lived. Who his children were. Where his father lived.

Sam struggled to control the fury rising up inside him. He could feel his heart thumping against his chest, and the same sense of cold determination that he felt before a hit. Somebody is going to die for this.

He took a deep breath and walked back into the house. *Who?* he wondered. Rotanski? Hassim?

Elena was standing at his side.

'What is it, Sam?' she said.

He could hear the anxiety in her voice.

He passed across the picture, then reached out a hand to steady her. She was staring at the picture, at first puzzled by it, then looking at it with horror as she slowly deciphered its meaning. 'We've got to get you and the kids out of here,' said Sam. 'Right now.'

The lobby of the Banque Laboucherd was simple enough. The walls were wood-panelled, and the sofas were freshly upholstered. On a coffee table, there was a display of British, American and local Swiss papers. Everything about the place smelt of money. If I was offered another life, I might well be a Swiss banker, thought Sam. Good money, beautiful surroundings, low taxes. And all you have to do is keep your mouth shut. *How hard could that be?*

'Mr Kurer will see you in five minutes,' said the receptionist. 'He sends his apologies for the delay. Another client has run over the allotted time.'

Both Sam and Michael nodded. There was no need to hurry, Sam decided. *I spent five years making this money. Another five minutes won't matter.*

Five years ago, when the mission started, he'd chosen Lucerne, preferring it to the two better known Swiss financial centres, Geneva and Zurich. It was smaller, tucked into the side of Lake Lucerne, home to a dozen private banks, managing the money mostly of Italian and German businessmen who liked to keep their assets away from the tax authorities in their own countries. It rarely attracted any of the big, international money, the way that Zurich did. Sam didn't mind that. He liked local, and small-scale. I am, after all, small-time myself. *And happy to keep it that way.*

'So,' said Michael, looking towards the receptionist with a broad grin on his face, 'this guy called Abe, he goes to see his rabbi, and says, "Rabbi, something terrible is happening and I have to talk to you about it." "What's wrong, Abe?" the rabbi asks. "My wife is poisoning me," Abe replies. The rabbi was very surprised by this. "How can that be?" he says. "I'm telling you," Abe pleads, "I'm certain she's poisoning me, what should I do?" The rabbi then offers, "Tell you what. Let me talk to her, I'll see what I can find out and I'll let you know." A week later the rabbi calls Abe and says, "Well, I spoke to your wife. I spoke to her on the phone for three hours. You want my advice?" "Yes," says Abe anxiously. "Take the poison," says the rabbi.'

Michael laughed out loud as he delivered the punchline, and the receptionist laughed with him. I'm going to miss this idiot, thought Sam, smiling at the joke, even though he'd heard it a couple of times before.

The previous day had been spent getting Elena and the kids out of Frankfurt. He'd sent them to stay with one of her cousins who lived just outside Vienna. Even though her Mossad allowance would stop, there was enough money in her account for them to live for a few months. As soon as he could organise it, he would find a place for them in London. I can use the money deposited here to get us sorted out. *And to find out who is threatening my family's life.*

'Mr Kurer will see you now,' said the girl.

Sam stood up. When the mission had been set up, it was agreed that the salaries of the team would be paid through a dummy company in Germany. It was important that nothing should connect the five of them back to Mossad, so they had to be taken off the official payroll. Once the money was paid into the German company, it was then paid out to an account in this bank. Sam checked it every few months. Since all expenses were paid for, and Elena had been given a separate allowance to live on, he had been building up some tidy savings.

'Good to see you,' said Kurer.

He was almost six feet tall, with a dimpled, delicate face, and skin that was so smooth it was as if he never set foot outside. Sam shook his hand, as they walked through to his office. 'We need to withdraw our money,' he said, coming straight to the point. 'I have an account in London, but I'd like to have the money in cash. In American dollars.'

Kurer nodded curtly, pursing his lips together as if in thought. 'Quite so, Mr Wolfman,' he said. 'As you wish.'

'You keep enough in cash, I hope,' said Sam. 'If necessary, I can stay in Lucerne for a couple of days.'

A smile flashed across Kurer's lips. 'I think we have enough funds,' he said. 'Excuse me, while I go to the vaults.'

Sam sat down. From the window, he could see a clear view of the lake, with the mountains rising from all sides. One hundred and fifty thousand dollars, thought Sam, turning the number over in his mind. Thirteen thousand, six hundred for each man we took down. Their lives were sold cheaply. The way they should be.

Kurer came back into the room. Sam stood up, walking over to the desk. Carefully, Kurer opened an attaché case, then glanced up at Sam as he counted out three bills. One ten-dollar note. And two singles. 'Here is your money, Mr Wolfman,' he said. 'Twelve dollars. Actually, the balance on your account as of this morning was eleven dollars and thirty-eight cents. I decided to round it up.'

Sam looked down at the money. It took a moment for the words to connect. Even when they did, Sam wasn't sure he had heard right. Twelve dollars. It was impossible. 'There must be some mistake,' he said quickly.

'No mistake,' said Kurer.

'But the last time I checked there was a hundred and fifty

59

thousand in the account. That was only a couple of months ago.'

'Well, I imagine there was a withdrawal.'

'A withdrawal?'

'That's when a customer takes money from an account.'

Swiss bankers, thought Sam. As soon as your account is empty, they turn on the sarcasm as easily as they turned on the charm.

'But who . . .'

Sam didn't need to finish the sentence. Suddenly, it was all clear in his mind. The account was set up with two signatories. Sam, of course. Plus the dummy company in Germany. The company that was controlled by Mossad to launder the money it was paying to Sam.

Rotanski. *The bastard had emptied out the account . . .*

'The other signatory, of course,' said Kurer. 'FBH Holdings AG, of Stuggart. The money was withdrawn two days ago, sent to an account at the Dresdner Bank in Stuggart.'

Sam could feel the pulse beating within him. Keep steady, he warned himself. Anger will get you nowhere. 'Who took it?'

'I just told you, the company.'

'Who at the company?'

Kurer cast a steely eye at him. 'Bankers are occasionally caught in the middle of disputes between signatories to accounts, Mr Wolfman,' he said, a pompous, self-satisfied expression playing on his face. 'I can assure you that all my experience has told me it is better never to take sides. If there has been a misunderstanding between the two signatories to this account, then I'm afraid you'll have to sort that out between yourselves.'

He backed away, standing behind his desk, as if it were a protective wall, shielding him from the anger that was evident in Sam's eyes. 'All I can tell you is that the money has been legitimately withdrawn.'

'And my money,' said Michael quickly. 'What's happened to my account?'

'Your account is in order,' said Kurer. 'The balance as of this morning is ninety-two thousand, three hundred and thirty-eight dollars.' His eyes turned sharply from Michael to Sam. 'Now, is there anything else I can help you with today?'

Sam stood looking down at the water of the lake swirling beneath him. There was an old wooden footbridge at the far end of Lucerne, where the lake narrowed to just fifty metres, and the water rushed beneath it. A single thought was echoing through his mind. *The bastards. You step out of line for one minute, and they strip you of everything.*

'You going to be OK?' said Michael.

Sam attempted a grin, but the muscles in his face weren't working. 'They took everything,' he said. 'The money I was going to use to start again. All of it. Just because I disagreed with them. Just because I told that idiot Rotanski that it was useless, that we couldn't go on any more.'

'You sure it was him?'

'I told him three days ago I was quitting. A day after I speak to him the account gets drained. The only people who had access to the German company were Mossad. They set the damned thing up. It has to be them.'

'For revenge?'

'Of course. That's what Rotanski's like,' said Sam. 'He's just a bloody desk jockey. All he knows is how to shuffle paper around. He wants to punish me. And to be an example to the others. To show that you put one foot out of line, this is what they'll do to you.'

'Maybe he wants you back,' said Michael. 'This is his way of forcing you back into the fold.'

Sam shook his head. 'Even Rotanski's not that stupid,' he said. 'You don't win a man back by stealing from him.'

Sam started walking. It was better to walk, he told himself.

Keep your head clear. Decide what to do next. Make each move as if your life depended on it.

'I can help you,' said Michael.

'I'll be OK. I'm a big boy, I can look after myself.'

'I have more than ninety thousand. Really, I don't need it. No family, not even a girlfriend. I've got my next posting, so there's nothing I need to worry about. Look, you need a loan until the antiques business starts making money, take it.'

'I don't need it.'

'Hey, don't be a fool. We spent five years together. It's only the two of us left. Take the damned money.'

Sam turned to face his friend. 'I got myself into this mess. I'll find my own way out.'

Michael nodded. 'So what are you going to do?'

'I've got a thousand dollars in cash, and a plane ticket back to London,' said Sam. 'And with that, I'm going to rebuild my life.'

SEVEN

The boards were hammered roughly across the front of the shop. Put up quickly, noted Sam as he looked at the nails spliced through the wood. *By someone who wanted to make sure another part of my life was sealed up in a tomb.*

He stepped forwards, standing in front of the small, narrow window behind which he had sat for much of the last three years. A sign on the shopfront said it had closed. Another sign advertised premises to rent. Through the gaps between the boards he could see the floor of the shop was empty. The stock had already been taken away. Maybe even sold.

Don't look back, he told himself.

With his hands dug deep into the pockets of his overcoat, Sam started walking. He'd landed at Heathrow at ten this morning, then taken the tube to Sloane Square, and walked to the shop from there. The plan had been forming in his mind. He'd come back to London. He'd reopen the shop, transferring the lease from the dummy company set up by Mossad into his own name. He'd get a bank loan, and get in some fresh stock. Some of those little half-tables to slot into hallways, and cheesy oil paintings of dogs and hounds: the kind of stuff the English liked, and which would walk out of the shop without much trouble. He'd put his head down and turn it into a business. Within a few months, he'd be turning enough of a profit for Elena and the kids to join him. Put a deposit down on a house out in the burbs. They'd be OK. *Just.*

Sam walked past the Royal Hospital, nodding to a couple of the Chelsea Pensioners wearing their red ornamental tunics. The world is full of old soldiers, he thought. At least the British give them a nice uniform.

That Rotanski was responsible for the closure of the shop, Sam had no doubt. The lease had been taken out via a British subsidiary of the Stuggart holding company. The stock was all owned by the same vehicle. From the looks of it, the lease had been cancelled, and the stock had all been sold off. There was no shortage of auction houses in London where you could get rid of a shopful of antiques quickly.

I'm being written out of the script. As if I never existed.

Sam crossed the river, walking over Chelsea Bridge, passing by Battersea Park, and down on to the Queenstown Road leading towards Clapham. It led him through one of the sharp transitions he'd grown used to in the five years he'd been living in London. The opulence and wealth of Chelsea melted away into the poverty and grime of Battersea. A few streets of old Victorian terraces were starting to be spruced up, but right behind the park, there were acres of grim housing estates stretching back for half a mile at least. The landscape was grey concrete.

I had a thousand dollars and a plane ticket and a shop with some stock in it. Now, I've got nine hundred and forty dollars, and nothing except my own wits.

He stopped outside a newsagent's. The window was grubby, but there was a collection of scribbled postcards on display. A lawnmower for sale. A woman who did cleaning. Some kittens looking for homes. And rooms to rent. Thirty pounds a week, plus electricity in a coin-operated meter.

I'll do the only thing I can do. I'll start rebuilding my life, block by block. *Until I have something I can be proud of again.*

Sam sealed the letter, and dropped it into the postbox. Like many decisions in his life, he'd felt better once he'd made it.

Once or twice during a largely sleepless night he'd felt a damp touch of doubt creeping across his mind. Maybe he should go back to Mossad. Complete the mission, kill Hassim. Do a deal to get his money back. Buy the shop from them. Do anything to get his life back on the rails from which it had been so brutally shaken.

No. That wasn't an option.

There is always something satisfying about slamming a door shut.

The letter was addressed to a shipping company in Marseille. Just one of the vast network of front organisations Mossad had established across Europe. It would get to Rotanski in due course. And the content was clear enough. Sam Wolfman formally resigned from the organisation. No more reasons, no more explanations. Just a polite farewell. *It was over.*

Rotanski could be left in no doubt of his decision. They could keep his money if they wanted to; there was nothing Sam could do legally to recover it anyway, and there was no way he was going to try to fight Mossad single-handed. It made no difference. He wasn't going to work for them again.

The bedsit he'd rented had a single bed, which creaked with age. In one corner there was a single electric ring. In another, there was a single basin. The windows were covered with a plastic blind on which a thick layer of grease had embedded itself. Looking out, you could see the back rows of small terraced houses, and above that a gas works and a railway line. Who the other lodgers were, Sam had not yet assessed. One thing was clear. Their luck must have all but run out. Otherwise they wouldn't be here.

Thirty-five years into your life, and you find yourself alone and living in a slum. *You have to work your way out of this. And quickly.*

The Man in the Moon pub was at the bottom of Chelsea's

King's Road. Sam recognised the man as soon as he sat down. David Grise was approaching forty, and had left Mossad four years earlier, after a decade working undercover in Africa and Asia. His face was tanned, and he'd grown a beard since the last time Sam had seen him. Looking good, thought Sam. Then again, I probably look all right myself. Looks tell you nothing.

'You're out,' said Grise, collecting two glasses of orange juice from the bar, and handing one to Sam.

'About time too,' said Sam.

It was a Thursday afternoon, and customers were sparse. A couple of old men were sipping on pints and smoking cheap cigars in one corner of the bar. A black guy was sitting by himself with a glass of gin. Otherwise empty. Sam looked at Grise. Civilian life was suiting him. He seemed relaxed.

'You fixed all right financially?'

Sam shrugged. 'Who is?'

Grise laughed. 'Nobody who worked for those bastards, that's for sure.'

Sam had first met Grise in the army, then come across him again when he was bodyguarding Israeli government ministers. He was a rough, humorous character, always complaining about the long hours and the lousy pay. Several times he'd tried to persuade Sam to get involved with one of the countless entrepreneurial schemes being run by one of his many cousins. After bodyguarding, he'd gone off to work in data collection – a polite bureaucratic term for spying – attached to Israeli embassies across South-East Asia. Then for a while back in Tel Aviv, Grise had been in charge of 'babblers', the anti-bugging devices that were planted in every senior cabinet minister's office. After that, he'd mobbed on to 'false flagging', a sophisticated ploy Mossad had perfected for recruiting intelligence sources abroad by convincing them they were working for some country other than Israel. Grise had been particularly good at convincing Egyptians and Moroccans around Europe they were feeding information to the Palestinians when in fact it was going straight to Mossad. Although they hadn't worked together for nearly a decade, they'd stayed in touch as best they could.

'I need to know what I can do on the outside,' said Sam.

'Got anything lined up?'

'I did,' said Sam. 'But it's gone. So I need to make some money. Quickly.'

Grise laughed. 'That's always the hard kind, isn't it? The quick money.'

'That's what I need.'

'And how far are you prepared to go?'

'I'll do whatever it takes.'

There was a silence. Neither man needed to speak. They both knew what the consequences of leaving Mossad were. Grise certainly wasn't about to spell it out. Guys came out of the service in their mid-thirties. They had no qualifications, except for the black arts of phone-tapping, mail interception, bugging, surveillance and, occasionally, assassination. Of course they had 'legends' – the elaborate cover stories and false identities provided by Mossad – but they had no CVs. If they went to a job interview, they couldn't tell anyone what they had been doing for the last decade. It was all secret. They had nothing to offer.

Grise looked at Sam sympathetically. 'It's worse out there than you think.'

'Explain.'

'There isn't much work for men like us. There's a lot of talk among the guys about private security work, but the truth is, it's pretty thin on the ground. Most companies don't need people who do what we do. Why would they? They sell soap powder and washing machines and bank accounts and all the rest of it. What do they need surveillance and wiretapping for? There's bodyguarding, but not as much as there used to be. And when there is, it doesn't pay that great. Five hundred dollars a day. Maximum.'

'You look OK,' said Sam.

Grise laughed. 'There's always a niche,' he said. 'If you know where to find it. I lucked out, but not everyone does that.'

He handed over a sheet of paper. Sam looked down. On it there was a neatly typed list of names, and next to each one an address and a phone number. 'Call them,' he said. 'They're the people I know who might be able to help you out.'

'I'll do that.'

'Good luck,' Grise said, standing up to leave. 'I hope it works out for you.'

Sam looked at the man sitting opposite him. He was forty-five, with sandy hair, and a scar down the left-hand side of his cheek. Bob Herbert had been in the SAS for a decade, and had picked up some shiny medals in the Falklands. Now he was running the London base of Surgical Security Ltd, a small company that pretended to be in the corporate protection business while mainly hiring out mercenaries to whichever government might be able to afford its exorbitant fees.

'Handy with a gun, Mr Wolfman?' he said.

Sam nodded. 'I can show you the medals from my time in the Israeli Army.'

Herbert smiled. 'No need,' he said crisply. 'We know you Israeli boys always give everyone a good thumping.' He glanced at the sheet of paper on his desk, a letter Sam had written introducing himself. 'And the last ten years, that's with Mossad right. Doing what?'

'I can't speak about it.'

'I understand,' said Herbert. 'Just give me the general flavour.'

'Undercover,' said Sam. 'There are people the Israeli government would prefer not to have around any more. They told me their names. And then . . .'

Herbert leaned back in his chair. He was wearing jeans, but a formal shirt, with a pair of gold cuff links that caught the light streaming in from the window. His office was just a pair of rooms in an anonymous block just behind Baker Street. There was a phone but no computer, just a big map of the world on the wall and an atlas on his desk.

'And you need money, fast?'

Sam nodded.

'You don't mind if it gets rough?'

'I'm used to that.'

'Then I might have something for you. It would be a couple of months' work in Africa. Might be some shooting involved, and you might have to take orders from a wog. You can handle that?'

'So long as the orders aren't suicidal.'

Herbert laughed. 'Well, if they're coming from a blackie, they might well be bloody stupid, but if they're suicidal then you could always just ignore them.' He paused, jotting some notes down on a pad of paper on his desk. 'OK, we could offer you, say, eight weeks' work to start with, and we'd pay you a thousand a week, cash. Airfares and everything thrown in of course. So when you get home you've got eight grand in cash in your pocket. What do you say?'

Sam tried to smile, but his lips could scarcely move. Cannon fodder, that's all you're looking for. Someone to risk his life while you sit behind this tidy desk collecting a tidy 30 per cent.

My life may not be worth much, but I'd put a higher tag than eight grand on it.

'I'll think about it, if I may,' said Sam politely. He stood up to leave. 'I've got your number.'

★

'The thing about bodyguarding is it's bloody boring,' said John Clusky. 'Jesus, sometimes you hope there might be an attempted kidnapping or something just to liven up the bloody monotony of the day.'

He was standing in a corner of a crowded bar just off Tottenham Court Road. The pub was packed with after-work drinkers, yet Clusky had insisted they go down there to talk rather than stay in his single-room office on Charlotte Street, where he ran a company called Belgravia Security. He was already on to his second double whisky, although Sam was still only halfway through his first half-pint of lager.

'Can you drive?' said Clusky.

'Of course.'

'And shoot?'

Sam nodded.

'Then you've got the bloody basics covered,' said Clusky.

Clusky's own background wasn't clear, even though Sam had made a couple of phone calls to try and check him out before their meeting. A Scotsman, he claimed to have been a major in the Black Watch, yet from his appearance it must have been some time since he left the regiment. His hair was growing down beyond the collar of his shirt. His stomach was flabby. And his skin was red and blotchy.

The company provided bodyguards throughout London. Twenty-four hours a day, seven days a week, it boasted that none of its clients had ever been harmed. Then again, since kidnapping was virtually unheard of in Britain, that wasn't much of a boast. 'Truth is, we have two types of clients,' Clusky replied when Sam asked him about it. 'We get a few bored Arab housewives who want someone to look after them. That usually means three days traipsing around Harrods, helping to carry their shopping. Then we get American executives who think anywhere east of New York is a bit foreign and dangerous. That usually means a couple of days sitting outside boardrooms in the City, then reminding them they have to take their passports with them when they go to Paris because it's a different bloody country. The hardest thing about this job is not losing your patience with the morons and tossers we end up working for.'

'So do you think you might have anything for me?' said Sam.

'The point about bodyguarding is it's mostly just marketing,' said Clusky. He turned towards the barman and ordered another drink. 'We use a lot of ex-SAS guys because the punters love it. They think they're getting a real hard man. The bored housewives like that in particular. I don't think they actually shag them, but it gives them a bit of thrill to think they've got a real killer taking them shopping for the afternoon.' He paused. 'Now, Mossad is hard all right, as hard as they come. I'm not disputing that. But obviously the Arabs are out of the question. They're not going to like it. Then again, we get a few big-shot Jewish American bankers and businessmen. Some of them might be impressed.' He looked straight at Sam. 'I think if we were to use you, we'd have to talk about how many people you'd knocked off. Build you up. Give it a bit of colour.'

'I couldn't do that.'

'There's no point being fussy in this business, mate,' said Clusky. 'You have to sell yourself a bit.'

'I can't talk about my past work.'

Clusky downed his drink. His eyes suddenly narrowed. 'Then we can't use you, mate,' he said. 'There's no space here for bloody prima donnas. Either you give the punters what they want, or you can naff off.'

Sam put his half-pint of lager back down on the counter. He'd only taken two sips. 'Then I'm sorry for wasting your time,' he said firmly.

Sam walked away from the pub and started heading back towards the tube. He could get the Northern Line back to

Clapham, then walk to the bedsit from there. It was only nine thirty, but there was nothing else for him to do. Let's see what tomorrow brings, he thought grimly. There are still names on the list. Maybe something will turn up.

Sam hesitated before pushing the doorbell. The flat was number 7 in a series of eight-in-one big, stucco-fronted houses, on Sutherland Avenue in Maida Vale. There was no name on the bell, just a number.

'I'm looking for Ben Dutton?'

'Who is it?'

'Sam Wolfman.'

'Come up.'

The buzzer opened the door, and Sam stepped over the piles of unopened mail and the bike in the hallway, and started climbing the stairs to the third floor. Along the way, he'd stopped off on the Edgware Road, glancing towards the street where Joe had died just a couple of weeks earlier. It had returned to normal. Any barriers the police had put up had been taken down. Where Joe was now, Sam had no idea. Nobody had claimed the body. Mossad corpses could never be named. Probably they'll wait until they had written 'Case Unsolved' on his file, then they'll take him down to the crematorium, and put his ashes in a box somewhere.

He deserved better, thought Sam as he climbed the last flight of stairs. *We all do.*

'Cup of tea?' said Dutton. 'I've got one brewing.'

Sam nodded, and stepped into the flat. It was sparsely furnished: a sofa, a pile of magazines, a big TV and video recorder, and the remains of a pizza on the floor. Dutton was a small man, just over five feet. His hair was jet black, and swept back over his forehead. Hard to place his origins. Not English, that's for sure, and Dutton was certainly not his real name. Maybe Italian. Maybe Hungarian or Albanian. One of the hordes of Eastern European gangsters who'd started to swan into London since the Berlin Wall came down the previous year. Men who were so used to dealing in the black market and dodging the secret police of the regimes they'd grown up with it was as if they'd been given a master's degree in the arts of smuggling, prostitution and money laundering. And now they were all being let into Western Europe.

A few weeks ago, I might have been tracking a guy like this. Not looking to work with him. *Or for him.*

'David tells me you're pretty useful,' said Dutton, putting down a mug with the tea bag still floating in it.

'I know my way around,' said Sam with a shrug.

Dutton looked at him cautiously, examining his reaction. He looked like a man used to making snap judgements on the trustworthiness or otherwise of everyone he met, yet looked to be having trouble with Sam. 'Ever done any transportation?'

'What kind?'

'Stuff that you don't want customs to know about. Doesn't matter what it is. Just a few boxes, that's all. Some things some men in Hungary would like delivered to Britain.'

'I've done that kind of thing, yes.'

There was nothing untrue about the answer. Usually the team had sourced whatever weapons or explosives they needed in the country where the hit was staged – more often than not through Papa. That was one of the rules of the trade: buy local. Not because it was better, but because carrying anything illegal across a border was just a pointless risk. Still, there had been times when it had been necessary, and Sam knew most of the tricks. For the right money, he might consider it.

'What do you want shipped?'

'Like I said, just some boxes,' said Dutton. 'No need to look inside them.'

'I like to know what I'm delivering.'

'And I like mules that don't ask questions,' snapped Dutton.

Sam fell silent. A mule. I'm being described as a mule by some irrelevant Hungarian gangster. *And I'm not even bothering to disagree.*

'When do you need it?'

'What?'

'The stuff,' said Sam. 'From where to where? And when?'

'You fly to Budapest. I'll give you the name of a guy there. He'll take you to a van with some kit in the back. You drive it to London, then deliver it to me. I'll give you a grand in cash to cover your expenses for the trip. Then I'll give you two grand on delivery for your trouble.' Dutton grinned, revealing two glistening gold teeth. 'Not bad for a week's work.'

'Same van?'

'Well, of course the same bloody van.'

'Let me see,' said Sam. 'From Budapest to London. I'm crossing into Austria, then up into Germany, down into Belgium, then through either France or Holland to get back to Britain. I make that at least five border crossings. I'd have thought you'd need to change the van at least a couple of times, to reduce your chances of detection.'

'Well, it's just the one van, mate,' snapped Dutton. 'We're not made of money.'

'And how about the plates,' pressed Sam. 'Is this a Hungarian-registered van? Because that's a lot more likely to be searched. I'd have thought you'd be better to start out with German plates and then switch to Dutch plates. That's just a matter of stealing some then sticking them on the van.'

'Listen, we just want a mule to drive the bloody van, OK?'

'I'll tell you something,' said Sam. 'I don't mind working with gangsters, smugglers or murderers, but I'm not interested in working with fucking amateurs. Goodbye.'

He turned round, and walked out of the flat.

'I heard you were all right, shouted Dutton. 'But you're just a tosser.'

Sam kept on walking silently down the staircase. The words were just washing over him. There are limits to how low a man can sink, he told himself. And I've just found them.

Mrs Stevens was a woman in her mid-fifties, with permed black hair and the grey, tired skin of a hardened smoker. In the three days Sam had been living in the bedsit now, she appeared to spend most of her life pacing around the hall-way, a cup of tea attached to her left hand, inspecting the comings and goings of the different lodgers in the house. Sam smiled at her weakly as he stepped through the door. He had so far managed to avoid any conversation that contained more than three sentences.

'The hot water is on the blink, love,' she said.

Sam nodded.

'And there's no heating,' she added. 'Sorry about that. I've got a bloke coming in, but he won't be here until tomorrow.'

'I'll survive,' said Sam.

He started to walk up the stairs. The carpets were faded and threadbare, and although the paint on the walls was new, patches of damp were starting to show through. There was a lingering smell of boiled potatoes in the air. On the way up, he passed another of the lodgers. A woman with red hair, approaching forty, wearing a tight leather miniskirt and a black jacket with thick shoulder pads. She nodded at Sam and seemed to be about to say something, but he just looked away.

'Mr Wolfman,' Mrs Stevens shouted up at him.

Sam stopped.

'I forgot, there was a call for you.'

A call, thought Sam. *I've told no one I'm here.*

'A man called David,' continued Mrs Stevens. 'Said he had something to add to your conversation the other day. He said to give him a call.'

Sam turned round. There was a phone that the lodgers used to make and receive calls, but Sam didn't want to use that. Too much chance of being overheard by the ever-pacing Mrs Stevens. He stepped out on to the street, and walked the two blocks to the nearest phone booth.

Putting a coin into the slot, he dialled Grise's number.

'How did you know where to find me?' he asked as soon as the phone was answered.

'It wasn't that hard,' replied Grise. 'You said you'd walked to the King's Road. I know you don't have much money. So I figured you must be staying in some cheap lodgings just on the other side of the river. There's only about a dozen of them. I found you in the fourth call.'

Mossad training, thought Sam. All the field agents were smart. *They knew how to track down the people they wanted.*

'I'm not really hiding,' said Sam lightly. 'Just saving money. Until I get things sorted out.'

'How's it going?'

Sam paused. There was no point in saying just how badly it had gone. 'OK,' he said. 'Nothing substantial yet. Some leads.'

'It's tough, right.'

'No joking.'

'Listen,' said Grise. 'There's one more person you should call. His name is Benjamin Naved.'

'Who is he?' said Sam.

'Rich guy, well connected, but used to be one of us,' said Grise. 'Trust me, you'll like him.'

Sam jotted down the number, then put the phone down. He started walking back towards the bedsit. Along the way, he picked up some bread and cheese, and a few apples. I'll

76

have supper in my room, he decided. I have 587 pounds left in cash. No point in blowing the money on meals in restaurants. At the rate I'm going, that might have to last me for years.

Another minor arms merchant, maybe. A drug trafficker or a pimp. Whoever he is, he's probably just another one of the minor lowlifes and losers who Grise seems to associate himself with these days. I'll leave calling Naved until tomorrow.

There's only so much humiliation a man can digest in one day.

He turned the corner, approaching the street where he was staying.

A man in the shadows.

He was standing just opposite, then began moving along the pavement. Sam's eyes flickered up towards him. About thirty, wearing a thick grey coat. He had brown hair, with some stubble on his chin, and he was playing with a cigarette lighter in the fingers of his left hand.

Sam kept walking, monitoring the pavement opposite. The man was walking at a slow to moderate pace. He was looking straight ahead of himself. You've made one mistake, thought Sam. You're acting too casual. I've made that walk too many times myself. *I could spot it anywhere.*

He stepped inside the front door of the house. 'Get what you needed?' said Mrs Stevens, walking away from the kitchen towards her own rooms.

Sam nodded, then waited until she closed the door behind her. He headed for the kitchen, where there was enough light seeping through the windows for him to see clearly. He walked swiftly towards the back, unbolted the door and stepped into the garden. It measured about thirty feet, with a few shrubs around its borders and a back fence that led into a side alley, filled with bins, old bikes and weeds. Sam scaled the fence, and landed softly on the other side. He walked towards the end of the alley, hesitating as he approached the street, then peered round the corner. The man was there again. Just walking, slowly up and down. *The way you would if you were watching the place.*

Sam dived back into the alley and waited. He took one of the dustbins, and emptied the contents of a black bin bag on to the ground. Next, he rolled up the bag and slipped it into his pocket. The man would have completed one circuit of the street and be starting another. The same slow, practised movement. Up and down. Within ten, maybe fifteen seconds, he would be passing the alley. I can wait, thought Sam. *And then I'll have you.*

Now he could hear the man drawing closer. Sam tensed his muscles. He was just yards away. He could hear the footsteps moving past him. With a sudden swift movement, Sam moved forwards. He locked his arms around the man's neck, dragging him backwards. His hand reached up to the man's mouth, but he wasn't even trying to scream. He was strong, with the shoulder muscles of a man who lifted weights, but he had been taken by surprise, and it would take a minute for him to summon the strength to resist. Sam pushed him down on to the ground. His knee barrelled into the man's chest, knocking the wind out of his lungs. A groan of pain erupted from his lips. In the same second, Sam whipped the bin bag over the man's head. It still smelt of the rubbish that had been tipped out of it: takeaway curry, noted Sam with distaste. Pulling it tight, he closed it around the man's head, then gripped his arms. 'Within twenty seconds, you're going to be dead,' said Sam.

The man was struggling, but Sam was holding on tight to his arms. His lungs were gasping for oxygen, but the bag was too tight around his neck. He was just sucking into a vacuum.

'. . . five . . . six . . . seven . . .'

Sam stopped at fifteen. Already he could feel the man's limbs start to loosen as the oxygen drained out of him. He relaxed his grip just enough to let some air into the bag. The man was gasping desperately. 'Who the fuck are you working for?' said Sam.

'Piss off,' the man spat through the bag.

Sam tightened his grip on the bag, '. . . fifteen . . . sixteen . . . seventeen . . .'

He loosened the bag, letting in a small gust of air. 'For the last time, who the fuck are you working for?'

The man was still struggling to breathe. 'Foreign guy. Maybe Italian. He paid me to follow you and report back on your movements.' The man took another gulp of air. 'Christ, please don't kill me. I'm nothing, just a watchman.'

'Where can I find him?'

The man was trembling with fear.

Sam tightened the bag again. 'I said, where can I find him?'

He loosened the bag again. The man gasped for air, but he had taken no more than one breath before Sam closed it again. 'Now, this time just tell me,' he said.

'The Holloway Road,' said the man. 'Number 172. It's a kebab shop. I'm supposed to meet the guy there tomorrow night. One in the morning.'

Sam wrapped the bag even tighter around the man's neck. 'Well, you're not going to make it,' he said.

He could feel the strength draining out of the man. For a moment he toyed with the idea of killing him. No, he told himself. The guy's just a runner. A nobody. He relaxed his grip, letting the air back in. Next, he released the man's arms. The man reached up, and tore at the plastic, scratching it the way a man who had been buried alive would scratch at the mud. 'Now, fuck off,' said Sam. 'If you even think about going to that meeting, you're a dead man.'

Sam scaled the fence. He knew that he was no longer protected by Mossad. Maybe Mossad even intended to kill him. The foreign guy could be Italian – but more likely Israeli, or Hassim.

Sam had never felt more alone.

EIGHT

The house was a double-fronted Georgian building on Church Row in Hampstead. There was a Land-Rover in the driveway, next to a Mini. The door was painted black, decorated with gleaming ornamental brass work, and from the look of the place, money had been lavished on every square inch of the building. At least some of the old Mossad guys are doing all right for themselves, Sam thought as he walked up the steps that led to the front door. *What's their secret? I wonder.*

He rang the bell, and the door was opened by a Spanish girl, maybe eighteen or nineteen. She could have been a maid, but her casual manner suggested she was more likely the au pair to Naved's three children. 'Wait in the study,' she said. 'Ben will be down in a minute.'

Sam walked through to the smallest of three rooms that led off the main hallway. Late last night, he'd taken his kit from the lodging house, and moved to another cheap hotel towards Stockwell. If Hassim knew where he was, he needed to melt back into the City. First thing this morning, he'd called Naved and arranged to meet him at ten. Then deal with Hassim tonight.

The room was simply furnished, with a desk, a couple of chairs, a sofa, two phones. There was a gilt mirror hanging over a marble fireplace, and on the mantelpiece some pictures of Naved. One showed him shaking hands with Margaret Thatcher, another with Lord Hanson. A couple of calls back to Tel Aviv had established Naved's background. He worked for Mossad between 1975 and 1985, some of the toughest years in the organisation's history. He'd started in the field, then moved into counter-intelligence, before spending his final two years with the Directory, a unit of Mossad that kept track of all its spies, agents, informers and friends around the world. He'd acquired a reputation as a hard, methodical operator, according to the people Sam had spoken with. Yet he'd also acquired a taste for the lifestyle of the people his work led him to mix with. It was common enough in intelligence work, Sam had noticed. Agents smell the money. After a while, they wanted some of it for themselves.

By the looks of things, Naved wasn't just smelling the money these days. *He was eating it as well.*

'Pleased to meet you, Sam,' said Naved, walking into the room.

Sam stood, and the two men shook hands. Naved was a tall, thin man in his early fifties, with a tanned face and the body of someone who worked out regularly. 'Thanks for seeing me.'

Naved pulled up a chair, while Sam sat down on the sofa. 'I've heard a lot about you.'

'Who from?'

'I keep my ear to the ground. Ten years in the service, five undercover here in Europe. One of Mossad's best men. They'd never say that of course, they never do. But they gave you the most difficult job they have, so they must think something of you.'

The Spanish girl came into the room, putting down a tray of tea and biscuits. Naved poured two cups, waited until the girl had left, then looked back at Sam. 'Heard you had a bit of a falling-out with Rotanski. I don't blame you. He's a mean son of a bitch. And not nearly as clever as he thinks he is.'

'It doesn't matter now,' said Sam. 'He's the power. Once you've quarrelled with him, then you've quarrelled with the power. There's nothing else to do except go your own way.'

Naved nodded. 'The question is what to do next.' He put down his cup of tea. 'You're good, Sam, from what I hear. But you're also a loner. You play by your own rules. That limits your options.' He paused, glancing out of the window, as if turning an issue over in his mind before deciding whether to speak. 'I might know of something that could interest you.'

Sam drained the tea from his cup. Whatever it was – arms smuggling, assassinations, bank robbery – it couldn't be any worse than the work he'd been offered in the last few days. 'What?' he said softly.

'The Robertson File,' said Naved. 'Ever heard of it?'

'Max Robertson?' said Sam.

He thought for a moment about how he had been approached by Selima Robertson. A coincidence? *Maybe* . . .

'That's the one.'

'I've heard the name.' Sam paused before continuing. 'But what's the file?'

A slow smile started to ease on to Naved's lips, as if he'd just thought of something else. 'I'll give you the name of the man who can explain it to you.'

I'm going up in the world, thought Sam as he stepped into the offices of Merriman & Dowler. The reception area was lined with oak panelling, the orchids in a vase in the corner were freshly cut, and the receptionist looked as if she'd just stepped off the catwalk.

'Mr Dowler will be with you shortly, sir,' said the receptionist with a catwalk smile.

Sam nodded and took a seat. The appointment had taken only a few hours to arrange. He'd called straight after he left Naved's house, and Dowler had told him to be in his office at two that afternoon. Suddenly everybody wants to know me, thought Sam.

Maurice Dowler was another former Mossad man, who'd left the service and set up Merriman & Dowler, an upmarket City investigations agency. After struggling for a few years, it had made a name for itself during some of the big hostile takeover battles of the 1980s. Several tycoons had retreated wounded after investigators from Merriman & Dowler had unearthed details of Liechtenstein trusts, illicit tax deals or mistresses living luxuriously on the company payroll, and threatened to leak them all to the business sections of the Sunday papers. If you wanted to dig up some dirt, then Merriman & Dowler were the men with the spades.

'Coffee or tea?' said the receptionist as she ushered Sam into the office.

'Coffee,' said Sam briskly.

Dowler shook him warmly by the hand. He was a short man, running to fat now that he was moving through his fifties. Too many City lunches, guessed Sam. His hair was gone, and the thick black spectacles he wore turned his face into a series of circles. But his smile was genuine. Of all the people he had met in the past few days, Dowler was the first one who Sam felt might actually be pleased to see him.

'How much do you know about Max Robertson?' he asked, sitting down opposite Sam on one of a pair of armchairs in the corner of his office.

Only that a couple of weeks ago his stepdaughter walked into my shop asking me to investigate his death. *And I still don't know how the hell she found out who I was.*

'Just general knowledge,' he said.

'Then I'll start at the beginning.'

Dowler took a sip on the coffee the receptionist had just brought in, then settled back into his chair with the expression of a man who enjoys telling stories.

'You'll hear lots of tales about Robertson, and they'll all

83

have one thing in common,' he began. 'None of them will be good.'

'He was a swindler,' said Sam.

'One of the best. Maybe the greatest of the twentieth century. He was Hungarian by birth, but made his fortune in Britain. Scientific publishing was what gave him his start, mainly buying up research work from the Soviet bloc, and selling it in the West. But that was just the beginning. He expanded into other media. His greatest coup was buying the *Daily Echo* five years ago. I don't know if he made any money out of it, but it certainly did a hell of a lot for his profile. Then four months ago he mysteriously died. Fell off his boat. Suicide, or an accident, that was the official verdict.' Dowler shrugged, the motion suggesting he was not a man who placed much weight on official versions. 'Who knows? Anyway, as soon as he was buried, the whole Robertson empire started to unravel. It turned out he was up to his ears in debt, and the banks were closing down on him. He'd been raiding the pension fund of the *Echo*. Five hundred million pounds went missing. Where to? Nobody knows.'

'I know all that,' said Sam. 'Anyone who's been reading the papers for the past few months knows that.'

'Of course,' said Dowler.

'Then what's the file?'

Dowler glanced out of the window, looking at the rain that was beating down on the city. From his office, there was a view stretching out across Cheapside to St Paul's. 'The administrators to Robertson Communications Corporation have hired this firm to find out what happened to the money. All five hundred million of it. They want it back, naturally. To repay the bankers, and the pensioners.'

'And haven't you found it?'

Dowler shook his head. 'Sadly not. We have chased down every avenue we can, but all we've hit are blank walls.

Nothing. The administrators have even offered us a deal. They will pay us two per cent of the money, if we can find out what happened to it.'

'Like bounty hunters?'

'But without the Stetsons.' He paused, his expression turning serious. 'We in turn are offering one per cent of the money to anyone who can find out what happened to the money. That's the file. We give you what we know, you solve the riddle and, like I said, you get one per cent.'

'Five million,' said Sam. 'For one job?'

Instinctively, he started making the calculations in his head. After the humiliation of the past couple of days, he'd already downgraded his market value. This morning, he'd have been happy to take any work he was offered for a thousand a week. He could probably have been negotiated down to five hundred. Now there was five million on the table. Enough money to set him up for life. Enough money to restart the antiques business. To buy Elena that Poggenpohl kitchen she was always talking about. Get the family one of the big Mercedes everyone else in the Frankfurt suburbs drove.

All I have to do is reach out and take it.

'The issue,' said Dowler carefully, 'is whether it is worth it.'

Sam laughed: a tense, nervous laugh, reflecting his relief that this meeting was actually going somewhere, that he could finally see a way of clawing his way out of the hole into which he had been cast. 'Is it worth it? Five million for one job? I don't think you've been checking the employment prospects for ex-Mossad men recently.'

'Oh, I know the market all right. No one knows that market better, let me assure you,' said Dowler severely. 'And right now it's a bear market. But there is something I must tell you.'

'I know, I know, I may well come up against a brick wall as well,' said Sam. 'I may do months of work and come away with nothing. Believe me, I'm ready to take that risk.'

'That wasn't what I meant,' said Dowler. He looked at Sam. 'In the past two months, five men have sat opposite me in that chair. I've had the same conversation with all of them. I've told them about the file, and offered them the same deal.' He paused, as if weighing the next sentence. 'Within a week of walking out of here, all of them were dead.'

Sam stood in the phone booth, punching the number into the dial. 'Selima Robertson, please,' he said as soon as the phone was answered.

'She's away.'

'Can you give her a message? Tell her Sam Wolfman called. Tell her I'll take the case.'

He left the number of the digs he'd checked into last night, then started walking down the street. *First, I'm offered the case by Selima, then by someone else.* He remembered one of the first things Papa had said to him: *There are no coincidences.*

It was about five miles from Dowler's office to the Holloway Road: enough distance for a man to think as well as wear out some shoe leather. That Hassim was planning to kill him, Sam no longer had any doubt. He was out on his own now. Mossad wasn't around to protect him, neither was his unit. He was just one man. If he didn't deal with it now, then the Palestinian would always be lurking in the shadows. When a confrontation was inevitable, it was better to get it over with.

By the time he reached the kebab shop, it was already early evening. Darkness had fallen, and the rush-hour traffic was queuing up along the busy street. Sam walked past on the opposite side of the road. Whoever owned the shop hadn't even bothered with a name: it just said 'kebabs', 'burgers', 'fried chicken' and 'chips' on the stained, plastic signs. Sam could smell it even between the fumes from the cars: a thick, greasy aroma of roasting mutton and baked, dried bread. He kept walking. There was a stretch of London from the Holloway Road up towards Green Lanes that was like the Mediterranean in miniature. There were Greeks, Cypriots, Lebanese and a dozen different Arab races all pitching for their own few yards of territory. A natural place for Hassim to base himself, thought Sam. He could lose himself here as easily as he could back in the Palestinian camps along the Israeli borders.

He kept walking. The plan was slowly forming in Sam's mind. I'll take out his driver, and finish him in the car. All Sam's training had taught him to work out every move, to prepare every hit meticulously and to consider every possibility. Not tonight, he told himself. I'm going to get one more shot at Hassim. If I don't make, I'm a dead man. *It's just a question of when.*

The site was two miles away. After the team had arrived in London, one of its first tasks had been to drop four sets of weapons in strategic locations, forming a circle around the city. You never knew when you might need a gun in a hurry. Like this evening.

The *mislashim*, or dead-letter box, was located at an undertaker's office run by a *sayan*. It was an old and traditional place, which mainly served the Jewish community around Finchley. Five years ago, Sam had arranged for one single Beretta 92 to be stored there, complete with ammunition: the Italian-made pistol was one of the commonest handguns in the world, and seldom identified its user as belonging to any particular agency or army.

Two hours later, Sam was back on the Holloway Road. The Beretta 92 was tucked into the inside pocket of his overcoat. It was half past seven already. The rush hour was thinning out, but the street was still crowded. He circled the kebab shop twice: enough to give him an idea of the layout, but not too much surveillance to alert anyone.

Sam went to a café and sat down. Coffee followed coffee. He could feel the adrenalin surging through his veins. Seize the moment, he told himself. In a few hours either your enemies will be dead. *Or you will be.*

The hours dragged by. Ten gave way to eleven and then to twelve. By three o'clock the coffee he'd drunk was sitting like lead in the pit of Sam's stomach.

The watchman, if that was what he was, had warned off his paymaster, and Sam was left with the feeling that he was being watched from the shadows.

NINE

The file was neatly typed, on thick white paper. Sam flicked through the pages, glancing down at the rows of words. At least they gave me a fresh copy, he reflected. They don't just recycle copies from the other guys who've read through these pages. *The dead ones.*

He walked across the faded pink carpet of his tiny room. There was a two-bar electric fire in the corner. Sam fed a fifty-pence piece into the slot, then switched the fire back on. He spiked a slice of white sliced bread on to the grate, waiting for it to toast, then spread a thin layer of margarine on to it. He chewed slowly on the food. The next few weeks may be the most testing of my life. Yet at the end of it there may be five million pounds. *Enough money for a man to stake his life on.*

The first part of the file was a summary of Max Robertson's life. It could have been put together by any competent researcher trawling through the hundreds of newspaper articles to be found in any archive, or the pair of hack biographies on the man's life, one of which had been rushed back into print since his death.

Robertson had been born in Hungary in 1920, to a Jewish family. The family name was Klein: Robertson was a later invention. He was one of eight children, brought up in a small farming village in the east of the country. His father, Jacob, worked first as a miner, then as a tenant farmer. There was never much money: certainly not enough for young

Max to be educated beyond the village school. At sixteen he left for Budapest and started an apprenticeship as a printer. He claimed to have already started a publishing venture on the side, but since the only source for that was Robertson himself, there was no way of knowing whether it was just another of the myths with which he liked to embroider his own life. Doesn't matter much now, thought Sam. It was what happened after the war that provided Robertson with the perfect arena to nurture his peculiar talent for self-aggrandisement and self-promotion.

After the Nazis occupied Hungary, Robertson joined the Resistance, and was soon captured by the Germans. There were some reports he'd actually been arrested for trading on the black market, but once again Sam decided that didn't matter now. He'd spent six months in a prison camp before escaping, then made his way, via Greece and North Africa, to Britain, where he enlisted in the British Army. That was in 1941, when the British were recruiting every able-bodied man who came their way. Robertson was certainly that. At six foot two, with a thick, solid build and dark hair, he was already physically imposing. And he had already developed the steadiness of nerve, the ability to hold his head amid the rattle of gunfire, that was to distinguish his career as a soldier, then later as a businessman. Holding your nerve, thought Sam. Next to that quality, brains, strength and guile count for very little. *It is the warrior's supreme virtue.*

The officer who recruited him made the first name change. Maximilian Klein became Max Kenward, for the simple reason that it was the first name that came into the officer's head. Two years later, he changed it himself to Max Robertson, because he'd read somewhere that three syllables in a surname made a man appear more trustworthy. Like all conmen, he knew instinctively that winning trust was the one crucial skill he had to master. *Once he had that, he could rob people blind.*

The war record was distinguished, if you believed it. Robertson had fought in North Africa, then in the Normandy campaign. He was wounded once in the leg, and captured briefly by the Germans, although his unit was liberated after three days. He was awarded a King's Medal, created to honour foreigners fighting in the British Army during the Second World War, and was mentioned in dispatches. By 1944, he had been promoted to the rank of major.

Decades later, Robertson would often start a sentence: 'When I was fighting the Nazis . . .' It was all part of the man's act, designed to engage, impress and then subdue his audience. That was another standard part of the conman's tool kit. *Establish your own moral superiority. Then pick their pockets.*

Sam found himself wondering whether any of it was true. He'd been a soldier himself, and he knew that on the battle-field truth was the last thing anyone worried about. Nobody was taking notes. Stories got told and retold, with new twists and fabrications each time. Some men got medals just for showing up on the day. Others performed acts of incredible, gut-wrenching bravery and yet went unrewarded just because there had been nobody around to witness them, and they were too shattered or numbed to speak of them afterwards.

The battlefield was not so different from any other arena of human contest. It was the pushy, the ambitious and the self-promoting who got the prizes. Even as a young man, those were arts of which Robertson was already a master.

As the war closed, he was posted to Berlin, working in liaison in the eastern sector of the city, establishing contacts with the Communist regime then being assembled and which he would use so effectively in later life. Next, he was posted back to England, to barracks in Kettering. He was briefly married to Selima's mother Marie, but after she died, he met and married Anna, who was to be his long-suffering wife through his rages and infidelities of the next forty years. The daughter of a district judge, from an impeccably respectable, suburban family, she added a thin coating of respectability to Robertson's swagger, energy and panache. His reinvention as an English gentleman had begun, and so too had his assault on society.

Sam knelt down next to the electric fire, spiking another slice of bread on to the bars. These are just the dry, dusty bones of the man's life. I need to get up close. I need to be able to smell the man.

Only then will I get a sense of what game he was really playing.

Sitting back down on the creaky single bed, he leafed through some more pages. Robertson had spent another two years in the army after the war, then struck out on his own. He set up Gradus Publishing, putting out industrial journals and books, which many people suspected was just a cover for industrial espionage. In the early 1960s, he'd been elected to Parliament as a Labour MP for a seat in Birmingham, but had to stand down at the 1970 election as his company, by then floated on the London Stock Exchange, had come close to bankruptcy. In 1972, the business was near to bust, and the Department of Trade and Industry published a report condemning Robertson as 'unfit to be a director of a public company'. His career lay in broken pieces. Most people assumed Robertson was finished.

But a man is never finished, thought Sam. Not until he is dead. *And sometimes not even then.*

Robertson clawed his way back with a tenaciousness, strength and ambition that impressed even his most per-sistent critics. By the turn of 1980, the publishing business was spitting out profits again. Its credit had been restored. And the City's bankers were working for it again. As the global economy recovered, Gradus became just a subsidiary of the Robertson Communications Corporation. Robertson distinguished himself as one of the flourishing asset strippers in that decade. He would move in on old, established but declining companies, usually in printing or trade publishing. He would buy them on the cheap. Then the management would be fired, the workforce slimmed down, and most of the factories closed, leaving the land free for redevelopment. Robertson would turn a handsome profit before moving on to his next target. It was the kind of business that didn't win you many friends. But it did make you a lot of money. *Then you could buy friends.*

The biggest breakthrough came when he bought the *Daily Echo*. A red-top tabloid, it was Britain's biggest selling paper in the 1960s, and although Rupert Murdoch's *Sun* had overtaken it, the *Echo* was still an influential paper. On taking control, Robertson immediately started using it as a vehicle of self-promotion. The paper was constantly filled with tales of the proprietor's magnificence. His trips abroad were reported as if he was the Prime Minister. He dictated leaders himself, pursuing his own interests and vendettas. The paper rewarded his friends, and punished his rivals. Often, the coverage bordered on the ridiculous, yet it allowed Robertson to swagger through the world as a man of global importance. His voracious ego was fed every day with the food it found most nourishing: publicity, flattery and power.

As the decade approached its close, he was hitting the height of his powers. Newspapers in Israel, Canada, the US and Asia had been added to the empire. So too had publishers, broadcasters, computing companies, and a string of businesses supplying information and intelligence. Outwardly, he was fast becoming one of the most influential tycoons in the world. Then, on 15 November 1989, Robertson died.

Sam held the sheet of paper in his hand. It was dark now, and as he glanced out of the window of his small room, he could see nothing but rooftops and above the flashing lights of a plane dropping out of the clouds as it started its descent into Heathrow. A man's death is always mysterious. Yet Robertson's death was extravagantly theatrical. Almost as if it had been staged.

The bare facts were simple enough. He had been on board his boat, the *Guinea*. It was moored off the Amalfi coast, in southern Italy. The crew had been dismissed for the evening, and Robertson had been drinking heavily. The bar was stocked with bottles of vintage champagne and mounds of caviar, the two staples of his voracious nocturnal appetite. Robertson had been pacing around on the deck. Then he slipped and fell into the water. A huge, overweight man, with a bulk of at least three hundred pounds, and in poor physical shape, he drowned quickly. His body was found floating face down off the coast next morning.

Sam read the description once, then read it again. He'd read about it at the time, naturally: Robertson's death had been the lead story on the news everywhere in the world, but nowhere more so than in Britain where he had made his career. Yet he had paid little attention at the time. His mind had been elsewhere: on his mission, and his antiques business. It was only now, studying it afresh, that he could see how strange Robertson's demise had been.

The day after he drowned, Robertson's body was claimed by the Israeli authorities. It was flown back to Tel Aviv, the autopsy completed, and within three days he had been buried. Robertson had taken out Israeli citizenship in the early 1970s, and so that country had first claim on his body. The Italians could have held on to him if they had wanted to, but from the notes in the file, it looked as if they wanted him off their territory as soon as possible.

And who can blame them? *Because it turned out that he was even more trouble dead than he was alive.*

In the days and weeks after his death, Robertson Communications started to unravel. The company had a

Byzantine structure, all ultimately controlled through a private family trust in Liechtenstein. Assets were constantly being shifted from different units and subsidiaries, and money was flowing through a thousand different bank accounts. At the time, many people assumed the complexity was to reduce taxes: that was the usual reason big companies shuffled their money through hundreds of subsidiaries. It turned out Robertson wasn't hiding from the taxman. He was hiding from his bankers. *And he was hiding from the truth.*

The company was as fictitious as many of the stories Robertson told about himself: a series of deceptions carefully stacked on top of each other to create an impression of solidity when there was nothing underneath. Money was stuffed into one business to make it look profitable, then quickly switched to another. In reality, very few of Robertson's businesses made any money. He paid handsome prices for plain assets, then ran them ineptly. Every time he bought a company, he drank the blood out of it, then started to chew up its bones. Every Robertson company was run on a high-octane mix of fear, paranoia and sloth. Senior directors were fired immediately. Divisions were scrapped overnight. Staff were fired pointlessly, and replacements found on nothing more than a whim.

The impact was much the same as Stalin's constant purges of the Red Army. Few were left who knew what they were doing. Many that remained did nothing but take long lunch hours and get drunk until they were fired as well.

Robertson had held the whole contraption together through will-power alone. Once he disappeared beneath the waves, there was nobody left within the business of any substance. The bankers, for so long overawed by Robertson's financial showmanship, started to move in. At first they started asking for interest payments to be met more promptly. Next, they started calling in their loans. Then the company's bonds collapsed. Within a few days, its credit had completely evaporated. And without credit there was no business.

Six weeks after Robertson died, the company was in receivership.

Sam looked down at the collection of notes in his wallet. Only a little over five hundred pounds, in tens and fives. Meagre resources with which to crack open a story that had already consumed dozens of investigators, the world's finest journalists, and various intelligence agencies and police forces around the world. And one on which five of Dowler's freelancers had already sacrificed their lives.

My only shot. If I had any other choices I'd take them.

Sam looked out of the window again, and into the drizzle that was gently falling across the rooftops stretching out into the distance. Robertson was a brilliant man, he thought to himself. Evil, for sure, but brilliant as well in his own way. *And brilliant men don't waste their lives. Not like that.*

That's the riddle. If I just gnaw on that bone, maybe I'll get somewhere.

Sam fished out his membership card, and showed it to the girl at the reception desk. She glanced at it, smiled, then looked back at the magazine on her desk. 'If you need a towel, there's a pile on the way into the changing room.'

'It's OK,' said Sam. 'I've got one in my locker.'

He walked towards the changing room. The Oasis gym was just on the outskirts of Reading, one of dozens of new health clubs that had sprung up on the outskirts of every British city in the past couple of years. Sam needed a safe place where he could stash a few things that he might need one day. Station locker rooms were the stuff of spy novels, and anyway, they were so disorganised these days you couldn't guarantee you would get the stuff back when you needed it. Bank safe-deposit boxes were too risky. Whatever they told you, the bank always kept records of who owned which box, and the British banks would always cooperate with their own intelligence agencies. If asked, they would open it. But gyms didn't run any checks on their members, and most of them had private lockers you could rent for a small fee. Leave something there, with a membership taken out in a false name, and it was untraceable.

Two guys were showering in the changing room, but Sam ignored them, making straight for his locker. The two-foot metal case was secured with a combination padlock. Sam twisted the four digits into place, then opened the door. Everything was just as he had left it the last time he'd been here six months ago. There were two white towels, a pair of swimming trunks, some cheap trainers and a T-shirt. Lifting up the T-shirt, he pulled out the black leather wallet. Inside there were three passports, one British, one Irish and one Dutch. He glanced at the Dutch passport, made out in the name of Henk Sosa, and slipped it into the pocket of his jacket.

Mossad had supplied him with various identities for travelling around Europe, each with their own credit card, which were good for up to five thousand pounds. Back in Tel Aviv, the institute had a whole department devoted to supplying false identities for its agents around the world. There was no more professional operation anywhere. Each identity was crafted from scratch. A complete background for the person was supplied, complete with a false address, a family and a profession. Bank accounts would be created, and used at least once every six months to stop them from being classed as dormant. Robertson himself may well have helped out, thought Sam: Mossad agents regularly travelled as journalists, and his papers would supply the credentials.

Sam took Henk's ABN Amro Visa card, slipped that into his wallet alongside the passport, then folded the black wallet back inside the T-shirt. He assumed the card would have been stopped and if he did try to use it he could be traced.

Better destroy it. He lifted up the first towel, and looked underneath. Nestling between the two layers of white cotton was a small Browning FN-49 hand pistol, less than twenty centimetres long. Next to it was a stack of six ten-round cartridges. Sam put the towel down. Always good to have a gun hidden somewhere, particularly in a country with tough gun laws like Britain. You never knew when you might need one.

Sam took off his clothes, and put on the trunks. Ten lengths he told himself. It would look suspicious to visit the gym without using it. A shower, then Henk Sosa is on his way to Israel. On the trail of Max Robertson.

TEN

Sam looked out of the window of the Optima Tower hotel, a functional concrete block close to the commercial centre of Tel Aviv. The streets where he had grown up were just a couple of miles in the distance, and all the smells and sights of the city had been comfortably familiar as he took the bus from the airport to the hotel.

He turned back towards the simple black desk and the Robertson File. Sam had read it once in London, then again on the plane, and now he was reading it for the third time. It's like a money box, he told himself. Shake it enough times, and eventually some cash will drop out.

He started to turn the pages once more. The final section of the dossier reviewed the speculation surrounding Robertson's death. In the weeks and months that followed his drowning, and the collapse of the empire, there had been a wave of speculation about what might have really happened. Much of it was just the gossipy chatter that always fills newspaper offices and the trading floors of banks. Still, Dowler's researchers had done a diligent job of tabulating each piece of guesswork. Laid out before him was a tableau of conspiracies. If Robertson wasn't paranoid by the time he died, he should have been. *It sounded like everyone wanted to kill him.*

Although the official verdict had been that Robertson committed suicide by throwing himself from the boat, that did not ring true. Robertson was not the kind of man to kill himself. The most obvious answer was that someone had murdered him. But who? *And why?*

The dossier grouped the potential assassins into four main categories.

Sam took out a pad of paper, and started to write them down. Notes would help to clarify the issues in his own mind. *The Russians*, he wrote in neat block letters. Robertson had extensive dealings behind the Iron Curtain. His companies bought scientific papers from the Eastern bloc, and that had been the basis of his fortune. He had made huge investments in countries such as Hungary and Bulgaria, and published grovelling biographies of minor Communist dictators. Sam thought for a moment. It was a possibility. He could have been trading in nuclear or military secrets. Any one of those deals could have turned sour. If it had, neither the Russians nor any of the Eastern European satellite states would hesitate to assassinate Robertson. In their world, the price of failure was death. They knew no other currency.

The Mafia, wrote Sam on the next sheet of paper. Again, there were stories that Robertson had close links with the mob. Some people thought the media business was in reality a money-laundering racket. They couldn't understand how an essentially small-scale business such as scientific publishing could ever have been transformed into such a huge enterprise. Again, possible. The Mafia used lots of businesses to launder their profits. They were generous to their friends, and ruthless to their enemies. If Robertson had crossed them, then his life was as disposable as a Bic razor.

The banks. The mass of debts accumulated by Robertson Communications were still unravelling. It had borrowed money from a minimum of 180 different banks around the world. It had slightly more than three hundred bond issues outstanding. There could be few financial institutions anywhere that didn't have a small and toxic parcel of Robertson debt somewhere in its portfolio. Some of the wilder theorists speculated that the banks might have had him killed. The trouble with that theory, thought Sam, was that Robertson was probably worth more to them alive than dead. As a tycoon, there was still a chance he could somehow manage to pay back at least some of his debts, but as a corpse, he was bankrupt, and the loans were as dead as he was. Still, one footnote caught Sam's eyes. Among the largest lenders to Robertson Communications were a couple of the biggest French state-owned banks. One of the few organisations Mossad had learned to respect as almost as ruthless as itself in defence of its country's interests was the DGSE, the Direction Générale de la Sécurité Extérieure. Once you were classified as a problem to the French state, it was only a matter of time and circumstances before the DGSE came up with its own lethal solution.

Investigate, Sam told himself. Follow every lead, no matter how trivial. *That's the only way to crack this.*

He turned the page, and made one more note, again in neat block letters. *Husbands.* Robertson was a womaniser, his carnal appetites as gargantuan as his financial greed. The offices of his companies were riddled with stories of sexual intrigue. Women were hired purely for their beauty, then pressurised into sleeping with Robertson. Mistresses were maintained in a dozen cities around the world; and in London, according to one source, there were five women permanently on the payroll. A fixer made it his business to hire an expensive hooker in any city Robertson was visiting. Each tart was then required to act the part of an ordinary woman, bowled over by Robertson's charms, and willing to share his bed for the night. Robertson almost certainly knew of the deception, but, as in the rest of his life, lived in such twilight between reality and fantasy he no longer cared. He must, anyway, have known about the bills. As Robertson became more and more obese, and his sexual demands more disturbing, even the hookers were reluctant to entertain him. The prices were getting higher and higher as every month passed. By the end, the payroll was running to tens of thousands a month.

A husband, pondered Sam. Or a boyfriend. It's possible. Many of the women bullied into sleeping with Robertson were married. Although it was hard to imagine the relationship meant anything to them, that didn't mean there wasn't a husband out there somewhere driven to seek his own vengeance. Never underestimate the power of passion betrayed, Sam reminded himself. *The human heart has no darker impulse.*

Sitting by the bed, Sam put a call through to London. Selima Robertson's house. Not there, said the maid. She was still on holiday. She'd make sure she got Sam's message.

Sam dialled another number. The phone was answered on the second ring. 'Zvi here,' said the voice on the line.

Sam hesitated. If it was possible for a man to have two fathers, then Zvi Imer would take his place alongside Yoram. They were both his creators: Yoram had created his genes and Imer his character. Now in his seventies, a thin and wiry man with chestnut-brown eyes, Imer had been the head of Mossad training up until failing health had finally forced him out of the service. He had taken Sam as a raw recruit straight out of the army, and spent a year turning him into the hardened agent he would later become. It was a process that was as much psychological as physical: Imer took his recruits apart piece by piece, then re-engineered them as the perfect servants of the Israeli state.

Imer, Sam sometimes felt, had Israel in his blood: cut open his chest, and his heart would be shaped like a thin slither of land nestling precariously on the edge of the Mediterranean. He'd been born in the Ukraine in 1917, a fact that he would often refer to with a hollow laugh. 'Imagine it,' he'd say, as they shared a meal after a long day of training. 'A Jew born in the Ukraine in 1917. Can history deal a tougher hand to play than that? And you boys think you have it tough when I make you do fifty press-ups before breakfast. I tell you, you don't even know how to spell the word tough.' There was much truth in that, Sam would later realise, as he gradually learned the facts about Imer's life. The man himself never spoke about it, but Sam put together some of the details from talking to his father and his friends among Israel's old warriors. As a child, Imer lived through the collectivisation of the farms in the Ukraine, and the famine that followed it; then the purges of the 1930s that saw millions deported to the camps; then the Nazi invasion that swept brutally through the country; then the round-up of the Jews in Nazi-occupied Ukraine. Imer himself was sent to Dachau, and managed to survive there for two years, until the camp was finally liberated by the Allies. He was one of just a handful of Jews left alive at the end of the war. From there, he made his way to Palestine, and joined the fighters battling to found an independent state. He was wounded twice, but both times went straight back into action.

It was not surprising, his father had told him, that the man was prepared to fight to have a country where he could feel safe among his own people. Nor that he expected others to do the same.

'It's Sam, I need to see you.' He waited a split second before delivering the next line. 'I need some help.'

'Sam Wolfman?'

'Like I said, I need some help.'

Imer did not hesitate before replying: 'Then you better come and see me.'

The block was close to the Yarkon Park, on the northern edge of Tel Aviv. Sam checked the passageway before stepping inside. Whether there were any other old Mossad men living here, he had no way of knowing, but it was a possibility. Everyone likes to stick with their old kind, and of no breed of men is that more true than old soldiers.

103

Anyone recognises me here, then I could be in more trouble than I imagine.

The passage was empty. It was just after two in the afternoon, and the midday heat was fierce. There were some bikes parked in the hall of the concrete apartment block, and some cheap cars in the car park outside. But at least half the spaces were empty. This was one of the roughest areas of town: anyone who had the money for a decent car would be living somewhere else.

Imer lived on the eighth floor. Sam took the lift up, then turned left. He knocked softly and the door was opened almost immediately. 'Sam,' Imer said, a broad grin breaking out on his thin, leathery face. 'Come in, come in.'

It had been five years since they had last seen each other. Sam had always suspected that retirement aged a man, yet he had never seen the evidence so clearly demonstrated as it was now. Take away a man's purpose and the life started to drain out of him. Five years ago, Imer had been a fit, if ageing man, his skin polished, and his eyes bright and alert. Now his skin was grey, the stubble was spiking his chin, and his eyes were shot with exhaustion. 'Here,' he said, 'I'll get you something to drink.'

Sam followed him through the hallway. The apartment had just one room. There was a kitchenette off to one side, and next to that a shower room in which a man could just about stand. The living space contained a television and radio on a stand, a small desk, and a futon laid out on the floor to sleep on. The only ornament was a picture of Imer's two daughters: Ruth, who now lived in Boston, and was married with two children; and Hannah, who was working at one of the American investment banks in London. Imer, Sam knew, had divorced almost twenty years ago, and the girls were the only family he had, yet he hardly ever saw them. From the looks of this place, he hardly saw anybody.

The only luxury was a noisy air-conditioning unit stuck

through the single front window. Sam stood next to it, grateful for the blast of cool air.

So this is what a lifetime in the service of Mossad gets you, Sam thought as he cast his eyes around the apartment. *Absolutely nothing.*

'I heard you quit,' said Imer, taking a carton of orange juice from the tiny fridge.

Sam nodded. 'I'm freelancing.'

Imer scrutinised his face. It was a look Sam well remembered. In training, Imer put his recruits through a punishing schedule. You were woken at the crack of dawn, bashed out a series of press-ups, before being sent on a six-mile run, followed by three hours of lessons. After lunch, you skipped for two hours: there was no better way, they were always told, of achieving the eye-to-hand coordination that a marksman needed. Afterwards you went back to the classroom for another three hours of lectures on the basic craft of your new trade: surveillance, interceptions, kidnapping, money laundering, assassinations and forging.

At the end of it, Imer would look into your eyes and ask you one question. 'Can you take it?' The answer didn't matter but the expression did: he was looking for signs of weakness. At least one recruit a month would be quietly removed from the course. No reason would be given. The person would not appear to his comrades to have failed in any way, and everyone would be puzzled as to why they had been kicked out. But Sam knew. Imer had looked into their eyes and found them wanting. *That was enough.*

He can look into my eyes as long as he wants to, thought Sam. *He won't find any signs of weakness.*

'What went wrong?'

'We were betrayed.'

'Betrayed?' said Imer archly. 'Who by?'

'Twice over,' said Sam, taking a sip on his orange juice.

'Somebody set us up for a fall when we went for Hassim. Then by Rotanski. He cleared out my bank account.'

Imer stood against the wall, looking out of the window. 'Let me tell you what I think,' he said slowly. 'You go back, and you sort this mess out. The service needs men like you. And you know what? A man like you needs the service as well.'

'I tell you, I'm finished,' said Sam firmly. 'I've done my time. It's over.'

'You finish the mission,' snapped Imer. He leaned forward, so close that Sam could smell the sweat on the old man's skin. 'What will you do otherwise? Carry bags for rich ladies who want a bodyguard for a few days at a time. Become one of those self-important security consultants for a big company. Bah, it's nothing, Sam. Nothing, I tell you. You'll just be a nightwatchman with a tie and collar and fancy title.'

'At least I'll be making money for myself. And for my family.'

'No, you can't work for yourself, Sam,' said Imer, his tone touched with anger. 'When you get to my age you'll realise that. If you haven't lived for a cause, then you haven't lived at all.'

'Really?' Sam cast his eyes around the tiny apartment. 'And what kind of life did you live? You never saw your family, so they all left you. Your wife left you twenty years ago. Your daughters both moved out of the country. When did they last call you?'

Imer remained silent.

'When?' Sam paced through the room, unable to manage more than five steps from one end of the apartment to the other. 'When did they last call? Six months ago, a year? You never saw them when they were growing up, and now it's too late. They don't really know who you are. Mossad left you an old man with nothing. Just like they did my father.'

Sam stopped walking, as if suddenly frozen in his tracks. 'I'm not going to end up like you.'

A silence descended on the room. Sam realised the cruelty of what he had just said. The truth hurts, he thought to himself. That's why, of all the weapons at our disposal, it is the one we are most reluctant to use.

With a quarter-smile on his lips that said he understood, Imer said, 'So what did you want my help with?'

'The Robertson File,' said Sam, turning round to look at Imer again. 'There's a bounty out from the men who are trying to clear up the mess he left behind. All I have to do is find how and why he died, and what happened to all the money within his company.'

Imer laughed. 'Good luck.'

Sam laughed too. The argument, he sensed, was now buried. Imer might never accept his decision to leave Mossad, but there would be no grudge. Their relationship was like father and son. They could argue bitterly with one another yet remain close. 'I was wondering if you might know anything about it.'

'Me? About Robertson?' said Imer 'Why should I?'

'There were always stories,' said Sam. 'About Robertson and Mossad. About how he was working for us.' He paused, looking straight at Imer. 'Is that true?'

Imer shrugged. 'How would I know?'

'How would you know? What kind of question is that? Of course you would know. You've been with the organisation since it was founded. You know everything. There isn't a skeleton hidden in that place without you knowing about it.'

'You overestimate me, Sam, you always did. That's one of the reasons I liked you.'

'So you heard nothing?'

'I heard lots of things.'

'Like what.'

Imer paused. 'There were always stories about Robertson. He was one of the richest men in the world, even when his creditors were chasing him, and he never seemed to have the ability to pay them. And he was always a friend of Israel, even before he took out citizenship. He bought companies here. He met constantly with our politicians. He set up endowments at our universities. So Mossad would have taken at least an interest, of course. He might even have been one of the thousands of people around the world who gave us help and assistance informally when we needed it.'

'I know all that,' said Sam. He looked hard at Imer. 'What I need is a doorway. Something that is going to take me inside this mystery.'

'Then look at his grave,' said Imer suddenly.

'His grave? What would I find there?'

'Well, ask yourself where it is for starters.'

Sam paused. He had read it in the files and the fact was lodged in his mind. 'On the Mount of Olives. Robertson was given a full state funeral. It was in all the papers.'

'And doesn't something strike you as odd about that?'

'Like you said, he was a citizen and friend of the country. He brought a lot of money into the country. Why shouldn't they give him a state funeral? They hand them out to men who have done far less.'

'You've been out of the country too long, Sam. You're forgetting things.'

'Like what?'

'Well, how did Robertson die?'

'Suicide – well, that was the official verdict. He threw himself off the boat, but no one believes that.'

'Our government certainly doesn't.'

Sam realised now why he had come here. If he'd been a gold prospector, he'd have always struck it rich. Imer had a genius for spotting the tiny nugget of information amid the rubble. 'Because they gave him a state funeral, right? Under

108

Jewish law, a man who commits suicide can't be given a religious funeral. It's against the rules.'

Imer nodded, but his eyes remained cast down on the floor. 'So they didn't believe he committed suicide.'

'Maybe they weren't bothered,' said Sam. 'Maybe they just figured he'd done a lot for the country, and he deserved a decent burial.'

Imer laughed. 'Since when did our government take the faith that lightly. No, they wouldn't have given him that funeral unless they knew for sure that Robertson hadn't taken his own life.'

'Meaning that he's not dead?'

'Well, that's one possibility. All the theories surrounding Robertson's death are just conjecture spun out of thin air. There is only one way to know for sure whether the man committed suicide or not.'

'Which is . . .?'

'Either you've spirited him away and staged his funeral. Or else you killed him yourself.'

ELEVEN

Sam slotted the video into the machine, but paused before pressing the play button. The words that Imer had left him with were still rattling around inside his mind. The only way you could be certain that a man hadn't killed himself was if *you* had killed him. Or if you had faked his death.

Sam sat back in the cheap hotel chair, and started watching. The tape was the Israeli television broadcast of Robertson's funeral. Sam had called up the station, telling them he was a Spanish journalist researching a documentary on Robertson's death, and they'd sent a tape round to the hotel. Using the remote, Sam fast-forwarded through the opening shots. They showed the entrance of the King David hotel, then Robertson's wife Anna stepping out of the lobby, dressed immaculately in black. Flanking her were her two godsons, Simon and Robert, and behind them, her stepdaughter: Ann never had any children of her own with Robertson. Underneath her broad black hat, Sam recognised Selima. She was walking steadily forward, like the others, getting into one of the waiting black limousines. They drove to the Hall of Nations, one of the most imposing modern buildings in the city, where the body was lying in a side room, Robertson's face was covered by a tallith, a traditional Jewish prayer shawl. The corpse was surrounded by candles, as the family traipsed through the room, paying their last respects before the body. Next came the first of the hundreds of mourners. Sam recognised a few of the more famous faces. Chaim Herzog, the President of Israel. The Prime Minister, Yitzhak Shamir. The leader of the opposition, Shimon Peres. Following them were a small galaxy of Israel's most important businessmen, politicians and diplomats, the faces blurring into a grey mass. Sam searched around for Rotanski, but could see no sign of him. Surely he wouldn't have missed this? Even if he didn't want to pay his respects to Robertson – and Rotanski didn't pay respects to many men – he wouldn't have wanted to miss the chance to network with so many influential people.

It took an hour for the mourners to file past the coffin. Sam fast-forwarded – one bowing dignitary kitted out in black quickly looked much like another. Next came the Kaddish, the prayer for the dead. Then Chaim Herzog took to the podium, and delivered the first of the homilies. His voice was touched with what Sam judged to be genuine emotion as he described Robertson's achievements. 'In his life, we find a parable,' Herzog concluded. 'From the most humble of origins, he scaled the greatest heights, yet he never forgot who he was, nor looked down upon those who had not risen as far. The people of Israel had no greater champion, nor any truer friend.'

The eight pall-bearers lifted the body up, and started carrying it towards the waiting hearse. Sam watched them closely, wishing he had the machinery to blow up the pictures. Robertson was a huge bear of a man, and his corpse would weigh at least three hundred pounds, maybe more. Sam hadn't spent five years in the assassination business without learning that the dead were surprisingly heavy. He looked closely at the pall-bearers. They seemed to be carrying the coffin with ease. Perhaps there is nothing in there except air. *Even his stepdaughter thinks he might still be alive.*

Just as the coffin was being carried from the hall, a young rabbi ran out and started shouting at the body, but was

111

quickly dragged away by the plain-clothes security guards circling the building. Sam paused, watching that slice of tape three times over, but he still couldn't make out the rabbi's face clearly, or hear what he was saying.

On the Mount of Olives, Anna led the family towards the grave, followed by hundreds of silent mourners. The pall-bearers carried the body to the edge of the pit, while the gravediggers stood aside. Through the crowd, Shimon Peres walked silently, his head bowed in respect. Peres stood next to the grave. 'He has done more for Israel than we can speak of at this time or in the place,' he said out loud.

One of the gravediggers stepped down into the pit. Then four of the mourners came forward, gently removing the tallith from Robertson's face. The gravediggers tilted the stretcher, so that the body began to slide into the open grave. The one below guided it into position, until the corpse was lying flat in the ground. The tallith was held over the pit, so that only those closest could witness what was happening, while slabs of Jerusalem stone were placed one by one over the body, until it was completely covered. Without another word being spoken, and with the sun setting in the background, the ceremony was over. One by one, the mourners started to drift away.

That's some send-off, thought Sam. A dead president couldn't hope for anything better. And all for a swindler who had done as much to blacken the name of Israel as he had to promote it. And who had broken, at least according to the official verdict, one of the most sacred of our religious laws by taking his own life.

Who the hell was Robertson really? The official record said that in Israel he owned one small newspaper and a football team in the country. *What did he do for the state to earn him this kind of funeral?*

Sam hit the rewind button, taking the tape right back to the beginning. He watched the coffin being lifted, then watched the young rabbi come out and start shouting. The coffin still looked light to his eyes. He rewound again, this time concentrating on the rabbi. He tried to follow the words on his lips, but it was almost impossible to decipher what he was saying. 'Fraud?' Sam wondered, as he looked at the scene yet again. *Is he trying to tell us it's a fraud?*

The Mount of Olives had the special kind of quiet you only find in graveyards: a suffocating sense of peace that commanded everyone to speak in whispers. The wind was rustling through the branches of the trees, and even though it was still early in the morning the sun was bright and the day was already warming up. Sam walked slowly towards the grave, using the route he had already memorised. There were few people around: two women on the far side of the hillside, a mother and daughter, Sam guessed, visiting the grave of their husband and father; a gardener weeding the space between the graves; and an old man walking without any seeming purpose or direction between the slabs of rock arranged in neat rows on either side of him.

What did you take into that grave with you? Sam wondered as he glanced down at the grey slabs of stone that marked Robertson's last resting place.

There was nothing remarkable about the grave, just one among hundreds. The earth around it was still fresh, but in the months since the funeral, some grass had started to grow over it. Another year, and it would be indistinguishable from all the others. It looked genuine enough, thought Sam, but the only way to be certain was to dig it up.

If Robertson was being chased by his creditors, and the Israeli state owed him a favour, maybe they staged his death. *It's no more unlikely than any of the other theories.*

Sam spun round. He suddenly sensed he was being watched. He had taken a risk in coming here: the place was almost certainly monitored by Mossad and if they identified him, he would be in trouble. He remembered the photo of his daughter with the target mark on it. If they'd kill his daughter, they certainly wouldn't hesitate to kill him. His eyes scanned the graveyard. Fifty yards away, a boy in blue jeans and a black T-shirt was kneeling in front of a tombstone, muttering something under his breath. He looked up, and saw Sam staring across at him. He scowled, then looked away.

Is someone following me? Does somebody know I'm here?

Assassins should stay out of graveyards, Sam told himself as he walked quickly back towards the bus stop.

The bus took only a few minutes to arrive. Sam rode it back into the centre of town, then picked up another bus to take him out towards the eastern side of Tel Aviv. There were three people on his list to see today. *If I start now, I might get a lead by nightfall.*

Ben Feldman lived by himself. The apartment was smarter than Imer's but only just. Two rooms, a small bathroom and a view of the hills. From the cushions spread out across the sofa, Sam guessed there was a girlfriend who maybe stayed over from time to time, but there was no sign of her now, nor was there a clue to who she might be in the pictures displayed on the dresser. 'Let's get a coffee,' said Ben, soon after Sam stepped into the apartment. 'It's too crowded to think in here.'

Sam nodded, and walked alongside Ben as they headed round the corner to the coffee shop. They had been in the army together, but that had been ten years ago, and though they had stayed in touch they had rarely seen each other since then. It didn't matter: they were still close enough for Sam to trust him, for him to feel certain that Ben wouldn't simply tell Rotanski he was back in the country. Ben had spent three more years than Sam in the army, and joined Mossad straight afterwards. He'd spent the last two years on the senior body-guarding team, arranging security for the most senior members of the government. Close to the centre of the action, thought Sam. *That's why I want to talk to him.*

'I'm trying to find out what happened to Max Robertson,' said Sam after they had drunk their coffee and spent twenty minutes swapping news of their families and old war stories.

Ben laughed. He was a thin man, with thick, dark hair and eyes that sparkled with humour. 'Then you'll be needing some protection yourself.'

'Not yet,' said Sam sharply. 'I'm not even close.'

'So what do you want to know?'

'Was he working for us?'

'For Israel?'

Sam nodded. 'For Mossad.'

Ben shook his head. 'Not that I know of,' he said. 'You heard anything?'

'Just following every lead.'

They continued talking for another twenty minutes, but Sam already knew the conversation was over. Ben didn't know anything. He said goodbye, promised to keep in touch, then went back to the bus stop. Try another contact, he told himself. *Keep working the leads until you get somewhere.*

Leon Barnea was living close to the centre of town, in a modern apartment block. Expensive, thought Sam, as he stepped through the marble, air-conditioned lobby and pressed the gilded button on the lift. The door was opened by Alina, a Russian girl. Sam had heard she'd moved in with Barnea six months ago. Tall and slim, with short blonde hair, and bright brown eyes, she had the high cheekbones that were common in Russia but rare out here in Israel. Apparently he'd been working in Russia on some oil contracts, and managed to get her a visa out. Cost a bundle, from what Sam had heard on the grapevine. And from the look of the end product, worth every last rouble.

'He's just washing,' she said, looking sympathetically at Sam as she showed him in. 'I'll get him.'

Some guys get all the breaks, thought Sam as he watched Alina's high heels clip across the expensive parquet of the apartment. Great job, plenty of money, sexy girlfriend. Some of us know how to get what we want in life, and some of us don't. *It comes naturally, or it doesn't come at all.*

Sam checked his watch. Just before eleven in the morning. Whatever line of business Barnea had found himself in, it clearly didn't involve getting up early. The first time Sam had met him had been in the army, then later in Mossad. Barnea had done two years bodyguarding in Israel, then got himself an attachment to the Israeli consulate in Kiev, and spent three years there, supposedly processing applications from Ukrainian Jews trying to leave the country, but mainly trying to collect whatever information he could on the collapse of the Soviet Empire. In the last year, he'd been out of the service, living and working in Tel Aviv. Like many people with links to the disintegrating Soviet Empire, he seemed to be making a lot of money very quickly.

'We thought we'd never see you again,' said Barnea as he walked into the main room.

He was wearing blue jeans and dark polo shirt, and looked freshly scrubbed. His skin was tanned and healthy, and his eyes sparkled with the easygoing contentment of a man who has suddenly found that life is more fun than he ever expected.

'Yes, you go on that mission, you don't necessarily come back,' said Sam.

Within the organisation, most people knew what Sam and his team were doing. They were treated with respect by the rest of the men. They all knew there was no harder, more dangerous, nor more thankless mission. And, in truth, they were all grateful not to have been chosen for it. 'How many of you are left?'

'Just me and Michael.'

'Shit, that's bad.'

Alina put two glasses of freshly squeezed orange juice on the glass coffee table, then tactfully withdrew from the room. Probably got some new dresses to try on, thought Sam.

'We got more of them than they did of us,' said Sam. 'And they were somebody, while we were nobody. I'd call that a win.'

Barnea nodded. 'There aren't any winners though, are there?' he said. 'Not between nations. Only between men.' He paused, looking straight at Sam. 'What are you looking for?'

'Max Robertson.'

'He's dead.'

'Really?' Sam paused, waiting to see if Barnea would rise to that bait, but his expression remained impassive. 'I'm rooting around, looking for anything that might tell me why.'

Barnea shrugged. 'Search me.'

'I heard he might be working for us.'

'For me and you?'

Sam shook his head. He was surprised by Barnea's reaction. They had been friends in the army, and had kept in touch. He had thought he was someone he could rely on. Now, it seemed, everything had changed.

'No, of course not,' Sam said quickly. 'For Mossad.'

'Not that I know of.'

'He did a lot of work in the Soviet Union,' persisted Sam. 'He was there all the time, talking to their leaders, publishing their books. Our men there must have taken a pretty close interest in what he was up to.'

Barnea was making a show of looking bored, but Sam could sense the hostility in his manner. 'Not that I know of,' he repeated. 'We kept tabs on everything that was going on, naturally, but I don't remember singling out Robertson for any special attention.'

'Even when he started doing deals there?'

Barnea shook his head.

'Using Israeli companies?'

'I don't think so,' said Barnea. 'The Finance Ministry might have taken an interest. Not Mossad.'

Sam hesitated. He remembered something Imer had said to him when he first started his training for the service. Get to know the sound of a lie, he'd told his class. You won't always be able to see it. And you won't always be able to unravel it. But you should be able to hear it, because most people become lazy when they start lying. Barnea must have skipped that lesson, thought Sam. Because he's lying now. He can't even take the trouble to spin me a decent story.

If I was looking for confirmation that Robertson was working for us, I just got it.

'OK,' said Sam. 'I'm just checking up leads, that's all.' He stood up, and walked towards the door. 'Thanks for your help.'

'No trouble,' said Barnea smoothly. 'I'll be in touch if I hear anything. I've got your number.'

I haven't got a number, thought Sam as he shut the door. That's how likely you are to be in touch.

Outside, the sun had risen, and the temperature was already beyond thirty degrees. He wiped a bead of sweat from his forehead and pulled down his shades as he started to walk back towards the bus stop. Friendships evaporate in the heat, he decided. He'd thought Barnea was a man he could rely on, but that was a long time ago. He owes me nothing. And that's precisely what he's prepared to offer me. Maybe if I was in his boots I'd do the same.

The bus journey took twenty minutes. By the time Sam got off, it was past midday, and the office workers in the centre of the city were pouring out of the offices for their lunch. Sam decided to get a sandwich and a juice. Alik Netzer was working at a coffee bar, twelve blocks down from the King David hotel. It was five years since Sam had last seen him, but in the army, then Mossad, the two men had been close. He'd quit three years ago, and Sam had heard nothing about him since then. Circles of gossip allowed most Mossad men to keep tabs on each other's progress back into the real world: they were all fascinated by the different fates that lay in store for them. On Alik, there had been nothing: it was as if he had been sucked from the face of the planet. It had taken a couple of hours of phone calls to track him down, and then Sam discovered he'd been working in Tel Aviv all this time.

I'll let him finish his shift.

The Onami sandwich shop was nothing special. A few tables, a coffee machine, and piles of cheap lunches for the office workers: it served mostly falafel in pitta, and salt-beef sandwiches. The place was thinning out by the time Sam walked in: just a few desk cowboys grabbing a bite to take back to the office. 'Sam Wolfman,' said Alik, looking at him over the counter. 'What the hell are you doing here?'

'Looking for you,' said Sam.

Alik looked tanned and fit. His sandy hair was growing down to his collar and his face was bright and alert. He was a tall man, over six foot, with a thick nose and sharp angular features, but with eyes that were boyish for a man now pushing forty. He was one of those guys who never seem to grow up. In the army, he'd been one of their best gunners, and when he joined Mossad he'd made a name for himself in the newly emerging field of electronic surveillance. He was a demon with computers, devising bugs to place on the personal computers that were then just starting to be found on people's desks at work and even occasionally at home. His colleagues assumed he'd go far; he'd never acquired much of a taste for fieldwork, but then Mossad had always been an organisation that favoured brains over brute strength. If you were clever, and signed up to their view of the world, you went far.

Then he'd quit, disappearing out of the service without a trace.

'Let's get a coffee,' said Alik.

'Where?'

Alik laughed. 'Here of course. It's free.'

There was a room at the back of the café, filled with the smells of a million different sandwiches. Alik pushed aside a pile of tins, clearing some space between them, then put down two cups of milky coffee. 'You as well?' he said looking at Sam.

'Me as well, what?'

'You've had enough?'

'Is that what happened to you?' asked Sam.

His eyes moved around the back room. No doubt they did their best to keep it clean, but the place was filled with the chaos you get in any kitchen. Bins were overflowing, and every surface was covered in a thick layer of grease. Alik was one of the cleverest men Sam had ever met. In the three years since he'd last heard from him, he'd sometimes wondered where he might have gone. Usually he imagined he'd flown off to California, and was making millions by now in the booming computer industry. Or maybe doing some brilliant research at a university somewhere.

Why here? Sam wondered. *Why throw your life away in a sandwich bar?*

Alik took a sip on his coffee. 'I couldn't see the point in what I was doing any more,' he said flatly. 'I tried. I went through all the rationales, tried to look at it from every angle, but the way I saw it there were just two sides locked into a game. We killed them, they killed us. I think we'd all forgotten what it was about. So I stopped. I just couldn't carry on.'

'And you didn't want to do something . . . else?'

'Something better than working in a sandwich shop, you mean?'

Sam nodded.

'I couldn't do that either. I didn't want to work for Mossad any more because I couldn't support what we'd become. But I didn't want to work anywhere else, because that would be abandoning the service. So here I am. I'm close by, if they need me.'

Sam nodded. Like everything Alik said, it made its own kind of sense. Mossad was like the old joke about women: you couldn't work for them, but you couldn't work without them either. *I've felt that way many times myself.*

'And you?'

'Trying to put myself back on track.' He looked at Alik. 'I'm investigating what happened to Max Robertson,' he said. 'I've heard he might have been working for us.'

'What makes you say that?'

'Couple of things. We gave him a state funeral. Then I went to see Barnea this morning. He used to work for us in the Soviet Union. I asked him about Robertson and he lied to me.'

'That figures,' said Alik quickly. 'You shouldn't talk to him.'

Sam nodded. 'I know that now.'

'He's dropped down into the sewers,' said Alik. 'He got to know quite a few people when he was stationed in Kiev. Black-market guys, gangsters, all that. They've been pouring into Tel Aviv in the past few years. The Soviet Empire is coming down. The people at the top haven't noticed yet, but the people at the bottom have. They're stripping the place before it crashes, and Barnea is helping them.'

'I didn't stay longer than I had to,' said Sam. 'So, what do you reckon? Was Robertson working for the team?'

Alik shrugged. 'He sold us some software. He owned a company called Information Dynamics. They did tracking systems. You inputted a lot of data into the machine, and it tried to find patterns for you.'

'Like artificial intelligence.'

'Right. But like most of those systems, it was a con. The emphasis should have been on the artificial, not the intelligence. The program just came up with random word associations. It was nothing you couldn't do for yourself. And when you checked them out, they were all meaningless. Maybe one day someone will come up with a program that can replace human intelligence gathering, but that wasn't it.'

'So?'

'So, Mossad wouldn't have bought it unless they trusted Robertson absolutely. We'd already been working on putting bugs into computer systems, so that we could collect all the information on them. That was one of the things I was working on before I left. We knew it was possible, so there was no way we'd buy in a computer system unless we knew for sure who it was coming from. Too risky. We'd build it ourselves rather than take that chance.'

'Then he was working for us?'

Alik nodded. 'I reckon,' he said.

'Then why would we kill him?'

Alik shrugged. 'Maybe we didn't. Maybe we rescued him.'

'Mr Sosa.'

Sam looked up sharply at the desk clerk. He was standing in the lobby of the Optima Tower hotel. His jacket was slung over his shoulder, and he could feel the sweat on his skin as he stepped out of the heat of the day and into the air-conditioned lobby. 'Yes.'

'There's a message for you.'

Sam paused. He had told nobody he was staying here. Absolutely nobody. And he was travelling under a false name. *There shouldn't be any messages.*

He moved over to the desk and took the envelope with his name stencilled on the front. Slicing it open, he glanced down at the words written out in neat black letters. 'Call Mr Barnea.'

Sam walked quickly back to his room. It was late afternoon now, and the corridor was empty. He hesitated, holding the key in his hand, then knocked twice. 'Room service,' he said, then knocked again.

Silence.

If anyone was inside they'd answer the door, pretend to be me, then tell me to go away. That's what I'd do. *And the chances are they had the same training I did.*

Sam opened the door. His eyes swept the room, scanning it for any signs of disturbance. Nothing. Reaching inside the cupboard, he collected his two changes of clothes, his notebook and videotapes, and slung them into his black canvas travel case. He picked up the phone and punched in the only number he'd memorised since he'd been back in Tel Aviv. Imer answered on the second ring. 'I've got something for you,' he said as soon as Sam said hello.

'What?' said Sam.

'A lead, that's all. It might be nothing.'

Sam hesitated, glancing anxiously out of the window. 'What?'

'A guy called Perelman,' he said. 'Daniel Perelman. Mossad, of course, but he worked for the Directory, so he was mostly caught up in internal affairs. Apparently he was talking a lot about Robertson a few months ago. Just before he died.'

'Saying what?'

'I don't know, just sounding off. But if there is a link, he might be it.'

'Where can I find him?'

'That's up to you,' said Imer firmly.

Sam nodded. He knew there was no point arguing with

the old guy. Nothing would make him hand over more than he wanted.

'I've been tracked,' said Sam. 'Did you tell anyone I was staying here?'

'No,' said Imer quickly.

Too quickly? Briefly, Sam wondered if he had been wrong to trust Imer. The old man loved him, of that there could be no question, but he loved Mossad more fiercely.

'Who by?' said Imer, breaking into the silence.

'Barnea.'

'Then leave,' said Imer. 'Leave at once.'

Sam threw the remains of his belongings into a bag, went down to the hotel lobby and handed the clerk the cash for his room. 'There's a call waiting for you,' said the clerk.

'Who?'

'Mr Barnea.'

'Tell him I'm on my way to the airport.'

Sam could feel the air hitting him in the face as he stepped out of the hotel. He needed to find Perelman and to do that he needed help. A single question was burning through him. *Is there anyone I can trust any more?*

TWELVE

His father was sitting by himself, in the same canvas chair he always sat in. The garden to the apartment was tiny, but Yoram always maintained it with meticulous care. The grass was trimmed twice a week, and watered once a day. Along its borders there were rows of tulips, two yellow ones, followed by two red ones, with the same pattern stretching right around the garden. A book of military history was open on his lap, and there was a glass of juice sitting on the coffee table, but Yoram was neither drinking nor reading. He was just looking up at the blue sky, his eyes half closed, a look of puzzlement playing across his face.

Sam glanced for a moment at his father. Even by coming here, he knew he was potentially putting him at risk: he had taken care to make sure no one was following him, but you could never be certain. If there had been any other choice he would have taken it, but right now his father was the only person he could think of who might be able to push the investigation forwards.

It was more than a year since the two had seen each other, and ever since he'd retired Sam had been struck by how fast Yoram was ageing. It was as if all the years had been bottled up inside when he was on active service, and now they had been uncorked. The lines in his skin had grown deeper, and his eyes were sagging, as if he no longer had the strength to keep them open.

'Sam,' he growled. 'What the hell are you doing here?'

125

Sam pulled up the other chair. It was always this way with Yoram. No pleasantries. No catching up. No small talk. Just straight down to business. *Maybe I'll be like that with Luke one day.*

'I'm looking for someone,' said Sam. 'I thought you might be able to help me.'

He could feel his father scrutinising him. He always said very little, and asked few questions, but Sam could tell he was examining him, checking out his appearance, his mood, his manner. Afterwards, every word he said would be chewed up and analysed. Any mistakes would be logged carefully, and used against him years later. *Nobody held a grudge longer than Yoram.*

Why don't you just ask me how I am? he said to himself.

'Who's the guy?' said Yoram.

'He's called Daniel Perelman.'

'Is he one of us?'

Sam nodded, looking for signs of recognition in his father's eyes. Mossad was like a series of closed compartments. You knew the people in your unit, and you got to know the guys you trained with, but as far as possible the operators were kept to themselves. That way it was harder for them to betray one another – and Mossad lived in a constant state of suspicion, even of its own people.

Yoram rolled his eyes backwards, as if searching through the cluttered rooms of his memory. 'It's a common enough name.'

'I know,' said Sam.

'How old?'

'Twenty-nine.'

Yoram's eyes suddenly turned on Sam. 'Ruth Perelman,' he said. 'Her husband worked for Mossad. He was killed in 1981, on a mission. I know he had a boy, called Daniel. Ruth lived on the coast, in Hadera. Probably still does.'

'Think it's the same family?'

Yoram shrugged. 'The service is a family business.' He smiled. 'You should know that.'

'I quit.'

Yoram paused. Sam could tell his father was pleased. He'd never wanted him to join Mossad in the first place: he'd hardly spoken to Sam for a year after he discovered that he'd signed up. Mossad was like no other organisation in the world. It didn't have the bloated staffs, and compartmentalised attitudes, of the CIA, the KGB or MI6. The founders insisted it should never have a permanent staff of more than twelve hundred. Each man would be hand-picked after the most rigorous assessment, and each would be capable of multiple roles: scientists would be able to work in the field, an agent could work in analysis or training. They were all *memune*, or 'first among equals'. It was the quality that quickly built such a fearful reputation. It allowed Mossad to provide the information that enabled the Israeli Air Force to knock out the entire Eygptian Air Force before the Six Day War even started; it enabled them to put together the mission that lifted Adolf Eichmann out of Argentina and brought him back to Israel to stand trial; it gave them the confidence to send in a hit squad to rescue a planeload of hostages at Entebbe airport in Uganda. Although Sam knew his father was proud of what he and the founders of Mossad had created, he knew he didn't like what it had become, nor the way it treated its veterans.

That was why, every time they met, he'd tell him how Mossad betrayed him, how it took the best years of your life and gave you nothing back, how Sam should be working on building a proper life for Elena and his grandchildren.

'You know what I was doing?'

Yoram nodded. Sam had never discussed his mission with his father, but old soldiers were like any other network, they kept tabs on the younger men, and there was no question that Yoram knew. But did he approve? Sam would have liked the answer to that question.

'I heard.'

'I got tired of it,' said Sam. 'We kill them, they kill us, we kill some more of them. It's just a groove you get stuck in. It doesn't *change* anything.'

'Sure it does.'

'What does it change?'

'It changes *you*. It makes you a killer, just like them.' Yoram smiled, but it was a smile of regret not pleasure. 'Once you cross that line, you can't go back. You can get close, so close that the rest of the world probably won't notice, but you'll always be on the other side. Where the assassins live.'

'You never came back.'

'I know. I'm sorry.'

'That's why I quit. Before I got trapped there.'

'Then why do you want to find Perelman? You should be giving up that kind of work. Just cut loose, put it all behind you.'

'I'm working on something.'

'For yourself?'

'For myself, yes.'

Yoram hesitated. 'At last,' he said. 'You trust those people, then you end up like me. With nothing.'

Sam rang the bell again, but there was still no response. He glanced around the lobby of the building. A woman was leaving an apartment further down the corridor. 'Is Mrs Perelman away?' he asked her. 'She's not answering the door, maybe she's on holiday?'

'Who are you?' the woman replied, looking at Sam suspiciously.

Sam had noticed that change in Israel. It was only five years since he had left the country, but the security situation just got worse and worse. Everyone was suspicious of one another. The police and army were in a visible state of alert. The year of terrorism was starting to drain all the warmth and humanity out of the nation. One more reason why I don't want to come back, thought Sam to himself.

'There's an insurance claim that needs to be settled,' said Sam. 'I just need to get her to sign some papers.'

The woman kept her eyes firmly on Sam, as if she was appraising him. Then she moved forward, standing close to the door. 'We've had a couple of robberies in the block,' she said. 'She doesn't like to answer the door unless she knows who it is.'

She knocked twice on the door. 'Mrs Perelman,' she shouted. 'It's OK. Just someone to see you.'

The door opened slightly. The woman who looked out was thin, with grey hair, and wearing a pale blue smock. Her eyes darted up towards Sam.

'My name is Sam Wolfman,' he said. 'I think you knew my father, Yoram.'

A smile suddenly broke on the old woman's face. 'Come inside,' she said quickly. 'I'll get you something.'

The apartment smelt of disinfectant. Sam walked across the pale wooden floor into the main room. Up on the mantelpiece he could see pictures of Mrs Perelman and her husband when they were younger, holding their young son. All the pictures were at least twenty years old, he noted. Nothing that showed Daniel as a grown man.

'I wanted to speak to Daniel,' said Sam. 'I don't know where to find him. Dad thought you might know.'

The silence froze the air. Sam could see the woman shudder, as if a blast of cold air had blown through the room. The skin, already loose on her bones, started to shake. Sam glanced quickly back towards the mantelpiece. There were dust marks along the shelves. Where some picture used to be. *The pictures of Daniel as a grown man.*

129

'I'm sorry,' he said quickly. He paused, struggling for the next sentence. 'Something's happened to him, hasn't it?'

He moved swiftly across the floor. Mrs Perelman had collapsed in a faint. Sam just caught her in time, grabbing her with one arm, then another. He laid her across the chair, then went quickly to the kitchen, returning with a glass of water. He leaned across her. The pulse was still there, but faint. She was breathing. He tipped the glass of water towards her lips. 'It's OK,' he said.

Her eyes opened, and suddenly Sam could see how tired and bloodshot they were. There could be no doubt. Daniel was dead. This woman was entirely alone, both her husband and her son now dead.

More meat for the grinder.

'Do you want to tell me what's happened?'

She sat upright, grasping for the glass of water and drinking it down. The liquid was dribbling down her face, running in tiny rivers through the deeply etched grooves on her skin. 'Daniel is dead. Two weeks ago.'

'How?'

She hesitated. 'You're Yoram's son?'

Sam nodded.

'Then you're Mossad as well?' The question was delivered in a tone that was both breathless and harsh.

Sam nodded again.

'They all are,' she said sourly. 'The sons follow the fathers. Straight to their deaths.'

'What happened to Daniel?' Sam repeated.

'You know what it's like,' Mrs Perelman continued. 'You're on the inside, so you should know. They don't tell the mothers anything.' She paused, drinking the last of the water. 'You married?'

Sam nodded.

'I pity her,' said Mrs Perelman. 'I pity the poor woman. They won't tell her anything when the time comes.

Nothing. She'll never know how you died or why.'

Sam gripped her hand. He could feel the anger rippling through her. 'What did they say?'

'An accident. They said he'd been on a training mission. Something had gone wrong. He'd been killed along with three other men. There might be a medal apparently, although right now nobody is even supposed to know that he's died.' A thin laugh rose up from her lungs. 'There's always a medal, isn't there? His father got one when he died, and now Daniel as well. I'll have two medals to keep me company.'

'I might be able to help find something out.'

'What?'

Sam could feel her nails gripping into the skin of his hand.

'Did he ever say anything about Max Robertson?'

'How did you know that?'

Sam paused, deciding how much to reveal.

'Where did you hear that?' Her voice was louder this time.

'From men, in the service.' Sam unhooked her fingers from his hand, but kept hold of her. 'What did he say about Robertson?'

'It doesn't matter now. It won't bring him back.'

'It matters,' said Sam.

It matters to me anyway.

'That he was a bad man, that he wasn't a friend of Israel.'

You press the advantage. That's the first rule of interrogation. As soon as someone starts talking, you press the advantage. Squeeze as much from them as you can before they realise what they're saying. Then relax, soften them up, make them think they are your friend, then press them some more. Sources are like fruit, he could remember his trainers telling them. *The harder you squeeze them the more juice you get.*

'Was there a mission?' said Sam quickly.

'I don't know,' said Mrs Perelman.

'Was there a mission?' Sam repeated. 'Was Robertson classed as an enemy?'

'I tell you I don't know.' Her tone was turning cold.

'If I could find that out, I might be able to find out what happened to Daniel.'

A tear started to run down the woman's face. 'But I know what happened to him. I've seen the corpse. So what difference does it make now?'

As Sam walked towards the bus stop, the sun was setting across the Mediterranean, streaking the horizon with patchy smudges of red. The words Mrs Perelman had left with him were still rattling through his mind. Daniel had been talking about Robertson. About how he was an enemy of Israel. *And now he was dead as well.*

Sam glanced ahead. The bus stop for Tel Aviv was fifty yards down the seafront. On the other side of the road, a man was walking slowly towards him, his hands dug deep into his pockets.

There hadn't been any more information to extract from Mrs Perelman. Mossad had told her that Daniel had died on a training accident, nothing more. Sam didn't believe it for a moment. The puzzle was starting to take shape. They didn't help Robertson disappear, they killed him. Perhaps Daniel was one of the men who killed him? Perhaps they took him out as well to stop him from talking.

If I could just find out who he'd been working with. *Maybe I'd find out how they killed Robertson, and why.*

Sam turned and looked around. The man walking down the other side of the road had paused to tie his shoelace. Sam hesitated, watching as the man bent over.

Nothing, thought Sam. *Maybe it's nothing.*

He kept walking. The bus stop was just thirty yards away now. The man stood up, straightening himself out, then glanced once towards Sam, before hurriedly looking away.

The training, thought Sam. Once you've had the training, you recognise it everywhere.

He's following me.

He stopped, looking at the bus timetable. Six fifteen. A bus for Tel Aviv was due in ten minutes. The wind from the sea was rustling through his hair. Sam studied the map attached to the side of the bus stop. The man had crossed the road, and was now walking towards him. There was an expression of studied indifference on his face, and he was walking at just below average pace. *The same way I would.*

The man stood next to him. He took a pack of cigarettes from his pocket, lit one, then glanced at Sam. His skin was tanned but smooth, yet his eyes were hard: the eyes of a man used to surveillance. 'Have I missed a bus?'

Sam swung his right arm up. His forearm connected with the man's throat. He was five foot eight, with thick muscles and a lean, tough body, but the movement caught him by surprise. He was knocked hard against the bus stop. The cigarette sailed into the air as the wind emptied out of his throat. Sam leaned forwards, using the strength in his back to increase the pressure on the thin pipe connecting the man's mouth to his heart. The oxygen was slowly draining out of him, and though the man was trying to push and kick him away, he no longer had enough space to work up a blow with any force in it.

'Who the fuck are you?' said Sam, spitting in his face.

The man was now incapable of speech. His breath was gone, and although his lips were moving no sound could escape: the vocal chords were too starved of air to work properly. Sam relaxed his grip on the neck just a fraction, running a torturer's calculation through his mind. *Just enough easing to let him speak. Not so much he gets his strength back.*

'Why the fuck are you following me?'

The man's head was turning from side to side as he tried

133

to gasp down a lungful of air. 'You're a fucking psycho, man,' he said eventually. Saliva was dribbling down the side of his cheek. 'I'm just getting the bus.'

'Are you Mossad? Did Rotanski send you to get me?'

He scrutinised the man's face as he used Rotanski's name, looking for just a glimmer of recognition.

Nothing.

'Did Barnea send you?'

Again, *nothing.*

'I'm just getting the bus,' the man spluttered. 'Let the fuck go.'

Sam could feel the fear sweating out of the man. His body was trembling, and his eyes were shot through with hatred. He was lying. Sam could feel it in his expression, in his manner and in his body pressed up against him. 'You followed me,' growled Sam. 'Why?'

'Fuck off,' spat the man.

Sam leaned harder into his body, pressing the bone of his forearm tightly into the man's neck. He could feel the skin tighten then buckle under the blow, and he could sense the muscle of the windpipe closing in on itself. The oxygen was draining out of him. 'Please.' The man was choking.

'Tell me,' said Sam.

'Please.' The word was barely audible.

'Tell me,' Sam repeated.

The man was trying to speak but the words died on his lips.

Across the street, Sam could see a man looking out of the window on the third floor of an apartment block. He was maybe sixty, dressed just in shorts and a T-shirt, with a phone in his hand. He's calling the police, Sam realised.

In another minute, I'll have been taken.

'Tell me.' Sam was trying not to raise his voice.

The man's eyes flashed up defiantly towards him.

It's useless.

He leaned harder into the man's throat. His body thrashed, kicking outwards, but Sam had enough strength to contain him. The man slumped to the ground, unconscious. Sam checked he was still breathing, then moved swiftly to the wall separating the street from the beach. He vaulted across it, landing on the sand. The sun had almost set, and there were few people about: one woman walking her dog, and a man out jogging.

Sam started walking at a steady measured pace: by the time the police arrived, he'd be just another desk cowboy stretching his legs after a sedentary day in the office.

They're following me, Sam thought, as he jogged towards the sunset. Next time they'll kill me. The same way they did Robertson.

You work for Mossad, eventually they devour you. Just as my father always told me they would.

THIRTEEN

Sam folded the passport back into the locker. Goodbye, Mr Sosa, he said to himself with a brief smile. It was good to know you.

There were three other men in the changing room of the Oasis, but two of them were talking, and the other was in a hurry. Sam felt confident no one would notice him. He took out the second of the three passports. This one was Irish, made out in the name of Alan Godson, who described his profession as a businessman. Checking the small brown envelope, Sam made sure the passport was in order, then slipped the envelope into the inside pocket of his jacket.

After ten laps in the pool – again, there was no point arousing suspicions by visiting a gym without using it – Sam was on the train back from Reading to Paddington. Mr Godson had some people to talk to.

And this time he needed some answers.

Sitting on the train, Sam reflected on what he'd learned in the last few days. He'd been compromised while in Israel. Somebody knew he'd travelled into the country as Henk Sosa, and was starting to make connections. So from Israel, he'd made his way across the border to Lebanon, and from there caught a flight to Athens, making a connection on to a flight into London. He knew that someone was following him in Israel – maybe Mossad, maybe Barnea's gangsters – and he had to disguise his route out of the country. That Robertson had been working for Mossad in some capacity, he had no doubt. It wasn't that surprising. The organisation maintained a network of influential figures around the world who could be relied upon to provide help when it was needed: it was one of the advantages of working for a nation with people scattered across the globe. The question was whether they had killed him. Sam also knew that the Russian connection must be important. Barnea was involved he felt sure – but how?

Five million, Sam reminded himself as he stepped off the train. Enough to set you up for life. *For that you will keep pushing until you get some answers.*

He wanted to ask Papa, but without Mossad behind him, he knew he had no way to pay the old man – if he could still trust him anyway. He had to call Selima Robertson again. A maid said she was still travelling. She would pass on the message. Maybe, thought Sam. If you can be bothered. Sam was running out of leads.

The tube delivered him quickly to the Newton Arms, a dismal modern pub just off Holborn Circus. Eddie Mitchell had been a sub-editor for a decade or more on the *Daily Echo*, before becoming foreign editor for a year under Robertson. Sam had met him once before, while trying to recruit some friendly journalists who might be able to give him some leads into the PLO. The meeting had gone nowhere – Mitchell was a drunk, Sam had quickly realised, who knew nothing except for what he read on the wires – but for a few months he'd been happy enough to collect a small Mossad retainer. With two divorces behind him, Mitchell wasn't in a position to refuse any offers of money.

'People always want to know about the fat bastard,' said Mitchell, taking the first sip of the double Scotch and soda that Sam had just bought for him. 'I've had at least a dozen people come and ask me questions since he went under. I'm having trouble staying sober so many people are buying me drinks.'

Mitchell was a good-humoured, attractive man, which might explain why he had two divorces behind him: women liked him. Mitchell was one of those men unable to resist any chance of a conquest. He was tall and slim, with sandy hair, patrician features and a rumpled, intellectual manner. He lit a cigarette and looked at Sam. 'So your mob are trying to find out what happened to him as well?'

Sam nodded. 'When you became foreign editor, did you get involved in any of Robertson's trips abroad?'

Mitchell laughed. 'Did I hell. This bloody rag stopped being a newspaper, and just became an arm of the fat bugger's foreign policy. That's what he called it, you know. "Eddie" he used to boom out across the office. "Cook me up some words. Robertson Communications is changing its foreign policy."'

Sam took a sip on his beer. 'What did that involve?'

Mitchell shook his head. 'Don't get me started,' he said with a grin. 'There was always some kind of buggering around. The fat bastard used to arrange all these trips. A famine in Africa: we'd arrange a planeload of relief. "The *Echo* saves the starving millions, Robertson to the rescue." That was the kind of crap we'd have to put on the front page. Then I'd have to start ringing up the Foreign Office and all the bloody embassies to organise the trip. The local president or prime minister had to be there to meet him, and he liked to take a few MPs along with him as well. Next up, he'd be talking about some huge deal with one of those tinpot little Eastern European states. Bulgaria was a favourite. We always seemed to be going to Bulgaria to finance a new dam, or a power station, or some other bit of buggering around. "Robertson builds a bridge between East and West." Again, I'd be the poor sod who had to arrange all the details, line up the Foreign Office, get the ambassador to lay on a bash and all the other rubbish.'

'They didn't mind?'

'It didn't matter whether they bloody minded or not. Let me tell you something about Robertson. He was a sodding animal. He had this helicopter landing pad built on top of the headquarters, so he could fly right into the building. But the best bit was the railing. He used to go up there, stand next to the railing, and piss. Right down, sprinkling his piss on the heads of his employees as they left the building for the evening. That's the kind of guy he was. So it didn't really matter whether any of these tinpot little ambassadors minded or not. Raw power, that's what the fat bugger was all about. He snapped his fingers, they jumped.'

'How about the Soviet Union? Were there many dealings there?'

Again, Mitchell laughed. 'That was the worst. The last couple of years, we were constantly flying off to Moscow. Lining up a few ambassadors in the Congo or Bulgaria wasn't so bad. The buggers didn't have much to do all day anyway. Moscow was different. They really were important. The fat bugger would be saying things like, "Get the American ambassador to Moscow on the line for me, Eddie." Yeah, right. How the hell am I going to get the bugger on the phone? Not available, I'd tell him eventually. Then the fat bugger would go crazy. Start shouting and sweating and yelling. Called me every name under the sun. "What's the use of a foreign editor who doesn't know the American ambassador to Moscow?" he'd yell at me. "Haven't you any contacts, you fool? You're just a bloody cretin. The *Echo* needs proper journalists. You're fired. Hear that, Mitchell? Fired." Of course, it never happened. Only new recruits worried about being fired. The rest of us just turned up for work the next day. The fat bugger fired hundreds of people every day, but he rarely bothered to check whether they were still there at the end of the week. That's what it was like. Think of it as hell, but with very bad organisational skills. You'll get the picture.'

Sam noticed Mitchell's glass was empty, and went to the bar to get him another Scotch. Mitchell was drifting off into irrelevant anecdotes. *What I need is information.*

'What was he doing there?' said Sam. 'Why was he in Moscow all the time?'

Mitchell shrugged. 'Search me. Showboating, I reckon. The point about Robertson was that he loved power. Exercising it. Studying it. Getting close to it, any way he could. The Politburo understood raw, brutal power better than anyone. I think the fat bugger liked to hang out with his own kind.'

'But what did they want from him?'

'Money,' said Mitchell. 'The trouble with being a commie is that you have no understanding of business. I think here in London a lot of people guessed the fat bugger was a bit of a fraud. The Russkins, though, thought he was the genuine article, a financial genius. They wanted access to some of his cash.'

'Any deals that could have led to his death?'

'I don't know. I reckon you're barking up the wrong bloody tree. My theory is that it is one of the husbands who killed him.'

'The husbands?'

'The fat bugger was shagging women by the dozen. The way he went about it was close to statutory rape. Think about it: one of the beauties goes home and complains to her husband, and he decides to finish the fat bugger off.'

'On a boat in the Med?'

Mitchell shrugged. 'It's just a theory. Who says one of the birds wasn't married to an SAS guy or something? With the fat bastard, anything's possible.'

'Even that he's still alive.'

'Jesus, I hope not,' groaned Mitchell. 'That's the last thing the world needs.'

The drinks were finished, and Sam was in no mood for

another one. In his judgement he'd pumped as much as he could from Mitchell. Keep in touch, he said as he left, along with a promise that if Mossad needed anyone on a British newspaper they'd contact him. Some chance, he thought as he walked out of the pub. *Mossad won't be using me to hand out any more retainers.*

From Holborn, it was just a short bus ride down to Trafalgar House. He was meeting Sir Jeremy Brammel for tea at three at the Oxford & Cambridge Club in St James's. Brammel had had a glittering early career. He had been an MP in his native Australia at the age of twenty-seven, he had been a junior minister in the Australian government by the time he was thirty. Then it had all gone wrong. Some bad investments, had left him painfully short of money. He'd been forced to resign his seat and drifted from one failed City venture to another, kept afloat only by the fast-dwindling value of his reputation. For the past five years, he had been one of Robertson's main advisers.

Mitchell was wrong, Sam said to himself as he stepped from the bus. Killing a man such as Robertson required sophisticated organisation. It took a team, with training.

Brammel was already sitting at a table at the back of the club's bar. In his late forties, age had not been kind to him. His hair had greyed and thinned out, and lines had creased up his skin. But it was in the eyes that you could see the battering that life had served up. They sagged into their sockets, with an expression that was both hunted and dejected at the same time. That's the trouble with early promise, Sam thought as he introduced himself and ordered some tea. It's too much to deal with when you can't deliver on the contract.

'The banks,' said Brammel. 'That's where you need to be looking.'

'Which banks?' asked Sam softly.

'It was all kept afloat on a sea of debt,' said Brammel, with the tone of a man who knew a fair bit about borrowing money himself. 'There was very little substance to anything the man owned. We just shuffled money around from company to company. We made acquisitions using borrowed money, just so we could get our hands on some cash in another company's bank account. We defaulted on loans and bonds all the time. The whole thing was just one great big conjuring trick, with Robertson at the centre of it. He was the only one who really had any idea what was going on.' He paused, pouring from the pot of Earl Grey tea the waitress had just put down on their table. 'Robertson bullied the banks the same way he bullied everyone else. First he charmed them, then he tormented them. When they made the first loan, they were drawn into the web. Lending officers were shouted and screamed at. Sometimes they were even threatened. I can tell you one thing. By the end, they all hated him and they just wanted out.'

'Surely Robertson was worth more to the banks alive than dead?' said Sam.

'Don't count on it.'

'But they had more chance of getting their money back if the empire was still afloat.'

Brammel shook his head. 'In your organisation, I suspect finance is not the first thing you learn about,' he said, adopting an air that was quickly grating on Sam. 'Robertson Communications was writing new banking covenants every day. Each time we took out a loan, we gave a different set of guarantees. Not everything in the business was worthless, remember. There are some perfectly respectable little units in there, doing good business and making good profits. So some of those banks would have charges over those units. Each loan came with a different set of claims on different assets, usually the more valuable one. That meant a few of them stood a good chance of getting some money back. *If* Robertson was out of the way.'

'You're saying the banks might have someone killed?' It wouldn't have surprised Sam in the slightest to hear of a man being killed by his bankers. Sometimes, however, if you feigned surprise, a man could be goaded into telling you more than he planned to.

Brammel looked at him. 'I would have thought your organisation would know that sometimes it doesn't take very much provocation to get a man killed.'

Sam let it pass. 'So which banks should I be looking at?'

Brammel was holding his teacup between his fingers, a thoughtful expression on his face. He knows, thought Sam. He's just deciding whether to tell me.

'Which banks?'

'Now, why should I want to tell you that, Mr Godson?'

It hadn't been easy to arrange a meeting. Life had been hard for Brammel since Robertson died. He'd lost his job after the company went bust. All his share options and bonuses had evaporated. He was the subject of countless investigations. He was the butt of much of the anger of the tens of thousands of pensioners Robertson had swindled. His career was finished – even more finished than it had been when he took the job with Robertson in the first place. The last thing he needed was yet another investigator eating up his time and energy. Yet Sam remembered the files he had seen in Mossad's London office several years earlier. There were notes on every significant man in London, usually with some incriminating detail that could be used against them when the moment required it. Brammel's file included two very dodgy Arab arms deals – one routed through Libya, the other through Iraq – that Brammel had been party to. It was only when he mentioned those on the phone that he'd agreed to meet. Now that Sam was face to face with the man, he could tell he wasn't going to tell him anything. *Not unless he was squeezed.*

'Because I want to know,' answered Sam calmly. 'Now,

which banks stood to get their money back if Robertson died?'

Brammel put his cup down. 'You're Mossad, aren't you?'

'I told you on the phone, I'm investigating Robertson's death. As a private individual.'

Brammel leaned forward. 'Listen, I heard enough bollocks working with Robertson to last me a lifetime. I don't care any more. Robertson broke me, like he broke all of us. He found out how weak we were, how easily we could be bought with money and flattery, and then he used us and destroyed us.'

'Which banks had the greatest motive for killing him?' Sam persisted.

'Look up your own bloody files,' said Brammel. 'I don't understand why you're asking me these questions.'

He stood up, leaving the bill unpaid on the table. Sam put down a five-pound note and stood up next to him. 'It's important to find out why he died.'

'Not to me it isn't.'

Sam reached out for his arm, but Brammel pushed him aside. From the corner of his eyes, Sam could see the head waiter looking at them disapprovingly. 'I don't think anyone really knows whether he's alive or dead,' he said.

'And if you find out, Mr Godson, then send me a bloody postcard.'

Brammel brushed past him, collected his coat from the desk and walked briskly out into the street. Sam followed a few paces behind. He turned left out of the club, then started walking towards Green Park tube. Could one of the banks have structured a loan so that they would be better off if he died? he wondered to himself. He got off the tube at Liverpool Street and walked around the area. It was just before six, and the City offices that lined the streets were still full. In this part of London, nobody left the offices until seven at the earliest. He had one drink, then walked back to the station.

The train for Colchester left at six twenty-five. Sam walked through to the third carriage, as arranged, then sat down next to a man of around forty, with light brown hair and a double-breasted suit that might have been fashionable a couple of years ago, but was starting to look out of place even among the commuters heading back to Essex for the evening.

'Thanks for agreeing to see me,' said Sam. 'How's the office?'

'OK,' answered Stayfield. 'And yours?'

'Not bad. It's a living.'

'I know how that feels.'

Stayfield worked for one of the largest British clearing banks as a senior lending officer. That gave him access not only to the credit records of everyone who banked with his own institution, but also to the records of most of the other British banks as well. They all swapped information with one another for a simple reason. None of them wanted to be stuck with a bad loan, and it made sense to pool their knowledge on who was and wasn't a good credit risk. Sam had met Stayfield twice before. Like many men in the informal network Mossad maintained, he helped out partly from a sense of loyalty to the cause, partly for the small sums of money Mossad paid for the work and partly in hope of advancing his career. The Jewish members of the network would always help another take the next step up the ladder if they could: that way their influence would always grow, and the sources of information would multiply.

'We're trying to find out what to Max Robertson,' said Sam.

'You and everyone else,' said Stayfield. 'One of your colleagues was asking me about Robertson only a month ago.'

'Who?'

'Guy called Heaton. David Heaton.'

Sam had heard of him. A Mossad desk officer who'd spent a couple of years in London. He'd quit the service two years ago. If he was poking around Robertson's death, he must have been one of the five men Dowler had previously hired to crack open the mystery. *One of the five who died . . .*

Stayfield glanced around the carriage. Sam knew he always arranged to meet his Mossad contacts on the train home, and that he had no way of knowing Sam had left the organisation. The carriage was full, as always, but everyone else was reading the paper, or talking to the friends they'd made on the train. Nobody was paying any attention to what the two men at the back of the carriage were saying.

'There's a theory some of the bankers might have been behind it,' said Sam.

'Christ knows he deserved it.'

'Do you think we should be checking that out?'

Stayfield shook his head. 'Not as far as I know. The old bastard stitched us up completely. I don't think anyone at any of the banks had any real idea just how much he'd borrowed. If they had they'd never have lent him so much. He was an expert at bullying people into doing what he wanted. I can tell you, there are a lot of broken careers around London right now. A lot of guys aren't ever going to get promoted after agreeing to lend money to Robertson. In fact, they're going to be branch managers in Preston – that's the best they can hope for.'

'Isn't that enough to kill a man?'

'No,' said Stayfield firmly. 'Because none of them knew how much shit he was in. He conned them so well, I think they actually believed it was a solid company. Sometimes I think he must have even believed it himself. Right up until the end.' He looked across at Sam. 'You know what I think? I think it's just another con. I don't think he's dead at all.'

146

'Not dead?'

Sam suddenly found himself thinking back to the graveyard. *And the strange sensation he had of being watched.*

'It's a rumour, that's all,' said Stayfield. 'But I wonder whether there might be something in it.'

'Would he do something like that?'

Stayfield laughed. 'He was capable of anything. You should see some of the lending documents. The man lied through his teeth. He was pledging assets that didn't exist, inflating balance sheets, creating subsidiaries with nothing in them, the works. There are rats in the sewers with more scruples than Robertson.' He moved closer to Sam. 'I was talking to one of the other bankers, a guy called Simon Abell. The guy is up to his neck in this thing. His bank lent Robertson a hundred and fifty million, most of it authorised by Abell personally. He's going to lose his job for sure, and the guy's got three boys at boarding school. Anyway, Abell says he was talking to Robertson one day just as the extent of the mess was starting to emerge. Robertson was his usual self, blustering through everything. Then he looked up at Abell, and said, "You know, Simon, when it's time to face the music I'll just hire myself a different band."'

Stayfield paused, making way for a woman who was trying to get past him to the next carriage. 'Now, maybe he was just talking. He did a lot of that. But maybe he realised the whole thing was about to come crashing down and decided to exit stage left. Stash some money away somewhere secret, live quietly for a few years, maybe re-emerge one day, maybe not. It has to be better than being a bankrupt. I don't think Robertson could have handled that. So many people hated the man, once he didn't have his money to protect him any more, they would have descended on him like wolves.'

'He was buried,' said Sam. 'In Israel.'

'Right,' said Stayfield. 'And they were his friends. If

147

anyone would help Robertson stage-manage his own death, it would be the Israeli government.'

As the train pulled up at Stratford station, Sam thanked Stayfield for his time. It was still early evening. He switched back on to the tube, and started travelling towards Kilburn. He'd arranged another bedsit, somewhere he could stay for the week, just off the high road. Along the way he picked up some bread and cheese at a corner shop. It was cold and damp back in his room, and he had to feed two coins into the electricity slot before the fire came to life.

He knelt down before the fire. It took a few minutes before the chill had emptied out of the room enough for Sam to take his coat off. It had been days now since he stayed anywhere where he could have a proper bath and meal. Don't worry about it, he told himself grimly. Focus on the endgame.

Taking his notebook from his bag, Sam started to jot down what he had learned. The day had brought him into contact with men who knew Robertson, and who in their different ways had been broken by him. He was starting to get a fuller picture of the man. A brutal, tyrannical bully, driven by greed and vanity, and able to dominate any situation through a titanic will-power. There was no question that he was a monster. Yet everyone already knew that.

I have nothing. Just more stale rumours and old gossip.

OK, he thought, scribbling a few notes on to the paper. I've established that Robertson had extensive contacts in the Soviet Union. That must be worth investigating further. That's progress. But perhaps the most intriguing suggestion is that he isn't dead at all. Maybe Mossad helped him stage his own death. Maybe that's the secret they're protecting.

★

The *Guinea* was sitting glimmering in the dock. Next to the other boats in the Gosport marina, just across the bay from Portsmouth harbour, it looked like an elephant in a pet shop. Gosport was home to the yachts of Londoners who came down to sail at the weekend. Forty- and fifty-footers, they were boats for cruising out to the Isle of Wight on a sunny afternoon. The *Guinea* was in a class of its own: fifty million pounds of yacht that you could sail anywhere in the world.

Sam had read about it in the files, and in the press cuttings he'd been studying. Two hundred feet long, it had been built to order by a yard in Toulon. It weighed five hundred tons, and hit a top speed of eighteen knots, the same as a destroyer. The massive fuel tanks gave it a range of three thousand miles, enough to cross any ocean. The yacht had been fitted out with every luxury imaginable. It had its own telephone switchboard and satellite communications system. Inside, there was a fully equipped gym, six separate bedrooms, each with its own dressing room and bathroom, as well as a dining room and two sitting rooms. The stateroom was where Robertson himself slept: it had a study and two bathrooms; the dressing rooms were kept stocked with freshly pressed clothes, and the fridge was always filled with champagne and caviar.

Some dark clouds were starting to swirl off the English Channel as he walked along the quayside towards the boat. After Robertson's death, and the collapse of the company, the boat had been impounded by the administrators: it was one of the few assets left that might actually be worth something. When they sorted out who would get the money, the boat would be sold. Until then, it was docked here, locked up like a dog in a pound.

'Nice boat,' said Sam, glancing towards a man tying up a small yacht.

The man nodded.

'You ever crew her?'

The man shook his head.

'Know anyone who did?'

The man stood up, looking at Sam suspiciously. 'Are you a journalist?'

Sam shook his head.

'What are you then?'

'Just curious, that's all.'

The man stared at him for a second, then lost interest. 'There's a guy called Jim used to crew the *Guinea* sometimes. You'll find him at the bar up on dock. But he prefers to talk to journalists, they pay him. Or at least they might buy him a drink.'

Sam nodded. He had eighty pounds left. Better to stick to buying some drinks, he thought to himself.

He glanced up at the quay. Landon's was a smart, modern-looking bar, designed for the Londoners coming down for the weekend rather than the locals who crewed the big boats. Sam kept walking to the station. It was just after two in the afternoon. A few people were finishing their lunch. At the bar, a small group of sailors were sitting with their pints of bitter: rough-looking men, with weather-beaten skin, who'd come out of the navy and now made an easy living sailing the chartered boats across the Channel. 'I'm looking for Jim,' said Sam as he ordered himself a pint.

A man somewhere between forty and fifty looked up towards Sam. His green eyes were sunk deep into his head, and his hair was combed back across his head, as if it had been caught permanently in the wind. 'Can I buy you a drink?' said Sam.

Sitting next to Sam at a table in the corner of the bar, Jim took a sip on his beer. 'Is it Robertson you want to know about?' he said.

Sam nodded.

'You a reporter?'

Sam shook his head.

'An insurance investigator?'

Sam shook his head again. 'Just curious, that's all.'

'About the man? Or the boat?'

Sam paused for a second. The boat was the man, he

thought to himself. That much was clear as soon as you stood on the quay. Every man has a cave he crawls back into when he needs to. A study, a bar, a mistress: a place where they go to shield themselves from the world. For Robertson, it was the *Guinea*: a great, ugly, floating monstrosity that could disappear into the night at a single command.

'The boat,' said Sam. 'What did he use it for?'

Jim laughed. 'We took it out of here, then sailed it into the Med and picked up the old bugger in Majorca. He came on board, stayed for a couple of days, then told us to sail it out to the Aegean. We dropped him in Sicily and he flew back to London. We didn't see him again for another month, and didn't want to. Spent a month sunning ourselves and chatting up the local birds. That was how it went for the whole year I was on board.'

Sam signalled to the barmaid to bring them another pair of pints: Jim had already finished his and was looking thirsty. 'Sounds like nice work.'

Jim shrugged. 'It was all right when he wasn't there. Soon as the old bugger arrived, it was a bloody nightmare. He was always barking orders at everyone. Then he'd take to his room for a couple of days and refuse to come out. Next thing, there would be a pair of birds flown out to see him. We felt sorry for them. I'm sure it was well paid, but it must have been miserable work. He was in a good mood when he had a girl with him, but whenever he was feeling good, it was even worse. He'd start firing people. He'd walk along the deck, see you working on the rigging, or whatever, and then he'd fire you there and then. No questions, no arguments. The captain would give you a couple of grand to soften the blow, but you'd be on your arse in some dock in Sicily or Malta. Happened all the time. Made for a miserable atmosphere on the bloody ship. None of the blokes liked it. We were always looking for another berth, even though he paid good money.' Jim paused, taking a swig of the pint that had just been put down in front of him. 'He wasn't a happy man for all his money. Couple of times, I was up on the deck at night, doing a watch, and I saw him sitting looking out at the sea, and he was crying. The boat was his refuge. It was the place he escaped to. But he was still miserable.'

'Did Selima Robertson ever come on board?'

Jim smiled. 'Nice-looking girl.'

'You met her?'

'She didn't come on to the boat, not while I was crewing it,' said Jim. 'None of the family were allowed. It was the old bugger's private place. But she's been down a few times since. I guess she's interested in who's going to buy it.'

'When was she last here?'

'Three days ago.'

Sam leaned forwards. 'Right here?'

'Hanging around the boat, asking questions. Who'd been to see it, what were they like, that kind of thing. Even left a number, said to call her if there were any serious buyers.'

'Another pint,' said Sam, nodding towards the barmaid. Jim took two gulps on the beer, then looked back at Sam. 'You want it, don't you?' he said. 'The number.'

'Of course.'

Sam took the number, thanked Jim for his time, paid for the drinks, then left the bar. There was a payphone a little way up the street. He glanced at the digits Jim had written down for him. It was different from the number she had given him, but had the same first three digits, so must be in the same area. 'Selima Robertson,' he said as soon as he heard a woman's voice on the line. 'It's Sam. Sam Wolfman.'

A pause. Surprised, he glanced out towards the sea, where the wind was starting to whip some foam into the waves.

'You found the desk?'

Sam laughed. 'No,' he replied. 'But I'm ready to take the case.'

'Then I'll come and see you tomorrow. At your shop.'

'It's being renovated.'

'Then my house,' said Selima. 'At five.'

Sam started to walk up towards the ferry that would take him back towards the train station. He could feel the wind rustling across him, and smell the salt in the air. Out on the Channel he could see the lights of the Isle of Wight ferry as it approached the harbour. Maybe Selima will have some clues. After all, it was Selima who had first raised the possibility that her stepfather might still be alive.

Two men were walking down the side of the pier. Sam glanced towards them, but then looked away. For the past few days, he'd been strung out on a wire, peering into shadows, calculating where the next hit would come from. Hassim and his men would certainly be looking for revenge. One whisper of where he was, and they would put him down like a stray dog.

Sam kept walking, paying the two men no visible attention, but watching their movements closely all the same. The larger of the two had black hair, and the shorter had shaved his head: they were wearing jeans and sweatshirt, and carrying cans of lager in their hands. Sailors on shore leave, reckoned Sam. *Nothing to worry about.*

One of the men knocked Sam's shoulder. There was a smell of beer on his breath, and a sullen, malevolent look in his eyes. Sam ignored it and walked on. 'Here, watch where you're fucking walking, you cunt,' shouted the shorter of the two men.

Sam kept going. Don't look at them, don't respond, he told himself. The last thing you need is a fight.

'I said, watch where you're fucking walking, cunt,' shouted the man again, louder this time.

The pier was abandoned. In the distance, Sam could see a man walking his dog, but as he heard what sounded like the beginning of a fight, he started to move swiftly away. Sam turned round. The two men were standing next to each other, about ten yards back from him, with their cans tight in their fists. 'There's no need for any trouble,' he said quietly but firmly. 'Now leave me alone.'

The larger of the two men hurled his can to the ground, and started running towards Sam. 'You fucking tosser,' he growled. 'You don't talk to my mate like that.'

He was surprisingly swift for a big man, and the drink didn't appear to have slowed him down. He covered the ten yards in a fraction of a second, hurling himself into Sam's side. He could feel the man's thick skull crashing into his ribs like a cannonball, and for a second the air emptied from his lungs. He coughed, struggling to hold on to his balance. The smaller man was running towards him, a six-inch steel knife already sticking from his right fist. Sam regained his balance. The bigger man was standing straight in front of him, his hand reaching back to deliver a blow. The punch swung towards him, but Sam had anticipated it and ducked out of the way, leaving the man to swing into thin air. He pulled himself back up, pushed his two fists together to create a hammer of flesh and bone, then crashed them hard into the side of the man's neck.

Just at that moment the smaller man jabbed his knife forwards. The blade ripped a hole in the side of Sam's sweatshirt, but narrowly missed the skin. Sam kicked out, trying to hit the knife with his boot, but missed. He slammed his foot back down on the ground to steady himself. The larger man had recovered from his failed punch, and was now behind Sam, grabbing hold of his arms. Sam struggled, but the man had the strength of a bull. He was gripping Sam hard, making it impossible for him to move, and thrusting him forwards. 'Slice the fucker,' shouted the bigger man. 'Slice the fucker now.'

Sam could see the second man advancing steadily towards him, he could see the cold steel of the blade, and sensed the look of murder in the man's eyes. He knew the expression of cold-blood determination that came naturally to assassins in the moment before they dispatched their prey, and he could see it now. These aren't drunken sailors, thought Sam. They're trained killers. *Sent to find me.*

He poised himself, waiting until the man was two yards in front of him, his blade flashing in his hand. Then, with a roar to summon up his strength, he threw his legs up into the air. He could feel the muscles in his back starting to stretch and tear as the man behind tried to cling on to his arms. His legs swung down, crashing into the man's hands, knocking the knife clean from his grip and throwing him off balance. As Sam fell to the ground, he could see the knife just inches away from him. He reached across and grabbed it, holding it tight, and then in one swift movement rolled across the ground, took aim, then flung the knife. It arced through the air, planting itself in the centre of the larger man's chest. He choked, blood spurting instantly from his mouth. Sam leapt up and rushed towards him, then pulled the knife from his chest and jabbed it hard into the side of his neck. He twisted it twice, severing his windpipe, then with one heave, pushed him up over the side of the pier, letting him fall into the dark and murky water below. If you're not dead already, you soon will be, he thought to himself.

The smaller man took a step towards him but the look of defiance in his eyes had faded, replaced by one of fear. Sam jabbed the knife in front of him. The man was jumping around, swerving to avoid the blade flashing out from Sam's hand. Sam swiped with the knife, missed, then swiped again. On the third attempt, the man tried to grab Sam's wrist, but Sam was too quick and the blade stabbed deep into the palm of his hand. The man cried out as the pain inflicted by the wound shot through him. Sam knew that he had the advantage: he must seize it. He lunged forward, grabbing the man's wrist and cutting into the skin. He twisted the knife until he found the artery, then slashed it open.

The man fell to the ground, and Sam fell on top of him, smothering the body with his own. Blood was pouring out of the opened wrist, and the man was moaning in agony. Sam held his knife to his throat. 'If I don't bind up that wound in the next minute you're going to fucking die,' he growled into the man's ear. 'Now tell me, who the fuck sent you here to kill me?'

Sam could see the pain on the man's face. The life was draining out of him by the second. He sensed he was about to die and, as it did for most dying men, the bravery had emptied out of him. Sam had seen it often enough: they were alone, and afraid, and they wanted to live. 'Tell me now,' he growled again.

'Guy called Max Robertson,' said the man.

Sam paused. 'Robertson himself?' said Sam. 'Big fat guy? He paid you?'

The man shook his head. 'Please help me,' he whimpered. 'Bind up my hand. I'm fucking dying here.'

'Answer the bloody question first,' snapped Sam. 'Who paid you?'

'Local guy,' said the man. 'Paid us two hundred a day. Told us to deal with anyone suspicious who seemed to be asking too many questions. We were just going to frighten you off.'

'What's his name?'

'I don't know.'

'What's his name?' spat Sam, his voice louder this time.

'I don't know. He just said he was an agent for Robertson, that's all . . .' His voice trailed off.

'The name?' repeated Sam.

Nothing.

He looked down. The man had lost consciousness already. Another minute and he'd be dead. Sam started walking away. Somehow he had to get himself cleaned up and back on the train. Max Robertson's alive! he said to himself. He's alive, and has access to enough money to have anyone killed who might come close to unravelling that secret. That must be what happened to Dowler's last five agents. *And, if I'm not careful, I'll be the next name to be crossed off that list.*

FOURTEEN

Although there was no blood relationship, if you looked at Selima Robertson in a certain way you could recognise the likeness to her stepfather. It wasn't there in the blonde hair of course, nor the high, sculpted cheekbones. Nor was it there in the slim, toned body, which although she was nearing forty had not an inch of fat on it. It was not there in her manner either, which seemed welcoming, close even to flirtatious.

It was in the eyes. Hard and intense, with a way of looking through you, as if drilling through rock. They were the eyes of someone with the ability to command obedience.

Selima smiled and offered Sam a drink. 'A cocktail, maybe,' she said. 'Hell, it's after five. Down here in Wimbledon, that counts as the cocktail hour.'

The house was larger and more opulent than Sam had expected. If the Robertson family had crashed to a spectacular bankruptcy since her stepfather's death, or disappearance, it evidently hadn't affected her lifestyle too badly yet. A detached Edwardian villa, in one of the leafy suburban streets leading away from the tennis club, there was a Land–Rover and a Mercedes parked in the driveway, and a maid to answer the door. From what he'd read in the files, Selima was Robertson's only stepchild. She had been married and divorced twice: the first husband was a banker, who was now remarried and held a senior job in the City; the second described himself as a film producer, although he'd never actually made a film. There were two children, aged eleven and nine, both from the first marriage. The house was expensively but blandly furnished, with lots of oriental rugs and fitted furnishings. As he stepped from the hallway to the drawing room, Sam couldn't help himself noticing one simple fact, perhaps surprising in a woman tracking down a Gastou writing desk. Her furniture was all modern. *There weren't any antiques.*

'I'll have what you're having.'

Selima returned two minutes later with a glass of pale green liquid. Sam took one sip. A Gimlet, a mixture of gin and lime. And a strong one. 'You've changed your mind?' she said.

Sam raised a hand. 'I'm certainly willing to discuss it. If you still want me.'

'Of course I still want you,' snapped Selima. 'Like I said, you're the best in the world.'

Sam ignored the remark: there are many things I can be seduced by, but flattery is not one of them. 'You didn't return my calls.'

Selima cast him a glance that melted from anger to amusement in an instant. 'I have two numbers,' she said. 'I switched, to stop the press calling me all the time.'

She was just making me wait. *This is a woman who knows all about men and how to control them.*

'You think you can find out what happened to my stepfather?'

'I can try,' he said.

'You'll be well paid, of course.'

'The Robertson family is still solvent then?'

She cast him a sharp look. 'We're surviving. It's my stepdad that went bust, not me. His debts aren't my debts.'

'I'll need a thousand a week, plus expenses,' said Sam. 'It's the expenses that are the important thing. Tracking a man down is costly work. Particularly when they're dead.'

'Like I said, I'm not sure he is.'

159

'I remember.'

Sam saw that Selima was looking at him closely. From the pier, Sam had walked into town, and found an Asda supermarket that stayed open late. Although his bloodstained condition attracted some strange and mostly frightened looks, he managed to avoid any policemen, and bought himself some cheap jeans and a sweatshirt, changing into them in the loo. He'd taken the train back to London and cleaned himself up at his lodging house. But there was still some bruising on his face that would stay for a few days at least. I imagine Selima isn't used to dealing with men who get into a fight for a living.

'Why did you change your mind?'

'It's personal.'

Selima was sitting on the sofa, her legs crossed, but Sam preferred to remain standing. 'The money's fine,' she said. 'I'll arrange payment in the morning. How long do you think you'll need?'

Sam laughed. He was surprised by the coolness with which she could discuss her stepfather's disappearance. Maybe she doesn't care about finding him. Maybe she just wants to find out where he stashed his money. Perhaps she thinks he faked his own death with the help of Mossad, and that there is nobody better to unravel a Mossad plot than one of their own agents.

'A month, two months,' said Sam with a shrug. 'Perhaps we'll find him tomorrow. It depends how much help I get.'

Selima drained the last of her drink, and looked up at Sam. 'Another?'

Her body felt warm and supple beneath his. She smelt of alcohol, and nicotine, and passion. Selima pushed upwards, bucking against him until she had reached her own climax and had satisfied him. Then she rolled over, lighting up a cigarette and pouring herself a gin.

'You're not an antique in bed anyway,' she said with a mischievous smile, blowing a ring of smoke out of her smudged lipstick-stained mouth.

That they had ended up in bed together had taken Sam by surprise. Over the drinks at her house, they had talked for a couple of hours about her stepfather, and how she'd taken his disappearance. At the end, it seemed natural enough to suggest dinner. They'd gone to a small Italian place in Wimbledon village, where they'd shared two bottles of red wine. Sam reckoned he'd had half a bottle, Selima the rest. The conversation flowed as smoothly as the wine. Selima had charm in bundles: something else, Sam suspected, she inherited from her stepfather. Her manner was flirty yet vulnerable: straight out of the seduction instruction manual. The conversation hadn't been about much in particular: her children, what a loser her second husband had been, the Italian restaurants in London. Sam spun her a carefully fabricated version of his own life, which included ten years in the Israeli Army before being posted to London and getting into the antiques trade – of course she knew he was a Mossad agent but, he said, that wasn't something he was willing to talk to her about until he knew her much better. She seemed interested in the army, particularly how many men he might have killed. At no stage of the evening, he noticed, did she ask him whether he was married or not. Maybe she assumes I'm not, otherwise I wouldn't be here. *No, more likely she doesn't care.*

As Sam picked up the tab – fifty pounds was a blow, but possibly a good investment – she insisted they go back to her house. The children were with their father for half-term, she announced as they stepped through the door. She was lonely. We're all lonely, thought Sam, as he sat down next to her. *Get used to it.*

They'd been in bed within half an hour, Sam surprised at how greedy she was – another trait he supposed she learned from her stepfather. She chewed him up with relish, as if he were a new toy she'd just discovered. He'd also been surprised at how good she was. Whatever made those two husbands leave her, it wasn't the sex.

Afterwards, Sam lay still and silent for a moment. That he had enjoyed himself was undeniable, but that was beside the point. Mossad always taught its agents that sex was a weapon just like any other: you pointed, aimed and fired, and then you threw it away. You were no more attached to the person you were sleeping with than to the pistol you were carrying in your holster. So although he felt some guilt about betraying his wife, he quickly dismissed that from his mind. When you've accepted that you assassinate people for a living, it was surprising how all other moral issues faded into insignificance.

Sam was not so vain as to suppose that Selima found him irresistible. *She's in this bed for a reason.* He reckoned that she wanted him to be emotionally committed to the mission. *So that I don't mind taking a bullet if I have to.*

'Your stepfather must have managed to salt away some of the money,' said Sam, letting some of the smoke from her cigarette drift into his lungs. 'If that's not a personal question.'

Selima reached across for the bottle of gin, and poured another shot into the empty tumbler. 'It's a fucking personal question.'

Sam paused, aware that he needed to win her trust, yet at the same time slowly squeeze enough information out of her that it would give him a substantial lead on her stepfather.

'Your stepfather knew the empire was in trouble,' he said. 'He must have had some kind of contingency plan. Men like that always do.'

'Dad?' said Selima with a smile. 'The old bastard thought he was immortal. And who knows, maybe he was?'

Sam closed his eyes. 'I saw him being buried on TV. You were there.'

Selima finished her gin, and rolled over on to her back. 'Let's not talk about him now,' she said.

The wind was blowing in off Brighton pier: harsh, blustery gusts of air that whistled up through Selima's hair. She turned round to look at him, her eyes suddenly intense and questioning. 'Can I ask you something?' she said.

Sam slipped his arm around her waist. They had come down to Brighton for the weekend, at his suggestion: they were staying at the Imperial hotel, since she was paying for it. There was an antiques fair on, he told her, so why not come along, since the children are away. Who knows, maybe we'll track down that Gastou?

He needed to spend more time with her.

'Sure,' he replied.

'Can I trust you?'

He turned to face her, delivering his answer with easy confidence. 'Of course you can trust me.'

She paused, then smiled.

'Why?' he said.

'Oh, nothing,' Selima shrugged. 'Just wanted to ask.'

They carried on walking down the promenade. It was a foul day, but neither seemed to mind, and Selima began to talk about her stepfather. The cruelty of the man was beyond question. She told Sam stories about how he used to beat her regularly, for no good reason. His wife would be at her side, begging him to stop. She'd be criticised constantly for not being good enough at school, for not doing her homework. She could remember being starved for a whole day when she was four because she'd refused to finish her supper the night before. Her stepfather gave her a long lecture about how there had been no food in the village he grew up in, then confined her to her room. She could still remember the terror as she imagined she was going to starve to death. It didn't get any better as she grew into a teenager.

She recalled inviting a friend from school round for lunch when she was seventeen. She said something that annoyed her stepfather, and he called her up to the head of the table, made her hold out her hand, then pulled out a ruler and smacked her palm six times. The humiliation had been unendurable. She'd never felt able to invite a friend back again.

Selima pushed a key across the table. 'Here,' she said. 'What do you think it is?'

A candle was burning between them. They were back in the same Italian restaurant in Wimbledon. They were sitting in the same quiet corner where Selima always sat, drinking the same bottle of Chianti she always ordered. Sam picked up the slim piece of metal and held it up to the light of the candle.

He shrugged. 'It's a key.' He was thinking: *It means she's starting to trust me.*

'What's it for?'

Sam laughed. 'What's this, twenty questions.' He pushed the key back across the table. 'For a lock, presumably.'

'Which lock?'

Sam took a sip of his wine. 'You don't know?'

Selima shook her head.

'Your stepfather gave it to you, didn't he?'

There was a pause. Sam could tell what she was thinking before she replied. In the brief time he'd known her, she'd talked about everything imaginable. She was one of those women who hated a silence, immediately filling it with her own voice. Except when you asked her about her stepfather.

'About two months before he died,' she said finally.

'And he didn't tell you what it was for?'

She shook her head again.

Sam looked at her hard, trying to read her expression. 'He just gave you the key?'

'That's right,' said Selima. 'It was after lunch, one Sunday afternoon, at their house. I'd taken the kids round for the day. He suddenly took me aside, and said he wanted me to look after this key for him. I asked why, naturally. He said he couldn't say. Just to hold on to it. I asked him what it was for, and he said he didn't want to discuss that either. So I put the thing in my handbag and didn't think any more about it.'

'And you really don't know what it's for?'

'I didn't know he was going to bloody disappear, did I?' said Selima crossly. 'Anyway, you don't know what the old bastard was like. You did what he asked you. That was the way it was.'

Sam picked up the key again. It was a slim, brass object, with a traditional three-point turning mechanism. There was nothing remarkable about it. 'So what do you want me to do?'

'You agreed to investigate the death of my step-father,' she said sharply. 'Find out what it's for.'

Sam laughed. 'There are, who knows, maybe a couple of billion locks in the world,' he said. 'And you want me to find out which one this fits?'

From her expression, he could tell she didn't appreciate the tone. 'Why not?' she said. 'You're good at finding things.' She reached out across the table, taking Sam's hand in hers. He could feel the tension in the slight sweatiness of her palm. 'If anyone can find it, you can.'

Sam folded the key into the breast pocket of his jacket. 'And what do you think I might find?'

'My stepfather was full of secrets,' she said softly. 'It could be anything.'

Joel Lazaran turned the key over in his hand. He picked up an eyeglass from the table, squinting as he focused his attention on the slim piece of metal. He sighed, putting it back down. 'Sod it, Sam,' he said. 'It could be from any-where.'

'I know that,' said Sam. 'But if you had to start some-where, where would you start looking?'

They were standing in the back room of Lazaran's jewellery business on Hatton Garden, a small street full of gold and diamond merchants just up from Holborn Circus. Sam had met Lazaran many times before. He helped out Mossad informally, although he had little time for the organisation: one of his three sons had been killed while serving in the Israeli Army, and Lazaran was convinced Mossad had been responsible for sending his unit out on what turned into a suicide mission. Still, he liked Sam, and was always willing to do him a favour. He'd been working in the jewellery and precious stones trade all his life, as had his father and his grandfather before him. Nobody knows more about locks than a goldsmith, Sam had told himself as he left Chancery Lane tube station and started walking towards the shop. *They are constantly on guard against thieves.*

'Why do you want to know, anyway?' said Lazaran.

Sam remained silent. This was something only he and Selima could know about. It would be their secret, he'd promised as he left her house that morning. *If I find anything out, I'll let you know.*

Lazaran looked up and smiled. 'Don't want to say, eh? I understand.' He leaned over, scratching the surface of the key. 'How much do you know about metals?'

Sam shrugged. 'Not much.'

'This is brass,' said Lazaran. 'You know about brass?'

Sam shook his head again. He was familiar with the Lazaran manner: an endless series of rhetorical questions, before you finally got to the answer he had all along. 'Of course not,' he said.

Lazaran scratched the key some more, sending a few shavings of the metal down on to his desk. 'Well, I do,' he said. 'Brass is a standard base for any kind of gold plate, so you see a lot of it in this trade. It's also very good for making locks, and has been since Roman times. That's because it's very strong, yet you can work it at relatively low temperatures. So if you've got something fiddly to make, brass is what you need. Now, brass is usually made from a combination of copper and zinc. It's an alloy. The alloys vary from country to country, and manufacturer to manufacturer. The more zinc you put in, the more elastic it becomes.' He rubbed the metal dust on his desk between his thumb and his forefinger. 'Now, this has a relatively high zinc content. You can tell because the zinc gives it this yellow colour.'

'What does that tell us?'

'I reckon it was made in Belgium. Maybe Antwerp. There have always been a lot of metalworking firms there, it's the local industry. And the Belgians have always specialised in high-zinc-content brasses.'

'So the key might open a lock in Belgium?'

Lazaran shook his head. 'You know what I think this is?'

There was pause. Another rhetorical question. 'No,' he said quickly.

'Well, look at the key,' said Lazaran. 'It's not for a door, is it? Too slim, too weak. A door needs a bigger, heavier lock than anything this opens. It's not for a chest, it's the wrong shape. It's not a car, obviously. Yet it's a properly made key. No expense spared. So what else do people have keys for, apart from their houses and their cars?'

'A safe?'

Lazaran shook his head. 'A safe has a combination. Nobody would put a key on it. Too easy to pick.' He pointed to the serrated edge of the key. 'You see, this key isn't designed to offer very much protection at all. As if it was for a place that already had protection.' He looked up at Sam, and threw his arms open. 'Like a safe-deposit box. In a bank.'

Sam nodded. *Of course.*

Lazaran handed the key back to Sam. 'That's my guess –
a key for a bank deposit box. Probably in Luxembourg.'

'Luxembourg?' said Sam.

'Of course,' said Lazaran. 'It's made in Belgium, right?
But Belgium doesn't have any banks – at least none that
you'd trust. And where's the closest place that does?
Luxembourg. Lots of secured banks. Just down the road
from Antwerp.'

Sam slipped the key back into his breast pocket. A safe-
deposit box in Luxembourg. *The same tiny city where
Robertson kept many of his offshore trusts.*

FIFTEEN

Karel Mey looked across his desk at Sam, his expression blank. He was a young man, less than thirty, with thick black hair and heavy glasses. 'And what do you wish to put in the box, Mr Godson?'

'Personal effects,' answered Sam.

They were sitting in an office of the Ivry Trust, a private bank on the Grand Rue, in the centre of Luxembourg. Sam had arrived that morning, travelling on Alan Godson's passport. Before leaving, he'd researched a list of the banks in the city with which Robertson was known to have dealings. It was a long shot, he knew that much, but if the man had a safe-deposit box, it might well be with a bank he already knew. *If so, I have the key.*

Mey nodded. 'If you wouldn't mind filling out a form.'

The sheet was just one side of A4 paper. For the sake of the money-laundering regulators, the Ivry Trust might be going through the formalities of checking its customers, but Sam felt certain it was just a sham. So long as you could pay the fee for the box, and show that you had credit, they were happy enough to do business with you. Luxembourg hadn't made itself one of the richest cities in the world by being too fastidious about how people made their money.

Sam gave the sheet back to Mey, along with the passport made out in Alan Godson's name. Mey looked inside, checked the photograph, then glanced back at Sam. Next he handed over the five hundred Deutschmarks the bank charged as an annual fee for each of its deposit boxes, before following Mey through the offices and down two flights of stairs.

'This is Mr Godson,' he said to the guard outside the vault. 'He's taking a new box. Number 653.'

He handed Sam the key with a curt nod of his head. 'Do let me know if I can be of any further assistance.'

Sam took the key between his hand. The wrong bank, he told himself. The key was made from brass, but was a different shape and design to the one nestling in his pocket. *No point in wasting any more time here.*

Sam folded six sheets of blank paper into box 653, then walked swiftly out of the bank. It was a cold Tuesday morning on the Grande Rue, and there were only a few shoppers weaving their way through the mass of banking offices that made up the main economy of the town. He'd established that Robertson had regular dealings with five of those banks. Shoe leather, he told himself. *The first rule of detection is that you patiently work your way through all the options until you make a breakthrough.*

He walked towards the next bank on his list. Even by Luxembourg standards, the Julius Plessis bank was small. One office, ten staff and probably not more than a hundred accounts. That didn't mean it lacked money. A hundred accounts was enough for a bank. So long as they were the right hundred accounts.

Ten minutes later, Sam was back on the Grande Rue. The bank was closed to new customers, he'd learned. It offered safe-deposit boxes, but only for existing customers. Maybe I could open an account, Sam had suggested. No. The bank only opened accounts for people who had recommendations from two existing clients. Return with those, and they'd be happy to make an appointment for him to meet Mr Plessis. *In the meantime, the door was that way.*

Sam sunk a coffee at the bar of a café, then moved on to

the Banque Populaire du Luxembourg. Stepping inside the marble-and-stone hall of its main building, it was the closest thing he'd seen to a proper bank so far. Tellers, desks, people paying cheques in and out: the kind of things normal banks did. It took him twenty minutes to complete all the forms necessary to acquire a safe-deposit box. And another ten minutes to discover that this bank as well used a different set of keys.

More shoe leather, he reminded himself as he walked back on to the street. That's all it takes.

By lunchtime, he'd visited the five banks on his list and had no luck at any of them. Each time, the same routine. Take out a safe-deposit box, then head down into the vaults. Each time, there had been the same sense of disappointment as he was handed a key that was very different to the one tucked into his jacket pocket. In the café where he'd ordered a sandwich, the phone book listed 146 different banks in Luxembourg. This could take weeks, he thought glumly. *And at five hundred Deutschmarks for every box, it could cost a fortune as well.*

He cast his eyes around the café. It was mostly filled with prosperous bank workers. Luxembourg was basically a French province and, like the French, everyone believed in a proper three-course cooked lunch, enjoyed for at least an hour.

Dammit. Anywhere else, I could find a bank worker to bribe. I'd just offer one of them some money until they found someone who recognised this key. Not here. Luxembourg has plenty of greedy people, that's for sure, but I don't have the cash available to tempt them. *The place is too rich.*

I have got my brains though, thought Sam, finishing off his sandwich. *When your cash is not good enough, you just have to fall back on your wits.*

He walked out of the café, and started strolling the mile

from the Grande Rue to the Gare de Luxembourg, an ornate, nineteenth-century building, with lines running out of the city towards Brussels, Metz and Liège. It was early afternoon, and there were only a few people around. Sam went into the station, bought himself a cheap disposable camera, then walked towards the strip of cheap hotels on the two side streets running away from the station.

He sat down outside a café, ordered a coffee and waited. Always the same in this job, he thought. *Waiting.*

There were six hotels within eye range, ranging from one star up to three. None of them looked like the kind of place you wanted to stay in. Not unless you'd just got off the train late at night. Or you were looking for a cheap place to spend a couple of hours with your mistress in the afternoon.

That's my prey.

He sipped slowly on his coffee, keeping his eyes trained on the street. A woman walked past with her dog. Another woman, pushing a pram. A man carrying a suitcase, checking the prices at three hotels before making his choice. Sam watched them all go by without moving, then ordered himself another coffee.

It doesn't matter how long it takes. I've got all day. All week. All month, if that's what it takes.

He patted the key in his pocket. *This is the only lead I have right now, and I'm not going to lose it.*

It was three fifteen before he saw anything that interested him. A man and a woman, walking down the street together. Both were in their mid-thirties, the man possibly slightly older, smartly dressed as if they had just come from the office. They weren't holding hands, or touching or even talking. But they were glancing at each other. The way lovers do, noted Sam.

He took the camera from his pocket, and took one picture of them side by side. He watched as the man walked into the Hôtel Metz, while the woman walked once around the block. He took another picture of her standing alone as she stood under the hotel's porch. She glanced around twice before stepping inside, but Sam felt sure she hadn't noticed him.

No more coffee, thought Sam as he signalled the waitress in the café. 'An orange juice, please,' he said.

It was just after five when the couple emerged from the hotel. *Time to get back to your desks before the day ends.* He stood up, put two notes on the table and started walking. The couple headed across the street, past the station and through the shopping district that led towards the Grande Rue. Sam followed at a discreet distance, always thirty paces behind his target, always on the other side of the road and always at just below average pace. The streets were starting to fill up as people left work. *The chances of my being detected are zero.*

The couple split at the entrance to the Grande Rue. Not so much as a kiss or a peck on the cheek. Just a glance. Sad, thought Sam. They care about each other, but can never reveal it in public. *Their problem, not mine.*

Staying on the opposite side of the road, he walked slowly, keeping his eyes on the man as he headed down the street. He turned into the headquarters of Banque Fresnius, one of the medium-sized private banks that filled the area. Five twenty-five, Sam noted, checking his watch. *I won't have long to wait.*

Twenty minutes passed before the man came out again, this time wearing a raincoat and carrying a briefcase. He turned right, heading towards a bus stop ferrying the bank workers out of town. Sam hopped on the same bus just as it was pulling out, taking a seat near the back. It was six stops before the man climbed out. Stressen, Sam noted, looking up at the name of the stop. He remained in his seat, watching the man as he walked slowly towards the rows of neat suburban houses that led away from the main street. *I'll see you in the morning.*

The man was reading the business pages of the German-language daily, the *Luxemburger Wort*, when Sam sat down next to him on the bus. It was just after eight in the morning. Sam had no way of knowing when he took the bus to work, and he'd been waiting at the café opposite the bus stop since seven, ready to jump on the same bus as his target.

'These pictures should interest you,' said Sam softly.

The man glanced first into Sam's eyes. He looked startled, then annoyed at being disturbed. Next, his eyes flicked down towards the picture Sam was holding in the palm of his hand. In a six-inch by four-inch colour print, it showed the man and the woman standing together on the street.

'We need to talk,' said Sam. 'In private.'

Anger had been replaced by fear in the man's expression. His eyes looked suddenly hunted, and a bead of sweat was starting to form on his neck.

'Don't be afraid,' said Sam, standing up. 'Here, follow me.'

He walked towards the door as the bus pulled up at a stop. They were still some distance from the centre of town, and not many people were getting off. Sam stepped down, checked the man was following him, then pointed towards a café. 'There,' he said flatly.

They were already sitting down, a pair of coffees on the table in front of them, before the man was able to speak. 'Who the hell are you?' he said eventually. 'And where the hell did you get those pictures?'

'It doesn't matter who I am, or how I got them. All that matters is how we are going to resolve this situation.'

The man drank his coffee in one gulp. Sam could see the caffeine making him more nervous: that was the main reason he'd brought him to the café. Always interrogate people over a coffee, Imer had told him in training. *It makes everyone jumpy.*

'We were just going to a business meeting together,' the man snapped. 'It means nothing.'

'I don't care,' said Sam. 'It doesn't matter to me. I'm just going to lay out your choices. I can give this picture to your wife, and you can explain to her how it means nothing. Or else you can do one simple thing for me.' Sam looked up sympathetically. 'Nothing illegal. Nothing corrupt. Just a favour. And in return I'll do a favour for you. Destroy this picture, plus the negative.'

Sam could see the man pondering what he'd said. What's to think about? he thought to himself. A guy doesn't want his wife looking at a picture like that. Nobody needs that kind of trouble. *Not when it can be avoided.*

'What?' said the man, hesitantly. 'What do you want me to do?'

Sam pulled out the key and placed it on the saucer of the man's coffee cup. 'This opens a safe-deposit box at a bank in Luxembourg. I want you to find out which one.'

The man picked up the key, holding it between his fingers as if it might be toxic. 'I can't go into a customer's box for you,' he said nervously. 'In Luxembourg, we take the privacy of our customers' affairs very seriously.'

'I'm not asking you to,' said Sam. 'All I want to know is which bank would issue this key. That's all.'

The man fingered the key nervously. 'Why?'

'It doesn't matter.'

'Then why me?'

'It doesn't matter,' Sam repeated. 'All that matters is whether you'll do it, or whether I give that picture to your wife.'

The man took the key and stood up. 'I'll see what I can do,' he said. 'I can't guarantee anything. There are a lot of banks in Luxembourg.'

Sam smiled, and followed the man towards the bus stop. 'Meet me back at the café at six,' he said. The man nodded.

175

Behind him, the bus was just pulling up. 'You've only seen my nice side,' said Sam slowly. 'So don't fuck with me.'

Sam's eyes ran up and down the street, scanning the commuters stepping off the buses. It was almost six fifteen, and he had been waiting for twenty minutes already. Where is he? he wondered.

He had no idea what his name was, nor where he lived. Who his mistress was, he neither knew nor cared. It wasn't his business. His threats were just bluffs. Most threats were. The issue was whether the man knew that. If he was smart, he'd just walk away. *But he didn't look that smart.*

Sam checked his watch. Six twenty. If he wasn't here by half past, he had to leave. But the man had the key, the one solid lead he had: he had to get that back. Then he saw the man emerging from the Gents. Sam glanced around, wondering briefly if he'd decided to go to the police. Or spoken to his bank, and decided to bring along some heavies. He looked behind, scanning the back of the café. Nothing. He was alone.

He walked up to Sam and looked down contemptuously. The man pushed the key across the table. 'A coffee?' said Sam.

The man shook his head. 'It's the Banque Azoni,' he said.

Sam nodded. 'Where is it?' he asked.

'You'll find it in the phone book,' the man snapped in reply. 'I can do nothing more for you.'

The vault had a musty smell, a mixture of metal, grease and decaying paper. There must have been about two hundred boxes, Sam reckoned, each one measuring ten inches across and eight inches high. Enough space to put some papers. Maybe a false passport or two. Some diamonds. And some spare cash.

The usual private treasures of the rich and nervous.

Sam had opened an account at the Banque Azoni that morning. As the name suggested, it dealt mainly with Italians. The manager seemed surprised that an Irishman wanted to open an account, but had been happy to take his money. There is no more determined nation of tax evaders in the whole of Europe than the Italians, thought Sam smiling to himself. *They need to keep their money somewhere, and it's certainly not at home.*

The guard had shut the door behind him. Sam had explained that he had some private papers he wanted to deposit in the box. If there was one thing they understood in the Luxembourg banking industry it was discretion. *If a man wanted to be left alone, that was always his privilege.*

He scanned his eyes quickly along the boxes. In his right hand, he was holding the key for Robertson's box. The match was identical: the same type of key, made from the same metal, to the same design. *Now I just need to know which box it fits.*

He started from the middle. The guard had said he could be left alone for five minutes in the room to arrange his papers, then he would open the door to let him out. Sam tried one box, then another, then another. The key didn't fit. He tried the next row, slotting the key into the boxes in neat, steady movements. No good. It still didn't fit.

Don't rush, he told himself. *Don't get flustered.*

Another row, then another.

Three minutes had ticked by on the clock.

Sam wiped a bead of sweat away from his brow. He could feel his palm getting sticky, and his heart thumping within his chest.

Suddenly the key slotted into place. Box 161. *He'd found it.*

He turned the key with one swift movement, then pulled the contents out. He placed them straight into his own box, then slammed it shut, turning the key. He replaced

Robertson's box, turned its key and dropped it back into his pocket.

Ten seconds left. He could hear the guard at the door. Sam wiped his hands clean and turned to face him. Taking a quick lungful of oxygen, he willed his expression to change from one of anxiety to one of calm.

'Everything OK, sir?' said the guard.

'Perfect, thank you,' said Sam.

There have been more dangerous days in my life, thought Sam as he sat down behind the desk. Days when I had to stand up to some of the world's deadliest assassins. Days when I faced death minute by minute. Yet I don't think I have ever passed twenty-four hours of such consistent, mind-numbing tension as I have just been through.

He'd switched the contents of Robertson's box into his own the day before because there had been no time to examine it in the room. To go back on the same day and make a withdrawal would be too suspicious. There was no choice but to wait until the following day. At least I have plenty of practice. *Waiting around is what I do best.*

'You wish to close the box already?' said Monsieur Fornier, the sub-manager of the Banque Azoni.

Sam nodded, and attempted a weak smile. 'Plans change,' he said. 'It turns out I need those papers after all.'

Fornier nodded. He was a thin man, with pale, intense eyes that burned through the thick spectacles that covered them. 'There'll be another charge,' he said. 'It was all in the agreement you signed.'

'It's OK,' said Sam quickly. 'I quite understand.'

'I'll need the key,' he said. 'When customers close a box, we return the belongings to this office. A security pre-caution, you understand.'

'I understand,' said Sam, handing over the key.

It was ten fifteen. Five minutes passed, then ten. Sam

poured himself a glass of water from the jug on the side table. Just another few minutes. *Then at least some of Robertson's secrets will be mine.*

'I'll need you to sign some papers,' said Fornier.

He put a stack of brown envelopes down on the desk. Reaching across, Sam signed the sheet of paper Fornier had just handed him, then collected the envelopes into his briefcase. 'Thanks,' he said, turning crisply on his heels and walking out of the bank.

The cold morning air hit him straight in the face as he stepped out on to the street. He turned swiftly towards the hotel he'd checked into the night before. The briefcase felt heavier in his hand. Anticipation, he told himself. Nothing weighs more.

On reaching his room, Sam laid the case out on the bed. A single room at the Hôtel Flanders measured just eight feet by ten, with a small desk in the corner, a radio and a window looking out on to the bins from a restaurant behind. Greedily, Sam opened the first envelope. *There is no appetite,* he thought, *that needs to be satiated more quickly than a hunger for information.*

Sixteen sheets of paper slipped from the first envelope. Sam held them up. Bank statements printed on the note-paper of the Banque Azoni. There was no name on the account, just a number, but the address was given as Robertson's Oxfordshire mansion. There could be no doubting that this was his account. Quickly glancing through them, Sam established that the account had been open for three years. It had started in 1987, with a deposit of five million dollars, three million of which had then been subdivided into sterling, Deutschmarks and Swiss francs. For the first year, the account looked to have been dormant, with just some small amounts of interest credited to it. Around the summer of 1988 it became more interesting. There were a series of payments into the account, several of up to half a million dollars. No withdrawals.

Sam turned the pages, his mind ticking as he did so. Through the spring of 1989, there was another series of payments, plus a number of withdrawals, the largest of them for two hundred thousand in sterling. From the statements, it was impossible to tell either who the money was paid to, or where it came from. All the transfers were from numbered accounts, either in Luxembourg or Switzerland.

Robertson had some secret money stashed away. And here's the evidence.

Sam leafed through the pages, his eyes scanning through the numbers. There was information here that might take days to sort through. Pausing, he looked at the last entry. A withdrawal of fifty thousand Deutschmarks. Made two months ago.

Let me get this straight. There were payments out of the account four months after Robertson died.

Sam hesitated, checking the numbers again. There could be no doubt. The account was still being used.

He's alive, thought Sam. *Here's the evidence.*

He glanced up at the window, but could only see some drizzle starting to drip against the pane. Why had Robertson given his stepdaughter this key? Was he trying to tell her he was still alive? That would be madness, surely? Yet if he was hiding somewhere, living quietly on some of the money tucked away in this account, maybe he'd want his stepdaughter to know that. *Even the worst monsters care about their children.*

Sam took a few seconds to ponder the implications. *If I could deliver Robertson alive back to Merriman & Dowler I'd have certainly earned the five million.*

Sam opened up the second envelope. He could feel the tension rippling through him as he carefully unsealed the brown paper. He tipped it open, letting the contents fall on to the desk. Disks, he realised, looking at the three square black plastic objects in front of him. Computer disks.

He held one up in his hand. Sam was no expert on computers, but he knew enough to recognise which disk fitted into which machine. He could tell an IBM disk from an Apple disk. *This wasn't any kind of disk he'd ever seen before.*

Sam opened the next envelope. Three more disks, again all of the same unknown make.

Where the hell am I going to find a computer they'll fit? Sam asked himself.

At that moment there was a noise by the restaurant bins and two men and a woman walked past his window. Sam could not be sure if they had seen him. Time to move on. Time to disappear.

SIXTEEN

Sam folded the passport into his jacket. He'd double-checked the likeness in the photograph, and judged it good enough. The document had been made overnight by Bertrand Leski, a jeweller by trade who ran a profitable sideline forging passports, identity cards, driving licences, and any other documentation required by the French state. Sam had dealt with him a couple of times before when his team had needed new documents in a hurry, and found him a reliable operator. More importantly, he was an independent: most of his business was done for local Parisian gangsters. He had no links to Mossad.

Albert Brunier, Sam noted, memorising his new name. A Belgian businessman. Right now, I reckon I have Mossad on my trail, no doubt Hassim's men and perhaps even Robertson himself. *But they should have no way of tracing Brunier.*

Walking past the station, Sam noticed two disabled people: one selling flowers, the other collecting donations next to a sign saying he was a veteran of the Algerian wars. Sam increased his speed slightly. Papa kept his network of observers at every major transport hub in Europe. If they spotted him, then Papa would know right away where he was and what he was doing. *And right now, all my movements must be made in secret.*

He stopped at a call box and phoned Selima. There was no response from either number. She's disappeared from contact again. When she wants to speak to you, she does. *And when she doesn't, she vanishes from the scene.*

Andrei Usmanov lived twenty minutes' walk from the station, in one of the maze of tiny streets just behind the Bastille. A Russian by birth, he'd turned agent for Mossad, then fled the country five years ago when he feared being unmasked as a spy. He'd now settled in Paris, working as a computer consultant, mainly for private companies but also freelancing for security agencies. When Sam knocked on the door, his wife said he was out for the day. Ask him to meet me in the café on the corner, said Sam. About six. Tell him it's important.

The day passed slowly. Sam walked through the city, ate some lunch, then spent a couple of hours browsing through some of the antique shops on the Left Bank. Trade was brisk, he could tell that much just by chatting to some of the dealers. There was a lot of newly minted money sloshing around the world. *If I could only crack this case, there's a market for me there.*

Usmanov was already sitting in the café when Sam arrived, even though he was ten minutes early. Paris seemed to have thrown the ageing process into reverse, as it did for many men. He had never asked Usmanov his age, but last time he'd seen him he'd have guessed about forty. Now he'd guess about thirty-five. His beard had been shaved off, he looked thinner and fitter, and the shapeless suit he wore back in Russia had been replaced by stylish jeans and a leather jacket.

'You're looking well,' said Sam.

'Better than you, anyway,' said Usmanov with a wide grin.

Russians. They don't bother with the normal pleasantries of life. They get straight to the point. 'I was wondering if you might know what this is?'

He pushed one of the disks taken from Robertson's

183

collection across the table. Usmanov took it between his fingers, examined it for just a fraction of a second, then put it down. 'Christ, I was hoping never to see one of them again.' He glanced at Sam. 'You really don't know what it is?'

'Well, it's a computer disk, obviously. But not any make I recognise. I took it into a couple of shops but they didn't recognise it either.'

'No, they wouldn't.'

Sam leaned forward. 'Because it's for an intelligence agency machine? Or a military machine?'

Usmanov laughed, taking a hit on his drink. 'No, because it's for a fucking crap machine.' He pushed the disk back towards Sam. 'That's for an Agat.'

'What's the hell's that?'

'The Soviet computer. It was a rip off of the Apple II, except not nearly as good, like everything my late lamented motherland copies from the West. The machine that was going to introduce a generation of Soviet schoolchildren to computing. About half a million of them were supposed to be manufactured, but needless to say, only about half of them got made, and half of those didn't work.'

Sam nodded. Robertson was writing something, or storing some information, on a Soviet computer? Why? He could buy all the IBMs or Apples he wanted. 'Can you read this disk?'

Still grinning, Usmanov shook his head. 'Not unless you can find me an Agat to plug it into. It wasn't compatible with anything else. To tell you the truth, the Agat was hardly compatible with itself. The fucker usually crashed before you even tried to turn it on.' He drained his glass. 'I suggest you try Moscow. You'll find one there.'

SEVENTEEN

It was three years since Sam had last walked through Red Square, but he was surprised by how much it had changed. The same buildings, true. The same surly policemen, true. The same shabbily dressed people, also true. But the air was different. The unmistakable smell of collapse was clinging to every surface.

Sam took a couple of pictures of the Kremlin on the cheap camera he'd picked up at the airport that morning, then moved on. He was playing the tourist and doing so carefully: he walked in the slightly lost way that tourists walk, and kept his head high as if admiring the sights. But after an hour or so, he was no longer certain he needed to bother. On his previous visits to Moscow, he'd sensed immediately the ruthless professionalism of the security services. You could feel them all around you. Their eyes were sharpened to perfection, and their ears alert to every murmur. They would notice instantly anyone pretending to be a tourist, anyone who was not actually looking at the monuments. And now? Standards looked to have slipped. A few guards were standing around the square, but they were paying little attention. *Like any army, once their morale has snapped they are useless.*

He thought back to what Barnea had told him. The whole place is falling apart. The people at the top haven't seen it, but the people at the bottom already know. The guards in the square certainly knew. The Berlin Wall had

185

come down last year. Eastern Europe had been let go. Gorbachev was still hanging on to power, but the place was rife with rumours of coups by the hardliners, and counter-coups by the democrats. Those guards aren't bothering to protect anything, because they know there is nothing left to protect. *In a looted city, the police lose interest.*

Barnea might think the men at the top don't know the house is about to come down on their heads, but maybe they do know. *Maybe Robertson knew.*

Valeri Vinchel was living in a ten-storey apartment block, six subway stops from Red Square. Sam climbed out of the Begovaya subway station and started walking. This was a different Moscow from the tourist strip leading away from Red Square. Out here, the city had been shelled to the ground by the Nazis and had been rebuilt out of the rubble and dust during the 1950s. The architecture was high Stalinism: a style, Sam thought, that managed to be both imposing and comic at the same time. 'Did anyone see you?' said Vinchel, opening the door.

He was a small man with a pinched, tired face. He was wearing a grey suit, with a pair of mittens on, even though the spring weather was relatively mild for Moscow. He was another of the *sayanim*, another ordinary man going about his job, whom a field agent could call upon when help was needed.

Last time they'd met, Vinchel had been working in the Ministry of Internal Affairs, processing visa applications. Sam had been tracking down leads on PLO agents, and had hoped to find them in Moscow: most of the Palestinian leadership had been trained in the Soviet Union, and they returned regularly to regroup, retrain and rearm themselves. Nothing much had come of it. Vinchel had been able to supply him with a dozen false identities used by Palestinians visiting Moscow, but by the time Sam started tracking them down, they had already been changed. The men on his list were all experts: they never travelled under the same name for more than a few weeks at a time. Still, the contact had been made. Vinchel was a source, Sam had figured at the time, who might be useful one day. *Like now.*

'I didn't get the impression security was that tight.'

Vinchel beckoned him into the three-room apartment. The place smelt of cheap Georgian red wine and stew. Some music was playing on the radio, the volume turned up way too high. Sam recognised the Shostakovich string quartet, the theme managing to sound both melancholic and hopeful at the same time. Judging by the state of the apartment, Vinchel had lost his job. It looked like a place where a man spent the best part of twenty-four hours a day: the floor was covered with books and papers; the kitchen was piled with dishes; and there was a trail of clothes leading towards the bedroom. A place doesn't turn into this kind of a dump all by itself. *You have to work at it.*

'Don't you believe it,' said Vinchel as he led Sam into the kitchen. The stew was bubbling on the two-ring gas stove, its smell a sweaty mix of pork, eggs, cabbage and spices. Sam checked his watch. Just after twelve. *With luck I can be out of here before he offers me any lunch.*

'None of the guards I saw at the airport or along Red Square seemed to be paying attention to anything.'

'That means nothing. They don't bother checking up on the tourists any more. And they certainly don't bother with the criminals. There isn't any point. But the KGB and the army are on high alert. They've turned paranoid, the way any cornered animal will do. There have been arrests, of the kind we haven't seen since the 1950s. Knocks on the door at midnight, whole families being taken away, the works. The whole place is coming apart, and everyone knows it. All that's happening now is people are trying to get themselves into position. For day one of the new Russia.'

'And you? What's your position?'

Vinchel laughed. 'There isn't one for men like me. Russia now belongs to the young and the old. I was born in 1940. A war baby. I'm too young to be in a senior position now, so I don't have the power to start looting what remains of the place. And I'm too old to become one of the young entrepreneurs who are going to take over the place when the system gets swept aside.' He shrugged. 'So I stay home and listen to Shostakovich. What else can I do?'

'You could make some money.'

He looked at Sam. 'Are you about to make me an offer?'

Sam nodded.

'Then let's have some lunch.'

Sam winced. The smell of the stew as the plate was put down in front of him was overpowering. What looked like a pork knuckle was resting in the centre of the plate, surrounded by some grey liquid and the remnants of some vegetables that had been boiled down to a mush. Sam prodded the knuckle with his fork, flaking away a piece of meat, then putting it gently to his mouth. It tasted like old diesel fuel. He swallowed hard, then looked up at Vinchel. 'I need help finding out some information.'

'What kind?'

'Computer disks,' said Sam. 'I need someone who can plug them into an Agat for me, then maybe help me out if they need translating.' Sam took a bit of the vegetable mush, which seemed to be flavoured with orange peel. 'I'll pay you a hundred dollars a day to work with me while I'm in Moscow. Cash.'

'Excellent, excellent,' said Vinchel. 'You should stay here. No need to worry about the expense of a hotel. And this stew will last us for days.' He paused, wolfing back a mouthful. 'You know, the more often you reheat it, the better it tastes.'

Tatiana Breyeva was the thinnest women Sam had ever seen. She was sitting behind a mesh of wires, stripped-down

188

metal boxes and angled lamps. On the workbench next to her was a tiny soldering iron, smelling of hot metal. Next to that was a cold cup of coffee, with some lumps of powdered milk floating on its surface.

'An Agat,' she said, smiling at Sam. 'Of course we've got one somewhere. It's just a question of getting it to work.'

Sam had travelled with Vinchel on the blue metro line that led out of Moscow towards the Krylatskoe suburb. Along the way, Sam had noticed one flower seller who looked as if he could be one of Papa's informers, but otherwise the journey was uneventful. It was a nasty area, to the south of the city, dominated by high-rise apartment blocks and factories. Dozens of skateboarders congregated around the subway station, weaving through the crumbling concrete, and Sam had to dodge his way through the teenagers whizzing by. The building where Breyeva lived seemed to be a squat. It could have been some kind of office originally, Sam thought as they stepped inside, but it had long since been abandoned. There was some anarchist graffiti on the wall, and a collection of bikes along the corridor. A couple of skinheads were playing reggae, and in the basement, a band was rehearsing. Judging from the noise, only the drummer seemed to have any idea what tune they were playing.

'I just need to read this disk,' said Sam, handing it across.

Breyeva nodded, and started looking around. The room was painted a pale green, with patches of damp. From the mess of components on her desk, Sam guessed she was building PCs from scratch. He could see what looked like silicon chips, and memory boards, and graphics cards. Where she got them all from, he couldn't imagine. But pieced together with a soldering iron, they'd make a brand new computer.

'Here,' she said rummaging around the jumble of equipment at the back of the room. 'The comrades managed to liberate some surplus stock a couple of weeks ago. The Agat is crap, as you probably know. The worst computer ever made. Completely unusable. However, the memory chips aren't too bad, and some of the wiring is OK. We bring them in here, take out the kit that we want, then put it together with Taiwanese components to make a decent machine. The only question is whether I can find one we haven't cannibalised yet.'

Sam watched her while she worked. She was six feet tall, with sharp, angular arms and legs, but couldn't have weighed more than ninety pounds. She had no breasts that he could make out underneath her plain black T-shirt, and no hips that he could see below her baggy black jeans. Her face was thin and pointy, but her green eyes were lively, and her smile as wide as she was narrow. 'I could give you money to get a new one if you haven't got one here,' said Sam.

'Fuck that, we'll just nick one,' she said. 'Anyway, people are always pleased to get rid of an Agat. They're crap, I tell you. One look at this rubbish, and you realise why our system is finished.'

She pushed aside some broken plastic casings, then walked back to the workbench carrying what looked like an intact machine. It was, Sam observed, a horrible piece of design. The computer itself was a clunky, pale brown plastic box, on top of which sat an adapted twelve-inch Soviet TV screen. The keyboard had thirty-three characters, in a mixture of Latin and Cyrillic characters. 'Crap, right,' said Breyeva triumphantly.

Sam nodded. 'I just need it to read the disk.'

Breyeva started searching around for a plug. 'We call it the Yablotchko, the Small Apple,' she said. 'If you look inside the operating system, it still has the signature of Steve Wozniak in it, one of the original Apple designers. They just nicked it. Shame they didn't make a proper one.'

The screen hissed then flicked into life as Breyeva plugged the machine into the socket. Sam could hear its hard disk cranking into action. Both he and Vinchel leaned forward as she plugged the floppy into the machine. There was a scratching sound as the machine started to read the disk, then a series of files jumped up on to the screen. 'Open one,' said Sam quickly.

He stared at the screen as Breyeva opened up the first file. A series of numbers filled up the screen. Digit after digit, after digit, in an unending row. 'Another one,' he said.

Breyeva's fingers tapped on the ugly keyboard. Her fingers were so thin, you could see the bones jabbing out of her knuckles. The screen flickered, and Sam could hear a slight crunching sound as the hard drive bit into the disk. Another series of numbers started to scroll across the screen. No words, just numbers. Sam ground his fist together. 'Try another disk,' he muttered.

The files flashed up on to the screen, then, as Breyeva opened them, another series of numbers. Vinchel looked at Sam. 'You came all the way over here just to look at this?' he said.

Sam continued to stare at the screen. He started reading the numbers aloud. 'Twenty-two, six, thirty-one, two hundred and fifty-seven, thirteen . . .' He paused. 'It's a code,' he said.

Breyeva glanced up at him. 'I can't see a pattern,' she said. 'The numbers look entirely random to me.'

Sam shook his head. 'It's a code,' he repeated. 'Nobody goes to this amount of trouble just to put some meaningless numbers up on the screen. It means something. It *has* to.'

He looked harder at the screen. When he joined Mossad he'd been given some basic lessons in code-craft. The music boxes he received from head office were the way he'd always communicated: that was a music-based code, this one was obviously numerical. 'Don't try to figure them out yourself,' that had been the lesson the code instructor always gave to the recruits. 'If you can break it, it's not worth breaking. If there's any information in there worth having, you'll have to get an expert.'

Sam turned towards Breyeva. 'You know about computers, right?' he said. 'But do you know anyone who knows about codes. I can pay good money.'

'How much?'

'Fifty dollars a day. I have to find out what's on this disk.'

'Wait right here,' she said.

Sam paced around the small room. An old curtain was strung across the one window, and it looked as if it would fall down if you touched it. Little light was coming through, and only the soft electronic glow from the four different computers Breyeva was working on at the same time were illuminating the room. A code, thought Sam. Written on to a Soviet computer? *What kind of game was Robertson playing?*

Down below, Sam could hear the band racking up another song. The chords crashed into each other like a motorway pile-up, until, within seconds, the tune had disintegrated into an ugly wall of white noise. Then he could hear some shouting, and what sounded like Breyeva's voice, trying to make itself heard above the racket. Great, thought Sam. She's getting one of the band. Let's hope it's the drummer, he's the only one that seems to have anything resembling a brain.

The boy was walking a few paces behind Breyeva when she came back into the room. His head was shaved, and there were some anarchist tattoos on his forearms. If it was possible, he looked even thinner than she did. 'You know about codes?' said Sam.

'I . . .'

He looked nervously towards Breyeva, as if asking for permission to speak.

'It's OK,' she said quickly.

'I . . . I think . . .'

The sentence died on his lips.

'It's OK, you don't need to say anything.'

Sam guided him towards the Agat's screen. The boy sat down nervously, his fingers tapping against the plastic screen.

'What's your name?' asked Sam.

He looked as if he couldn't remember. 'I . . . it's . . .'

'He's called Dimitri,' said Breyeva. 'Really, he's a lot smarter than he sounds. I just make these things, but Dimitri can program them, rewrite American codes, the works. He graduated from the Soviet Academy of Sciences with first-class honours in computing, and he was told he had to go and work for the KGB. That's what they do to all the best programmers in this shit country, get them to work for the police. That's all they think computers are good for, a more efficient way to spy on their own people. Dimitri managed to leave after six months, and came to live with us.' She looked down at him affectionately. 'Really, he's a genius.'

'Fine, fine,' said Sam impatiently. 'Just see if you can make any sense of what's on the screen.'

'I . . . it takes . . . there's . . .' stuttered Dimitri.

'He'll need a little time,' said Breyeva.

Sam glared at her. He was calculating how long he could safely stay here before the local secret police became aware of him. They might tolerate a bunch of drop-out kids, but if they knew there was a foreigner among them, they'd want to know who he was. 'Time is the one currency I don't have.'

Breyeva walked quickly into the restaurant. 'Dimitri's got it,' she said. 'I told you he would.'

Vinchel put a ten-rouble note on the table, and he and Sam stood up. They had been sitting there for three hours. Sam knew that code crackers worked best when they were by themselves. Like chess players, they needed total concentration. Just the presence of another person was enough to distract them. So they took themselves off to the closest restaurant. Sam ordered a big gammon steak – the most expensive thing on the menu – which tasted as if it came from a tin. For the next few hours, they talked about the gradual disintegration of the Soviet Union. Vinchel described how the officials had stopped running the system, and for the past year had only worried about lining their own pockets. Who would take over from Gorbachev was the question everyone was asking, and who would make the money once everything was privatised. Vinchel reckoned they had it all wrong. The army would move in soon, and there would be a new Stalin: someone who could reimpose the command economy. 'Listen to me,' he said glumly. 'They'll be reopening the camps soon.'

The boy was still sitting in front of the Agat, still staring at the screen, when Sam walked back into the room. 'I heard you found something, Dimitri,' he said.

Dimitri nodded. He looked up at Sam, and the shyness seemed to have drained out of him. His manner was suddenly clear and confident. Information, thought Sam. It has made him powerful.

'Look at these numbers,' he said. 'It looks like just a random collection of figures.' He rested his finger on the screen. 'But one number keeps re-emerging. Sixteen.'

Sam followed his fingers. He was right. Sixteen cropped up every ten to thirty numbers. You'd have to run a statistical analysis, but it certainly looked as if sixteen was the most frequent number in the series.

'Ever heard of a guy called Felix Dzerzhinsky?' said Dimitri.

'Of course,' said Sam. Anyone in the intelligence world would have heard of Dzerzhinsky, the founder of the Cheka, the organisation that evolved into the KGB. He turned the question over in his mind, until its meaning became clear to him. 'And there are sixteen letters in the name Felix Dzerzhinsky.'

'It's like their own personal code. The KGB uses hundreds of different codes, some of them number-based, others letter-based, some rooted in pictures. Whatever. But they always use the number sixteen for a full stop. It's a kind of marker.'

'You're telling me this is a KGB code?'

Dimitri nodded. 'I worked there for a few months, I know their systems.'

'But can you crack it?'

'Crack it?' Dimitri laughed, and Sam could tell that the answer was not going to be good. 'A KGB code? No way.'

'I have to find a way of cracking this code,' Sam reiterated.

Dimitri turned round to look at him. 'Then you'll have to find a way of getting inside the KGB,' he said slowly. 'Because there's no other way you're going to do it.'

Sam pondered the implications. Robertson had been in deep with the KGB. Had he played the KGB off against another outfit? Had he been killed because he had betrayed one to the other? Perhaps he had been assaulted by the KGB and that was why Israel had given him a hero's funeral?

EIGHTEEN

Andrei Shenkov sipped his tea. He looked at Sam with the eyes of a man for whom suspicion has become so ingrained it was an instinct: it was as if he would look at his own face in the mirror in the morning and start wondering what he was concealing from himself. That's what life in the KGB does for you, thought Sam. Suspicion is wired into your soul.

'You want what exactly?' he said.

Sam paused. He was sitting with Vinchel in a café a few hundred yards from the Sokol metro station to the north of the city. Just by getting in touch with Shenkov, Sam knew he was taking a risk. The man was what Mossad referred to as a coma patient: someone who was in such a deep sleep he'd probably never come out of it. He'd been recruited more than a decade ago, and had since risen to the rank of deputy commandant in the KGB. Mossad had never used him, and probably never would. He was there as a back-up policy, to be made use of only in the most extreme circumstances. If the Soviets were equipping the Syrians or the Iraqis with a nuclear weapon, they'd expect Shenkov to tell them. Otherwise he would be left alone. An asset as valuable as that was too precious to be wasted on anything that didn't threaten the very existence of the Israeli state.

'I need to access the KGB codes.'

Shenkov kept his eyes fixed on Sam. 'The codes?'

Sam nodded. 'Some material has fallen into our hands,' he

continued. 'But it's been encoded by your organisation. We need it translated.'

'We?' said Shenkov. 'You mean Mossad?'

Sam nodded. It was a lie, of course, but the only shot he had. *How else am I going to get access to the KGB codes?*

Shenkov took another sip of his tea. The café was quiet. Some workmen were sitting in one corner, a pair of women gossiping in another. There was a smell of grease on the old tablecloth. 'But you don't work for Mossad any more,' he said quietly. There was a thread of steel running through his voice. 'You resigned. So what the fuck are you playing at?'

'That's for cover,' snapped Sam. He leaned forward. 'We need those codes.'

'Who the fuck are you working for? Yourself?'

Sam paused. Shenkov knew something. As soon as Sam set up this meeting, he must have checked in with head office. Who his controller was, Sam had no idea. Rotanski possibly. They must have told him Sam was out in the cold. Shenkov had no intention of giving him those codes. He'd only come here to find out what Sam was doing.

It's me that's under interrogation.

'What are you doing in Moscow?' pressed Shenkov. 'What's your game?'

'Listen,' said Sam. 'If you don't give me the codes, I'll blow your cover.'

Shenkov looked at him. 'Are you for real, Wolfman? I'm the best asset Israel has in the whole fucking Soviet Union. And you'll blow that just so you can push forward some petty little moneymaking scheme you're involved in? You can work for yourself if you want to, but you don't have to turn yourself into a traitor.'

'There's only one traitor in this room. You've been betraying your country since the day you were born.'

Shenkov stared at Sam, his eyes emptied of every emotion apart from one. Contempt. 'You've become like all the freelancers. A nasty, grubby little man, only interested in looking after himself,' he spat. 'Now piss off. We can still have people shot in this country. We might have bloody perestroika to deal with, but in my organisation we still have some backbone.'

The smell of the stew hit Sam straight in the face. As soon as he turned the key on Vinchel's apartment, he could feel the stink rising up from the surface of the floor. His eyes glanced left, then right. 'Stop,' he said to Vinchel. 'The place has been ransacked.'

Sam held himself still by the door. He'd already turned the key in the lock, and pushed the door ten inches open. Anyone inside waiting for them would have been alerted to their presence. Just hold it right here, Sam told himself. If they want you, they'll have to come and get you.

Silence. He counted to ten, then ten again. Nothing. Sam pushed the door further open. Then he stepped into the hallway. He could see and hear nothing.

They've been and gone.

Vinchel followed behind him. He was a man of few possessions. Now he had nothing. The few bits of furniture in the apartment had been broken apart. The mattress and cushions had been knifed, the stuffing left on the floor. The kitchen cupboards had been flung open, the contents strewn on the floor. Even the stew had been searched and tossed across the table.

'Shenkov,' said Sam. 'I should never have contacted him.'

'We'd better get the hell out of here,' said Vinchel.

'No,' snapped Sam. 'I have to find out what's on those disks.'

'This is the fucking KGB you're talking about. This is Moscow. Nobody fights them, nobody.'

'Have it your way, I'm cracking that code.'

Vinchel thrust his fist into Sam's chest. 'I was living here quietly until you showed up. Now look at the mess I'm in.'

'Listen, you better help me,' said Sam. 'Because right now, I'm the only lifeline you've got.'

Sam counted out the money. A hundred and fifty dollars was easily affordable, even from the fast-dwindling stash of money he'd brought into the country with him. That's one advantage of Communism, he thought. *The place is so broke that life is cheap.*

Dimitri folded the money into his pocket, then glanced at Breyeva. 'OK,' he said. 'We'll take him in.'

The house was ten miles outside Moscow, in the woods that started to the east of the city. Like the last place, it was now a squat, with a shifting population of draft dodgers and skateboarders. The fact that such places existed at all was a certain sign of the way the Soviet system had degenerated in the last five years. A decade ago, it would have been shut down on the spot. These boys would have been rounded up for the army, and the girls sent off to the canning factory. Now they could just do what they liked.

That doesn't mean the KGB isn't still dangerous, Sam reminded himself. *A wounded animal still has bite.*

'How are you going to get me in?' he said.

'The library is what you need,' said Dimitri. 'That's where they keep the codes. I know that much from the few months I worked there.'

'You're taking me in?'

Dimitri's lips creased up into a hollow smile. 'You haven't got enough money to pay me to do that. We're going to take you to see a guy called Roman Sereditsky. He works in the library at the Lubyanka. You don't look so different. With the right clothes, I think that can get you inside the building.'

Sam looked into Sereditsky's eyes. They were the same height and a similar build. The clothes would fit, and the manner was easily copied. But the eyes will tell us apart, thought Sam. Anyone looks too closely into my eyes, then I'm just a corpse searching for a coffin.

I've gambled my life before. At least this time, I'm playing to win.

Dimitri unrolled a map on to the tablecloth. 'This is . . .' he started hesitantly.

'The Lubyanka,' said Sereditsky. 'They've been torturing people in there since before the revolution. It was Stalin's personal killing field.'

'Just tell me how to get in,' said Sam.

Sereditsky pointed to the map. 'What you see from the street, the big yellow building, is the main headquarters. The head of the KGB always has his office on the third floor; there are offices all around it, and the prison down below. Two other buildings are set around an inner courtyard. On the right-hand side you'll find the museum that Andropov opened to try and improve our image. There's also a clubroom in there, and even a small disco. To the left, you'll find the military stockroom. That's where all the weapons are stored, plus a permanent contingent of assault troops. The library is in there. You'll find all the KGB's archives stored in a series of underground vaults. Those papers are so sensitive that even the Politburo aren't allowed access to them. I certainly can't get into that section. Next to that you find a general reference library. That's where I work. We look up everything for agents around the world. On the same floor, you'll find codes. There are about ten people working there. We use a complex system of numerical codes. There are a set of equations that translate the numbers into words, using five different keys. The key your disk uses will be embedded in the first few lines of numbers.'

Sam looked at Sereditsky. He could tell already what made him a good librarian: this was a man who revelled in precision. Every detail counted for him.

'My shift starts at eight tonight. The library is open twenty-four hours, but there are only two people on duty at night. Sacha is sick, so it'll just be me, or rather you. You should have the place to yourself. Just present my papers at the gate, and hope to hell they don't look at them too closely. If they just glance, you'll be all right. If they stop to study them, then you're a dead man.'

'I'll take my chances,' said Sam. 'How can I read the codes?'

'You know much about computers?'

Sam shook his head. 'Just general knowledge.'

'I'll give you a lesson,' said Breyeva.

Sam counted out the money from his pocket. Two thousand French francs, in crisp, colourful notes. Sereditsky would have preferred dollars, but Sam was only carrying large stacks of French money. So long as it wasn't roubles, it would do. Sam was going to go into the Lubyanka at eight. At ten, Sereditsky was going to report that his papers had been stolen, and there might be an intruder in the building: by then, Sam would have to be clear of the place or face the consequences.

He watched while Sereditsky counted out the money, each note weighed in his hand, as if it was made out of metal, and then folded it into his pocket. Money is heavier when you are staking your life on it, thought Sam. Sereditsky must know the kind of risk he's taking, but with the system so close to collapse, he doesn't have any other choice. You sell out now, while there's still something to sell.

Sam glanced over to Dimitri. 'For another fifty dollars, can you get me some pharmaceuticals?'

Dimitri shrugged. 'Sure, for that kind of money, I can get whatever you want. Some dope, some speed, some LSD or smack, whatever.'

'A cyanide tablet,' said Sam. 'Two, just to be on the safe

side. I don't know what they do to men that try to break into the Lubyanka. But I don't think I want to live through it.'

It's in the walk, thought Sam.

He gazed up at the Lubyanka. In a strange way, it was like meeting a famous person, they were always shorter than you expected. Same with the KGB headquarters. The yellow façade of the main building occupied the whole of the block, built in an oppressive, serious brick. It was four storeys high, with a basement sunk deep into the ground, but it was squatter and less substantial than Sam had expected. It could just as well be a museum, or a corporate office. *Not the most brutal killing machine ever created.*

The walk, he reminded himself, as he approached the front entrance. Imer had taught him about the walk when he'd been in training, and the advice was as good now as it was then. It was no good just acting calm. You had to be calm. For real. Security guards are trained to smell fear. To detect the slightest flicker of tension. Only by draining all the fear out of yourself can you hope to survive. 'Fear is a soldier's most basic instinct, and his most useful,' Imer always concluded his lectures. 'It's what keeps him alert. Fear is the most vital shield. A good solider learns how to overcome his fear, but not to banish it. For an agent, it's different. You must learn not how to combat, overcome or ignore fear. You must learn to make it go away.'

If I can live up to that advice, maybe I can get away with this.

Another night on the job, he thought as he took another few paces forward. He could see the gates to the building ahead of him. On either side stood soldiers in grey uniforms. Both were equipped with the AN-49s, which the Red Army's elite troops used in place of the more famous AK-47. I'm bored, Sam told himself. My mind is on what my kids are doing at school. I'm thinking about how to pay the rent, and why my wife has pissed me off. All the things that guys think about as they trudge into the office.

He focused his eyes on the square, slowing down his pace until he saw another pair of men approach the Lubyanka. As they neared the building, Sam quickened slightly, making sure he steered himself in front of them.

He flashed the ID card as he stepped into the main entrance. The guard stopped, looked down at the card, then glanced briefly up at Sam. A thick grey coat was pulled up high around his collar, shielding him from the cold. A woollen hat was pulled down over his head. Gloves were wrapped around his fingers. All three had been borrowed from Sereditsky to blend in as naturally as possible. Behind him the two other men were waiting impatiently, waving the cards. Make sure the guard is under pressure for time. That was the point of steering himself ahead of the other men. That way the guard was under pressure not to spend too much time looking at his papers.

The guard waved him through, then turned to the two men behind. Sam buried the temptation to smile. Show no reaction, he reminded himself, as he casually walked on. He glanced around. The inner courtyard was created from grey stone, with high windows looking down on the square. There were maybe a dozen people walking through it. An enclosed world, thought Sam. Like every intelligence agency, it was interested mainly in itself.

The map had been imprinted on Sam's mind. He knew that he had to walk without thinking. Any sign of unfamiliarity would immediately alert suspicion. He turned left, and kept walking. He could see the stockroom, and hear the sounds of some soldiers eating and drinking. He turned left again through a black door, descending one flight of stairs, then walking two hundred metres along the corridor that stretched out in front of him. As he stepped into the library, he could see a woman in thick black glasses get up to collect her coat. Sereditsky had warned him about her. Mrs Bogdanchikov. You'll be taking over from her shift. Just nod in her direction. She never says anything.

Sam nodded as he was told to, then turned his face away and headed into the Gents: that was fifteen yards away, down a corridor. So long as she didn't actually look at him, he should be OK. Luckily there was no one in the Gents. When he returned, she'd already left. The library was empty. And, next to it, so was the computer room.

Sam permitted himself a fleeting smile. So far so good. Now I just have to find the codes.

The library was a long narrow room, with a desk at its front; it stretched back a hundred yards, and was filled with long rows of metal bookshelves. Next to each shelf there was a light you could turn on, but since it was empty, all the lights were off, and only the front desk was illuminated. It had a dead, hushed quality to it, like all libraries, but here it felt especially lifeless. Ten Agat computers were positioned through the room, each one on its own desk. From the pale light glowing from their screens, Sam could tell they were still switched on. He sat down next to the first computer. Pausing for a moment, he listened to the room. There were some footsteps rattling through the concrete, but they were at least fifty yards away. Maybe in the corridor. Sam turned back towards the screen. He took the disk from his inside coat pocket, then slipped it into the floppy drive. The instructions Breyeva had given him were still lodged in his head. Plug the disk in and let the machine run. Once it has identified the code, slot another disk into the Agat and tap download into the keyboard. It should identify the code you need, then start downloading it on to the floppy. It shouldn't take more than ten minutes – and since the Agat was copied straight from the Apple, all the programming language is in English.

Sam watched as the numbers scrolled up on to the screen.

He could hear the hard drive of the machine clanking into action as it read the information, then the screen offered him two options: 'Translate' and 'Save Code'.

Somewhere in the distance, Sam could hear the footsteps again. *Closer.*

He hit the 'Save Code' button, and some symbols started to flash across the screen. Something appeared to be written on the floppy. Sam hesitated, hardly breathing. His ears remained alert. The steps were drawing closer still. *Maybe as close as fifty metres.*

A message came up on the screen. 'This program has hit an unexpected error. It will close immediately.' Within a second, the Agat had shut itself down.

'Fuck it,' Sam muttered under his breath. Breyeva had warned him that it might take two or three attempts to download the code. 'If it crashes, just try another one,' she'd told him.

Sam took the floppy from the Agat, and moved quickly to the next desk. He punched up the program, and started to download the code. The disk started crunching. At its side, Sam was tapping his fingers anxiously against the table top.

He glanced up towards the door. The footsteps had fallen silent.

A breathing space.

He looked back at the screen. The numbers were dancing across it, and he could feel the heat of its cathode-ray tube hitting him in the face. His coat was still on, and the hat still pulled down over his face. Faster, he muttered, willing the tiny Agat to complete its task. *Just download the code so I can get out of here.*

'Download complete,' flashed a message on the screen.

Sam ripped the disk from the computer, slipping it into his coat pocket. He stood up, glancing at the clock above the librarian's desk. It was twenty past eight. Sereditsky's shift was meant to last until five in the morning, when the first of

205

the day librarians would take over. Doesn't matter, Sam told himself. *This one's finishing early.*

The footsteps again. They were even closer now. Maybe thirty metres. *At most.*

Sam hesitated. His mind was racing towards a decision. Shall I try and get out now before anyone comes in? No, if they see the library is not manned, they might raise the alarm. Then I'll never get out of here. But if I stay, they might realise I'm not Sereditsky. Then they'll raise the alarm for sure.

Better to bluff it out. And pray.

He sat down at the desk, and started leafing through the pages of a book. Calm, he told himself. It's all in the attitude. If you can make yourself feel as if you belong here, there's just a chance you'll get away with this. Most people don't talk to the librarian, Sereditsky had briefed him, they know what they are looking for and they go straight to it. With luck, they'll do no more than nod in your direction.

A man walked into the room. He was short, with thinning grey hair and half-moon spectacles balanced on the end of his nose. His expression was intense, as he glanced towards Sam. Sam nodded, then looked back towards his book. His eyes tracked the man as he walked to the shelves of reference books at the back of the library.

Sam looked at the clock again. Eight twenty-three. Maybe I can just get up and go. The guy will just think I'm going to the Gents. *Get out of here while I still can.*

'*Arnac*,' said the man, turning round to look at Sam.

Sam's Russian was adequate, but this was not a word he'd heard before. There was a pause. It lasted no more than a fraction of a second, but Sam already suspected it was fatal.

'*Arnac*,' said the man again, louder this time.

From the look on his face, he was growing irritated at being made to wait for an answer.

Sam stood up. Maybe I can bluff my way through, he

thought, walking over to the reference section. The books were a mixture of Russian, English and French: encyclopedias, dictionaries and atlases mostly. Sam cast his eyes across them. What the guy might be asking for he had no idea. A place, perhaps. He wanted details about a place.

Sam took one of the dictionaries from the shelf and handed it to the man, who glanced down at the cover crossly. '*Nyet*,' he snapped.

He looked back at Sam, standing just five feet away from him. He could feel his eyes scrutinising, burrowing through his thick coat and woolly hat, and staring into his eyes. Slowly, his expression changed: irritation was replaced by curiosity, then by shock.

He knows, thought Sam. *He knows I'm an impostor.*

'*Govno*,' he said slowly. Then, switching into clipped English, 'Who . . . what.'

Sam reached forward. There was no time to think or plan. In a moment like this we drive only on instinct: like trapped animals, we fight back using whatever weapons we can. His arms reached out, gripping the man tight by the neck, and squeezing hard into the skin around his windpipe. The man was at least ten inches shorter than Sam, and fifty pounds lighter. Another of the desk jockeys you find in every intelligence agency: one of the pen pushers, not one of the warriors. Sam pulled him closer into his chest, draining the blood from his neck and squeezing the oxygen out of his lungs.

Then, still grasping the man's neck with one hand, he slipped the other into his pocket. There were the two cyanide tablets Dimitri had sold him: small white pills, no bigger than an aspirin. Sam gripped one tablet between his thumb and his index finger. He held it tightly. With his right hand, he snapped the man's head back, then jabbed his thumb into the side of his gum. The man was struggling, kicking out with his legs, but it was in his upper body that he needed to strengthen if he was to loosen Sam's grip. Sam kept his right thumb pressed into the man's mouth, then with his left hand pressed the cyanide tablet into the wet flesh just inside the gum. The man was stretching backwards with his neck, but lacked the strength to break free. The small white tablet was already starting to dissolve into the saliva.

With one swift movement, Sam yanked his head back, then punched him in the stomach. The man coughed violently, then swallowed. The cyanide on his gums was digested. The chances were he had no idea what he'd been given: cyanide was odourless and tasteless, precisely the reason it had always been the poison of choice for assassins. Suddenly his stomach started to heave, as if he was about to vomit. Sam glanced towards the door, making sure no one was approaching. The man's face convulsed, as he tried to vomit, but his lungs closed up. A smell of burnt almonds escaped from his lips. Sam held the man tight, as the last embers of life died within him. He checked his pulse, making sure he was dead, then rested him on the floor.

Stepping over the body, Sam moved over to the door. It was him or me. If I hadn't killed the man, I would have been taken prisoner, and tortured slowly to death. There would be nothing else to do with a foreigner who had broken into their headquarters. Kill or be killed. *It was all part of the dismal routine of our trade.*

He checked the corridor, his eyes sweeping along it, then started walking. One person passed him, but Sam kept his head down and the man paid him no attention. He climbed the stairs, and walked across the open courtyard. Never run, he reminded himself. But always walk quickly. In any organisation, the important people walk quickly. So long as they think you count, they won't stop you.

The guards were standing in the same position by the main gate, the AN-49s slung across their chests. One guard flashed his eyes up towards Sam. He showed him Sereditsky's pass. The guard nodded. In the next instant, Sam was back on the street.

He could feel the blood rushing through him, a heady mixture of adrenalin and oxygen. *I've made it.*

Except that I killed one of their men. And that will neither be forgiven, nor forgotten.

NINETEEN

Sam looked anxiously at the clock. It was twenty past nine in the evening. Breyeva and Dimitri had been working for close on twenty-four hours, their bodies fuelled on coffee, pork sandwiches and the occasional shot of vodka. So far they hadn't translated the disks.

'More time, more time,' Breyeva kept saying. 'All we need is time.'

'We don't have time,' Sam snapped back.

The KGB must have found that body by now. *They are going to be searching this city with a toothcomb.*

'Well, if the Agat wasn't such a crap computer it would work quicker,' she said. 'Our genius planners managed to copy the Apple design, but they halved the clock speed of the computer. They didn't understand that the whole point of computing is speed. They thought it was about power, because that's what they always think.'

Spare me the lessons in computing, thought Sam to himself. I need that code, and I need to get out of the country before they catch on to me.

They were sitting in yet another squat. Sam was surprised by how Moscow seemed to be encircled by alternative communities made up of free spirits who couldn't face a life in whatever ministry they were assigned to after they finished university. A whole alternative ruling class, thought Sam. Just waiting to emerge once this place finally falls apart.

The building was part of a collective farm that had been

abandoned. There was a grain store, barns for the animals, some rusted tractors and threshing machines, and a three-storey concrete apartment block where the farm workers were housed. Each family was allotted a three-room apartment. A strange, looking-glass world, thought Sam as he walked through the place. In the middle of an empty countryside, they created a collective farm, and built a tower block as if they were in an industrial slum. *No wonder their people despise them.*

He sat back in the chair, watching Dimitri and Breyeva while they worked. He'd already given both of them five thousand francs, with the promise of another five thousand if they managed to crack the code. They both kept reassuring him they could do it now they had the disks from the Lubyanka. Still, Sam was suspicious. Offer people money, and they'll tell you what you want to hear. *Coming from a capitalist system, that's one lesson you learn.*

'You're in big trouble, Sam,' said Vinchel, as soon as he walked into the room.

'I've been in trouble all my life,' said Sam. 'Tell me something new.'

'This is different,' said Vinchel. 'You've never been in this kind of trouble before.'

Sam pulled the collar of his coat higher around his neck. Several windows were broken in the decaying apartment block, and a chill wind was blowing through the building. 'The Lubyanka, they know there's been a break-in. I heard about it from a contact of mine. Shenkov isn't stupid. He can put two and two together. First you're looking for the codes. Next thing there's a break-in at the library, and a poisoned corpse is left behind. He knows it's you.'

Sam stood up. In the corner, Breyeva was still working on the computer, using the power from the farm's own generator. He could tell she was listening but pretending to concentrate on her work. 'What's he going to do?'

'He's already sent one of the KGB's best men to find you,' said Vinchel grimly. 'A guy called Oleksander Kersch.'

'Is he any good?'

Vinchel laughed, but it was just gallows humour. There was clearly nothing amusing about Kersch. 'The guy's a legend,' said Vinchel. 'He made his name in Afghanistan. Two years working behind the lines, tracking and assassinating the leaders of the resistance. Then a spell in Chechnya, dealing with some of the troublemakers down there. Next they sent him to the West. He took out at least four agents who'd defected. He's brilliant. A couple of guys had been put in deep hiding by the CIA. New faces, new names, new identities, the works. It didn't make any difference. Kersch tracked them down and then he killed them. Sometimes he works alone, sometimes in a team, but always with the same deadly results. The KGB has always had one assassin it keeps in reserve, a weapon of last resort. Right now, it's Kersch. And they've sent him after you.'

Sam shook his head. Sounds a bit like me, he thought. Only a Russian. There must be something on those disks. *And they must know I've got them.*

'I spent five years dodging the PLO,' said Sam with a shrug.

'That's different,' snapped Vinchel. 'You're in Russia now. With the KGB's top assassin on your trail. You're a fucking dead man.'

'I've been that for weeks,' he said wearily. 'I'm just waiting for someone to start kicking some dirt over the coffin.' He looked straight at Vinchel. 'Is it safe to stay here?'

'It's not safe to stay anywhere.'

'Looks pretty obscure to me.'

'Listen. They're going to take Sereditsky into the Lubyanka. They're not going to believe his bullshit story about being robbed. They're going to torture the miserable bastard until he speaks. That'll lead them to us, and pretty soon they'll be here.'

He turned, walking around. 'And I'm not going to be here when they arrive.' He looked towards Breyeva and Dimitri. 'And neither should you.'

'Wait,' said Sam. 'We just need to get away, lose the trail. Find somewhere to lie low.'

Vinchel laughed. 'This the Soviet Union. The original police state. We don't have any hiding places.'

'A few days at most,' said Sam. 'That's all we need.'

'You're on your own,' said Vinchel sourly. 'Nobody can help you any more.'

Sam watched as the man walked from the building. From the window, he could see him tramping into the empty countryside. He's made his own choice, thought Sam. He looked back at Dimitri and Breyeva. 'You don't have to stay if you don't want to,' he said. 'I can find someone else to decode those disks. Or, if I have to, I can do it myself.'

'How much money do you have?' asked Dimitri.

Sam paused. 'Another twenty thousand French francs. That's about four thousand American dollars.'

Dimitri stood up and walked closer to Sam. 'If we help you, it's ours.'

'Sure,' said Sam. 'Take it. Take the lot. I just need to read those disks. And maybe get out of this country alive.'

Liski, reflected Sam as he walked through the square, was the kind of place that made you realise why you'd been fighting the Cold War. A bleak industrial town on the River Don, it was a stop on the main railway line linking Moscow to Rostov. A canning factory filled up the west of the city, and stretching away from it were rows of monumental apartment blocks all built from the same grey concrete. As you approached the main square, dominated by a statue of Stalin, there were three department stores, their windows shabby and unclean, and their displays pitiful. Next to it, there was one hotel, with a restaurant attached to it. There were no small shops. No bars or cafés. At three thirty on a Tuesday afternoon, only a few people were out shopping. What was the point? There wasn't much to buy.

Better dead than red, thought Sam with a half-smile. *If you wanted proof of that cliché, then you'd find it right here.*

The journey had been long and tough, and Sam's limbs were still aching. That they had to get out of Moscow, he had no doubt. If Vinchel was to be believed, there was no doubt the KGB would track down the farm soon enough. Some friends of Dimitri's had put them in touch with a gang that took draft dodgers out of the country. For thirty dollars, paid in French francs, they were happy to spirit the three of them away from the capital. Anywhere, Sam had told them. Just so long as we can grab a couple of days to decode these disks, and then where I have a shot at getting out of the country alive.

A truck had been organised. It was taking machine tools from a factory near Moscow down to the Black Sea, and would stop at Liski on the way. It was a big, three-ton vehicle, with one driver and a full load that smelt of grease, oil and iron. Sam, Breyeva and Dimitri were packed into the back, inside a dummy crate. They were given ten bottles of water, six loaves of bread, ten tins of sardines, two bottles of vodka and two cartons of cigarettes. From the smell of the stuff, you'd be better off smoking the sardines and eating the cigarettes, Sam thought. Never mind. Just so long as it keeps us alive.

You can't come out for two days, their driver had warned them. It's too dangerous. Just keep still and keep quiet, and you'll be OK.

Sam had slept most of the way. A few smuggling routes for draft dodgers avoiding the Afghan war had been established in the past few years, and this was one of them. The last Soviet troops had left Afghanistan in February 1989, but the Red Army was still patrolling the borders. It was mostly young factory workers who were escaping military service, Dimitri explained. The sons of party officials could avoid the draft, and anyone with professional parents could secure themselves a cushy two years, mostly spent on engineering courses. It was the factory and farm workers who got sent to the front line. They paid what they could to a truck driver to ferry them south, hiding out in the back of the vehicle, then they were smuggled on to one of the boats crossing the Black Sea. Most of them ended up in Turkey. From there, they were on their own. Many of the Jews made their way to Israel. Others travelled to Western Europe and tried to find work. When an army can't enforce its draft, thought Sam, then it should know it's beaten.

By the time they were dumped out of the truck, it was Thursday morning: they had been driving for almost thirty-six hours. The trucker left them outside an abandoned factory, now occupied by a few squatters. It was much smaller and more peaceful than the places in Moscow: a dozen people, two of them women with children, in a community that seemed to have the tacit approval of the local police. Providing temporary lodgings for draft dodgers was one of their main sources of income, one of the men explained. The police didn't care: nobody made any pretence of supporting the army any more, and since most people in this part of the country assumed it was only a matter of time before the hardliners ousted Gorbachev, took control again and ordered the invasion of Poland and Czechoslovakia, they might as well take advantage of the brief moment of relative liberty. 'Freedom doesn't come around very often in Russia,' the man who showed them around explained with a smile. 'We take it while we can get it.'

Sam left Breyeva and Dimitri to get back to work on the Agat, while he took himself for a short walk around the town, keeping his hat pulled down low enough over his forehead to obscure the bulk of his face.

There was a smell of cooking as Sam stepped back into the building: some kind of dumplings, mixed with pork and fruit. One of the women offered Sam a plate, but he declined. He walked straight into the back room where Breyeva had hooked up the Agat to the factory's power supply. She looked more relaxed than the last time he'd seen her at work. There was a glow to her thin cheeks. 'I think we got something,' she said, turning to Sam.

It was like having a vein plugged into the wall: a sudden bolt of electricity jabbed through Sam. 'A full transcript?' he said.

'In English,' she said. 'Word for word. Once you get the right stretch of code, the numbers just dissolve into letters.' She stood up, walking across to Sam. 'Here, I printed it out for you.'

'Have you read it?'

Breyeva shook her head. 'I didn't think I should.'

'Don't,' said Sam quickly. 'Whatever comes off the screen, don't read it. It's too dangerous.'

The chair rocked back slightly as Sam sat down. The room looked out on to a stretch of railway track, and somewhere in the distance he could see a locomotive start to loom into view. It couldn't have been doing more than forty miles an hour, carrying wagon upon wagon of heavy industrial goods.

He looked down at the sheets of paper Breyeva had given him. Twelve sides of A4. Sam's eyes scanned through the letters. This is the secret, he thought to himself. *The one that could have me killed.*

15 August 1988

This is the diary of Max Robertson, Chairman and Chief Executive of Robertson Communications Corporation.

A diary. *The old man kept a diary.*

I arrived in Moscow last night on the British Airways flight. From there I was ferried by chauffeured car straight to my own suite within the Kremlin. Usually, on my visits to Moscow, I bring my own retinue, and stay in a hotel, or take an apartment. But this time, it is different. This time my visit is absolutely secret, and must remain so.

My first meeting of the day was scheduled with Roman Trusov . . .

Sam leaned back in his chair. Trusov was the head of the KGB, and had been for twelve years. According to all the reports Sam had read about him, Trusov was the one crucial figure keeping the regime afloat. While Gorbachev liberalised, Trusov repressed. One analyst described his job as keeping people 'just afraid enough' to stop the system from collapsing. In all the reports of a coup by the hardliners, Trusov was the man most often spoken of as leading it.

Why would Robertson be meeting with Trusov?

We are, of course, old friends, and we greeted each other in a manner becoming old comrades. I first met Trusov in Berlin in 1947, when I was with the British Army and he was a young political officer in the Red Army. We liked each other immediately. He had the air of a man who intended to make something of himself in the post-war world, and so, of course, did I. He had neither my charm nor my intelligence, but he had the same will-power. We recognised then that one day we might be useful to one another, and have remained in contact ever since.

We didn't meet in the Lubyanka, as we had in the past. Or in the Kremlin. The car collected me and drove me along the Tverskaya, that great long boulevard that leads away from the Kremlin towards the north of the city. We stopped outside one of the apartment buildings. I didn't recognise it, but if I had to guess, I'd say it was occupied by KGB men. The chauffeur took me to the top floor, and showed me into the penthouse apartment. Like me, Trusov clearly feels most comfortable at the top of a building. A man of substance should always make sure everyone else is beneath him.

When I entered Trusov was sitting by himself. There were no secretaries, and no guards. We talked for a while about politics and business. I told him that although Margaret Thatcher had just won another British election, the Labour leader Neil Kinnock shouldn't be written off. He would certainly be Prime Minister one day, probably as early as 1990. Trusov disagreed. Kinnock was a lightweight, he argued: none of the KGB's moles in the Labour Party thought he had a chance. George Bush, who both of us knew personally, we agreed would be shoo-in as next President of the United States. Both of us felt that Bush would certainly overshadow Ronald Reagan, who neither of us felt had achieved much in his presidency. It was all pleasant enough, but so far just cocktail-party chatter. Then he looked me straight in the eye. 'Max,' he said, 'it is almost forty years since we first met. We have both risen in the world since then. And now we need to talk.'

And talk he did. For the next hour, he unburdened himself, describing the mess that the Soviet Union had become. The system, he said, was coming apart at the seams. The rot had started with the invasion of Afghanistan, tying the country down in an unnecessary and expensive war. The economy was sinking further and further into a mess. Don't believe any of the official figures, he warned me. Production is falling year on year. The farms aren't producing nearly enough grain, and what they do harvest gets sucked into the black market. In some provinces people have barely enough to eat. Half of the national output was going into the army and the security services, and it still wasn't enough. Eastern Europe was restive and there was nothing Moscow could do about it, because it didn't have the manpower any more. The KGB wanted to crush the Solidarity revolt in Poland with a swift invasion, but the generals couldn't spare the troops from Afghanistan. 'Trust me, Max,' he said. 'The KGB knows everything that happens in this country. And it's rotten the whole way through. Nobody works. Nobody believes. It's just corruption everywhere. The discipline is all gone. And, you know, discipline and will-power were all we had. Without that, we're nothing.'

I listened, but I mostly remained silent. Then when he seemed to have finished, I looked up and I said: 'That's all very interesting, Roman, but what do you want me to do about it?'

And he looked at me, and he said: 'It's very simple, Max. We want you to help us. We need to plan for the long term.'

Sam put the papers down. Outside, the train was finally rattling past, its massive, heavy wagons shaking the fragile glass in the windows of the abandoned factory.

Trusov wanted Robertson's help. He turned the information over in his mind, trying to figure out what it might mean. His help? *But with what?*

He walked back into the room where Breyeva and Dimitri were working. 'Any more?' he said.

Breyeva held up another sheaf of papers. 'Once you figure

out which codes to use, it's quite easy,' she said. 'Just a matter of crunching through all the numbers, and trying to make sure the Agat doesn't crash.'

Sam took the papers and returned to the room overlooking the railway track. As he sat back down by the window, he could see in the distance the train rumbling on towards the Black Sea. He looked down at the papers and started to read.

26 September 1988

I am back in Moscow, staying in the same suite Trusov arranged last time. I arrived on the BA flight two days ago, and I am scheduled to be here for three days in total. On the first day, I met with Trusov again. He seemed in slightly better spirits. Progress is being made towards taking the troops out of Afghanistan, and that will reduce the pressure on the army. Some contingency plans are being drawn up for an invasion of Poland. Trusov believes there has to be some firm action, before the whole situation spins out of control. They have already chosen the sites for the camps they'll build, he joked. But Gorbachev won't authorise it. 'The man has no guts. He doesn't seem to understand that socialism can only work with discipline and order.'

We discussed our strategy in more detail. Now that I have agreed to what Trusov wants, our discussions are mostly about logistics and planning. Ideally, I would have delegated much of this work to some of the operations people within the company. I have always been a man of vision: the detail is for smaller minds. Still, I above anyone should know how important absolute secrecy is. History is being made by the day. Nobody must know about it.

After seeing Trusov, I met with several people in the Kremlin. Two different members of the Politburo, and various officials from the planning agencies. Also, a shipping captain called Pavel Ryazanov, with whom I may have some dealings in the next few months. He seemed a rough, uncouth man, but then I suppose most seamen are. I only spoke to him for a few minutes, mostly about life in Odessa which I visited right after the war. There were maps, and charts to be studied, and details of the weather to be taken into account. It was hard and tiring work. In many ways it reminded me of my time as a staff officer in the Normandy campaign, when I was fighting the Nazis. The same rush of organisational excitement. The same detailed logistics. The same worry about whether the machinery would work. Now, at the end of two days' talk, I think we're ready. The work should begin before Christmas. It is, I believe, the most exciting undertaking of my life so far.

Sam looked up towards the dirty window, adjusting his eyes to the half-light that filtered through the accumulated grime around the glass. Some smoke was rising up from a bonfire next to the railway track, mixing with the low-lying clouds to obscure the view even further. Robertson was working directly with the Soviet leadership. But why? What the hell was he taking out?

Holding the sheets of paper tightly in hand, Sam read on. He knew what he had already was pure gold. He was deeper into the riddle of Robertson's life and death than anyone else had managed to get. And yet, even in his own personal diary, Robertson seemed to be concealing as much as he revealed. *As if he didn't even trust himself.*

4 October 1988

There is still more work to be done before the task is completed, but I feel it is important that I keep on with this record, so that future historians may have a proper grasp of the events that are unfolding, and their true importance. As Winston Churchill once said, when the history of these times comes to be written, you have to remember that I intend to be one of the historians.

At ten this morning, I attended the first of two meetings at 10 Downing Street. I had arranged a meeting with Sir Anthony Messier, the Cabinet secretary. Margaret Thatcher put her head round the door to say hello, and apologised for not being able to stay longer, but she had to prepare for Prime Minister's Questions in the House. Margaret and I have always got along well, despite the fact that I am a supporter of the Labour Party. She doesn't hold that against me. I think she recognises me as one of the men of action who are helping to make this country great again. And I suspect she finds me attractive. She said nothing about the work I have been doing with the Russian leadership, but mentioned something about how I should give my best wishes to her great friend Gorbachev. Or Mikey, as she affectionately refers to him.

Messier was quite forthcoming. Inevitably, I wasn't able to go into too many details. The essence of the plan must remain secret. That is part of the arrangement with Trusov. But it is impossible to move materials in this kind of quantity without creating some kind of stir. There are satellites tracking the movement of goods around the Soviet Union. There are spies deeply embedded into the system, most of them unknown to Trusov. In time, the British and the Americans would have found out what we were up to. The British, in particular, have a network of spies, reaching deep into the Soviet hierarchy.

I told Messier what we were doing. And he acknowledged that while it was impossible for the British government explicitly to approve of the plan, neither would it be doing anything to stop it. I took that as an acknowledgement that we had at least their tacit agreement. And we needn't worry that they would stand in our way.

Sam flipped over a page. The diary started again on a fresh sheet of paper.

26 October 1988

This weather is Washington is warm for the time of year. This morning I amused myself by playing with the idea of buying one of the Washington newspapers. Of course, they are not for sale, particularly the *Post*, which is the only one worth having. My main purpose was to meet with Paul Demowitz, Assistant Secretary of State. We met at the state department on C Street, early in the morning. The coffee was horrible American pap but the meeting went well enough. Very similar to the meeting I had in London. They can't explicitly acknowledge what I am doing. Were any word of it to leak out – which of course it mustn't – then they would deny ever knowing anything about it. He made it quite clear it was my head on the block, as if I were a man frightened of such things. Clearly he is not aware that Max Robertson is not the ordinary, timid tycoon, but a man who thinks on a much larger scale than other men.

History, I feel, is on my side. This will be Max Robertson's greatest triumph.

I only spent one hour there, yet I came away with the impression that we had their blessing. For all their rhetoric about destroying communism, the Americans are primarily interested in stability. Anything that maintains the world as they have always known it is in their interests. I ran into Vice-President Bush in the corridor as I was leaving. He was on his way to a meeting, or so he said. I formed the distinct impression that actually he might have contrived to be in the corridor at precisely that moment so that he could speak with me without it seeming prearranged. He said that he had heard of our plans and wished us well, then he mentioned that his eldest son might be available for some non-executive directorships should Robertson Communications need any. I said I'd think about it, and maybe I will. Then I went on my way.

Next time I see Trusov I shall be ready to inform him that we are ready to start moving. Max Robertson never breaks his word.

The diary ended right there. Sam put the papers down, then walked back to the room where Breyeva was working on the Agat. His head was still buzzing with the information contained within the documents. That it was explosive he had no doubt. Robertson was involved in a plan that involved the head of the KGB, and had to be cleared by the British and American governments. Both George Bush and Margaret Thatcher had given it their blessing. But what was it? Tantalisingly, the diary didn't say.

'The last disk?' said Sam. 'Have you managed to decode it.'

As she turned round, he could tell from her expression that he was about to be disappointed. Her face looked as if it had just been punched. 'It's different,' she said softly. 'The code . . .'

Sam walked over to the screen. He peered into the thin cube of glass, looking at the meaningless rows of numbers stretched out across it. 'Why,' he snapped, looking down at Dimitri. 'Why won't it translate this disk?'

'It's a . . . there is . . . I mean . . .' started Dimitri. He pointed at the screen. Sam looked at the computer. The words were written in English. 'There is no final disk. The rest of my diary has been entrusted to my stepdaughter Selima.'

Sam could feel the air growing colder around him. Selima must have known much more than she'd told him. Maybe she even knows where he is.

The closer he got, the more elusive the prey seemed to become.

Through the grimy window, he could see two men approaching the building. Both were in their early twenties and they were dressed in the pale grey uniform of the Soviet police force

'A gun,' said Sam. 'I need a rifle, and I need it now.'

He could feel his heart thumping inside his chest. He got this far, they weren't going to take him now.

'Don't be stupid,' hissed Dimitri. 'They're probably just making a random check on the place. Maybe just checking for draft dodgers.'

'There are no random checks, not while I am around,' said Sam. 'Find me a bloody gun.'

Sam held himself close to the window. He could see the two policemen moving closer to the derelict building. They were talking to one of the women. He couldn't make out what they were saying: his Russian wasn't good enough, and the distance was too great. But he could tell they were shouting. This was no ordinary police search. They were looking for something. *Or somebody.*

Dimitri came back into the room, holding a gun. Where he had found it, Sam had no idea, but there were enough army deserters passing through this house for it to be full enough of kit and ammo to arm a battalion. Sam recognised it at once, even though he had never fired one. An OSV-96 large-calibre sniper rifle, it looked like a giant piece of black metal tubing with a handle mounted on one end. It was used by the Soviet military – a few had made their way into the hands of the Palestinians – and it was accurate to a distance of a thousand metres. Its one-metre barrel was unwieldy, and there was a hinge to make it easier to carry into combat, but it was that which gave the gun its long-range accuracy. Sam took the rifle, holding it to his chest to get a feel of its weight. He could smell the oil on it, telling him it had been cleaned recently. He looked down on to the patch of scrubland at the front of the derelict building. The police-men were shouting at Mikhail, the Russian who ran the hideaway: Sam had been introduced to him earlier, and he was a no-nonsense former Red Army sergeant who had told Sam he'd seen enough boys killed pointlessly in Afghanistan to be willing to help anyone who was trying to escape the same fate for themselves. Now Mikhail was shouting back at the police who were looking more and more agitated. Eventually, Sam understood one word drifting upwards towards his window. Foreigner. It's me they're looking for, he realised. They know I'm here.

Sam took the disks and stuffed them into an envelope, addressing them to the gym in Reading. He handed the envelope and one thousand francs to Dimitri: 'Post this for me,' he said. 'And keep the rest of the money.'

He raised the OSV-96 to his shoulder, resting the barrel on the edge of the glass. The rifle was equipped with a telescopic lens. Sam raised it to his eye, then focused the rifle on to one of the policemen. The bullet was lined up to enter his shoulder, and should come clean out the other side. A nasty flesh wound. Nothing to do any permanent damage.

He could see the other policeman push past Mikhail, demanding entrance to the building. Sam paused for one second. Him or me, he told himself. The same choice that keeps facing me. He squeezed the trigger, and the bullet exploded from the gun barrel. The OSV had a kick on it like an angry mule, and he could feel the thing slamming hard into his shoulder. He held himself steady, looking down. The bullet had smashed into the policeman's shoulder, knocking him to the ground. The other policeman was running towards the window, his pistol in his hand. He fired once, then twice, but his aim was unsteady, and the bullets crashed into the walls. Sam put his eye to the lens once again. The man was moving, but was less than three hundred metres away, easy range for the OSV. Sam squeezed the trigger. The same recoil, but Sam was ready for it this time, relaxing the muscles in his shoulder to absorb the blow.

The policeman had fallen to the ground, a trickle of blood seeping from the open wound.

Down below, Mikhail was running into the house. All around him, people were shouting. Sam calmly put the gun down and started walking from the room. Dimitri and Breyeva were both looking at him, too frightened to speak. 'I'm sorry,' he said. 'I'm too dangerous to be around. Take the money I gave you, and forget you ever saw those disks. They're poison.'

He hit the stairway, as Mikhail was running up towards him. His face was red and panting with fury. 'Get the fuck out of here,' he shouted. 'Get the fuck out of here now. You might be going to hell, but you're not taking the rest of us with you.'

Sam was already on his way. He'd grabbed his kitbag, and started running towards the open ground. He glanced at the wounded policemen, but only briefly. He headed out towards the railway tracks, and slowed to a walk. His head was buried deep into his coat, and his hands were dug deep into his pockets. I'm on my own now, he thought. *With just my wits to survive on.*

TWENTY

Odessa had a quiet warmth to it. Spring was already arriving this far south, and the city's temperate, mild climate had always made an oasis of warmth for Russians more used to their own far harsher northern weather. There were crocuses growing in neat displays in the public spaces, and the hazy blue skies had only the slightest traces of cloud to block out the sunshine.

Robertson's diary had mentioned a sea captain called Ryazanov, based in Odessa. Whatever Robertson had been doing for Trusov, Ryazanov had been at the sharp end.

Sam stepped away from the main railway station, and started walking down the wide tree-lined Primorsky Boulevard. The station was a mammoth neoclassical building, painted a pale cream and topped with a round dome. As he turned into the wide street, he could smell the salty air of the sea hitting him in the face. In the corner, he noticed an old man loitering alone. He had only one leg, and was using a crutch to prop himself up against a wall, and seemed to be quietly whispering to people for money – begging was, of course, illegal in the Soviet Union, so that might be his only way of eking out a living. Maybe one of Papa's men, thought Sam, pulling his woolly hat down further over his head and quickening his pace. *Could his network of spies be operating even within the Soviet Union?*

The train had taken thirteen hours to travel down from Liski. After the shootout at the safe house, he knew it could only be a matter of time before the police descended in numbers: Sam just hoped that Dimitri and Breyeva managed to escape in time. He'd walked along the railway tracks for half an hour, before a freight train rumbled past. It was travelling at twenty miles an hour, slow enough for Sam to climb aboard and hide himself amid a consignment of newly manufactured tractors. There was no food, and no water, but Sam hadn't minded that. The train was taking him south. Deep south. *Where some of the answers to this mystery might be buried.*

He was down to two thousand francs in cash, and there was no chance of laying his hands on any more money out here. *That was about two hundred dollars. Hardly enough to live on, let alone escape.*

At least life was cheap, and on the black market, you got a lot of roubles for every scrap of hard currency. Sam kept on walking. He could see the main port terminal up ahead, and feel the wind blowing in from the sea. Along the journey, there had been plenty of time to think. During the two years before his death, or disappearance, Robertson had been caught up in some kind of plot with the Soviet leadership. That much was clear. But what was it? From the descriptions in the diary, it involved transporting something out of the Soviet Union. Again, what? Nuclear weapons? There were constant rumours in the intelligence trade that the Soviet's nuclear arsenal could be up for sale. Israel already had a nuclear weapons programme, but it would certainly be in the market for an upgrade. Or biological weapons? If Robertson had been involved in shipping out Soviet weapons, maybe in return the KGB helped him to disappear. Maybe they were hiding him right here in Odessa?

The one hard clue he had was the name of the ship's captain mentioned in the diaries. Pavel Ryazanov. Just a name. *But if I can find Ryazanov, then maybe I could find out what Robertson was shipping out of here. And where they've stashed the old bastard.*

He walked casually, painfully aware that he was stretching his self-reliance further than he had ever done in the past. Never do anything you haven't prepared for, that was one of the pieces of advice that Imer gave his new recruits. *An agent who isn't trained for every eventuality is a dead agent.*

Well, I'm not prepared for this, thought Sam glumly. I've no training for operating undercover in the Soviet Union. I don't speak the language well enough. I've no back-up. And no resources to call upon. *I'm winging it.*

The docks reared up from the side of the wharf in a series of giant slabs of concrete. The Black Sea smelt different to the Mediterranean that Sam was more used to: the spit from the waves crashing into the sea wall flicked up against his skin, and there was some real bite to the water from the levels of brine mixed into it. The ships lined up in the dock were mostly Russian, along with a few Turkish and Greek vessels. All of the foreign ships had a couple of policemen stationed next to their holds. Sam buttoned up his coat, and walked slowly on. What I need is a bar. Somewhere where the sailors hang out.

He kept walking through the jetties. There was a string of rough-looking hotels, but Sam couldn't be sure it was safe to check into any of them. In the Soviet Union, all hotel registrations went to the local KGB office every night. His papers were forged. Relying on them to survive that kind of scrutiny was risky.

The weather wasn't so bad. If he needed to, he'd sleep rough. Twenty-four hours, he told himself. Give yourself that long to find a lead to Ryazanov. If you haven't found anything by then, see if you have enough money to smuggle yourself on board a ship sailing into the Med. Any ship. So long as it gets you out of Soviet waters.

The bar was shabby. Any other port in the world, thought

Sam, the wharf would be lined with bars and brothels, but here there were just a few seedy drinking holes. He looked down the length of the bar, before taking up a position at the far end. It was just after eleven in the morning – early, but not too early for a sailor to ask for a drink.

'Beer,' he said to the man behind the bar.

The barman looked about fifty, with tanned, leathery skin and dark brown eyes. He was dressed in a black T-shirt, and spent a few moments polishing some glasses before looking back at Sam. He eyed him suspiciously, then walked up the length of the bar, stopping where Sam was standing.

He said something in Russian that Sam couldn't understand.

'Beer,' said Sam again.

Surely in every bar in the world they understand that word.

The man repeated the words, but Sam just shrugged. He knew he was taking a calculated risk. Speaking English in any of these bars was going to mark him out as a stranger, and that was going to attract the attention of the police. One look at his papers, and he was in trouble: a Russian sailor would of course speak Russian. Against that, most sailors had little time for the police anywhere. And most of them spoke at least a little English: when you spent your life stopping at different ports, it was the one language you always need.

'Anyone here speak English?' said Sam. 'I need someone who can show me around.'

'I speak some English.'

Sam took the beer that had just been poured, and looked round. The man standing behind him was maybe thirty, thirty-five. He was short, no more than five foot five, but with the thick, hardened torso that developed after years of hard physical work. His hair was black and his skin dark: one of the southern, semi-Asian races, Sam guessed. Maybe Azerbaijani, or even Mongolian.

231

'Let me buy you a beer,' said Sam.

He pushed a five-rouble note across the counter, waited for the beer to be poured, then passed it over. The man introduced himself as Vilayet, took one gulp, sinking half the beer, then looked at Sam. 'Where are you from?' he asked.

'Israel,' Sam replied. 'My ship's unloading, then heading back home. We've got two days ashore.'

'Be careful,' said Vilayet. 'There are police everywhere in Odessa. The foreigners are meant to stay on their ships.'

'I know. I'm looking for someone.'

Vilayet grinned. 'A woman?'

Sam shook his head. 'I've got one of those already. I'm looking for a captain. A Soviet captain. His name is Ryazanov. Runs cargo ships out of Odessa. Ever come across him?'

Vilayet paused, as if thinking. 'I don't think so. How old?'

Sam shrugged. 'Mid-forties.'

He was guessing, but he didn't want to give away how little he knew. All I have is the name. *Nothing more.*

'I don't know him,' said Vilayet. 'But it's a big port.'

Sam sunk his beer, and left the bar. He started to walk along the street. Coming to another bar, he glanced through the window, but he could only see one old guy sitting by himself. No point bothering, he told himself. He doesn't look as if he knows anything. He kept walking. He stepped into another bar, ordered a beer, and found himself in conversation with a Ukrainian ship's navigator. Had he heard of Ryazanov? No, the man told him. But ships called in from all over the world, and there were hundreds of captains. Many of them didn't last more than a few years: a single accident, or a single late delivery, often meant that they lost their command. Sam said goodbye, and kept walking. He found a seamen's hostel, where he ordered himself some cabbage soup and black bread for lunch. There were two men sitting to his left, both dressed in the thick black donkey jackets that marked them out as sailors. Both of them looked at him suspiciously when he tried to speak to them. Sam finished the rest of the meal in silence. He already had the feeling he was pushing his luck to the limit.

If I'm going to find Ryazanov, I'm going to need someone to help me.

On leaving the hostel, he started walking towards the docks. Maybe one of the sailors on a foreign ship would know something about Ryazanov. If not, maybe he could find himself a berth out of here.

A sound. Shouting. Sam spun round. He could see a policeman waving at him. He paused, his eyes glancing nervously towards the wharf. His mind was calculating the odds furiously. If he made a run for it, he had a chance of making it down to the water. But where can I go? No, I can't escape. I have to try and bluff this out.

The policeman was nearly six foot, dressed in a grey uniform, with a pistol at the side of his black leather belt. Sam walked up towards him, trying to look as innocent as possible, and struggling to get his pulse and breathing under control.

The man barked something in Russian. But it was too fast, and the accent unfamiliar.

He pulled out his papers, and handed them across. The policeman looked down, examining first the writing, then looking at the picture. He barked again.

Sam pulled a zipping motion across his mouth. Try to convince him I'm dumb, he told himself. *That's my only chance. If he realises I can't understand him, I'm done for.*

The man spoke again. This time he was shouting. Across the street, Sam could see two other policemen starting to join their colleague.

How the hell do I get out of this one?

He zipped his mouth again, gesticulating wildly. The

policeman shouted at him, then slammed his papers down on to the ground. Sam bent down to pick them up. As he stood up again, he could see the pistol had been drawn. The barrel of the gun was pointing straight into his forehead.

A police car had drawn up at the side of the road. And Sam was being ordered to climb inside it.

The cell smelt of boiled vegetables, flaking concrete and unwashed skin. Sam sat in the corner, lowering himself down on to the wooden bench that ran along one side of the small room. His head was throbbing, and there was a searing pain in the side of his ribcage where the policeman had delivered a couple of blows with the butt end of a rifle in the van that delivered him to the jail.

Maybe men have come out of here alive, thought Sam grimly as he surveyed the cell. But only if they had the luck of the Devil.

The room was twenty foot by ten, painted a rough white colour, but much of it had long since peeled away, leaving chunks of stained, exposed concrete. A single two-foot window was sited in the top left-hand corner, but the glass was so grimy, and bars across it so thick, only a little light could filter through. In one corner, there was a trough of water, and next to it a bucket to use as a latrine. There was already a powerful stench rising from it. There were six men in total in the room: two dark-skinned, maybe Georgians, or Azerbaijanis. The others were white Russians or Ukrainians: short, stocky men, with thick tattooed arms, and faces that were rough and savage, their skin a mixture of acne and scars. They looked up at Sam as the door was opened, watching him as he walked inside and took his place on the back bench. A couple of them muttered something in a language he couldn't understand. Then they laughed and went back to playing a game of cards.

Sam glanced at the thick steel door, the only object in the

room that looked to have been solidly built. The last couple of hours had gone by in a mixture of terror and confusion. Once pushed inside the police car, he had been driven straight to what looked like the local jail. Inside, the policemen had shouted at him again, growing more and more angry as he failed to understand their demands. They took his papers, studied them, then came back to the interrogation room where he was being held. Angrier again. They punched him a few times. Nothing serious. Just a couple of blows to the stomach and the neck. The really rough stuff would come later, he figured. Throughout, he stuck to his story of being dumb. He kept his mouth shut, refusing to say a word, even when they were hitting him. No matter what happened, he just zipped his lips. It was not much of a story, he reflected. *But it's all I've got and I'm sticking to it.*

Next, they had ordered him to take off his clothes, then thrown a couple of buckets of cold water over him. They found the French francs soon enough. As the policemen unfolded the brightly coloured notes, Sam suspected he was done for. Why would a mute Russian sailor be carrying phoney papers and French currency? *If there's a decent explanation for that, I'd like to hear it myself.*

They chucked his clothes back at him, waited for him to dress and then led him down into the cell. Sam kept looking at the door. He was trying to focus on his options. Telling them the truth would be impossible. *A former Mossad agent, freelancing in Russia, who'd stolen codes from the KGB? They would shoot me on the spot. I can't appeal to the Israeli Embassy for help. I'm not working for them any more. I have nothing. And no one to help me.*

Sam buried his face in his hands. *I should have listened to the advice I was given all those years ago by Imer. Never embark on any mission you haven't prepared for. It's never worth it.*

The door opened, and a guard pushed through a single tray of food. Around him, the men put down their playing cards and jumped to attention. On the tray there were seven metal bowls, with some kind of grey soup inside. Next to them were seven chunks of a thick, black bread. The men stood in turn, getting their bowls and grabbing some water from the trough. One of them took a piss in the bucket at the same time: a few droplets, Sam noted, splashed across to the water trough. They knelt on their haunches to eat, all remaining silent as they slurped on the soup and wolfed down the bread.

Sam bent down to pick up the one remaining bowl. It smelt of horse bones and potatoes. Suddenly, one of the men shouted something at him. Sam looked round. It was one of the Russians. He was a short man, with a face like a box and a few days of stubble on his chin. The words Sam couldn't understand. He attempted a smile, then zipped his lips. Dumb, he told himself. Try to convince them I'm dumb.

The man walked over to him. There was a swaggering, menacing look in his eyes: the expression of a bully tooling himself up for a fight. He reached out a hand. The soup, Sam realised. He wants the soup.

Sam gave it to him: if he made enemies of his cell mates, then he was finished. He couldn't take them all on. The man took it, grinned, then pointed at the bread. Sam knelt down, and handed it over. The man looked at Sam with an expression of malevolent brutality in his eyes, then tore off a hunk of the bread to give to the man sitting next to him.

Sam sunk down on the ground next to the bench. *Who the hell do I pray to now?*

Sam eased himself gently up. The door to the cell had just been opened. A guard was motioning to the men with his fist, and one by one they were standing up. None of them moved very fast. What time it was, he couldn't be certain: his watch had been taken when he was searched and hadn't been given back to him. Mid-morning, he guessed. He'd slept fitfully through the night, before being woken by his cell mates rushing for the breakfast that was pushed through the door. Needless to say, they hadn't let him eat anything. Doesn't matter, thought Sam. *If hunger is the worst thing I suffer in here, then I'm a lucky man.*

The guard shouted something at him. Sam shrugged and started walking. A long corridor stretched away from the cell, with a series of doors running off it. After fifty yards, the men were led into a shower room. They started taking off their clothes. The smell made his stomach churn: a vile mixture of sweat and food that suggested showers were only allowed once a week at most. They stepped forward, as the guard turned on the taps, then left the room. Thick jets of icy cold water spat down from the old metal pipes at the top of the room. Sam could feel his skin freezing as the water jetted on to him. He stood under it, letting it cascade across his body.

One of the men was jostling him with his arms, trying to take more space under the shower head. Sam slipped. His back fell against the side of the tiling, and he could feel the bone getting bruised. 'Fuck,' he muttered.

The man looked down at him. He was tall, with cropped sandy hair and blue eyes. He said something in Russian. Sam shook his head. The man kept looking at Sam. 'You speak English?'

The accent was thick, but the words recognisable all the same. Sam glanced at him. He pulled a zip across his mouth. The man shook his head from side to side. 'You speak English,' he said. 'I heard you say fuck.'

Sam shook his head again.

A punch landed in the centre of his stomach. He crashed back against the wall, his shoulder colliding hard against a rusting piece of piping. He could feel a trickle of blood get caught by the jets of water and spit down on to the ground. Sam pulled his fist back, coiled all his strength into his shoulder and delivered a glancing jab into the lower side of the man's jaw. It was a blow he'd learned when he was a commando: if struck at the right angle, the punch stunned the nerves in the jaw, sending bolts of pain shooting up into the brain. It was a blow that delivered maximum pain, while doing little long-term damage.

The man reeled backwards, slipping in the water. One of his mates made a move towards Sam, raising his fist, but the man on the ground shouted something at him. He stopped, turning round and helping his friend to his feet. The cold water was still splashing over all of them, numbing Sam's skin and senses. The man he'd struck nursed his chin, then looked at Sam. 'OK, we don't have to fight,' he said in slow, broken English. 'Just tell us who the fuck you are, and what you're doing here.'

Sam nodded. 'In the cell,' he said.

The water stopped as abruptly as it had started. He shivered as he waited for the other men to finish with the single towel, then quickly dressed himself. They were led out by the guard, and deposited back in their cell. It was almost lunchtime, Sam figured, but no sign of them being given any food. 'Who the hell are you then?' said the man as soon as they sat down.

'My name is Sam Wolfman,' Sam replied. He'd already observed that the prisoners never spoke to the guards, so there was little chance they'd pass on information he gave them. 'Who are you?'

The man grinned, revealing a set of teeth so broken it looked as if he'd lost more fights than he'd won. 'I'm a sailor, we all speak some English.' He looked hard at Sam. 'But what are you? American, British, an Aussie?'

'I'm Israeli,' said Sam.

'Then what the fuck are you doing here?'

Sam hesitated. 'I got lost from my boat,' he said. 'Then there were a few personal problems. With a woman. So here I am.'

'Can't your embassy help you?'

Sam shook his head. 'It's not that simple.'

The man laughed. 'Then you're fucked.' He rubbed the stubble growing on his chin. 'This place is for all the scum the police pick up off the streets. Drink too much and get in a fight, then this is where you end up. They keep us here for a week or two, then they sentence us.'

'To what? A proper jail?'

The man shook his head glumly. 'A prison boat.'

'A prison boat? What the hell's that?'

'There are a few boats that Russians can't get anybody to crew, not willingly. Mostly boats patrolling the Baring Sea, then sailing across the top of Siberia. Sometimes it's a supply ship to the bases they have up there. Other times it's a military vessel itself. They always need extra sailors to do the hard work. Six-month voyages in freezing weather and rough seas. If you're unlucky, you get iced up and get stranded for the winter. Most of us will get two years.'

'There's no escape?'

'From what? The boat?'

'No, from this place.'

'The only escape is a bullet. Make one wrong move, and that's what they'll put straight through you.'

The man chuckled, but it echoed with despair not humour.

Sam started wondering how long it would take them to connect him to the murder in the Lubyanka, and to the shooting of the two policemen in Liski. How long before Kersch showed up here? When that happens, the prison ship they all seem so afraid of will seem like a cruise. Maybe that's my best option. After two years, everything will have quietened down. I can take whatever punishment they throw at me. *So long as I still have my life, I'm in the game.*

The guard pointed at Sam. He stood up uneasily. Another day had passed, sitting alone in the corner, with nothing but his thoughts to occupy him. He thought about his father mostly. He had been one of the best Mossad agents in his day, but after he was captured he spent a decade languishing in an Eygptian jail. He had been working behind enemy lines in the 1960s, recruiting and training the networks of agents that helped Israel defeat its Arab enemies in two wars: it was thanks to Yoram's informers that the Israeli Army was always prepared for any attacks. Sometimes Sam felt it was no exaggeration to say that the government owed its very existence to his father's work. Despite that, the Israeli government refused to negotiate for his release: even to start a conversation with the Eygptians was interpreted as a sign of weakness, and no man was worth that. It was only after the Yom Kippur War of 1973 and 1974, under the terms of a general prisoner release, that he finally walked out of the jail. By then, Yoram was a broken man. The father Sam remembered from his childhood was a smiling, joking bear of a man, but after he came home Sam wasn't sure he ever saw him smile again.

The guard pointed down the corridor. Sam walked its length. Somewhere in the distance he could hear laughing, but not from any of the cells. He sat down in the interrogation room: a small, grey cell, with a picture of Gorbachev on one wall, and with only a desk and chair for furniture. He poured himself some water from the jug on the table and took a sip. It was more than twenty-four hours since he'd eaten. He could feel his stomach churning, but whether it was the nerves or the hunger it was impossible to tell. What difference did it make, anyway?

'What language do you want to speak?' said the man as he stepped into the room.

Sam zipped his lip.

The man was tall, over six foot, with jet-black hair, a strong, thin face. Maybe thirty, judged Sam. An officer, although he couldn't tell what rank from his uniform.

240

'I repeat, what language do you want to speak?'

Sam zipped his lip again.

I have just one story. My only chance is that they decide I'm an imbecile not worth wasting their time on and throw me back on to the street. Even a jail boat in Siberia would be better than what they'll do if they find out what I'm really doing here.

'Your name?' shouted the man.

Sam just looked bewildered.

The slap was delivered across the side of his face. It stung Sam's skin, but he managed to swallow his pain. No reaction, he warned himself. Say and do nothing. Just soak up their punishment. *The way an imbecile would.*

'I'll give you one more chance,' said the man. 'Then I'll turn nasty.'

Sam looked up towards the man as if pleading. Once again, with sad despairing eyes, he zipped his lip.

Not working, he told himself. This guy doesn't care.

The man pulled out a Russian Nagant revolver. Sam recognised it at once: originally a Belgian design, it had been manufactured in Russia since 1925, and was as lethal now as when it was first minted. He pointed it towards the wall and fired once. The bullet dug out a chunk of plaster that fell noisily towards the floor. For the first time, Sam noticed the wall was marked with dozens of gunshot holes.

Maybe this is the room they use to execute the hard cases.

He looked at Sam. 'That's just so you know I'm not firing blanks,' he said.

Sam remained silent, but he could feel his heart thumping furiously.

The man then opened the chamber of the gun. He showed it to Sam, before snapping it shut. There was one bullet inside: the other six spaces in the seven-chamber revolver were empty. 'We have a version of roulette in this country that I'm sure you're familiar with,' he said slowly. He spun the chamber round, waited for it to click into place,

241

then held it to Sam's head. He could feel the cold tip of the metal squeezing into the skin just below his ear. Sweat was pouring out of him.

'Now, one last time, before I pull the trigger,' said the man. 'What language do you want to use to start telling me who the hell you are?'

Sam zipped his lips.

With hesitation, the man squeezed his finger on the trigger. Sam could hear the hammer strike the chamber. He closed his eyes, muttering a silent prayer to himself.

Nothing.

The chamber was empty.

'You're a lucky son of a bitch,' said the man. 'Let's try it again.'

He held the chamber in front of Sam. He could see the single bullet: a ten-millimetre lump of brass-coloured metal. Slowly, the man spun the chamber until it clicked, then pressed it back to Sam's head. 'Now, I'll ask you one more time. What language do you want to start talking to me in?'

Sam zipped his lip.

Click.

For a moment, Sam was certain he could hear the bullet exploding inside the barrel of the revolver. He drew a sharp breath, waiting for the bullet to smash into the side of his head.

Nothing.

Another blank.

Sam opened his eyes again, surprised to still be alive. The man shouted something, his face reddening with anger, then walked out of the room.

'Would they have used a real bullet?' Sam asked, his new friend in the cell, who he'd discovered was called Leb.

'Oh, sure,' said Leb, with a rough grin. 'It's a common interrogation technique in here. Either they kill you, or you speak. Either way they come out ahead.'

Sam thought for a moment. Time, he knew, was fast running out. He could keep his lips sealed no matter what pressure they put on him. But surely it could only be a matter of time before they figured out who he was. The KGB knew he was in Russia, and they were looking for him. Sooner or later, they would connect him with the mysterious foreigner picked up in Odessa. When that happened, he could guarantee it would be a full revolver that was put to his head.

'I have access to money,' he said. 'If somebody knows how to get me out of here I could pay them well.'

Leb shook his head. 'Save it for your widow. Your money's no good in here.'

The door opened. Sam glanced up. It was late. Their food had already been served, and this evening Sam had been allowed a hunk of the bread, although none of the soup. The guard pointed to him, and Sam climbed to his feet, walking towards him.

'Give me a message for your wife,' said Leb, speaking in a hushed tone so as not to attract the attention of the guards. 'If I can, I'll see that it gets to her.'

'Why, what's happening?' said Sam.

'This time of night, it's a bullet for you,' said Leb, his expression grim. 'They always do the shootings at midnight, when the executioner is tooled up on vodka.'

Sam could feel a knot starting to form at the pit of his stomach: the same ugly mixture of fear and aggression he'd felt the first time he'd gone into battle. 'Then tell her I love her,' he said quickly. 'And tell her to find the better man she deserves.'

The guard stood at his side, as they walked down the corridor, with no expression on his face. In the silence, Sam thought furiously of some story that might buy himself out of the bullet he now felt certain was waiting for him. But no matter how many times he dived into the issue, he kept coming up blank. *There was only the truth, and that was no use to him now.*

'There's someone to see you,' said the guard, the same man who had interrogated him earlier that day. 'Called Markku Dalborg. He says he's a relative of yours. He's come to get you out.'

Sam stopped in his tracks. He looked straight ahead. A rough-looking man, with short blond hair and a scar on his left cheek was standing in the doorway. 'Get your kit,' he said in broken, hesitant English. 'There's not much time to lose.'

TWENTY-ONE

The waves were beating against the shore. A simple fishing boat was pulled up against the pebbled beach, its captain sitting on deck, with a cigarette hanging out of his mouth. The smell of salt filled the air, and in the clear night air, a half-moon was sending ripples of silver light shimmering out across the water.

'Here,' said Dalborg. 'This will get you out of here.'

From the jail, they had driven straight down to the coast: from the ten minutes they had spent in the car, Sam figured they were ten miles or so along the coastline running east from Odessa towards Yalta. His mind had been burning with questions, but when he asked Dalborg who he was and why he'd come to get him, he'd refused to answer. 'You're a free man,' he said simply. 'You can come with me, or stay in there. Your decision.'

Dalborg spoke in English, but Sam could tell that wasn't his native language. He could have been Finnish, or Swedish maybe: he had the blond hair, taut skin and clear blue eyes like little rocks of ice of a Scandinavian. His manner was brusque and businesslike: a man who was doing his job, and just wanted to get it over with as quickly as possible.

Now he was standing in front of the boat, Sam was aware he had a tough choice to make. The boat was certainly capable of making the overnight run across the Black Sea and into Turkish territory. And if Dalborg had good enough connections to get him out of that cell, he would certainly

245

know how to evade the Soviet coast guards that patrolled these waters.

'I'm not going,' said Sam.

A strong south-westerly wind was blowing in off the sea. Sam could feel the night air creasing up the skin on his face, and he knew that at least part of him wanted to climb on to that boat and sail to freedom. Yet another part, just as strong, was playing a different argument. Don't go back a failure. Don't just be another burnt-out, embittered agent, eking out a life on old war stories. *You are too close to turn back now.*

'I'm not going,' he repeated, looking straight at Dalborg. 'I came here to find a Soviet sea captain. I'm not leaving until I find him.'

'You're a bloody idiot,' snapped Dalborg. 'Now, get in the boat.'

Sam shook his head. 'I can't.'

'Listen, this is the one chance you'll get. It cost me a fortune to bribe your way out of that jail. I can't do it again. So you get into this fucking boat, or you take your own chances.'

Sam nodded. He heard what Dalborg was saying, and it spoke directly to the part of him that wanted to escape. 'Like I said, I can't.'

From inside his jacket, Dalborg pulled out a pistol: a small SPP-1, first developed by Russian Navy special forces, and one of the few handguns in the world you could use underwater, although it had to be loaded with particular ammunition. He pointed it at Sam. 'Now get in the damned boat,' he snapped.

A thin smile started to spread across Sam's lips. 'If you wanted me dead, you'd just have left me in that jail. They'd have done the job for you soon enough.' He turned round and started walking back towards the road. 'Now, I'm going to find Ryazanov. You can come with me. Or you can get in that boat. That's *your* decision.'

He was aware as he moved that he was breaking one of the most basic rules of his training. Never turn your back on a loaded gun. Dalborg wasn't going to shoot him. He wanted him alive. Why, Sam couldn't yet say. But of that one fact he could be certain.

'Have it your way,' said Dalborg. 'It's your bloody life.' He was walking beside him now, steering him towards the car.

'So who are you, and who are you working for?' said Sam.

'You're an ungrateful bugger, aren't you?' snapped Dalborg.

Sam shrugged. 'I'm not looking to graduate from charm school. Now, who the hell are you?'

'I'm just here to help you.'

'You don't want to tell me who you are, then I work alone.'

'I can help you find the captain.'

Sam switched direction, walking towards the car. 'Then let's go and get him.'

A roadblock was slung across the main coastal road leading into Odessa, manned by some ugly-looking soldiers, but Dalborg seemed to know a back road that took them into the docks without being stopped.

They were sitting in a Zaporozhet, a small Ukrainian car. It was, without question, the most uncomfortable vehicle Sam had ever been in: the seats were made from wood, with just a thin layer of cloth over them, and the engine coughed and spluttered as it struggled to climb over sixty kilometres an hour. Still, it would get them about. And, out here, a Zaporozhet didn't draw any attention to itself.

He was still trying to figure out who Dalborg might be. Perhaps he worked for Mossad. If they knew he was in a jail in Odessa, they wouldn't want him falling into the hands of the KGB. *There are too many secrets I might reveal. Or* maybe he worked with Papa: Le Groupe ran a huge smuggling operation within the Soviet Union, bringing in goods for the black market in exchange for gold, diamonds and weapons. He could work for MI6: they certainly had the best network of spies within the Soviet Union. Then, with a chill running down his spine, another thought flashed through Sam's mind. *Maybe he works for Robertson.*

Who knows, thought Sam. I'll take his help as long as it's useful. I'll keep as close a watch on him as I can. And as soon as I've found Ryazanov, I'll cut loose.

'Wait here,' said Dalborg. They had pulled up outside one of the bars in the docks. It was already close to midnight but, from the sound of the place, the bar seemed to be full. Sam pulled his jacket up around his neck. About a hundred yards ahead, he could see a policeman patrolling the street with a dog. He looked around the car, wondering if Dalborg might have left a gun behind. Nothing. *He doesn't trust me that much.*

'I've got something,' said Dalborg, climbing back into the car. 'One of the sailors in there used to sail with Ryazanov. He lives about ten miles outside town, two miles back from the coast.'

'Good work,' said Sam.

'It helps if you speak Ukrainian.'

The drive took twenty minutes. Dalborg stuck to the side roads, then headed along a dirt track to take them out of town. As he looked back down on the city, Sam could see a couple more roadblocks, but they managed to evade them. Within a few minutes, they were clear of Odessa, driving through hilly, dark countryside. The Zaporozhet bounced across the track, its suspension straining. In the distance, Sam could see a row of houses. There were five of them, in a small strip, with a long stretch of lawn in front. Each had maybe three, four rooms. A terrace of fishing cottages, thought Sam, looking at the way they overlooked a curve in the seafront. Down below, there was a jetty and a few simple-looking boats moored alongside.

'Here,' said Dalborg, pulling up the car. 'The second one from the left. That's where he lives.'

Sam climbed out of the car. With Dalborg at his side, they knocked on the door. Nothing. Sam knocked again, then threw a couple of pebbles against the window. A light flicked on. They waited. Sam could hear the sound of chains and locks being unbolted. The door swung open. In front of him, Sam could see a bear of a man: 250 pounds, with thick, heavy features, and muscles that bulged out of his dressing robe. 'My name is Sam Wolfman,' he said, looking straight at the man. 'I need to talk to you.'

Ryazanov muttered something in Ukrainian.

'I can make it worth your while,' said Sam, stepping cautiously into the hallway. 'I have access to money.'

For a moment he was certain Ryazanov was about to strike him. His muscles seemed to be flexing, and there was a look of murderous anger in his eye. 'Money,' repeated Sam. 'I can help you with money.'

The expression in Ryazanov's eyes slowly began to soften. 'A drink,' he said eventually, in thickly accented English. 'Why don't you come in for a drink?'

Sam was led to the main room of the house. There was just one light in the corner casting a few dim shadows across the shabby room. One sofa, one chair and a small table were the only furniture. There was no TV, but an old seventies-style music centre was encased in a fake wooden cabinet. Next to it was a stack of American jazz records that Ryazanov must have collected on his travels. He poured a shot of vodka into three glasses and handed one to Sam, another to Dalborg.

'What do you want to know?' he said.

Sam took a sip of the vodka. It tasted like wallpaper paste: a thick sludgy mixture that seemed to stick to his throat as he swallowed. It was the first drink he'd had in a couple of days, and he could feel the alcohol starting to kick into his veins. 'Between 1988 and 1989 you were running boats out of Odessa. A sensitive cargo.' Sam paused, wondering how quickly he could push the man. 'I want to know what it was.'

'All my cargoes were sensitive,' said Ryazanov angrily. He drained his vodka in one gulp and re-filled the tumbler. 'I was the best captain in Odessa. Still would be, if they would let me have a fucking boat.'

'They took your boat?' asked Sam. 'Why?'

'Why do they do anything,' snarled Ryazanov. 'Some bloody pen pusher in Moscow decides he doesn't like your face any more, and that's it. Suddenly you're nothing again.'

'Maybe it was something to do with the cargo?' pressed Sam. 'Maybe it was too sensitive?'

'Maybe,' said Ryazanov, with a heavy shrug of his shoulders. He finished the vodka and filled the tumbler again. 'It hardly matters any more.'

Like most alcoholics, Sam noted, he switched between the morose and the angry, with few emotions in between. 'You met a man called Max Robertson,' he said. 'In Moscow. In 1988. You did some work for him?'

Ryazanov shook his head. 'I never heard of the man.'

Sam reached into his kitbag and took out his wallet. He found a picture of Robertson and shoved it in front of Ryazanov. 'This man,' he said. 'Are you telling me you've never heard of him?'

Ryazanov held the picture in his hand. 'Ah, Mr Klein,' he said slowly. 'A great man. A very great man. How is he?'

Klein, thought Sam. That had been Robertson's name when he was born. Maybe he used that when he was dealing in the East. 'He's dead – or so they say,' said Sam. 'You didn't know?'

'Dead?' muttered Ryazanov morosely. For a few seconds Sam thought the old sea captain looked genuinely sad. He took a swig on his drink, and seemed to be swilling the alcohol around his mouth contemplatively. Then his expression changed. At sea you don't get to mourn a man for long, reflected Sam.

'How should I know he's dead?' said Ryazanov, pouring himself another drink. 'But I'll tell you this. He was a great man. I miss him.'

'What did you do for him?'

Ryazanov sat back on the sofa. 'What do I look like? A gardener? A musician?' He laughed. 'I'm a bloody sailor. I sailed a boat for him.'

'To where?' pressed Sam. 'And what were you carrying?'

A look of anger flashed across Ryazanov's face. His eyes were bulging, and his blotchy, swollen skin was turning red. 'Why the hell should I talk to you?'

Sam thought for a moment. 'There must be something I can get you?' he said. 'Something you want?'

'A boat,' replied Ryazanov sourly. 'I'm a sailor. I need a boat underneath me the way other men need a woman.' He waved his vodka bottle in the air. 'Get me a boat, then maybe I'll talk to you.'

Sam got up and moved closer to where Ryazanov was now sprawled across the sofa. 'I don't have a boat,' he said. 'But I could get you some money. Enough money to buy any brig in Odessa.'

'Let's see your cash,' said Ryazanov.

Sam hesitated. He'd had a few French francs left in his stash when he was arrested, but inevitably it was gone by the time he was released from the jail. He glanced at Dalborg. Unpeeling a wad of notes from his pocket, Dalborg counted out five hundred-dollar bills and put them down on the table in front of Ryazanov. 'Now talk,' he said softly.

Ryazanov picked up the money, caressing it between two

huge sweaty palms. 'I can't remember the question,' he said with a sly grin.

'The boat,' said Sam. 'Where did it go?'

As he spoke, he was aware of Dalborg listening intently to the conversation. *Whoever he is working for, he's going to report this back. So I better not say anything to Ryazanov that reveals how much I know. It can only be me who holds all the pieces of the jigsaw. Nobody else.*

'Israel,' said Ryazanov. 'The stuff arrived in trucks. We loaded it on to the boat. Then we took it out into the Black Sea, and across the Mediterranean to Israel. Four days there, and four days back again.'

Sam thought for a moment. *You worked for days, risked your life, and then the breakthrough came almost casually, the information tossed out as if it didn't really matter. But it did matter, of course.* Line by line, the story was starting to come together. Israel. Max Robertson was shipping stuff out of the Soviet Union and taking it to Israel.

'Which port?'

'I've told you what I know.'

'What were you carrying?'

Ryazanov shrugged. 'I don't know.'

Sam took a step forward, swiping the vodka bottle out of the man's hand. He was rapidly descending into drunkenness. 'A captain always knows what's on his boat.'

Ryazanov stared back up at him angrily. 'I can't tell you. None of the men were allowed to open any of the cases. We were told that if we did so we would die instantly.'

A single thought flashed through Sam's mind. Uranium. They were shipping uranium to Israel. Or maybe some other kind of nuclear material. *That would kill them.*

Dalborg was looking anxiously through the window. 'We have to go,' he said. 'I can hear a siren.'

'We still need information,' said Sam menacingly. 'He knows more than he's telling us.'

Dalborg grabbed him by the sleeve, tugging him towards the door. 'Get out of here, you idiot,' he snapped. 'If the police find you, you're dead.'

Sam looked once more towards Ryazanov. 'I paid you good money for information. Now tell me what was in those crates.'

Ryazanov stood up, grabbed the vodka bottle from Sam's hand and took a swig. 'In a few minutes, the police will be here. Then I'll just have your corpse to worry about.'

'Let's go,' shouted Dalborg. 'I'm not waiting here to be arrested.'

In the distance, Sam could hear the sirens himself: two loud peels of noise breaking out over the empty, dark countryside. He nodded towards Dalborg, and the two men slipped away. Dalborg slammed the door on the Zaporozhet, and gunned up the engine. The tiny car rattled into life. Dalborg pulled away from the road, and headed along the track. Glancing behind him, Sam could see the police cars heading towards the row of houses. Dalborg kept off the main road, and started driving down towards the coast. Sam could hear the sound of the sea looming up before them. 'We need to get out of the country,' said Dalborg, pulling up the car at the edge of the beach. 'It's not safe for us here. In the Soviet Union, you can't hide. They'll always find you.'

Sam climbed out of the car. Dalborg followed suit. The waves were lapping up at the shore. There was a small jetty leading out to the sea, with two small rowing boats tied up to it. It was now past two in the morning: the dead of the night, and, apart from the rustle of the wind, he couldn't hear a sound anywhere.

'Now,' said Sam, looking directly at Dalborg. 'Tell me who sent you? Was it Papa?'

'Who?' said Dalborg.

'Papa,' repeated Sam, pronouncing the word as two distinct syllables. 'The leader of Le Groupe in France.'

'Never heard of him,' said Dalborg, starting to walk towards the jetty.

'Why did Papa send you?' said Sam.

Dalborg carried on walking. 'If we take one of these boats, we can get back to that fishing vessel that was going to take us across to Turkey. It's our only chance. So stop wasting bloody time.'

Sam followed him out on to the jetty. He gripped the back of Dalborg's leather jacket and tugged hard. Dalborg spun round, and Sam could see the anger in the man's face: his eyes were filled with the cold venom of a snake about to bite. Sam gripped hard, squeezing his fists into the jacket. 'Why did Papa send you?' he shouted, his voice carrying out across the empty sea. 'What does he bloody want?'

Dalborg paused. 'You can come with me right now, or you can stay here and get shot by the Russians. Your choice . . .'

Sam pushed Dalborg forward so that he was leaning over the edge of the jetty. He could feel the strength in the man, but so far he wasn't resisting, just playing Sam along, seeing how far he wanted to push the fight. The sea was howling beneath them, a few specks of water spitting up on to both men. 'Tell me,' said Sam, his voice louder and more insistent.

'I don't know what you're talking about,' said Dalborg calmly. 'I'm getting the hell out of here.'

Sam could tell it was useless. Dalborg was a strong man. There was liquid steel running through his veins. Only torture would squeeze the information out of him, and maybe not even that. The chances were he didn't even know why he'd been sent here. None of Papa's men ever questioned what they were doing or why: they worked; they got paid; end of story. He loosened his grip, and Dalborg straightened up before climbing down into the small boat. 'You coming?' he snapped.

'I won't go with a man I can't trust,' said Sam. 'And I can't trust a man who won't tell me who he's working for.'

Dalborg untied the moorings, freeing the boat from the side of the jetty. 'Then you'll be dead by the morning.'

'So everyone keeps telling me,' said Sam as he walked back inland. 'And one day, I suppose they'll be right.'

He had walked for fifty yards, heading straight into the darkness. The field rose steeply up from the coastline, and in the moonlight, he could just see far enough forwards to stay out of the ditches. Then, behind him, he heard a sound. He looked back. Dalborg was still untying the fishing boat. A hundred yards away a man was walking straight towards him, advancing along the side of the jetty, but Dalborg hadn't seen him yet. The man was quiet, and the sound of the wind and the waves crashing in from the ocean was drowning out his approach.

Sam lay down close to the ground and watched. He could warn Dalborg, but only by revealing his own position. A cloud parted, and the bay was suddenly bathed in moonlight, allowing Sam to get a good look at the man. He was just under six foot, with close-cropped brown hair. He was wearing jeans and a black leather jacket, and from the bulge Sam could tell he was armed. He had delicate skin, and a boyish, innocent smile was playing on his lips. In an instant, Sam felt certain he knew who he was. Kersch.

He was standing still at the edge of the jetty now, just a couple of yards behind Dalborg. 'Wolfman,' he shouted.

The cry pierced the quiet of the night sky like a spear, and the wind carried it up the hillside so that it sounded to Sam as if the man was shouting right in his ear. He hunkered down closely into the field.

Dalborg looked round, his expression startled. In the same instant, Kersch pulled his gun from inside his jacket, levelled it and fired. He was quick, noted Sam. Under a second to draw and fire. And accurate. The bullet sliced through the centre of Dalborg's forehead, killing him instantly. With a quick stride, Kersch walked up to him, and fired two more bullets straight into the man's head.

Sam stayed where he was. They don't have a picture of me, he thought to himself. They didn't take one in the jail. Still, it doesn't matter. Sooner or later, that bastard is going to realise he's shot the wrong guy. And I don't want to stick around long enough for him to find the real Sam Wolfman.

TWENTY-TWO

The sound of the seagulls woke Sam. A flock of the birds had drifted in a few yards from the coast, and was circling around the tree under which Sam had rested for the night. He rubbed his eyes, and looked up towards the sun. From its position hanging just over the cusp of the horizon he reckoned it was seven, maybe seven fifteen in the morning. *Time to move on.*

As he stood up, he pulled the collar of his coat up high around his neck. Should have stocked up on supplies somewhere, he told himself. Some biscuits, some tinned meat, or just some water. Anything to help me get through the next few days.

He'd caught a few hours' badly needed sleep, and that had helped revive him. Of all the lessons the army had taught him, the ability to catch some rest just about anywhere was possibly the most valuable. After waiting quietly until Kersch had left the jetty, he'd walked for twenty minutes, tacking inland, until he found the tree. Curling himself up next to its roots, he'd sheltered himself from the wind, thrown his coat on top of him, and slept through until dawn.

Unfinished business, he thought as he paced steadily forward. Ryazanov knows more than he told me. *I just have to squeeze the information out of him.*

He could see the house about two miles ahead of him. He'd keep off the tracks and head across country. Just one more push. Ryazanov has the answer to this mystery somewhere, even if he doesn't know it.

He stopped next to the small row of houses. From the front door it was impossible to tell whether Ryazanov was at home: there was no car, but like many ordinary citizens in the Soviet Union he probably didn't have one. Sam walked round to the row of separate back gardens. He hopped over the two-foot wall and rapped on the back door. No answering sound. He tried again . . . nothing. Peering through the window, he could see a small, grimy kitchen. A cooker, a sink and a few unwashed pans on the draining board. A tabby cat was sleeping in the corner. Picking a rock from the ground, Sam wrapped his coat around his fist, then punched a hole straight through the window. With one swift movement, it was unbolted. He was inside.

The cat was looking up at him, half angry, half afraid. It was squealing, and scratching the floor. The kitchen smelt of cooking oil and dried fish. Sam glanced around. No sign of life. He listened hard. The sound of the breaking glass should have woken anyone. Except maybe a man who'd drunk a bottle of vodka the night before.

Sam picked up a carving knife from the draining board. It measured eight inches, and although the blade didn't look to have been sharpened, it would still spill a man's guts on to the floor if necessary. Gripping the knife in his hand, he stepped into the corridor. Still no sign of Ryazanov. Maybe the police took him last night. *Maybe just talking to me is enough to get a man arrested.*

The hallway showed some signs of a struggle. A couple of pictures on the walls, both of ships, had been knocked out of position, and the rug has been scuffed up. The police dragging a man out of here could have caused that, thought Sam. So could a drunk. He walked into the sitting room. A heavy smell of vodka filled the room: the alcohol had seeped into the furniture and the walls. You could get drunk just smelling the air.

Moving quickly, Sam stepped out of the sitting room and started climbing the stairs. As he turned the corner, he gripped the kitchen knife tightly in his hand. Ryazanov was a big man, but if he took him by surprise, he should be able to deal with him. Standing outside the one bedroom, he listened for the sound of snoring. Nothing. Looking inside, Sam understood why not. Ryazanov was lying face down on the bed, but he wasn't moving. There was no sign of any breath coming from his lips. You don't need to check his pulse to know what's happened, thought Sam.

Ryazanov is dead.

Someone killed him.

Why? Because maybe he did know what happened to Robertson.

A heavy smell of sweat and dirty socks filled the room. There was one cupboard along the back wall, and Sam pulled open its doors and started to rummage around the drawers and shelves inside. He had a clear idea of what he was looking for. Sailors were a sentimental breed of men. They loved to keep souvenirs of all the places they visited. If Ryazanov had been making regular runs from Odessa to Israel for a year or more, the chances were he would have kept some record of that. *I just have to find it.*

Sam pulled open the drawers, one after another. He rummaged his way through logbooks, old bills and old identity papers. He found a couple of albums and started leafing through them. From the look of the pictures, they were at least a decade old. They all showed a far younger, clean-shaven Ryazanov, when he was still an officer in the Soviet Navy: like most Russian sailors, he'd only switched to commercial shipping after a long spell in the forces. He put the albums back. Nothing.

Sam tossed aside the bedclothes, but again found nothing.

On the table next to the bed, there was a bottle of vodka – three-quarters drunk – an empty packet of cigarettes and a bulging ashtray, and a framed photograph. Sam picked it up, examining the picture closely. It showed Ryazanov and, from the look of him, it was clearly a recent picture. Next to him, with her arm around his back, was a woman. With black hair and dark brown eyes, she looked in her late thirties; attractive but with looks that were fading fast, even when this picture was taken. Sam looked beyond the two people, studying the background. They were standing on what was clearly a dockside. I've been there, thought Sam. He could make out the curve of the bay, and the arrangement of the piers that jutted into the sea. Ashdod Port, one of Israel's biggest freight terminals. He looked again at the picture. There was a curve to the woman's belly: an unmistakable shape that any father would recognise immediately. *She was pregnant when this picture was taken.*

Sam tapped the glass covering the picture with his knife, breaking it with one clean movement. He tucked the picture into his pocket. It was clear to him now. Ryazanov had been shipping something out of Russia and across to Israel. This woman had been his girlfriend when he was in port, and they had had a baby together. *She might know what he was shipping and where it was taken.*

I need to talk to her next, thought Sam, as he slipped back downstairs, and checked that the back of the house was clear. Women break easier than men. Not because they don't have the strength, but because they don't attach the same importance to secrets. *They break because they realise that ultimately life is more valuable than honour.*

A light drizzle was falling over the docks. Thick clouds were hanging low in the sky, and the waves were splashing up against the side of the docks. Sam crept steadily forward. He switched from container to crate, making sure that he slipped through the shadows of the cargo dock. *If anyone sees me now, I'm a dead man.*

From Ryazanov's house, Sam had trudged the ten miles back into Odessa on foot, going across country to sidestep the roadblocks that now seemed to be ringing the city. Before he left, he took a sleeping bag from the bedroom and as much food as he could stack into his kitbag from the kitchen. Ryazanov had a sailor's habit of stocking up on non-perishable foods: even though he'd lost his command, he still had plenty of thick, nourishing biscuits, bars of high-energy chocolate, and tins of beef, ham and fish. Sam arranged them all neatly in his bag and filled three plastic bottles with water. This would keep him alive over the rough few days ahead. Right now, that's all I care about.

As he approached the city, he slipped through gardens and vaulted his way across apartment blocks, to make sure he stayed as far away from the roads as possible. Stay out of sight, he told himself. You are just one man in a city of 300,000 people. *That makes you hard to find.*

Sam looked up from the container behind which he was hiding. He could see four ships being loaded. Two were clearly Russian, so they were to be avoided. Of the other two, one was flying Greek and the other Panamanian colours. Both were almost certainly flags of convenience. On instinct, he chose the Panamanian ship: the smaller of the two boats, it looked designed for a mixed, jobbing cargo, and hopefully would stop in Turkey, or Lebanon, or Greece, before completing its trip. Huge winches were swivelling across the docks, dropping the teeth of their cranes down to pick up the solid steel containers and the pallets of wooden boxes and lifting them up on to the ship. Sam chose his destination with care. About twenty yards ahead of him, he could see a group of boxes, stacked ten high and five wide on a pallet. Sam slipped across the concrete and climbed between the boxes. It was a tight fit, but he could just about squeeze in. Next, he levered free two thin planks of the balsa wood from which the boxes were constructed. Both came away easily enough, revealing the sacks of grain stacked inside. He pulled them across himself. To the casual eye, he would just blend into the expanse of balsa wood.

It was a wait of just an hour or so. He heard the crane approaching, and then, although he could not see it, he could hear the grinding of gears and metal as it lowered itself towards the pallet where he was hiding. Some men were shouting in Ukrainian, others in Turkish, steering it down. Then he heard the thump of metal clamping itself on to wood. The pallet shook violently as it was yanked suddenly into the air. Sam lay absolutely still. He could feel the wind gusting in off the sea, blowing through him. The pallet was swaying as the wind caught its sides. Up above him, he could hear the metal stretching and straining as it hoisted him higher and higher into the sky above the dockside.

Next he could feel himself moving sideways, then suddenly silence. Sam held his breath. All about him, the dock seemed to have fallen quiet. Have they spotted something suspicious? he wondered. Are they about to search the crates? He could feel a strong instinct to lift himself upwards, to steal a glance at what was happening. He fought it back, remaining absolutely still. Calm, he reminded himself. *There is no sharper weapon.*

The sound of the crane started up again. Sam could feel the pallet swaying and moving beneath him, followed by a sinking feeling in his stomach as it started its descent. It felt as if the very ground was disappearing beneath him. Next, he was plunged into darkness as he disappeared inside the cargo hold of the ship. He landed with a brutal suddenness that sent vibrations running up deep into his spine, and seemed to shake every bone in his body. Around him, he could hear shouting and swearing as two men unclamped the crane from the pallet.

Home, thought Sam as he listened to the darkness. *For the next few days at least.*

Spring was gathering pace, Sam noted, as he walked the length of the driveway that led up to Papa's chateau. The daffodils were in full bloom now, and he could see that the apple trees in the orchard just beyond the ornamental lake were already in blossom. There was a crisp, fresh smell to the air. After the past few days, Sam was filled with the sense of a man so surprised to find himself alive, he could take childish pleasure in even the most ordinary things.

'I'm here to see Papa,' he said to Jacques as he opened the door. Papa's elder son looked at him sourly.

Sam took his seat in the hallway. He had spent three days hiding on the boat, before it finally docked. Once it was harboured, he waited two hours, then slowly crawled out of the hold and made his way ashore. He was in Samsun, a port on Turkey's Black Sea coast. He had no money, and only a vague idea of where he was. That didn't matter. He was alive. He was free. And he knew what he had to do next.

Once onshore, he stole a credit card and passport from a drunken Belgian tourist. All Mossad agents were trained in basic card fraud. Using this he managed to get a cash advance from a local bank charged to the Visa card. He had two thousand dollars in Turkish lira. Better spend it quick, he told himself as he folded the notes into his pocket. Before it collapses in value any further.

From Samsun, he took a bus to Istanbul, then booked himself on a flight to Brussels. He had planned to go to France, but with a Belgian passport reckoned it was better to fly into Brussels than Paris: customs officers always looked a lot less closely at their own citizens than they did foreigners, and there were few border controls between Belgium and France. From there, he took a train across to Lille. Next, a pair of buses had taken him down to Orleans. He'd phoned

Papa from there. This time, there seemed to be no trouble getting an appointment to see the old man. No surprise, thought Sam. He's been playing me all along. For what ends? That's what I need to find out.

He knew it would be impossible to get back into Israel without Papa's help. If there was anyone else he could turn to for help he would, but there was no one. Mossad would be on full alert by now. The border guards would be looking for him. Every policeman would have his picture.

The nurse appeared as if from nowhere. The same severe woman, dressed entirely in black. 'Papa will see you now,' she said coldly. 'Remember, try not to excite him. His cold has cleared up with the warmer weather, but he is still very frail.'

'The old man is probably fitter than any of us,' growled Sam.

He walked through to the library. During the three days he'd spent by himself in the cargo hold of the boat, he had plenty of time to think. So much information had been collected during his time in Russia, it would take time to make sense of it all. That he was close to unravelling the mystery of Robertson's death he had no doubt. But why had Dalborg taken him out of jail in Odessa, then led him to Ryazanov? Who was paying him? Was it Papa? Or was it Robertson himself?

The old man was sitting by the window when Sam stepped into the room. There was a plate of goat's cheese and sausage in front of him, along with half a baguette and a jug of water. Pierre was sitting in his usual corner, but had no food in front of him. Both men looked up at him. A thin smile started to flicker across Papa's frail face.

'Why did you break me out of jail in Odessa?'

Sam sat down on a sofa as he delivered the question. He could see Papa reaching across for a piece of sausage, slicing it carefully with a steel knife and laying it flat on a small piece of bread. Through the window, Sam could see the gardener pushing a wheelbarrow overflowing with cuttings.

'Eat,' said Papa, offering Sam a slice of sausage.

Sam shook his head. 'Why did you break me out of Odessa?'

'You look thin,' said Papa. 'Pale.'

'I was in a bloody jail,' snapped Sam.

'I know,' said Papa.

'You broke me out. Why?'

'I look after my friends,' said Papa.

'So you don't deny it.'

Papa started to chew on the bread and sausage. 'At my age, you don't bother with denials. People believe what they choose to believe. You can rarely change their minds.'

'I'm tired of hearing about your age,' said Sam. 'It's no excuse for not answering a direct question.'

'Like I said, I look after my friends.'

'Who says I'm a friend.'

'Now now, Sam, don't be churlish.' He pushed out a slice of cheese and some bread. 'Here, have something to eat.'

Sam ignored the offer. Talking with the old man was like catching fish with your bare hands. 'I haven't asked for your help,' said Sam.

'But we have so much in common, Sam.'

'Like what?'

'Staying alive and making money,' said Papa. 'Simple enough to describe, but not always so easy to achieve.'

'I've done OK by myself so far.'

'Only because people have been helping you.'

'You?'

Papa pointed to a picture on the desk. It showed a thin man, with cropped brown hair and a boyish face. 'Have you seen this man?'

Sam took the picture, studying it for a few seconds. 'Oleksander Kersch.'

'You have seen him then?'

'He shot Dalborg, but he was looking for me,' said Sam. 'The KGB's top assassin. He's been sent to kill me.'

'Quite right,' said Papa. 'That should make you nervous.'

Sam shrugged. 'I've spent enough time in that trade to know the tricks.'

Papa waved a finger. 'So surely you should know how vulnerable you are. You've killed a few men yourself who also thought they knew the tricks. But they didn't know the one that killed them.'

'Are you about to sell me out to Kersch? said Sam, standing up and walking over to the tall window that overlooked the garden.'

'What are you looking for, Sam?'

'An answer.'

'To what?'

'I need to know what happened to Max Robertson.'

'He's dead.'

'Maybe, maybe not.'

'You think he's still alive?' said Papa archly.

Sam scrutinised his face, trying to judge whether there was any sign that Papa was concealing anything from him: if Robertson was still alive Papa might well know about it; who knows, they could even be working together? After all, Sam thought, the two men had much in common. They had both risen from nothing to control vast empires of inform-ation. They both loved secrecy, and riddles. They were bullies, intolerant of the opinions of others. The fact that one operated underground and the other in the open made no difference. They were like two sides of the same coin. *Maybe Papa is hiding Robertson?*

'It's one theory,' said Sam. 'All I know is there's a lot of money at stake if I can find out what happened to him.'

'Some things are more important than money.'

'Like what?'

Papa nodded. 'You'll see when you get there.'

Sam turned round to look at him. The old man's face was as inscrutable as ever: like an unfinished sculpture, you could see the lines and contours of the face, but as yet there was no emotion chiselled on to the rock. 'You know what he was doing?'

Papa's eyes were suddenly as bright as a child's. 'What have you found out?'

'Plenty,' said Sam sharply. 'But right now it's rumour, conjecture, theories. I haven't nailed it down. If I can stay alive, I might be able to do that. Maybe I need help.'

'Like I said, Sam, Le Groupe is always willing to offer help to its friends.'

Sam walked over to Papa, and he could see Pierre looking suddenly alert. We're about to reach an agreement, Sam realised. Pierre is memorising every word that is transacted between us: and I can be sure the contract will be enforced as ruthlessly as if it had been drawn up by the most overpaid lawyers in the world.

'There is a bounty of five million in sterling on this secret,' said Sam. 'If Le Groupe was willing to help me, then we could share the money.'

Papa smiled, cutting himself a slice of the cheese. 'I've spent most of my life thinking about how to make money. But from you, Sam?' He paused, as if thinking through the thought. 'When you were working for Mossad I was happy to take your money. But from you personally, it doesn't matter. All I want is for you to tell me what you know, as soon as you know it. The way a son would speak to his father . . .'

'You don't want any of the money?' said Sam. 'You don't even know what the information might be worth.'

Papa took a bite of his own cheese, and pushed a slice across to Sam. 'Let me be the judge of that,' he said. 'With respect, I have spent my life as an evaluator of information and its worth. You're investigating the greatest secret of the age. We deal in secrets. If you know half of what I suspect you know, then that would be of great interest to Le Groupe.'

Sam took the slice of cheese he was being offered and chewed on it. 'I need to go back to Israel,' he said. 'I need getting back in and out again. I'll need some money as well. Selima Robertson is paying me, but right now it's too dangerous for me to get in touch with her.' He paused. 'And a fresh identity.'

Papa raised a single hand. 'It will be arranged.' He leaned forward. 'Keep pushing, Sam. You're going in the right direction. I feel certain of it.'

'And I need to make sure that Elena is OK as well,' pressed Sam. He'd been worrying about her every day, and yet he also had enough discipline to know that he couldn't contact her: to do so would just place her and the children in greater danger. 'Could someone check on her and the kids?'

Again Papa nodded. He nodded towards Pierre, indicating that he was to memorise the instruction, and make sure it was acted upon.

'And Selima Robertson,' continued Sam. 'I'm also concerned for her. She could be at risk.'

Papa laughed. Sam was used to his sly smile, but in the time he'd known him had almost never heard him laugh. It was a thin sound, laced with malice more than humour. 'I think the Robertson family is more than able to look after itself,' he said sharply. 'They always have been.'

TWENTY-THREE

The darkness across the ocean was so thick and dense that Sam could feel it closing around him like a fist. He steered the tiny boat forwards, adjusting the diesel-fuelled outboard engine, looking down at the electronic compass he had strapped on to his arm to get a fix on his position. Just another twenty minutes at most. *Then I will be back in Israel.*

Clouds had rolled across the sky, obscuring both the moon and the stars. Sam could smell rain in the air, although for the moment it was dry. He pulled his cap down around his ears to protect himself from the wind blowing in from the west, and concentrated on his map. Keep heading south-east. Land is close enough.

Papa had equipped him with a new identity – he was travelling as an Austrian businessman call Max Venslden. From Orleans, he'd driven straight down to the south French coast and then taken a boat across the Mediterranean to Algeria. From there, he'd taken a local plane to Cairo, and from the Egyptian coast, Papa had arranged this boat to sail him into Israel. It was the only safe way to travel into the country. It was impossible to fly straight into Israel, or to come in by any conventional land route. From his last visit, he had to assume Mossad were looking for him, and if they knew he had returned, it wouldn't be long before there was a bullet lodged into his back. Travelling in under a false passport was no good either. Israel had the strictest border police in the world: it needed them. They knew how to spot phoney passports. So, the only safe route into the country was by boat: even the Israelis couldn't keep total control of a coastline that stretched for more than a hundred miles.

Sam listened to the wind, keeping his ears tuned for the sound of another vessel. He'd set out from Egypt two hours earlier, steering out into the Mediterranean to avoid the local coastguards, then steering back inland towards Israel. For the trip, he'd equipped himself with an Italian-made Beretta 900 handgun. He planned to make a landing near Ashqelon, about twenty miles down from Ashdod Port and a few miles up from the Gaza Strip. It was empty, desolate country: a place where a man could make a landing in the dead of night with little chance of being detected.

A noise. It was as if the boat had struck something. A rock, maybe, thought Sam. No, impossible. He was too far out to sea. A fish, perhaps. No, again. Only a shark or a dolphin could make that impact on a boat this size, and there were none of those in these waters. He killed the engine. It took a minute to stall, and for the single propeller to stop moving. The boat was drifting and a silence gradually started to descend over the boat. There was just the rustle of the wind. And the blackness.

Another noise, then a figure.

A hand.

He could see a set of fingers, encased in the black glove of a wetsuit, gripping on to the edge of the boat. Sam lunged forward, smashing his fist down. The hand withdrew, disappearing back down into the water. Sam looked wildly about. There was nothing he could see. Just the swell of the waves. And, in the distance, the first of the lights sparkling out from the shoreline.

But an enemy was out there. *Underneath the water.*

Sam took the Beretta from his pocket, gripping it tightly in his fist. Suddenly he heard an explosion. The sound of a gun being fired. He felt the bullet strike the side of the vessel, the boat swaying on impact. It rolled forward into a wave. Sam lost his balance, crashing down on to the floor of the boat. He could feel his skull hitting the stern. A slow trickle of blood started to ooze from the wound opening up on his forehead. Sam lay absolutely still, scared to even breathe. He rolled over on to his back, holding the Beretta in his hand. Let them come to me, he told himself.

Minutes ticked by. He could feel the sway of the boat as it drifted through the waves. Up above, he could make out the dark movement of the clouds as they drifted through the sky. Then the boat rocked. A man was holding on to its sides. With a whoosh of water, he rose up out of the sea like a rocket being fired from a silo. Sam steadied the gun in his hand, firing a single bullet. His aim was true. The man fell back into the water.

Sam lay still. Another movement. The boat rocked and swayed. Another figure, clad completely in a black wetsuit, rose up out of the water, clinging on to the side of the boat. Sam fired once, then again. The man fell backwards, only for the boat to shake again. Sam swivelled round, keeping his gun level, held between both fists. A third black figure was moving swiftly forwards. The man was gripping the edge of the boat, levering himself upwards. Through his face mask Sam could just see his lips, which were holding a twelve-inch steel-bladed hunting knife.

Sam fired the Beretta. Nothing. Water had crept into the firing mechanism, making it useless.

He threw the gun to the floor. The man had pulled himself clear of the water. Sam pushed himself forward, grabbing the man by the throat. He yanked hard at him, tugging him down into the boat. He was a strong, heavy fighter – at least two hundred pounds, all of it muscle. He was falling on top of Sam, using both his weight and gravity to give him the advantage. Sam took the fall, planning to use the strength in his back and his legs to kick the man back upwards. If he could stun him, then toss him back into the water, he'd be rid of the bastard. Sam steadied himself. He still had a good grip on the man's neck, but the weight was oppressive. He put all his force into his leg muscles, releasing the neck at the same time.

The knife dropped from the man's mouth, clattering to the floor of the boat. The man cried out as he took the force of Sam's blow into his stomach and chest. He flew backwards, crashing into the side. Sam scrambled to his feet. With the engine idle, the waves were rocking the boat, making it hard to get a grip. Water was starting to spill into its hold, and a vicious wind was starting to increase its force. Sam lunged for the man's throat. If he could squeeze the life out of him, he could finish him now.

But the man's punch took Sam by surprise. It had a speed and agility and force to it that he had not expected. His jaw felt as if it was fragmenting under the impact of the blow, and he could feel the nerves in his face start to numb. At least one tooth felt loose. The man had already leapt to his feet, delivering a punishing blow with his left hand. Sam stumbled. The fist, gloved in the black wetsuit, was like a rod of iron. The boat heaved over a wave, and a gust of wind wrapped itself around his stomach, tossing him left then right like a leaf caught up in a gale.

Only one organisation is trained for this kind of unarmed combat, thought Sam. *Mossad*

He felt his feet start to slip. Desperately, Sam's arms reached out, struggling to regain his balance. To slip now would, he knew, be fatal. *In any struggle, the man standing has the advantage.*

No good. The water had made the floor of the boat slippery and Sam crashed to the ground. In the next instant, the man had grabbed his knife and dropped to his knees, sitting on top of Sam's chest, pinning him down. Sam could kick his legs uselessly, but aside from that it was impossible to move. Trapped, he realised. *And dead.*

The man was pulling his knife back, holding it in his right hand with the expertise of a butcher about to slice open a side of beef. Let's just hope the bastard knows how to carve, thought Sam grimly. *And takes me out with one clean cut.*

He looked up into the night sky. The clouds were scurrying past, driven by the wind. At that moment, the moon suddenly broke through, casting its pale, silvery light out across the surface of the ocean. The man was holding the knife high above his shoulder, ready to plunge it down into Sam's heart. With the moonlight behind him, he looked down into Sam's face. And paused.

'Sam,' said the man. 'Is that Sam?'

Sam hesitated. He recognised the voice at once, but still, it was so unexpected it took a moment to make the connection. 'Michael?' he said. 'Fuck it, man, is that you?'

The knife was still in Michael's right hand. With his left hand, he ripped aside his face mask, revealing himself for the first time. 'I was about to kill you,' he muttered. 'They didn't tell us it was you.'

'Then what the fuck did they tell you?'

Sam stood up. He walked towards the back of the boat, pulling the cord on the outboard engine. It fired into life on the second attempt. Its power stabilised the boat, and Sam started to steer it towards the shoreline that was now clearly visible in the moonlight.

'They just told us what they always tell us,' said Michael. His voice sounded fractured and strained: the humour and bounce that Sam remembered from the five years they had spent working together had drained out of it. 'It's always the same. An enemy of the state, approaching Israeli waters. They give us the time and the place, and tell us to go and get him. Hell, we just assumed it was some Palestinian bastard. We didn't think it was one of our own.'

Sam was painfully conscious they were leaving two corpses behind in the rough waters: he'd killed before, and never lost any sleep over it, but these were men from his own side. That was different. *It was like killing a little bit of yourself.*

'What the hell are you doing here?' said Michael angrily.

Sam looked down into the water. Both men had disappeared: if they weren't dead already they soon would be. 'Practising my sailing.'

'Two of my team are dead.'

'They were trying to kill me.'

'Maybe it would have been better if they had.'

'Maybe,' said Sam grimly.

The boat was approaching land now: Sam could see the lights from the fishing village five hundred yards to his left, and was tacking right to make sure he gave it a wide berth. 'You've been there,' growled Michael. 'You know what it's like when a member of the team dies.'

The words stung because they were true. Sam was already ruminating on the tense debrief and the miserable visits to the mothers and widows that would follow this latest debacle. *Two more lives chucked into the grinder. It never ends.*

'What have you done that would make Mossad want to kill you?' said Michael.

'Discovered something,' said Sam.

'What?'

Sam could see the anger in Michael's eyes. They were approaching the shore now, the waves subsiding as they pulled into the cove where Sam intended to ditch the boat. 'It's about Max Robertson. He was shipping something from Russia to Israel. Boatloads of stuff, all sanctioned by both governments. I thought he might be still alive. Now, I think maybe Mossad killed him, just like you tried to kill me.'

'What was he shipping?'

'I don't know, Not yet. That's what I'm here to find out.'

Michael was looking down at the water. 'You just killed

274

one of your best witnesses,' he said. 'Mark was part of a small team trained in underwater assassinations. A four-man squad was sent out to kill Robertson on his boat, just the way they were going to kill you. The Code of Hammurabi, the iron law of retribution. Robertson had to be killed, and he had to be killed on his boat. That was the centre of his world, and the scene of his crimes as well.'

Sam paused for a moment, recovering his composure: the last few seconds were the closest to death he had ever been, and he was surprised how much the prospect had frightened him. So Robertson really was dead, he reflected. He wondered how Selima would take it. 'How was it done?' he asked.

'The team went in underwater, then climbed up on to the boat in the middle of the night. They'd observed the *Guinea* for three nights running. They knew that Robertson often wandered around on deck during the night. Couldn't sleep. As soon as they saw him, they knocked him out with gas. Then they dragged him to the water and took him down. Four men in frog suits, you can't fight that. They held him under until he had drowned, then left him to float away. To the rest of the world, it looked like suicide, or an accident.' He looked at Sam. 'Two of the men on the Robertson team were then killed in accidents.'

'Right,' said Sam bitterly. 'They want everyone who knows about it buried as well.' He looked back at Michael. 'What are you going to tell them?'

'That we made the attack, that you were heavily armed, two of us died and I lost you.'

Sam nodded. They would know he was in the country. That would make the next few days much harder.

'Thanks,' he said simply.

Michael remained silent. The bonds that had been forged between them during the years they had worked together ran too deep to be put into words. Neither man needed to express what he felt, nor would he have known how to find the words to do so.

'Hey, listen to this one,' said Michael as the boat pulled into the cove. 'This guy goes to the doctor for a check-up. After extensive tests the doctor tells him, "I'm afraid I have some bad news for you. You only have six months to live." The guy is dumbstruck. After a while he replies, "That's terrible, Doctor. But I must admit to you that I can't afford to pay your bill." "OK," says the doctor, "I'll give you a year to live."'

Sam laughed. It was good to know that Michael never changed. The jokes were as terrible as they had always been.

'What happened to the rabbi jokes?'

'I guess I finally ran out.'

Sam was looking out into the sun rising up over the Mediterranean, its bright orange beams rippling out across the water, when Imer walked along the pier to find him. The spring flowers were in bloom throughout the village, filling the air with a delicate, musty scent. Across the bay, he could see a couple of fishing boats returning with the night's catch. He looked across at one of the fishermen, as he tied his boat to the jetty. He looked weary from the night's work, his back sagging as he started to unload the heavy boxes of fish, but it struck Sam there was an honesty in his work that at this moment he could only envy. He wasn't always chasing shadows. *He never took any lives that he didn't need to.*

He put the picture down on the table: the picture of the woman he had taken from Ryazanov's house. 'Can you find her?' he asked.

'How long ago was this picture taken?' said Imer.

'Ryazanov was shipping stuff from Russia to Israel through 1988 and 1989,' said Sam. 'I reckon he met her during that time. She looks maybe seven or eight months pregnant in this picture. My guess is the baby was born in the summer of 1988. He or she would be almost two by now.'

Imer nodded, scrutinising the picture as if trying to read it for hidden clues. 'And in Ashdod?'

'So far as we know.'

'Then we check the playgroups,' said Imer. 'You want to find a young mother, then you go where the babies are.'

Sam drained his coffee, and put some money down on the table. 'Then let's get started.'

Imer looked at Sam suspiciously. 'Mossad want you,' he said.

'I know,' said Sam.

Imer nodded. Sam could tell the old man was wrestling with his loyalties: he had given his life to Mossad, and although he knew what cruelties the organisation was capable of, he would never do anything to harm it any more than he would harm his own child. 'You don't need to help me if you don't want to,' said Sam. 'I understand. I'll be fine by myself.'

Imer shook his head. He took out the keys to his ten-year-old BMW and walked towards the car, his shoulders hunched and his head bowed, oblivious to the bright sunshine now shining down on them. Like most soldiers, he was a man who had learned how to internalise his emotions. Sam knew that he would never catch more than a brief, fleeting glimpse of what he was actually thinking. By the time he'd turned the ignition in the car and pulled it out on to the road, his mood seemed to have lightened. Like most soldiers, although he might wrestle with a decision, once his mind was made up, Imer would stop agonising about his decision. *On a battlefield, there was no time for prevarication.* He was talking about his daughter in London, how she finally seemed to have met a guy, might even settle down and have some kids. 'London's not so far,' said Imer, steering the car out on to the main highway. 'I could spend a few months a year there, in the summer when it's too hot in Israel. A man needs to spend time with his grandchildren.'

It was only a twenty-minute drive towards Ashdod. They stopped first at a playground on one of the housing estates on the outskirts of the city. 'Let me handle this,' said Imer, as he climbed out of the car. 'Women are more likely to talk to an old guy like me. We're not a threat any more. They feel sorry for us.'

He spent just a few minutes chatting to the mothers grouped around the swings and roundabouts. There were four of them, watching their children, and Sam could see them smiling at Imer as he fired off a series of questions. 'No,' he said with a curt shake of the head, as he climbed back into the BMW. 'Nothing. Never seen her.'

'It's a big city,' said Sam. 'Maybe 150,000 people.'

'Cities are never very big for tiny kids,' said Imer. 'There's only a few places they go. Even in Tel Aviv there are only twenty or thirty places you'd want to take a two-year-old.'

The morning went by quickly. Playground followed playground, until Sam had seen enough climbing frames and seesaws to last him a lifetime. Imer had inexhaustible patience, however: that was what had made him such a fine tutor. He never minded how long something took, turning over stone after stone until he found what he was looking for.

'Esther,' he said, after visiting the ninth playground. 'Her name is Esther. And the kid is called Lilia.'

'Where?' said Sam.

'About a mile from here, in one of the new housing developments,' said Imer. 'They don't know the address, but they told me the block. We'll find her.'

Sam glanced through the windows as Imer steered the BMW back on to the main road. He could see a pair of policemen checking a car and he averted his eyes. He was used to being a fugitive: he'd spent the last five years under-cover, weaving a path through police forces all over Europe. But this was different. This time he was a fugitive within his own country. *There was nowhere he could call home any more.*

Imer pulled up outside a corner shop. The development was built to house the workers at the booming port. There were lawns between the twelve-storey apartment blocks, and flower beds that were neatly tended. The vehicles in the car park looked new. 'Number 23,' said Imer as he walked out of the shop. 'The girl behind the counter recognised her.'

They started climbing the stairs. It was just after four in the afternoon, and the sun was still high in the sky. Sam wiped a bead of sweat away from his forehead. He pressed the doorbell and waited. Just one more piece to the jigsaw, he told himself. And the picture will slot into place.

The woman who opened the door looked tired. She was wearing leggings and a black T-shirt, but there was some thick make-up around her cheeks and her eyes. In the background, Sam could hear the sound of the TV. 'We work for the government,' said Imer, looking straight at her. 'Could we talk to you for a few minutes?'

'Police?' said Esther.

From her tone, Sam judged she didn't have much time for the police.

Imer shook his head. He pulled out his wallet, and showed her the Mossad identification card he was still entitled to carry. Sam knew that, within Israel, Mossad still carried real weight. People who wouldn't talk to the police would talk to Mossad. The security of the nation depended on it, or so they thought. *It was a trust you could exploit.*

'It's nothing to worry about,' said Imer. 'We just want to ask you a few questions.' He paused, his expression turning grave. 'For national security.'

Esther nodded and led them into the hallway. The flat was

not large – two bedrooms, a sitting room and a kitchen – but it was smartly decorated, and there was a view of the sea from the balcony. The room smelt of jelly and Play-Doh: just like my house, thought Sam. He looked down at the little girl and smiled. She had dark hair, tied back in a plait, and sparkling brown eyes. She grinned at Sam, then looked back at the TV. He found himself thinking of Samantha. He had no idea when he would see her or the rest of his family again, or even whether they were OK. Sam pushed the thought from his mind. There will be a reckoning once this is all done, he told himself. *Save it for then.*

'There was a Russian sea captain,' said Sam. 'A man called Ryazanov. We believe you might know him.'

'Know him?' said Esther, tossing back her black hair angrily. She nodded down towards the girl. 'He's her father.'

'Tell us about him,' said Imer. 'About your relationship.'

'Not in front of Lilia,' said Esther. Sam and Imer followed her as she walked out to the balcony. At this height, a breeze was blowing in from the sea. Sam let the cool air waft over his face. 'What's he done?' said Esther. 'Not that anything would surprise me. He was a rotten drunk. Like most sailors.'

'He hasn't done anything,' said Sam gently. 'We're just trying to establish a better picture of the man. It's for our files.'

Esther nodded, but her expression suggested she was not convinced. She appeared certain Ryazanov had done something so terrible they couldn't even tell her what it was. Like most abandoned women, she was quick to assume the worst about her former lover. 'How long were you involved?' said Sam.

'Too long,' said Esther contemptuously. 'It started in '88. The summer. He was sailing into the port regularly. I'd never been out with a Russian before.' Her eyes rolled towards the sea. 'I mean, why would you? They drink like fish, they have no manners and they don't even have any money. Ryazanov was different, however. He drank all right. Even for a seaman, he poured alcohol down his throat like it was water. And, yes, his manners were atrocious. I could never introduce him to any of my friends, he just didn't know how to talk to people. He was a fine-looking man, though. And he had money.'

'How much money?' asked Sam.

Esther shrugged. 'A lot,' she replied. 'For a Russian. For anyone, really. That was how we first met. I was waitressing for a while, and he used to come in, order the best food we had, the best champagne, bottles of vodka, and pay for it all with cash. And leave a hundred-dollar tip. It was hard not to be impressed.' Her fingers reached up to her neck, and for the first time Sam noticed a thick gold necklace, with three diamonds studded into it. 'The first time we went out, he bought this. And that was how it went on. For Christmas he bought me this apartment. He said he needed somewhere to stay when he was docked and we moved in together. And I was already pregnant by then. We hadn't planned it, but once it happened he seemed happy enough.'

'How regularly was he here?' said Sam.

'About every two weeks,' said Esther. 'He'd bring his ship into port, stay here for a couple of nights while it was unloaded, then head back to Odessa. It was a regular run. Every two weeks, he'd be back. Always with more money in his pocket.'

'What was he bringing?'

Esther looked confused by the question. 'What? In his boat?' She looked out to sea, as if trying to remember something. 'How should I know? What do we import from Russia? Oil, maybe. Or grain, or something.'

'Did he talk about where the money came from?'

Esther shook her head.

'Or mention a man called Max Robertson?'

Again Esther shook her head.

'Or Klein? Maybe he mentioned a guy called Klein?'

'He didn't talk about his work,' said Esther sharply. 'Why should he? He was just a sailor.'

Sam could feel his spirit deflating. He'd steered into another dead end. *Every time the answer is approaching, it slips back into the night.*

'Listen, this may well be important,' said Imer, turning his eyes upon her. 'Nothing you say to us will go any further. Did Ryazanov ever give you anything?'

Esther paused.

'Anything at all?' said Imer.

'It's mine, right?' said Esther. 'Whatever he gave me is mine. It was honestly acquired.'

'It's yours,' said Sam. 'We don't want to take it. We just want to know what it is.'

She stepped back inside the apartment, leading them through the sitting room into the main bedroom. Pulling aside the rug next to the bed, she pointed down at the floor. 'Under there,' she said simply.

Sam knelt down. He could see a line cut out in the floorboards, three foot by two. Sam dug his fingers into the wood, levering the first floorboard gently upwards. He could feel himself tensing as he did so. One floorboard came away, then the next, then the next. Underneath, there was a small dark space, just over a foot deep. Lying inside it was a cloth bag. Sam glanced up towards Esther. 'Take a look,' she said.

Sam pulled at the bag. He was surprised at its weight, at least two kilos. He tugged it up on to the floor, then started to open it up.

Gold.

Hidden under the floorboards, there were four gold bars, each one weighing five hundred grams, the largest of the standard sizes. He felt one in his hand, turning it over in his hand. At the current gold price of about four dollars an ounce, each bar was worth around six thousand dollars. That meant twenty-four thousand dollars was stashed under the floorboards: a lot of money to keep lying around the house. 'Ryazanov gave you these?' asked Sam.

Esther nodded. 'He said it was a present for Lilia. To look after her, in case anything happened to him, and he couldn't come back.'

Sam studied the gold bar. It was plain, minted gold, its surface slightly tarnished – at a guess, he estimated it was at least two decades old, and because it hadn't been polished, it had long since lost its lustre. There were no markings of any sort on the bar. Since the early 1970s, Crédit Suisse had started putting a decorative motif on the side of the gold bars it manufactured, and the rest of the big Swiss banks that accounted for about a quarter of gold-bar production had followed suit. These bars had no markings, and there was no ready way of identifying them. So where did they come from? wondered Sam.

'When did you last see him?' said Imer.

'About two years ago,' said Esther. 'There were no goodbyes, nothing. He went back to Odessa, just as usual, and he never came back again. No explanations, no good-byes. It was over. I tried to contact him, but it was no good. He's in Russia. You can't just call people up over there, and anyway he never gave me an address. I wrote to him via the ship a couple of times, but I never got a reply. I sent him some pictures of Lilia as well.' She shrugged. 'That's men for you, isn't it? I shouldn't have expected anything better.'

Sam pondered the significance of the story. Whatever Robertson had been shipping to Israel, it had stopped very suddenly. Maybe there had been a disagreement, or a betrayal? Could that be what explained his death – or his disappearance? 'He didn't know the trips were ending?'

'No,' said Esther sharply. 'He would have said goodbye. He was a drunk, but sentimental.'

At the bottom of the sack, there was a plain white envelope. Sam held it up. 'May I look in here?' he said.

'Why not?' said Esther. 'It doesn't mean anything to me. I don't know why he left it. He said it was for the kid, for when she was grown up, but I could never see the point of it.'

Sam carefully opened up the envelope. Inside there was a single sheet of white paper. He opened it and held it to the light. It appeared to be some kind of a map. There were a series of passageways, linking square- and rectangular-shaped rooms. All of them looked to be encased within a triangular-shaped building. To Sam, it meant nothing. 'And Ryazanov gave no indication what this might be?' he said, looking at Esther.

She shook her head.

'You recognise it?' he asked, passing it across to Imer.

There was a silence.

Sam looked into the old man's eyes. He could see something there. A glimmer of recognition. 'You know what it is, don't you?' he said.

Another pause. Imer was holding the sheet of paper in his hands, and Sam could see that his fingers were trembling slightly. The best shot Mossad ever produced, thought Sam. His hands never shook. *What the hell has he seen?*

'What is it?' said Sam quietly.

Imer handed the sheet of paper back. 'You really don't recognise it?' he said.

Sam shook his head.

'Every senior Mossad man has that map imprinted on his mind,' said Imer. 'It's the interior of Mount Haifa. Where Israel keeps its nuclear weapons.'

TWENTY-FOUR

Sam looked out into the sea. The sun was just setting, streaking the sky with red, and the heat of the day was just starting to fade. He looked up and down the length of the beach. In the distance, he could see a man walking his dog. Further out, he could see a pair of big ships making their way into port. Otherwise, they were alone. Safe. *For now anyway*.

'What do you think it means?' said Sam.

He turned to look at Imer. The old man was sitting next to him, on the sea wall, looking down at the water below. He was concentrating, his brow furrowed, and his fingers tapping nervously against his knee. All the time they had been in training, Sam just assumed Imer knew everything. There was no danger so extreme, nor any mission so impossible that he couldn't point a way through it. Not any more. *We've found a mystery that even he can't fix.*

'Start with what we know for certain,' said Imer. 'Robertson was shipping something out of Russia and in to Israel. It was taken to Mount Haifa.'

'Maybe a nuclear weapon?' said Sam.

Imer shook his head slowly. 'Israel already has nuclear weapons. And why would the Russians want to give us any of theirs?'

'They could be selling us plutonium?'

Imer nodded. 'Possible,' he answered, in a tone that suggested he was far from convinced. 'It makes more sense,

285

Israel would always need plutonium, and the Russians have plenty of it.' He paused, flicking a pebble out into the sea and watching it skim across the water. 'But why would the Russians want to ship it here? That's one mystery. Next, why did they kill him? It doesn't make any sense. First, Robertson is working as a go-between between the Israelis and the Soviets. Next, they've killed him. Why?'

Sam stood up. He could feel the wind blowing on to his skin, helping him think. 'I'm going into the mountain to find out what's there,' he said. 'Follow the map, and see what Robertson stashed away. That's the only way I can solve this mystery.'

'Don't be an idiot, Sam,' said Imer. He was standing at his side now. 'You're talking about the interior of the mountain. Where our country keeps its nuclear missiles.'

'Of course I can do it,' snapped Sam. He could feel himself growing irritated. Until now, he would have trusted Imer with the lives of his children, but now he wasn't so sure. 'It's the only way I can crack this case for good.'

'This case,' snorted Imer. 'What does this case matter.'

'It matters to me,' growled Sam. 'I told you, there's five million at stake. I told myself I'd claim that bounty, and I bloody well plan to do so.'

'No,' said Imer. 'Listen to me, Sam. We're talking about the security of our nation. Go talk to Yoram. He'll tell you what to do. We're soldiers. We're all soldiers. We always put loyalty to our country above everything else.'

Sam laughed bitterly. 'I thought you knew. I'm not playing that game any more. The only wars I'm fighting are my own. And the only country I'm defending is my own family.'

Imer looked straight into Sam's eyes. 'The game never changes. You can disagree with Mossad as much as you like. Hell, I've done it myself. There are a lot of bastards in there, same as any organisation. But this is different. This is betraying your country.'

'I want the money,' said Sam. 'They took all my money from me, and now I'm damned well going to get some back. This is the only way I know. I owe it to Elena and the kids.'

'The money doesn't matter, Sam.'

'It matters to me.'

Imer looked away in disgust. He started walking along the seafront, along a road that led out of town, and up into the hill beyond. 'This country is your family, Sam,' he muttered, his voice seething with anger. 'You're Jewish, your family is Jewish. Israel is our home, and it has to be defended. Where are your kids going to go with all their money when they come after us Jews again? Answer me that, Sam?'

Sam remained silent. There was no answer, he thought. Except that Mossad had taken his money, and he couldn't let it drop. He didn't have Imer's blind loyalty, nor his father's: he'd looked within himself, but it just wasn't there. 'I'm going into the mountain,' he said flatly.

'I tell you, you can't.'

'And I tell you I can,' snapped Sam.

Imer grabbed Sam's arm. He'd pulled a Mauser M2 pistol from inside his jacket: the same pistol he'd always carried with him for the last forty years. Imer levelled the gun at Sam. 'I trained you, but damn me, if I have to, I'll kill you.'

Sam stepped away. 'You can't shoot me,' he said softly. 'It would be like killing one of your own children.'

'Don't believe it, Sam,' said Imer. His voice was loaded with emotion. 'I can put a bullet into any man I choose.'

Sam turned round and started walking away. 'Not into his back you can't.'

The jacket felt a little tight around Sam's shoulders, and he needed to bring the belt in a notch to make sure the trousers fitted properly. Otherwise, the uniform fitted fine. He looked up towards Michael. 'Thanks,' he said. 'I owe you big time.'

Michael nodded. 'One condition,' he said. 'You didn't get it from me.'

Sam shook hands, and stepped on to the road. He was a mile from Mount Haifa, dressed in the uniform of one of the fearsome army units that protected the entrance to the mountain. The mountain was protected by the Sayeret Tzanhanim, the elite commando unit of the Israeli Army. Sam had done a tour with them when he'd still been in the army, and found it the toughest three months of his life. He'd done two weeks as a guard at Mount Haifa, but had never been further than the barracks: he knew that only the most experienced guards were allowed into the interior of the mountain. Each of them would willingly lay down his life to protect the secrets the mountain contained. *At one point so would I.*

From Ashdod, Sam had travelled north to Haifa. He'd used local buses, changing frequently: that made it a long, torturous journey, but it reduced the risks of being stopped and checked. It was too risky to drive, and too dangerous to get a mainline bus that travelled from city to city. Along the way, he'd called Michael at a phone booth, asking him to find him a Sayeret uniform and some fake ID papers. That was the only favour he could ask for. *From now on, he was on his own.*

Sam kept walking along the road that wound through the side of the mountain. Other countries stored their nuclear weapons in silos out in the desert, or they buried them in submarines. Not Israel. There wasn't enough space. Other countries boasted of their weapons. Not Israel. The Israeli nuclear strike force was its greatest secret: a weapon of last resort, held in reserve, to be used only when the very existence of the state was threatened.

We keep our missiles among our own people, thought Sam. Where they should be.

Haifa was a bustling coastal city, with a large population, a port and a thriving university. The mountain rose up behind the city: it was not particularly high, but it had a dark, imposing presence, as if it was watching over everything around it. Even out here in the suburbs, late in the evening, there were still plenty of people around. Nobody paid any attention to Sam as he walked through the street: there were plenty of men in uniform around here, and one more made no difference.

The barracks loomed up ahead. To the outside world, it looked like a standard training camp for young Israeli recruits called up for their national service. In reality, few soldiers were ever posted here. A parade ground and a set of tin-roofed barrack rooms were just a façade for a complex series of passageways and tunnels that led deep into the heart of the mountain. A million tons of rock had been painstakingly carved out of the earth, creating the huge caverns in which the warheads and the missiles that would propel them towards the enemy were stored.

Sam flashed his ID to the guards at the gate, and stepped inside. It was ten years since he'd last been inside the compound but not much had changed. That was one aspect of military life you could rely on: the food never got any better, and they never updated the decor. It was just after eight in the evening, and the barracks was quiet. The men would have finished eating, and be playing cards or writing letters before lights out at ten. That didn't mean the place was unprotected though. The mountain had guards on it twenty-four hours a day.

The compound measured two hundred yards by three hundred. There was a wall around the perimeter, with barbed-wire fencing slung across it. Tarmac covered the surface of the ground. Up ahead, Sam could see two doors that looked ordinary enough from a distance. Made from regulation army-green cast metal, they could have concealed entry to some offices, an ammunition dump or the officers' quarters. Sam knew differently. That was the entrance.

The mountain had three layers of security. Israel's defence planners knew perfectly well that any aggressor would want to destroy its nuclear stockpile before launching a full-scale attack. The mountain was impenetrable to air attack: the bombs would just bounce off the side of the mountain. Only a deep, bunker-busting nuclear weapon had any chance of getting through, and only the Americans had those. Since the US wasn't likely to attack Israel, there was only one threat that had to be seriously planned for: a terrorist strike from within. In other words, thought Sam grimly, someone just like me.

The first layer of defence was relatively simple: the theory was that any attack would be drawn into a safe bubble, then dealt with while between layers one and two. Sam's ID card was good enough to get him through: there were several thousand soldiers who had access up to this point, and the guards couldn't be expected to know all of them. He showed his card to the soldier at the gate, and stepped through the smaller of the two metal doors. Inside, there was a cavernous, covered space, something like an aircraft hangar. The air was cold. Sam could feel the dampness inside the hangar. It measured about three hundred yards by one hundred. There was a small convoy of military trucks, and next to them Sam could see about thirty soldiers, all of them heavily armed. On a moment's notice, he knew from his own training, the whole area would be filled with bullets. It was a killing field. You walked across it at your peril.

Sam looked up towards the far side of the hangar. He walked straight towards it, looking neither left nor right. Inside his breast pocket, he had a copy of the map. My one advantage, he thought. Now I know the insides of this place even better than most of the soldiers do.

Six guards were standing around the lift shaft at the end of the hangar. Two of them were inspecting papers. The other four were just there as back-up. Sam nodded to the guard, and handed across the ID card Michael had given him. It was a Mossad security pass made out in the name of Ivan Rieden. Same age, same height and same picture as Sam. Just a different name.

'What are you doing here?' snapped the guard.

Sam looked coldly into the man's eyes. Mossad agents made regular trips into the mountain, Sam knew from his time within the organisation. Mossad had overall responsibility for state security. There were more than one thousand people, including scientists, technicians, weapons operators and back-up staff, working inside the mountain. They were all vetted before starting, but the mountain was so secret they were checked and checked again. That was Mossad's job. They were not popular with the Sayeret, however: the commandos guarded their turf jealously, and viewed the agents as nothing better than spies. *Probably because one of our main tasks is to check up on the Sayeret itself. We guard the guardians.*

'Security,' said Sam. 'Routine.'

The guard looked at his card, then back up at Sam. Yes, the Sayeret disliked Mossad, but they were also nervous of them: once they started investigating, it always caused trouble. 'Make sure you report to the guards below.'

Sam took his card back, and waited for the lift. There were three, depending on your level of security clearance: one lift for back-up staff; another for the scientists and technicians; a third for the security staff. Sam stepped into the third lift. There were no buttons inside: it only went to two places, and nobody was allowed to stop it. The lift started to descend automatically, the journey taking just a few seconds. When he stepped out, there was another guard waiting for him. He handed across his card. 'Chamber 278,' he said. 'Security check.'

The guard nodded and stepped aside. I'm inside the mountain, Sam told himself. *This is where it gets harder.*

A corridor led away from the lift, running both left and right. Sam started walking to the right. The tunnels inside the mountain had been carved out of rock, and although the surfaces of the walls were smooth, you could still see the stone from which they had been cut. The floor was filled in with steel girders, with railings running along the edge, and the corridor was illuminated by a series of light bulbs placed ten yards apart. Sam kept walking. He could feel a bead of sweat forming on his spine. One false move and they'll shoot me. I'm inside the mountain. *If they find an intruder in here, they don't ask questions. They shoot on sight.*

The right corridor led to another lift shaft, which would take you down another level to where the technicians and the scientists worked. The missiles were serviced down there, and the technicians worked constantly to make sure they were in perfect order. Israel was the one country that could never test its missiles, so the scientists had to service them constantly to make sure that, should they ever be needed, they would work as they were meant to.

There was no way he could get down there with just a Mossad ID card, Sam knew. They'll expect an appointment. If I don't have one, they'll phone Tel Aviv. Then I'm finished.

On the map, a service shaft was marked right next to the lift: it must have been drilled through the mountain at the same time. Sam looked left and then right. He could see the metal grille that covered the entrance to the shaft. He glanced around looking for CCTV cameras. Nothing. He ran his hands around the perimeter of the grille. Clean. Sam gripped the grille, tightening his fingers into the metal. He ripped it clean from the wall with one swift movement, then peered inside. It was completely dark. According to the map, it should bring him out into a network of service tunnels underneath the main missile silos: at the far end of that, there was a cavern where the cargo was stored.

Sam crawled into the tunnel. It measured four feet across: just enough space for a medium-sized man. It had been punched through the rock by a single boring machine, creating walls that were rough and irregular. You could still feel the grooves of the drill cut into its surface. Carefully, Sam pulled the grille back into place, then kicked back with his legs. He could feel himself starting to slide, his body starting to rush down into the interior of the mountain. Up ahead, the lights from the shaft opening rapidly faded, and within seconds he was plunged into complete darkness.

It was impossible to tell from the map how far down into the mountain this tunnel stretched, nor what he would find when he got there. He was travelling face first, using his arms to steady his progress. The surface of the walls was filled with jagged, sharp edges, and tiny cuts were being scissored into the palms of his hand as he descended. The darkness wrapped around him like a blanket.

Suddenly, he fell to the ground, hitting his shoulder on the rock. He emerged from the tunnel opening into some kind of cavern. There were no lights anywhere, nor could Sam hear any sounds. He pulled himself up, and switched on the torch he'd been carrying in his pocket. He flashed it through the cave. Mount Haifa was full of natural tunnels and caverns, carved into it when the sea had been far closer than it was today: that was one reason why it had been chosen as a missile dump, since there were already plenty of natural silos hidden within it. The rock swerved outwards from where he was standing, rising up to a height of thirty or forty feet at some points, then dipping down to just three or four feet, only just enough room for a man to crawl through. The rock was mostly grey, but smeared with tones of copper and iron from the traces of minerals in it.

Sam glanced down at his map. It took a few minutes to

locate his position. The shaft had taken him deep into the interior of the mountain. It showed a series of tunnels linking three large rectangular cylinders cut into the rock: Sam assumed that was where the missiles were actually stored. Beyond that, the map showed a series of eight large square rooms, each one with a series of smaller rooms leading off it. The stockrooms, thought Sam. For keeping warheads, plutonium, parts. *And Max Robertson's secret.*

Of the eight rooms, one was marked in bold pen. Sam started to walk the length of the tunnel. That must be where it was stored. Whatever the hell it was.

The path was dark, with the jagged edges of rock swooping down at regular intervals. Three times Sam had to kneel down and crawl, when the roof came down so low it was impossible for him to stand any more. The air around him was cold: this was rock that had never seen sunlight, and the temperature never rose above a few degrees centigrade even at the height of summer. Somewhere in the distance he could hear the sound of running water. Like most mountains, Haifa was cut through with underground rivers, streams and lakes. One of them must be close by. Sam kept walking, using his torch to illuminate the path ahead of him, but the darkness was so intense he could never make out more than few yards at a time. He paused as the path split. Looking down, he could see from the map he needed to take the left path. He walked another dozen yards, then dipped underneath a low rock and confronted a three-way fork. Again he studied the map, taking the middle path.

Without a map, a man would lose himself within minutes down here, Sam knew. The rocks had twisted themselves into a natural maze, the paths curling around on each other, protecting the rooms and silos above.

How did Ryazanov come into possession of this map? Robertson must have had a copy and given it to the sailor when he was making his deliveries into the mountain. So why had Ryazanov buried it at Esther's apartment along with the gold? Because he wanted it to go to his daughter one day. He knew it was valuable: it was, in effect, his insurance policy, although in the end it hadn't done him much good. Like most fathers, he wanted to leave something precious behind for his child. *This piece of paper was all he had.*

Sam negotiated his way through another two forks, and ducked through another low stretch of tunnel, crawling on his hands and knees. He could smell the dampness in the air. Suddenly, the tunnel opened up, and in front of him a river was flowing. Sam flashed the torch, the beam of light skimming across the dark water and filling the cave with a pale, deathly light. Kneeling down, Sam dipped his hands into the water, scooping it up and pressing it to his lips. The water was icy cold, but fresh and clean. He dabbed it on to his skin, and looked around the cave. There were four tunnels leading out of it. Checking the map, Sam selected the second one, and waded across the water to reach the other side. The water rose to his waist, and the ground beneath him felt slippery. The current was strong, pushing up against him, and he could feel his skin freezing under the impact. He reached the other side, and shook himself dry. The map gave him an outline of the direction, but there was no indication of distances. *These tunnels could stretch on for miles.*

Somewhere, he could hear a sound. A footstep? Or just some water tumbling through the exposed rock? Sam switched off the torch. He lay down against the wet ground, holding himself absolutely still. A voice? Sam strained his ears, trying to listen. No, he decided. It was just a murmur carried on the still air, and echoing through the cavernous chamber.

Working from memory, he started to crawl towards the tunnel leading away from the river. The sound had died away: whether it was real, or just a trick of the underground acoustics, it was impossible to say. But it was too dangerous to use the torch. The tunnel could be rigged with light sensors. There could be CCTV cameras hidden into the rock. The torch would locate him instantly. From now on, he would just use it to read the map: the rest of the journey would have to be completed in darkness.

Progress was steady, but painful. Sam used his hands to track the wall of the tunnel, steadily inching his way. Every few yards, he'd hit a rock, or get another tear on his skin, but he ignored the bruises and the pain, and pressed on. Only a few hundred more yards, he told himself. His eyes were gradually acclimatising to the darkness. The knocks annoyed him, but then became mundane. The human body could take a lot of punishment, Sam thought. It was just a matter of getting used to it. *And believing it had a purpose.*

As Sam stepped through a break in the rock, he was suddenly bathed in a pale blue light. He looked upwards. A gap in the roof of the tunnel, measuring three foot by one, had opened above him. The light was streaming down, catching the rock, highlighting the speckles of metal within it. Peering into the light, Sam could see a huge sheet of metal towering up into the sky. Light was pouring on to the metal from all sides, but the refraction through the rock was sending shafts of blue down into the tunnels below. The underside of a nuclear missile, Sam told himself grimly. Let's just hope nobody decides to fire it.

Sam pressed on. If he was passing the silos, then it wasn't much further to the storeroom. The light filtered through the tunnels, absorbed into the rock, lending it a strange luminous glow. For thirty or forty yards it lit up Sam's path like the lamps on a motorway, but soon the darkness engulfed him again, its cold silence wrapping itself around him. He stumbled on a crevice, and had to bite his lip, forcing himself not to cry out as the pain ripped through him.

One silo, then more light, then another. *Almost there.*

Sam paused fifty yards further on. He checked around him. The darkness was absolute. No lights anywhere. The silence was just as severe. He switched on the torch, adjusting his eyes to the sudden burst of light, then looked at the map. Three silos. Then the storerooms.

He switched off the light, and started kicking forward. The path was tough, and at several points he needed to crawl to get by. Up ahead, he could see the first signs of a properly constructed passageway. He flashed the torch to it. A set of rough metal steps had been smashed into the rock, leading up to a door. Sam passed it and kept on walking. The map told him it should be the fourth door. That was what he would aim for.

The steps, when he reached them, were not difficult to climb. The door was made of metal, with two thick bolts strung across it. Neither was locked. The tunnels underneath the complex were an escape route. Lock them, and they would be unusable. Sam slid the bolt back and stepped inside. At last, he told himself. *Robertson's secret.*

The room was vast. It had started as a natural cave, but the room, Sam could see clearly, had been hammered into shape with drills and dynamite. In total, Sam reckoned, it measured a hundred yards lengthwise and fifty yards across. Thick steel pillars had been erected at regular intervals to support the roof: the metal of the girders had gathered some rust, and there was a smell of dampness in the room from the moisture oozing through the rock. Along the ceiling, there was a string of electric light bulbs, ten of them in total, spread out in a line. No more than forty watts each, Sam judged, they filled the room with a pale, dismal light that struggled to illuminate the space beneath them.

At the far end of the room, Sam could see an elevator shaft. It was a thick, open machine, with a cage made out of steel mesh, the type you see in warehouses. A man could ride in it. But it was built for lifting stuff. Heavy stuff.

And then there were the boxes.

Sam looked to his right. The boxes were neatly stacked, one on top of the other. There were pallets between them to keep them level, and a carpenter had built a rough frame from timber to house them all. How many? Sam couldn't begin to count. It looked like hundreds and hundreds. Enough, anyway, to keep a boat sailing from Odessa to Ashdod for months at a stretch.

He could feel the pulse beating in his chest, the blood surging through his veins. He paused, looking at the first box in front of him. It was made from planking, maybe pine. It measured six feet lengthwise, two feet across and four feet deep. Sam gripped it with his arm. A single man couldn't lift it by himself, maybe not even two men. They must have used cranes and forklift trucks to get all this stuff in here.

The lids on the boxes were screwed into place. Sam took out the Swiss army knife he was carrying in his pocket, and started to twist the first screw. It was stuck firmly into the wood, and its thread had started to rust with age. It might have been moved here from Russia, but it must have been years, maybe even decades, since it was tightened down. He gripped the knife tightly, squeezing as much strength as he could into his finger. Nothing. The screw wouldn't budge.

Bugger it, thought Sam. He drew in his breath and summoned up his strength. Leaning into the knife, he made another attempt to shift the screw. Nothing.

I need a proper screwdriver.

Sam snapped the penknife away, silently cursing himself. I should have known I would need the kit to open boxes. He cast his eyes around the giant cave. Towards the back, some of the rock had fallen away. Walking quickly towards it, Sam saw a sprinkling of dust lying on the ground next to it. Amid the debris, Sam picked up a single shard of rock, measuring two foot in length. It had a jagged edge, and it cut the skin of Sam's palm as he gripped it.

Heck, it worked for the cavemen, he told himself as he walked back to the boxes.

Sam jammed the sharp end of the shard of rock down into the box. It splintered the plank. Sam hesitated. If this was plutonium that had been shipped from Russia, then even the slightest exposure would condemn him to death. No, he told himself, nuclear material would be stored in lead. And it wouldn't be in these kinds of quantities. There wasn't this much plutonium in the world, never mind in the Soviet Union.

It was something else Robertson had hidden away here.

Sam pushed his hand down hard on the rock. The wood of the plank groaned and creaked. Sam hit the rock. The wood splintered open, first one plank then another.

Taking the rock out, Sam jabbed into the other end of the box. The wood was weakening. One by one the planks came away.

The box was open.

Sam cast the wooden debris down on the ground.

On the top of the box, there was a simple grey cloth. His pulse quickening, Sam pulled it aside.

Gold.

Bar after bar of gold, laid out in neat rows. He reckoned there could be five thousand bars down here, worth about five billion dollars.

Sam lifted up one of the bars, holding it in his hand. From its weight and colour, he could tell at once it was pure. No markings. There was nothing to identify where the gold came from, or who it belonged to. There was no need. It was obvious.

The entire gold reserves of the Soviet Union had been shipped here to Israel. And Max Robertson had organised it.

Sam put the gold back into the box. Picking up the shard of rock, he started levering open the second box. For Sam, the mystery was staring to unravel. Trusov and the rest of the Soviet leadership wanted to ship the gold out of their own country. They knew the system was about to fall apart. That was what they had been talking about in the diaries he had seen. They were stripping the place of whatever they could get their hands on before it all came crashing down. *They might have started out as Communists, but they ended up as looters.*

Another box was open. Sam looked inside. More gold. Bar after bar of the stuff.

How much was it all worth? And what was the deal? What kind of hellish pact had Robertson brokered between the dying Soviet leadership and the Israeli government?

Whatever its terms, Robertson had paid for it with his life.

Sam looked again at the towering rows of boxes. If the entire Russian gold reserves are hidden here in Israel, that is a secret next to which no man's life is worth more than a breath of air. *Certainly not mine.*

Proof, he told himself. What I need is some form of proof that this gold is hidden down here.

A bar, maybe? No, gold could come from anywhere. A box, perhaps? No, that tells you nothing. A picture? Sam shook his head to himself. Even if I had a camera with me, it could easily be staged. Nobody would believe it.

He started looking through the boxes. *There must be something.*

A noise.

Sam's head spun round.

He could hear a loud screeching wall of electronic white noise. An alarm. His ears were starting to ache as the noise filled his brain.

Fuck it. *They know I'm here.*

He started running, heading towards the caves and tunnels

from which he had emerged. If I can find my way out through the mountain, maybe I have a chance.

From the ceiling, a thick sheet of metal was starting to descend. The exit was completely blocked. Sam turned round, running towards the lift that was the main exit from the storeroom. The alarm was growing louder, piercing Sam's skull. He raised his hands to his ears to try and block the noise, but the sound was splitting open his skull.

Looking up towards the lift, he could see it was descending. Through its metal grille he could see a troop of soldiers, their bodies covered in black body armour. In their arms Sam could see the American-made Colt Commando assault rifles that were standard throughout the Israeli Army. Sam had fired that gun in anger himself: he knew only too well its lethal efficiency as it sprayed bullets into the room. There were at least a dozen of them riding down in the lift. Enough to kill fifty men.

'Hold it right there, Sam,' shouted a voice.

Sam recognised it at once.

Imer.

He froze, his feet rooted to the ground.

'I may not be able to shoot you in the back,' he barked. 'But these guys will.'

TWENTY-FIVE

At the bottom of the shaft, the metal grille slid open and twelve soldiers walked out. The Colts were all pointed straight at Sam, six of them to his chest and six of them to his head. One by one they spread out, forming a neat semicircle. The men stood two feet apart, their guns raised to their shoulders.

I know that formation, thought Sam. *A firing squad.*

He remained still, with no expression on his face. Give nothing away, he told himself. If nothing else, meet your fate with dignity. *You owe yourself that much.*

From the back of the lift, three more men started to walk towards him. Imer was in the lead, followed by Rotanski. The third man was thin, with brown hair and a babyish face. Sam had already seen the smile on his face when he thought he was killing him. Kersch. *The KGB assassin sent to eliminate me.*

'Don't even think about moving so much as a muscle, Sam,' said Rotanski coldly.

Sam remained impassive. He had watched plenty of men die. He knew that few men could take a bullet calmly. All of them succumbed to panic in the end. The braver they were, the worse it was. They resisted the fear right up until the last moment, then, as they felt it take control of them, they were disgusted with themselves for surrendering to an emotion they had always thought they were immune from. When the bullet came, it was usually a relief. They just wanted the fear to end. *Like I do right now.*

Imer was glancing across at Rotanski. 'There,' he said. 'Just where I said you would find him.'

Rotanski nodded. 'You have my gratitude,' he said. 'Once again.'

'You betrayed me,' said Sam, looking towards Imer.

'You betrayed yourself,' said the old man slowly.

Sam could taste the venom in his voice. He'd heard anger on those lips many times. But this was different. *This was contempt.*

'I was your friend.'

'There are greater loyalties than friendship, Sam.'

'Not that I know of.'

Rotanski took a step closer to him, nodding towards the gold. 'And that's why you were never more than an agent,' he said. 'You were fine at pulling the trigger. But you could never be trusted to take decisions. You can't see the bigger picture.' He paused, and Sam could see he was searching for the right words. 'My loyalties are to the state of Israel. That's everything to me. You threatened that, and so you became my enemy. Simple as that.' Rotanski wiped a bead of perspiration from his forehead. 'Welcome to the Gokhran Vault.'

'The what?' said Sam.

'Gokhran is the Soviet Ministry for precious metals and minerals. As you can see, its vaults have been transferred here, temporarily at least.' He looked piercingly at Sam. 'You think we could take any chances with this secret? The entire Russian gold reserve shipped here to Israel? Imer knows we can't play games with information. Unfortunately, you don't.'

'I make my own decisions.'

Rotanski shrugged. 'So I've learned,' he said. 'Although the next decision is mine.' He turned away from Sam. 'What to do with you.'

Kersch stepped forward, holding a Czech-made CZ-75 pistol in his hand. Sam could see the man clearly for the first time. His eyes were blue and clear, and his hand rock steady. There were no traces of nerves or pity. The perfect assassin. *Pity he's on the other side.*

'We kill him,' said Kersch. 'Now. My country demands it. You know the arrangement. The gold is stored here on behalf of the Soviet people. It must remain secret. Anyone compromises that secret, then they die. We take no chances.' He took another step forward. 'We shoot him, right here, right now.'

Sam flinched. He could feel the muscles on his face start to twitch, and it took all his concentration to hold himself steady. Few men could listen to their own death sentence calmly. *I'm certainly not among them.*

'We shoot him right now,' repeated Kersch, his tone more insistent this time.

The twelve Colts were still trained on him. Sam could sense the bullets in their chambers, and could already imagine the dozen lumps of hardened steel that were about to shatter through his body.

Kersch's face was reddening, and the muscles in his chest were starting to pump up. 'Unless he dies, my country will demand its gold is returned immediately. If we can't trust you, then we need our property back.'

'I've already told you, we'll kill him if we need to,' said Rotanski. 'Until then, we need to know how much he has discovered.'

'He's discovered the gold, that's enough,' snapped Kersch.

'I know, and that will always remain secret, you have my word on it.' Rotanski turned to face the twelve guards. 'Take him away,' he said.

Sam sat back in the chair. The cell was just a hole carved into the rock, measuring twelve feet by six. At its front, there was a metal grille, with a door cut into it. There was no light in the cell, but a few pale beams drifted in from the corridor.

He wasn't sure quite how long he'd been sitting here. Three, maybe four hours. They'd taken his watch from him, as well as all his clothes, and given him a pair of army jogging pants and a sweatshirt to wear. A man may always have a weapon concealed somewhere within his own clothes, Sam knew. *They're not taking any chances with me.*

His mind was drifting. He could recall the stories he'd heard of how Mossad treated its rebels and traitors. It was a technique they had learned from MI6. They didn't torture them or try to break them. There were no splintered fingernails or electrodes strapped to the skin. They just put a man in a cell, with no windows and no contact with the outside world. For as long as it was necessary. Until he broke. Or was forgotten about.

Somewhere just like this.

Along the corridor, he could hear footsteps. Sam tensed up, unsure what to expect next.

Rotanski stood in the doorway, with one guard at his side. The guard opened the door, leaving it ajar, and then stepped away. His Colt was resting in his arms, his finger poised on the trigger. Sam couldn't help noticing that the safety catch had been released.

Sam shifted on his chair, as Rotanski looked down at him. 'You're a fucking idiot,' he spat.

'Then just let your Russian friend finish me off.'

'You're an Israeli solider.'

'I resigned,' snapped Sam. 'In case you've forgotten.'

'Nobody resigns,' said Rotanski. 'It's in the small print. I told you that once already. I'm sick of having to fucking repeat myself to everyone.'

Rotanski started to pace the tiny cell, turning in tight, concentric circles. 'Once you've signed up for active duty with Mossad, you're always on the reserve list.' He clicked his fingers. 'I just recalled you. That means you're legally under my control. I'm not going to let some Russian madman kill you. We'll give you a court martial, listen to the evidence.' He paused, looking straight at Sam. 'And then we'll bloody shoot you. With pleasure.'

'We're not assassins, right?' said Sam. 'We're Israelis, we're better than that.'

Rotanski nodded. 'We're not murderers, at least.'

'Then what was I doing for the past five years?'

'Protecting your damned country, just like you should be now.'

He started walking again, his head bowed down, looking at the floor. 'How did you know about the gold, Sam?'

'I followed the clues.'

'What clues?'

'You've shipped several hundred tons of gold from Russia to Israel. You think that doesn't leave a trail?'

'A trail can be covered.'

'This one hasn't been.'

'Why were you looking for it?'

Sam hesitated. The answer to that question was probably more complex than even he knew himself. 'For the money.'

'The money?' said Rotanski scornfully. 'You hoped to take some of the gold?'

'I'm not a thief.'

'Then what? A traitor? That's far worse.'

Sam fell silent. There was no point to this conversation. There never had been. 'What do you want to know?'

'I don't think you realise the kind of trouble you're in,' said Rotanski. Sam was certain he could detect a hint of malicious pleasure in his voice. 'By potentially revealing this secret, you put the security of the state at risk. For a soldier, there is no worse crime. No punishment is too severe.'

'Kill me if you want to,' said Sam. 'I've been one of your butchers myself. I know how easy it is.' He stood, jabbing a finger at Rotanski. 'But don't assume your secret will die with me.'

Rotanski chuckled. 'No threats please,' he said. 'I'm sure you've hidden away some records in a secret bank account somewhere. No doubt details of the gold will be posted to the newspapers in the event of your death. Everything will be exposed.' He paused. 'Well, I don't give a fuck. Nobody's going to believe you because you're nothing, a nobody. Just a piece of dog shit to be wiped off the pavement.'

'They might not believe me,' said Sam slowly. 'But they might believe Max Robertson.'

'He's dead,' snapped Rotanski.

'True enough,' said Sam. 'But they can read his diaries.'

'There aren't any diaries.'

'How do you know?'

Rotanski paused. 'I just told you, there aren't any diaries.'

Sam sat down on the single wooden chair. He looked at the stone floor. 'Fifteenth of August 1988,' he started, each word clearly enunciated. 'This is the diary of Max Robertson, Chairman and Chief Executive of Robertson Communications Corporation . . .' He glanced back up towards Rotanski. 'My first meeting of the day was scheduled with Roman Trusov . . .' Sam could feel Rotanski staring at him. 'Twenty-sixth of September 1988,' he continued, reciting the words he had committed to memory. 'I am back in Moscow, staying in the same suite Trusov arranged last time. I arrived on the BA flight two days ago, and I am scheduled to be here for three days in total. On the first day, I met with Trusov again.'

Sam stood up from the chair, then rested his arms on its wooden frame. 'So you can tell me there aren't any diaries if you want to, but that's a hell of a bet you're making with your career,' he said. 'And we all know how fucking precious that is to you.'

Without a flicker of regret or surprise, Rotanski spun round and walked out of the cell. 'Keep that gun trained on his brain,' he snapped to the guard as he headed down the corridor.

Sam could feel the hunger gnawing away at his stomach. It was at least twenty-four hours since he'd had anything to eat. The water from the river inside the mountain had been his last drink, and that was least a dozen hours ago. His throat was as dry as the desert sand, and his body felt weak and undernourished.

I can feel the strength draining away from me, as the water drains from a sieve.

He peered at the corridor. The guard was still standing there, his assault rifle pointing at Sam's head. Two hours or so ago the shift had changed, one soldier replaced by another. Apart from that nothing had happened. The cell was completely silent, and Sam had nothing but his own nightmares to surround him.

The same three thoughts kept rattling through his mind.

Maybe I pushed Rotanski too far.

Maybe he doesn't care about the diaries.

Maybe I'm about to die.

If I was Rotanski, I know what I would do. I'd send the pain masters down to this cell to squeeze the information out of me.

Footsteps.

Three guards were approaching, followed by a man dressed in the white coat of a lab technician.

The door was flung open. While the first guard kept his gun trained directly on Sam's head, the others moved swiftly into the cell. Sam could smell the thick, hardened plastic of their body armour. One guard grabbed him by the back of the head, while the other two gripped his left and right arms. With a coordinated heave, they lifted him clean from the chair and pushed him hard against the wall. Sam didn't try to resist. It was useless. Against three Sayeret warriors, he had no chance.

He could feel the rocks on the wall of the cave piercing the fabric of his sweatshirt and carving into the skin of his back. Ahead, he could see the technician placing a small metal case on the chair. Inside, there were six syringes, laid out in a neat row. Each one was filled with a colourless liquid. The technician had light brown hair, and a pale, featureless face. He looked down at the syringes as if he were choosing a toothbrush. Mossad had a dozen different poisons, Sam knew. He'd been trained in them himself: it had serums that could cause heart failure, lung failure, a stroke, blood clot or a brain rupture. It was just a question of deciding what you wanted it to say on the death certificate.

There's only one thing they need to put on mine, thought Sam grimly. *Cause of death: pig-headedness.*

The technician chose his syringe and held it between his thumb and index finger. Even in the pale half-light filtering through from the corridor Sam could see its steel tip glistening.

'What the hell is that?' he said.

'Quiet,' snapped one of the guards in his ear.

'What the hell is it?' Sam said again, louder this time.

He could feel the rock digging deeper into his skin as he was pushed harder into the wall.

'Stay fucking quiet,' shouted the guard.

Sam could feel himself starting to tremble. His legs were quivering, and he was starting to lose control of them. So intense was the fear starting to drive through him, it was a struggle to keep control of his bowels. 'A man has a right to know how he's going to die,' he said, his voice breathless.

'Don't worry, it's only the injection that's going to hurt,' said the technician, with a faint trace of a smile.

He knelt down. Two of the guards gripped Sam's legs, holding them still. He tried to kick out, but the hunger, the exhaustion and the fear of the last few hours had tamed his strength. They held him easily. The technician stabbed the needle into the fleshy skin at the top of his thigh. The needle pierced his skin, sinking through the muscle. A sharp bolt of pain ran up the side of his leg, jabbing into his spine. With a stab of his thumb, the technician squeezed the syringe.

As the liquid drained into his bloodstream, Sam could feel the pain ebbing away. First the feeling in his leg faded, then in his spine. The fear slowly disappeared, and so did the hunger: in their place was the relaxed contentment you got after a couple of glasses of wine.

Is this what dying feels like?

Sam struggled to keep his eyes open, the same way a flame struggles to stay alight on the embers of a fire. But the energy was draining out of him. His eyelids were closing. He was thinking about Elena and the children, then about his parents, but it was impossible to concentrate. The thoughts drifted in and out of his mind. The soldiers holding him slowly relaxed their grip. His ability to fight had long since emptied out of him.

As he watched the technician take the needle from his skin, Sam's last thought was that he might never wake up again.

TWENTY-SIX

Sam could feel the light hitting the outside of his eyelids. He kept both eyes closed, pausing a moment to emerge from the sleep into which he had fallen. His mouth was dry, and there was a churning pain in his stomach. His head felt as if it had been put through a shredding machine, and the muscles in his limbs were alive with discomfort and pain.

They didn't kill me, they just beat the hell out of me.

He opened one eye, then closed it again. The light was streaming in from the window straight ahead of him. Back in the darkness, Sam tried to collect his thoughts. He could remember the row with Rotanski. He could remember the walls of the cell. He could remember the needle piercing his skin. He could remember what it felt like to sense the life fading from you. And to be certain you were dying.

Opening his eyes again, he glanced around the room. It took a few seconds to bring everything into focus. The room was painted a dark green, with half-panelling up the walls. It was decorated with pictures and antiques. He was lying on a bed, but there were two armchairs, a writing desk and a coffee table right ahead of him. Sam struggled to his feet. He was dressed in beige chinos and a blue polo shirt, clothes he had never seen before but which seemed to fit him OK. Sitting down next to the table, he poured himself a cup of coffee from a silver pot. The cup was made from fine china. Sam took a sugar packet and stirred it into the coffee: he was aware of how long it had been since he'd eaten and he needed the mixture of caffeine and sugar in his bloodstream to bring him back to life again. He paused. There was a hotel logo on the sugar wrapper. Sam recognised it at once. The Hôtel des Bergues, the finest hotel in Geneva, right in the centre of the town, with a view overlooking the lake.

What the hell am I doing in Geneva?

Sam sipped the coffee and walked across to the window. The lake was looking placid and calm. Above it, the sun was just breaking through some light clouds, and although most of the snow had melted, if you looked into the distance, the caps of the far mountains behind the lake were still white.

A noise. Sam turned round. The door was opening. He stood with his back to the window. If there had been a weapon to hand, he would have grabbed it. He glanced at the writing desk. There was a pad of paper and some envelopes, but no pen or paper knife.

They don't trust me. They think I might kill them. Or myself.

'You're awake, Sam,' said Rotanski, walking into the room. 'I hope you slept well.'

Rotanski started pouring himself a coffee from the jug on the table, as Imer followed him into the room. Sam took another hit on the coffee, draining the cup. 'Only just,' he said.

Imer looked at Sam, running his eyes across him as if checking for damage. But there was a coldness to his expression. A bond had been severed, Sam could tell that. Would they ever get it back? It seemed unlikely now. *Those kinds of wounds don't heal.*

'You should start doing what you are told,' said Imer.

'And what's that?'

'We need to know where Robertson's diaries are,' said Rotanski.

Sam poured himself some more coffee. He was thinking on his feet. A series of questions were burning through his

312

mind. Why did they bring me here? What do they want? How much will they give me? Why didn't they kill me back in the mountain?

They want those diaries. My deck of cards has at least one trump in it.

'So you believe they exist now?'

Rotanski nodded. 'The dates tally,' he said, his tone guarded. 'They may be genuine, they may be forgeries. We'll determine that when you give them to us.'

'The diaries are genuine all right,' said Sam. 'They led me to the gold, didn't they? What more proof do you want?'

'To actually see them,' said Rotanski.

Sam laughed drily. 'Do you want to know what I think?' he said. 'Those diaries are my insurance policy. It's what's keeping me alive.'

Imer stepped forward. Sam could see the anger on the old man's face: he was starting to hate Sam, and hate himself for having helped him. 'Don't you get it?' he snapped. 'We need those diaries.'

'Not while they are keeping me alive.'

'Look, Sam,' said Rotanski. 'If we wanted to hurt you, we'd have done it back in Israel. We've brought you here to Geneva because we want to strike a deal. Just tell us where the diaries are.'

Sam shook his head.

'I spoke to your father,' said Imer coldly. 'He wants you to help us.'

'He's entitled to his opinion.'

'Dammit, man, don't push us too far,' said Imer.

'You broke my father,' said Sam. 'But you're not going to break me.'

Rotanski raised his hand. 'There are some other people who want to talk to you,' he said. 'Sit down.'

Sam sat back on one of the two chairs. He was aware of the stubble on his chin, and the headache still beating through his brain. He could use a wash and a shave. Anything to start making him feel alive again.

The door opened. The two men who walked in were instantly recognisable. Sam had seen their pictures. He'd never imagined he might actually meet them. And not like this.

William Landon led the way. In his sixties, with greying hair, a black, loose-fitting suit and a red tie, he had been director-general of the CIA for the last three years. By reputation, he was a man with a fierce temper and a determination to get his own way. He was followed by Henry McCormick, a younger man, in his early fifties, dressed in a double-breasted blue suit and a grey tie. A tall, thin man, with a drooping expression, Sam had seen photographs of the head of Britain's Secret Intelligence Service in Mossad files in London. After making his name penetrating the IRA's London cells in the early 1980s, McCormick had run the SIS for the past five years.

Both men looked at Sam warily. Just outside the door, Sam could hear footsteps. Bodyguards, he realised. These two don't travel anywhere without plenty of protection.

'I must be going up in the world,' said Sam, looking up at Landon and McCormick. 'For two such distinguished gentlemen to come and see me.'

'You have something we want,' said Landon.

His voice was terse, to the point.

'And we're willing to trade for it,' said McCormick.

'I don't get it,' said Sam. 'The entire Russian gold reserve is transferred to Israel. And you guys know about it?'

Landon nodded. 'These are dangerous times,' he said. 'The Soviet Union is close to collapse. We can all see that. Them and us. Even the ordinary Russians have caught on. The issue is how do we manage that collapse, and stop the place falling into complete anarchy. Of course we know about the Russian leadership shipping their gold out and we're damned glad we know. It gives us some leverage over them. And it helps them to leave power gracefully.' He paused. 'You know, a man is much more likely to quit when he knows he's got some money in the bank. Poor men — they are the dangerous ones.'

McCormick edged closer to Sam. 'The Russian gold reserves are an important part of the world financial system,' he said. 'If that gold starts coming on to the market, it will be very destabilising. Likewise, if it is known that Russia doesn't have the gold any more, the country will never get a loan again. It will be plunged into even worse chaos than it already faces.'

'So everyone's collaborating on this,' said Sam. 'The Russians, the Israelis, the British and the Americans. And everyone wants to keep it a secret.'

The reach of the conspiracy was starting to make sense to Sam now: it was like watching the fog clear away from a mountainside to reveal a completely unexpected view below. 'If a word of this gets out, then you're all in trouble,' he said.

'Quite so, Mr Wolfman,' said McCormick. 'The trouble is, you've put that secret in danger. You're a dangerous man. And ultimately you know what business we're in, because you've spent most of your life in the same trade yourself.' He paused, pouring himself some coffee. 'Tracking down dangerous men, and putting them out of action.'

'We don't have time to play games, Mr Wolfman,' added Landon. 'Those diaries are explosive. We want them.'

'Then answer me a question.'

Landon looked first annoyed, then amused by the remark. He nodded, sitting down. 'You've got five minutes,' he said, glancing down at his watch.

'Is Robertson dead?'

'Of course,' said Landon. 'We didn't want that fat greedy bastard running around any longer.'

'Mossad killed him?'

Landon glanced towards Rotanski.

'We had to,' said Rotanski.

'Even though he was working for Israel, shipping over the Russian gold so that it was on our territory?'

'He'd become a liability,' said Rotanski. 'You've investigated the man so you know what he was like. He drank too much, and he talked too much. He was only interested in himself. We couldn't trust him. Nobody could.'

'But you let him bring the gold in.'

'We had a deal with the Russians,' said Rotanski. 'We look after their gold for them. At the right moment, we'll give it back, but of course that moment may never arrive. Who knows? We are a small country, with few resources apart from the brains of our people, and plenty of enemies. We need to take our opportunities where we find them.'

'So you killed him. And then you buried him.'

'With a full state funeral, naturally,' said Rotanski with a thin smile. 'Although I didn't think it would be appropriate to go to the service myself. We decided it would be best to get the body out of Italy before there could be an autopsy. And the Italians were happy enough to get rid of him.'

Sam was trying to read the temper of Rotanski's voice. He sounded conspiratorial as he spoke, the tone of a man who was sharing secrets with someone he trusted. I'm not buying, thought Sam. He's trying too hard to make me feel we're on the same side. *There's something he's not telling me.*

'Maybe I'm just stupid, but I still don't get it,' said Sam. 'Why would the Russians transfer all their gold to Israel? How could they feel confident of getting it back?'

'I thought we'd explained,' said Landon. 'The Communist Party leaders know they're heading for a fall. It's unavoidable now. The system is too rotten. There are going to be a lot of Russian exiles in the next few years. They'll need something to live on.'

'But why Israel?' persisted Sam. 'Why not Switzerland, or France or the States? The Russians have never trusted the Israelis.'

Landon shrugged. 'Think about it,' he said. 'Where are you going to store all that gold? Not in Switzerland. The Swiss would just pocket it for themselves, the same way they did all that Jewish gold during the Second World War. Not the States. We're the old enemy, remember. Same for France, or the British. We might invade – hell, we've tried often enough. They might trust the Cubans, but that's not a stable place.'

'That leaves Israel,' interrupted Rotanski. 'A safe and impregnable state – in military terms. American protection, and nuclear weapons. They can trust us to keep it safe for them. And our central bankers can use the gold as collateral, so Israel can even make a profit on it. And in a financial crisis, it is always useful to have some gold reserves. Everyone wins. So long as nobody knows about it.'

'But, again,' said Sam, 'how could they be certain that Israel wouldn't just break the deal. The moment comes when Trusov and his gang want their gold back, and we tell them, tough. We've got it, and we're keeping it.'

'Because Russia has more Jews than any other country in the world,' said Rotanski. 'We betray them, they start killing our people. As simple as that. They've done it often enough in the past. A few more hundred thousand won't make any difference.'

There's something else.

'But –'

'Your five minutes are up, Mr Wolfman,' interrupted Landon.

Sam glanced at him. The charm had suddenly vanished. Now he could see a glimpse of the hardened steel that made up the man's core.

317

'We came here to offer you a trade, Mr Wolfman,' he continued. 'And it may be the last one you ever get.'

'We want the diaries,' said Rotanski. 'Now where are they?'

'I don't have them,' said Sam.

He delivered the line calmly and evenly, without any expression or emotion. Underneath, his heart was thumping. It was like taking your whole life and waging it on a roulette table. *With one spin of the wheel, your fate would be decided.*

No sooner had the words escaped his lips than he could feel the venom in Rotanski's expression. 'I know you have them,' he snapped. 'You gave me the time and dates of the meetings, and they all tally.'

Sam nodded. 'I said, I don't have them. But I know where they are, and what's in them.' With his right index finger, he tapped the side of his head. 'And that information is staying right here.'

At his side, Imer was leaning forward. 'They're willing to trade, Sam. Give them the diaries, and they let you live.' He paused, judging the weight with which he should deliver the next sentence. 'Believe me, it's a good trade. You're not going to get a better offer.'

Sam stood up and walked towards the window. The sun was higher now, and he could see a young family walking along the side of the lake. One of the children was in a buggy, and the father was pushing it with one hand, while the other was slipped around his wife's waist. He was suddenly gripped by a fierce will to survive. He had to see Elena and the kids again. He wanted them all to be safe again. Nothing else mattered. *Any deal that could deliver that was worth cutting.*

He turned round. Landon, McCormick and Rotanski were all looking at him intensely. Between them, Sam reflected, they represented the combined killing power of the three deadliest intelligence agencies in the world. But there's something else in those diaries. Something that has so far eluded me. *And they think I already know what it is.*

'There's only one deal I'm prepared to make, and this is it,' he said. 'I can't trust any of you. I keep the diaries. I'll store them in a safe place. No one need ever know the gold has been transferred from Russia to Israel. But I hold on to the proof. If anything ever happens to me, my friends are going to assume you guys were responsible. And the diaries are going to be released.'

'Not acceptable,' said Rotanski. The phrase was barked, the way a dog barks when its bone is snatched away from it. 'We need those diaries.'

'It's the only offer I'm making.'

'Then I think you're overestimating your negotiating position.'

He walked to a corner of the room. Picking up a black leather briefcase, he swivelled open the combination lock and pulled out two single sheets of paper. Walking quickly back across the room, he thrust them into Sam's hand. 'A secret military tribunal met last night in Tel Aviv,' said Rotanski. 'As you know, under Israeli law, any member of the armed forces, whether they have resigned or not, can be dealt with by the military courts. In your absence, you were charged with treason, and found guilty.'

Sam glanced down at the paper. Only a few words jumped out at him. 'Samuel Wolfman,' he read silently to himself. 'Sentence: Death.'

He looked back up at Rotanski. 'It's murder,' he said flatly.

'No, it's not,' said Rotanski with a swift shake of the head. 'What you did for us was murder. This is the law.'

Sam put the paper down. His stomach was churning. Even holding the paper made him feel queasy, as if he was giving it some legitimacy.

No man wants to read his own death sentence.

'Now,' Rotanski continued. 'I told you in the mountain when Kersch wanted to kill you that we don't assassinate our own men. We're better than that. But this is the verdict of the court, and whoever I choose to pull the trigger will just be carrying out his lawful orders. So, I give you a simple choice. You give us the diaries, and the sentence need never be carried out. You continue to resist us, and I have no alternative but to make sure it is implemented.'

He paused, and Sam noted the pleasure with which he slipped back into the dry, bureaucratic language of his training. It was as if he was discussing paper clips, not a man's life. He's never been in the field, thought Sam. *He doesn't know what death feels and smells like close up.*

'Immediately,' said Rotanski, finishing with a flourish.

'It makes no difference,' said Sam. He looked at Imer. 'You asked me a question five years ago when I accepted the mission to go undercover: "Can you reconcile yourself to dying?" I told you I could. Then you made another point. "Once a man crosses that line, he can't go back. A part of him will always be on the other side, where the corpses are." And you know what? It's true. I crossed that line five years ago, and I don't think I'll ever find my way back.'

Sam's eyes turned back towards Rotanski. 'So your threats mean nothing to me. It doesn't matter whether you execute me in accordance with your so-called law, or whether you murder me in cold blood. We can make a deal, but it has to be on my terms. That's final.'

'Don't be ridiculous, Sam,' said Imer angrily. 'There's a damned death sentence on you.'

'I said no.'

'You can trust us,' said Imer. 'Tell us where the diaries are and you'll be safe.'

Sam could feel the fury surging through his veins. 'No,' he snapped.

'Well, maybe you don't trust your own people, but you should listen to us,' said Landon. 'This offer is being guaranteed by the CIA. Mossad can't afford to offend us. So, c'mon, man, be reasonable . . .'

It wasn't every day you had the director of the CIA pleading with you. And it wasn't every day you turned him down. *Whatever they want in those diaries must have the explosive power of a nuclear warhead.*

'No,' said Sam coldly.

He turned to look at the lake again. The couple he'd been watching had disappeared, but the lakeside was still dotted with people. As Sam watched them, the will to live remained within him, but it was already qualified. *To live, sure, but only on my terms.*

'If I tell you where the diaries are you'll kill me,' he said. 'Just as soon as you have them. You'll betray me now the same way you betrayed me in Lucerne a few weeks ago.' He paused, turning back from the window. 'Only an idiot allows himself to be betrayed by the same man twice.'

'In Lucerne?' said Rotanski.

Sam could hear the surprise in his voice.

'Who betrayed you in Lucerne?'

'You did,' said Sam. 'You emptied all the money out of my account.'

A thin smile started to crease up Rotanski's lips. 'We don't assassinate our own people,' he said. 'And we don't steal from them either.'

Sam looked straight at him. 'After I said I was quitting the service. I went to the bank to take out the money that had been paid in during the five years I was undercover. But it was all gone.'

'Then it must have been someone else. Because it certainly wasn't Mossad who took your money.'

TWENTY-SEVEN

Sam struggled to control the anger rising in his chest. He didn't mind being drugged. He could tolerate being abducted. He didn't even care much any more if they killed him. *But I'm bloody through with being lied to.*

'I went to the bank in Lucerne,' he said. 'The one you'd been paying my salary into for five years while I was out risking my neck and my soul for my country. And the account was empty.' He stumbled over the word. 'Because you'd bloody taken it all. Only Mossad had access to those accounts.'

'And I'm assuring you that Mossad doesn't steal from its own men,' said Rotanski, his eyes flashing. 'I may have disagreed with your decision to resign from the service. I thought it was weak and short-sighted. But a man gets paid for his work. I may not have many principles, but I've always stuck to that one.'

'Well, somebody took that money. And somebody threatened my daughter.'

Rotanski stood so close to Sam that he could see the stubble on his cheeks. 'I'll tell you who took your money. But there's one string attached.'

'What?' snapped Sam.

'That you take revenge.'

For a moment, Sam remained silent. Then a smile started to spread over his lips: an expression that started in his guts and took a moment to travel up to his lips. 'At last,' he said, 'we're talking the same language.'

'You'll show no mercy?'

'Mossad trained me. Mercy wasn't on the curriculum.'

'I want to hear it from your own lips. No mercy.'

'Who was it?'

Rotanski paused. Likes all spies, he stored information away, hoarding it for the moment when it might turn out to be useful. Smokers don't like to give you a cigarette, drinkers don't share the bottle and misers won't lend you any money, thought Sam. And spies don't like to tell you the truth, even when it was in their own interests.

'Selima Robertson.'

Later, Sam couldn't be sure how long he'd remained silent. The words were there in his throat, but they couldn't make their way to his lips. His mind was working faster than his tongue could keep up.

'If you'd been paying attention,' said Rotanski, with just a hint of a sneer, 'you'd have seen it all along.' There was a mischievous look in his eye. 'How did you first meet her?'

'She came into my shop,' said Sam. 'That was ages ago, before the Hassim hit.'

'For what reason?'

'She wanted me to investigate her stepfather's death. I told her no. I wasn't in that business. Well, I wasn't then.'

Rotanski nodded. 'Then a few days later, the Hassim hit went wrong. Why was that? Because Papa and Le Groupe wanted it that way. They were working with Selima right from the start.

'Selima worked with Papa?'

'Why not? Papa is the biggest criminal in the world, but Robertson ran him a close second. I could never fathom their relationship, but I'm sure they worked together when they needed to.' He looked straight at Sam. 'Next, you went to collect your money. It was gone. She organised that as well?'

'How?'

Rotanski sighed. 'Robertson and Mossad went back a long way together. One of the things that he did for us was create dummy companies throughout Europe that we could use to pay our agents. One of them was the company in Germany we used to pay you.' His eyes remained fixed on Sam. 'So you see, the other party to that account was not Mossad, it was the Robertson family. She wanted you broke, because that would make you desperate for work.' He moved closer to Sam. 'Who introduced you to the Robertson File?'

'Naved,' said Sam. 'I think you know the guy.'

'Ben Naved? Of course I know him. He's another member of the flock that escaped the pen. Did you notice anything strange about him?'

Sam shook his head. 'Not really,' he said. 'Except that he looked very prosperous.'

'Right. And where do you think that money came from?' Rotanski waved a hand, brushing away any possible reply. 'The Robertson family. He was one of their fixers, brokering deals and taking his own slice. He has been for years. If he pointed you in the direction of the Robertson File it was because *she* wanted him to. So she knows for certain that you are going to start investigating. What choice do you have? You're broke, and you don't have many offers of work. Sooner or later you're going to call her because she's already given you her number and asked you to look into her father's death.'

'She didn't return my calls,' said Sam. 'I had to track her down.'

Rotanski laughed. 'A woman likes to be chased. It makes her feel more powerful.' He gave Sam a sly smile. 'She lets you seduce her, because a man is never thinking completely straight once his trousers are down. Then she supplies the critical information. She gives you the key to the safe-deposit box in Luxembourg.'

'Because she knew I'd find out what it was for?'

Rotanski nodded, more to himself than to anyone else. He was enjoying telling the story, Sam thought. Like any craftsman, he could take pleasure in the work of a rival – and Selima, it now appeared, could match any master in the subtle arts of intrigue, manipulation and deception.

'Once you get the disks, you head for Russia to find out what they mean. Along the way, Le Groupe help you out whenever you get into serious difficulties. So, it's obvious. Selima and Le Groupe have been controlling you all along. They played you like a violin. If only I could have recruited her to work for Israel like her stepfather.'

'Some men tried to kill me,' said Sam. 'They were watching his boat. They said they'd been paid by Robertson to eliminate anyone investigating his death.'

'They were paid by the Russians, not Robertson,' said Rotanski. 'After he died, they were terrified of anyone finding out about the gold. So they used local thugs to eliminate anyone getting close to cracking the real mystery of his death.'

'But why did Selima want me to investigate?' asked Sam. 'For the money?'

'The secret stash that her stepfather hid away?' said Rotanski, raising both eyebrows as he spoke. 'I'm not sure it ever existed. There might be a few dozen gold bars hidden away somewhere. In fact, I'm sure there are. But what she really wanted was the disks. I know she knew of their existence and she knew what was on them. Once she has that, she can blackmail us all. Whatever she asks for, we'll give her, rather than have the secret of the gold revealed.' He paused, glancing at Landon and McCormick. 'The secret is her passport back to wealth, status and position. All the things that went down to the bottom of the sea along with her father's corpse.'

Rotanski looked back towards Sam. 'Let me tell you

something about the rich. Anyone born into money has a terrible fear of poverty. The poor don't mind it, because they know it's not so bad. But the rich are scared to death of it. They can't face the humiliation.'

Humiliation, thought Sam, the word rolling around in his mind. *That's an emotion that comes in many different disguises.*

'So you see, Sam,' said Rotanski. 'You got it wrong from the beginning. We weren't your enemy, we never were.'

'You tried to kill me,' said Sam. 'On my way into Israel.'

Rotanski shrugged. 'By then, you were a threat to the state. It doesn't matter whether you were deceived or not, you were still a threat. You'd have made the same decision.'

'What about my daughter? You pinned a picture of her on my door, with a target around her face.'

'I'm not here to answer questions,' said Rotanski. 'Now, are you coming back?'

Sam shook his head. 'First I have to deal with Selima,' he said.

'For Mossad?' said Rotanski.

'No. For myself.' Sam was thinking on his feet, reshuffling his options as the information changed. 'I'll tell you what I'll do. I'll go and get the diaries. I know where they are, and only I can find them. I'll bring them back to you here, and you can destroy them, or lock them up, or do whatever you want with them. The secret will stay safely buried away, just like the gold itself.'

'We will fetch them,' snapped Rotanski. 'Just tell us where they are.'

'No,' said Sam. 'We do it my way. Only I can retrieve them.'

Rotanski paused, then nodded. 'You've got forty-eight hours,' he said. 'That's all. I want to see you back here by three thirty on Thursday afternoon. With the diaries.'

Behind him, Sam could see Landon and McCormick standing up. Their work was done. 'Don't even think about breaking this agreement,' said Landon. 'You'll have the CIA, Mossad and probably the KGB tracking you down. You might be good, but nobody's that good. We'll track you down, and when we do we'll kill you, in front of your family, if necessary.'

Sam nodded curtly. 'I've listened to enough threats in my life to tell the real ones from the bluffs.'

'This one's real,' snapped Landon. 'You better believe it.'

'Forty-eight hours,' said Sam. 'I'll be back.'

Rotanski took a roll of crisp dollar bills from his pocket and handed them to Sam. 'You might need some money,' he said, heading for the door. Landon and McCormick had already left, and Imer was by his side. Then he turned to look back at Sam and smiled. 'I'll need receipts for that money,' he said. 'So make sure you keep them.'

I'm back, thought Sam. *At least, that's what they think.*

With the dollar bills in his pocket, he started to walk from the hotel room. The plan was already taking shape in his mind. The odds of success, he knew, were slim: maybe no more than one in ten. Doesn't matter, he told himself. *A dead man doesn't argue with a second chance.*

TWENTY-EIGHT

He could see the alcohol in her eyes: the traces of red around the edge of the eyelids that only a bottle of wine could leave behind. Selima Robertson stood in the doorway, wearing a long black dress, with a string of bright pearls hanging elegantly from her neck. In the background, Sam could hear some piano music playing.

If I wasn't certain it was impossible, I'd swear she was expecting me.

She looked at Sam, and, after a momentary delay, a brilliant smile flashed on to her face. Yet she remained as inscrutable as ever.

'You better come in,' she said softly.

Sam had been travelling for hours. From Geneva, he'd flown on a scheduled flight to London. On landing, he got a bus to Reading where he retrieved the gun stored in the gym locker plus the disks, then took the train into central London, and checked himself into a cheap hotel so he could shower, shave and change his clothes before taking a cab down to Wimbledon.

When you're planning to kill a woman, you need to look your best.

He stepped into the hallway. Watching the sway of her hips, he followed Selima into the larger of the two sitting rooms that looked out on to the garden. It was just after ten at night, but in London it was never really dark: they were surrounded by the electronic haze of the city, and the lights from the planes descending into Heathrow were clearly visible in the sky. There was just one lamp on in the room, spreading a low light through it, and in one corner a scented candle was burning slowly, filling the room with the smell of charred herbs.

'A drink,' said Selima.

Sam shook his head. He'd trained himself to shoot straight with up to three units of alcohol in his bloodstream, because a bar was often the best place to hole up for a hit, and it looked odd if you stuck to orange juice. But a man's aim was never at its truest when he had alcohol rather than anger in his blood.

She poured some more red wine into her own glass and walked over to the hi-fi. Pressing restart on the CD player, the opening chords of Schubert's *Wanderer Fantasy* filled the room. For a few seconds, both of them just listened to the music, before Selima took a sip on her wine and moved closer to where Sam was standing.

'It's been a while,' she said. 'I was starting to wonder what was happening to my stepfather's disks.'

'They were more trouble than you can imagine.'

Selima laughed. 'I can imagine a hell of a lot of trouble.'

'That may be the only true thing you've ever said to me.'

Her expression changed in an instant. The welcoming look in her eyes closed down, replaced by an ugly mixture of fear and fury. Suddenly, she looked her age. 'What the fuck does that mean?' she said.

'It means you lied to me.'

'How dare you speak to me like that?'

Sam stepped closer, grabbing hold of her wrist. The wine glass fell from her hand, spreading a thick crimson stain out across the soft pale carpet. He twisted the wrist backwards, then yanked it into the air: a simple but effective manoeuvre for inflicting swift and sharp pain on your victim. 'You deceived me right from the start,' he said. 'What was the game?'

'Let go of me,' she snapped.

The rich, Sam noted, were different in the way they reacted to violence. Particularly the women. Where most people were frightened – quite rationally, since they were almost certainly about to be hurt – the rich were angry. They were confronted with somebody who wouldn't obey them – and had no idea how to handle that.

Sam released her hand. There was no need to hurt her any more. *You do it once, then the threat is always there.*

She sank down on the sofa, holding her wrist as if it might have been broken. 'Who the hell do you think you are?' she said.

'An errand boy for the Robertson family,' said Sam. 'And very nearly a corpse as well. Another one to add to the pyre.' He moved closer to her. 'You set me up. Just to get me to do your dirty work for you.'

The scowl on her face was replaced by a smile. 'I told you that on the first day.'

Sam looked at her questioningly.

'I came into your shop looking for a Gastou,' she continued, her tone lightening. 'What did he make?'

'Writing desks,' said Sam.

'What kind?'

Sam shrugged.

'Gastou was famous for making desks with hidden compartments,' she said. 'Little drawers tucked away where a woman could keep her love letters, or any other items she wished to keep to herself.' She laughed. 'He was a keeper of secrets. If you *actually* knew anything about antiques then you would of course have known that.'

Sam dipped his hand into his pocket. He pulled out the Browning FN-49 handgun he had retrieved from his hiding place in Reading, and lifted it slowly into the air. He wanted her to be able to feel its barrel pointing straight at her, to imagine the bullet crashing through her skin and cutting into her bone. He wanted her to realise how close she was to dying, and to start fearing the moment. Only that way would she bend to his will. 'Give me the final disk,' he said.

Selima looked at him, puzzled.

'What? You're being ridiculous.'

'Just bloody give it to me.'

Selima stared hard at him. All traces of the wine she'd been drinking had drained out of her eyes, replaced by a cold, sober assessment of her predicament. She's deciding how tough I am, Sam thought. *Whether I can shoot a woman in cold blood.*

'I don't have it,' she said firmly. 'I don't know what you're talking about.'

'Just give it to me.'

'I can't give you something I don't have.'

Sam took a step closer, the Browning still stretched out in front of him. He could see a bead of sweat forming on her neck, something he'd never seen on her before, not even when they were having sex. 'You chose me because I'm good,' he said slowly. 'So if you think I don't have the guts to shoot you right here and right now then think again. I've shot people who meant nothing to me, and slept well that same night. And you know what? I really haven't enjoyed being jerked around by you. So this bullet is going to be dispatched with pleasure.'

'Listen, Sam —'

'Just bloody give it to me,' snapped Sam, his voice stretched to breaking point.

'I . . . you . . .'

Sam flicked his hand, then squeezed the trigger. Just once. The bullet smashed into the side of the wall, ripping out a chunk of plaster and kicking up a cloud of dust. Selima flinched as she heard the sound of the bullet, and as Sam steadied the gun back on to her, he could see she was shaking. The fear has got to her, he noted with grim satisfaction. Like her stepfather, she has nerves of steel. She can lie as if she was born to it. But the fear gets to everyone eventually, no matter how strong they are. *Nobody wants to meet the bullet with their own name on it.*

'You've got ten seconds,' said Sam. 'Just tell me.'

He could see the hesitation in her face. She was wrestling with herself, trying to decide whether she should reveal the location of the code. And whether, robbed of possession of the secret, she wasn't condemning herself to a life of poverty and despair.

'Ten . . . nine . . .'

Maybe she would rather be dead than poor and powerless, perhaps that's what she decided. *Well, it's her choice.*

'Eight —'

A shot exploded through the room. Sam could see Selima ducking, convinced the bullet was aimed at her. Her whole body shook, and she crumpled to the floor. Sam spun round. The Browning had been knocked clean from his hand. It was lying five feet across the room, a twisted piece of metal. As it struck the floor, a bullet flew from its chamber, smashing into the ceiling, and breaking open a chunk of plaster.

Standing in the doorway was Kersch.

'Don't move a muscle,' he said, walking towards Sam.

Kersch was holding a Russian SVD sniper rifle slung into his arms, and nestling into his right fist there was a tint snub-nosed PSS pistol, developed for the special forces division of the KGB. Glancing at his trousers, Sam reckoned there was at least a grenade in there, and a hunting knife tucked into his shoe. Another pistol was strapped into a shoulder holster underneath his black shirt.

Not taking any chances.

Sam looked into his eyes. This was the third time he had

seen the man, and he could see now the qualities within him that made him the KGB's most trusted executioner. We know one another, he thought to himself grimly. There was a measured pace to the way he was walking towards him. The gun was steady and firm, but the grip relaxed enough for the aim to be true. There was no tension in him, but no joy either. Just work. Most of all, there was a ruthless professionalism. He could kill without compunction, as if he were just wiping up the stain from the carpet.

Like all professional killers, he was absorbed completely in himself. *The lives of other men meant nothing to him.*

'You have no business here,' said Sam.

Kersch nodded towards his gun, then looked back at Sam. 'This is my business,' he said.

'I've made a deal,' said Sam. He could hear the strain in his voice as he spoke. 'This is all agreed with Mossad, the CIA, the British SIS, the works.'

Kersch took another step forward.

'I'm going to deliver to them the diaries that Robertson left behind,' continued Sam. 'And then the secret is safe for ever.'

A thin smile started to spread out across Kersch's lips. 'I work for the KGB, remember,' he said slowly. 'The Cold War is not over yet. Whatever agreements you might have with the CIA or Mossad, they mean nothing to me. We're the enemy, after all.'

His finger was resting on the trigger. Sam glanced into his cold eyes, then looked across at Selima. He could see the tension on her face, as she anticipated the execution. *No one will be more pleased than her when my corpse hits her carpet.*

'I'm here to protect the secret, not to reveal it,' snapped Sam.

'The secret is safe when you're dead,' said Kersch.

'It's safe with the CIA and Mossad.'

Kersch's head swayed from side to side. 'The KGB hasn't

signed up to that agreement, that's why they've sent me here to kill you,' he said. A babyish smile was playing on his lips.

'Just do it,' said Selima. 'You can't trust him. He'll betray you.'

'Don't listen to her,' shouted Sam.

'Quiet,' said Kersch. He took another step forward, looking straight at Sam. 'Christ, you're a fucking assassin, man. You've delivered enough bullets. You should know how to take one.'

Sam stood still.

He closed his eyes.

Somehow, he'd always imagined it would end like this. *Maybe this is the death I deserve.*

A shot.

Another shot.

The raucous music of gunfire was so familiar to Sam that its rhythms, beats and melodies needed no explanation. He knew the explosive sound of a bullet exiting a gun barrel, the split second of silence as it cut through the air, and the sudden crescendo of impact. He steeled himself, expecting the shattering of his skull and the puncturing of his lungs. *That's what I'd do*, he reflected, able for the briefest of seconds to examine his own demise with professional detachment. *One to the head, another to the heart. Make sure the bugger is dead, then put another couple of rounds in him to make sure he stays that way.*

He waited.

A second passed.

Nothing.

Another second.

No bullet takes that long.

Sam heard a scream. A woman's voice. Selima.

He opened his eyes.

Selima was standing right behind him. Alive.

A trickle of red blood was snaking out across the carpet,

sinking into its soft fabric. His eyes followed the trickle until they reached its source.

Kersch.

The Russian was lying face down on the floor. A bullet had struck him in the back of his head, gone clean through him, smashing a hole through the front of his face, and only narrowly missing Sam before lodging itself in the wall opposite.

Standing next to him was Papa's son Jacques, a trail of smoke still evident on the tip of the MAS Mle., the standard pistol of the French Army, gripped to his hand.

And right behind him, propping himself up on a black wooden walking stick, was Papa.

TWENTY-NINE

The old man was walking slowly towards him, his expression serious and determined. With Papa, there was a price to be paid for everything, thought Sam. *For my own life, the bill will be a steep one.*

He remained rooted to the ground. He could see Selima cowering at his side, her expression bewildered. She was a strong woman, but not strong enough for this.

Papa looked down at the body, examining it for a moment with his practised eye. A simple nod of the head confirmed that Kersch no longer existed. Next he glanced at Selima. 'I will, of course, arrange for the carpet to be replaced.'

'I thought you never left France,' said Sam.

He chuckled. 'Not if I can help it. I was last here just after the war. The English still had rationing, of course, which presented a lot of interesting opportunities to a young man such as myself.'

'What brings you here, then?'

Papa looked at him curiously. 'To save your life, of course, Sam,' he said. 'Or didn't you notice?'

'I'm tired of listening to this shit,' snapped Sam.

The old man looked uneasy, thought Sam: he had a wide range of expressions but that one was rarely seen.

'You tricked me right from the start.' He looked towards Selima. 'The pair of you were working together all along.'

Papa walked slowly across the room and sat down on the

sofa. Jacques was at his side, the gun still in his hand, eyeing Sam suspiciously.

'I've made your life worth living, Sam,' said Papa. 'For that you should be grateful.'

The words were choking in Sam's throat as he struggled for a reply. 'I make my own choices about my own life, thanks,' he said sourly.

'That's because you're still young.' Papa shook his head sadly from side to side. 'Sometime I wish I was Chinese. Living somewhere where people respected the views of the old. I've known you for five years, Sam, and I've known your father for longer. Through that time, I've been helpful to you, yes? Of course I have. Why?' He paused, as if thinking through the answer to his own question. 'Because I wanted your money? Sure. But also because I saw something in you. A talent. In our line of business, there's a lot of brawn, and a lot of desire, but a talent is a rare and precious thing.'

He glanced towards the hallway, then, with difficulty, he walked across the room. 'Now,' he said with deliberate care. 'I think you'll find there's a Gastou writing desk somewhere in the house. Probably with a hidden drawer in it.'

He looked towards Selima. 'Are you going to tell us where it is?'

She remained silent.

'I think you should,' added Papa.

There was just a look between them, Sam noted, but it was enough. They communicated through glances, the way married couples do. There was an intimacy between them. Slowly, Selima started to move across the room, stepping over Kersch's prostrate corpse, then out into the hallway.

She turned left, heading for the library and study that overlooked the front lawn. Sam followed her, with Papa and Jacques bringing up the rear. Sam was acutely aware that Jacques was the only one of them with a gun in his hand.

Sam was also well aware that Jacques had never liked him.

Selima switched on the light in the study. The room measured about twenty feet by ten, but it seemed much smaller because it was so cluttered and cramped. Sam had never set foot in this room on his earlier visits to the house. Now he could see why. The room was a shrine to her stepfather. Pictures of him covered the wall, starting with him when he was still a handsome young man during the war, then of his first victory in Parliament, then of him shaking hands with global leaders as Robertson Communications became a media giant. There were headlines from the *Financial Times* and the *Wall Street Journal* recording his deals. And there were mementoes of the different newspapers, broadcasters and publishing houses he acquired as the empire grew.

Right at the back of the room was a Gastou desk. And next to it, a squat, ugly little computer that Sam now recognised instantly.

An Agat.

Sam took a moment to admire the craftsmanship of the desk. It was a beautiful piece of furniture, sculpted from maple, mahogany and oak, and polished until it gleamed. It was inlaid with a decorative motif that seemed to blend perfectly into the wood. He pulled down the front of the desk, and started to examine it. Inside, there was a complex nest of drawers. He opened them, one after another. Nothing.

'French, of course,' said Papa, looking at the open desk. 'We've always been good at hiding things.'

Sam started again. Some of the drawers had false bottoms built into them, a fact you could only establish when you tapped them from underneath. Others had fake sides. Below some of the drawers were hidden chambers, and they too had hidden sides, fake doors and concealed entrances. It was like a maze, thought Sam, a maze constructed from wood, and still impenetrable two hundred years after it was first designed.

'You better tell us where it is,' said Papa to Selima. 'Otherwise, this could take all night.'

Selima's fingers worked swiftly yet delicately. The wood was thin, and old, and all the concealed entrances were latched into place with just a single pin. Nothing could be pulled or yanked: the desk would only reveal its secrets to someone who knew it. Brute force would get you nowhere.

Sam watched her carefully as she pulled aside one piece of wood and then another. Even so, he had lost track by the time she finally stopped. Even if his life depended upon it, he wouldn't have been able to retrace her steps back into the desk.

'Here,' she said, handing over the disk.

Sam wished Breyeva were with him now. Reaching across the desk, he switched the power on to the Agat. The computer hummed into life. Its screen started to glow, and Sam could hear the hard disk scratching as it booted itself up. He slotted the disk just retrieved from the desk into its drive. More scratching. Don't pack up on me now, Sam muttered under his breath. *I need the one reliable Agat in the world.*

One by one, the words started to appear on the screen.

'Read it,' muttered Papa.

Sam started to focus. The Agat has not been used for a couple of years, and the screen was fuzzy. The words were swimming in front of him. One by one, his eyes adjusted to their shape, as their sense began to emerge. This, thought Sam, would be the last anyone ever heard from Max Robertson. *If this didn't tie up the mystery, then it died with him.*

'"14 January 1989,"' read Sam, pronouncing the words, slowly and carefully.

He glanced towards Selima. He could tell it was strange for her, hearing her stepfather's words on another man's lips. Her eyes were cast down on the floor, but her expression was intent: she'd gambled her life, and his, to force these disks to reveal their secrets, and she didn't want to miss a word now.

' "I have just landed in Moscow," ' continued Sam. ' "The weather is beastly, worse even than you expect from Russia in the winter. The airport was closed to commercial flights because of the snow, and it was only on Trusov's orders that it was opened for me. The landing was rocky, and the runway hadn't been properly cleared. Three Zil limousines were waiting for me, whisking me straight to my private suite. Some champagne and caviar was waiting for me, just as I would have expected, and I managed a decent night's sleep before the real work of my visit began." '

Sam paused, taking a deep breath, as the Agat slowly processed the words and spat them out on the screen.

' "15 January 1989. I spent the day with Trusov, reviewing the success of our mission so far. I must say, I am pleased with our progress. History will recall that Max Robertson was one of the men who helped to shape decisively the twentieth century. And I commit these words to silicon, safe in the knowledge that the codes that are used to encrypt them are absolutely impenetrable. Because what I am about to write must, of course, remain absolutely secret. The power they would confer on anyone who read them would be too terrifying to contemplate. Which is why only Max Robertson should ever be in complete possession of all the facts. No one else could ever be trusted to know the full truth, nor to use the power it would confer wisely. It is quite possible I am the only man in the world who can see clearly what is needed. It is a heavy responsibility, but I bear it well. The world is fortunate to have a man such as myself working on its behalf in times as troubled as these are.

' "We started with morning tea. Ever since our work together started, Trusov and I have been engaged in a game of bluff and double bluff. He is a secret policeman, and I am

340

a businessman, so we both know the rules of that trade." '

Sam reached across the desk for a water jug. He took a sip, letting it clear his throat. He was suddenly aware of the pictures of Robertson that surrounded him, the dead man's face peering suspiciously down on him from each side of the room.

' "Trusov was in melancholy mood. The system was reaching its last days, he told me. People were starting to trickle out of East Germany. They were making their way to Yugoslavia, then leaking out to the West. The Stasi had been told to stop them, but they lacked the will. It wasn't like the old days, he lamented. He'd offered to open up the camps in Siberia – they were all still there, still working, you just had to freshen up the barbed wire – but had been ignored. That was what they needed. Three hundred, maybe four hundred thousand East Germans and Poles sent to the camps. That would put some discipline into them, make them respect the party once again. But it wasn't going to happen. Socialism, ultimately, was about fear. The founders of the state had understood it, and the KGB had always been true to that insight. Their leaders had forgotten it: and without that truth, they were ultimately doomed.

' "That was as far as our small talk went. The gold had all been shipped now. All twenty-five thousand boxes of it. 'Max,' he said to me. 'We have come to trust each other over these last few months, so I feel I can speak freely to you.' 'Of course you may,' I replied. 'When I sold this plan to the rest of the party leadership, there were many questions I had to answer. In the KGB, we always pride ourselves on preparing for every eventuality, and this must be no different. Our big question was always, what should we do if the Israelis betray us? What happens if we ask them for the gold one day, and they just laugh at us? Then we should feel like fools, no?' 'You have the Jewish population of Russia and the Ukraine,' I replied. 'I thought that was to be the understanding. The gold would be guaranteed on the life of the five million Soviet Jews. If the Israelis tampered with the gold, you would punish those Jews. Heaven knows, we all know you're capable of that. It has happened often enough in the past. And ultimately the whole point of the state of Israel is to prevent more pogroms, more holocausts. They would never risk it.'

'"Trusov looked at me, and suddenly I could see in his eyes the qualities that had allowed him to rise to the top of the KGB, and to control that most ruthless of organisations for more than a decade: there was a thread of steel running through him that suggested no act was too cruel, no betrayal too monstrous, for him not to embrace it if it advanced his own cause by a single inch. 'No,' he said slowly. 'They have to let us check the gold. Once a year. And you, Max, have to arrange it.'"'

THIRTY

Sam paused. He could feel the silence in the room. Looking up at the clock, it was now eleven fifty. The day had almost expired, and soon, he sensed, the mystery would too. Robertson confided everything to this diary.

Sam started to read again.

' "16 January 1989. It started simply enough. The boats were ploughing their way across the Mediterranean, shipping the gold out of Russia and across to Israel. The empire was becoming more and more stretched. Ever since the stock market collapsed in 1988, the business has been under more and more pressure. The adverts aren't coming in. Circulations have been falling. I've shouted and raged at the managers but it makes no difference. I've changed a dozen editors in the last month alone, but each one is just as useless as the last. The cash flow just isn't there.

' "The bankers have been getting more and more restless. Over the years, I've hardened myself to the timid, insignificant squealings of financiers. They are small men, and once you have got your hands on their money you can usually treat them like the dirt they are. This time it's different, however. One of the French banks is threatening to seize one of the British titles. A German bank is demanding a fresh round of mortgages on all the properties. A British bank has closed all our financing facilities and is refusing to reopen them. It was only when I pleaded with the chairman that he agreed not to publish details: in the

343

City, that in itself would destroy what confidence remains in the company.

' "So I decided to borrow some of the gold." '

Sam hesitated, his eyes moving momentarily away from the screen of the Agat. A thief, he thought. He spent his life stealing from people. *It was in his blood.*

Sam returned his eyes to the screen. ' "Two crates were all I took in the first load. The *Guinea* was sent out from Athens to meet Ryazanov's boat as it journeyed out towards the Israeli coast. The boxes were deposited on board, then the *Guinea* sailed across to Sicily. The gold was sold to one of the local dealers there, a man called Giorgio Vicenzi who I first met when I was liberating his country from the Nazis. He paid me 1.5 million dollars in cash, money which I then deposited in one of my bank accounts in Geneva. Through a company there, I started booking ad space in some of the newspapers, funnelling the money into the company. Within days, there was enough cash in the accounts to stop the French bank from calling in its loans.

' "Once you start it's hard to stop. One part of me knew it was foolish, yet I have never viewed risk in the way that ordinary men have. My life has been built around it. I have an appetite for it, the way a wolf has an appetite for meat. On the next trip, I loaded the *Guinea* with ten crates. Vicenzi couldn't handle that much gold. It had to be distributed carefully around Europe, placed with different dealers and middlemen so as not to cause too much of a stir in the market. Within a month, I had taken and laundered 250 million dollars in gold. Most of it was funnelled through different accounts, and made its way into the company. Business was so bad that its appetite for cash just grew and grew. It was a monster that was impossible to feed. Only a small portion of the money was put aside for my own personal funds. And now Trusov wants to inspect the gold in the mountain. But at least 10 per cent of it is missing." '

Sam stopped. The words on the screen had stopped. He jabbed his fingers on the keyboard, scrolling down on the document to find the rest of the file. The words slowly took shape on the screen. Taking a sip of water, Sam started to read on.

' "17 January 1989. Even as I arrived in Tel Aviv, I was already starting to sense that I might have taken a step too far. On the plane I was reading an article in the *Wall Street Journal* about the sudden drop in the price of gold as new supplies mysteriously came on to the market. There were rumours that one of the central banks might have started selling to drive the price down. Of course, only Max Robertson knows the truth. The others are just fools.

' "I told Rotanski straight to his face. We were meeting at my suite in the Hilton. He was friendly enough, congratulating me on the job I had done, and of my importance to the state of Israel. Then, I said that Trusov wanted to send inspectors into the mountain to inspect the gold. 'It would be impossible, of course, I told him. Israel would never allow the Russians to come into the mountain. They would see our nuclear secrets.' 'On the contrary, I have no problem with that,' said Rotanski swiftly. 'I expected it. Their men can be shown into the vaults by a discreet route. Tell them it can be arranged.' 'There may be one problem,' I told him. 'I have diverted some of the gold to the accounts of Robertson Communications. Don't worry, it will be perfectly safe. We'll just have to delay Trusov until it can be replaced. It is a matter of a few months, that's all.' 'You have betrayed us,' he snapped. 'I betray nobody,' I bellowed. But Rotanski had already left the room.

' "18 January 1989. This morning, a car arrived at my suite. It took me straight to the headquarters of Mossad. I was shown straight up to Rotanski's private office. There were no pleasantries. He told me that overnight he had spoken with Trusov. He had told him nothing about the missing gold. But they had spoken about the security within the mountain. It had been made clear to him that if there was any question of the gold being tampered with there would be a terrible price to pay. It was not just an issue of retaliation against the Jews still living in the Soviet Union. There would be direct retaliation against Israel itself, up to and including the use of nuclear weapons. He looked at me. 'At this moment, you may well have put the state of Israel in the gravest peril it has ever been in. I want that gold back in forty-eight hours, or there will be a terrible price to pay.' For once I realised there was no line I could spin, nor any excuses I could fabricate out of thin air. 'It will be done,' I told him as I left his office.

' "But, of course, it won't. The gold isn't there. The money has all been spent. People will always believe that I have some secret store of money hidden somewhere. Apart from one Luxembourg account, there's nothing. It has all been spent.

' "19 January 1989. Today I am retreating for the *Guinea*. We are anchored some way from the Italian coast. I believe Mossad can't find me here. The sea is wide and deep, and can still hide a man if he chooses. I have been here for twenty-four hours, contemplating my fate. My options are evaporating fast. There is no prospect of getting the gold back. It is all sold. The company is still devouring cash. I stand on the brink of ruin. Whoever reads this document will know that fifty million dollars in gold bullion has been deposited in the account of Arbonne Holdings, a Luxembourg-controlled trust company. In the next few hours I will disappear from this boat, slipping ashore with nothing except for a new passport, a credit card in a fake name and the clothes that I am wearing. Just as I was in 1944, I will be a man with nothing but my own wits and guile to guide me. Except that I will have a lifetime's experience, and money stored in a secret bank account. I will use it to stage my own revival – just like the Communists who shipped it out of Russia in the first place. *If Mossad doesn't get to me first.*" '

Sam stopped reading. The document had finished, and so had the story. They knew now why Max Robertson had to die. He had placed Israel at risk. There weren't many crimes Mossad would forgive, and that certainly wasn't one of them.

There never was any secret stash of money. Apart from the account in Luxembourg which Selima must have been accessing herself – and presumably making the withdrawals he'd seen – there would be nothing to report back to Dowler. I'm not going to get the five million, he thought bitterly. For the last few weeks, I've been risking my neck for other people's causes. *Just as I was for Mossad.*

He turned round, looking first at Papa and then at Selima. 'Was she using you, or you her?' he asked.

'We all use each other,' Papa said. 'I knew there was some secret surrounding Robertson's death. Everyone knew that. I knew Selima probably knew about it but wouldn't tell me. So let's say I encouraged and assisted her. I suggested your name, because I knew you were the one man in the world with the strength and resourcefulness to get at those KGB codes, and so decode the diaries. Once she set you on the trail, then I knew in time the secret would emerge. And Le Groupe would be there to collect it.'

'For what purpose?' asked Sam.

Papa smiled. 'Secrecy is ultimately the source of all power. Think of the power this knowledge bestows on the man who possesses it. Start with the Russians. Anyone wants to smuggle anything into or out of Russia, they merely have to drop a quiet word with the authorities that they know about the gold, and suddenly they are immune from arrest. And trust me, a few men are going to get very, very rich in Russia in the next few years. Then there are the KGB archives. They've been spying on the entire world for eighty years. The greatest treasure trove in the world to a man such as myself. Whoever knows about the gold should be able to get into them. If this secret were ever to emerge, the Russians would be bankrupted. They will do anything for the man who is keeping the secret safe for them.'

Sam could see that he was starting to hit his stride: outlining a conspiracy stripped away the years from his face, until his expression was as fresh and as clear as a baby's.

'Then the Israelis,' Papa continued. 'They, of course, are equally desperate to keep this secret from emerging. Israel is the real power that controls the Middle East. Think of all those billions of petrodollars swilling around that part of the world. All the trade routes, all the smuggling scams, all the money-laundering loopholes – the Israelis know them all. And now they are indebted to us.'

Papa chuckled to himself. 'Next, there are the British and Americans to consider. They too would rather this secret was never revealed. And so they too are in our debt. A small favour here, a blind eye turned there. It all helps.' He looked at Sam. 'All the great powers of the world are colluding in keeping this secret under wraps. And the best thing of all is that it is controlled by Le Groupe.'

'And you'd use it?'

'You still have a few things to learn. A secret is like a moment. Once it's used, it's gone and you can't ever reclaim it.'

'If you can't use, then what's the purpose of it?'

'It is time you took a step up from being the hired gun of Mossad,' said Papa sharply. 'The world is controlled by secrets. Nothing is what it appears to be. I started my career in the sewers of Paris. And you know what, I've never really left them. There is the world of the surface, where most people live. Then there is the underground world, the world inhabited by people like me, where the truth is revealed.'

He rose from his chair, nodding at Jacques, who rose as well, following his father slowly as they left the room. 'And you know the greatest secret of them all?' Papa laughed. 'That all the secrets are known to Le Groupe. We store them away, and then when we need them, we deploy them to our own advantage.'

'I just plan to stay alive,' said Sam.

Papa nodded. 'With the right kind of secrets locked up inside his head, a man may do that for a very long time. No matter what the odds stacked up against him. We have one more thing to do now.' He looked at Jacques, then at Selima. 'We must get rid of the body.'

Sam watched as Selima followed him back towards the main sitting room. The lights were dim, and the scented candle had burnt out in the corner, but Kersch's body was still clearly visible lying stretched out on the floor. The blood had stopped seeping from his corpse, and the stain on the carpet had already started to thicken and dry. Selima was standing next to it, looking down distastefully. Her eyes were flicking, from the corpse to Papa. Suddenly her expression changed. From distate, to dread.

Sam suddenly realised what was happening – too late.

Jacques had pulled his MAS from inside his pocket. The first shot struck Selima on the side of her head, crashing into the bones of her cheek, crumpling them into a bloody pulp. Sloppy work, thought Sam, surprising even himself that his first reaction was a professional critique. The first shot should always be to the body. There is less chance of missing. And at least your victim should be disabled. *Ready for the next shot.*

'No . . .' she cried, her arms flailing out towards him.

Sam steadied his ground. She was looking directly at him, her eyes appealing for help. He remained rock still. His very stance was enough of an answer, he reflected: he wasn't prepared to twitch so much as a muscle to help her. She didn't deserve it. She should have known that the same fate awaited her as awaited her stepfather. *The secret had a life of* its own: it would take as many victims as was necessary to defend itself.

The second shot hit her in the forehead, throwing her head back with the impact of the bullet. The third struck in the neck, smashing open a hole in her windpipe. Sam was surprised at how poor a shot Jacques was, since he had managed to destroy Kersch with just two bullets.

Maybe that's why Papa doesn't completely trust his own son. *A man who can't shoot straight can't think straight either.*

Selima crumpled to the floor. Blood was seeping from her wounds, spreading out across the carpet, and the room was starting to fill with the wet, fleshy smell of an abattoir. Sam had witnessed plenty of killings, yet had seldom stuck around long to look at the bodies. Papa and Jacques looked completely at ease, he noted.

'Am I next?' said Sam, turning to face Papa.

His tone was cool and even, as if he was already reckoning on a fateful answer.

'You? Why?'

'You shot her because she knew the secret. Right?' said Sam. 'Well, so do I.'

'But you are now a member of Le Groupe.'

Sam shook his head. 'I don't belong to any organisation,' he said firmly. 'Nor do I ever want to join one. Not again.'

Papa smiled. 'But everyone who knows the secret belongs to Le Groupe. Regardless of whether they want to or not.' He paused. 'She betrayed me by not giving me that disk. But you will always do what I want.'

Sam nudged the door of the hotel room open.

His eyes swept through the room, checking it swiftly.

Nothing.

The place was empty.

He went inside quickly, and shut the door behind him. He'd hung on to the key of room 321 of the Hôtel des

Bergues, and none of the staff in the lobby had given him more than a cursory glance as he walked through the lobby. There were six hours to go before the appointed hour for his rendezvous with Rotanski. *Enough time to leave what I want to leave. And to make a clean getaway.*

He moved over to the window. Slowly, he started to feel the curtain. Nothing. Surely Rotanski wouldn't leave this room without any bugs in it. He must be watching me. *From somewhere.*

Sam checked the bed, then the bathroom.

Clean.

He shrugged. *It means nothing.*

Opening the small briefcase he was carrying with him, he took out the four disks and the printout he had made of Max Robertson's diary. He placed them down on the coffee table. On top, he put the handwritten note he had prepared on his journey here.

'Sorry not to make our appointment. Here are the diaries you wanted. Have I made a spare copy and hidden it somewhere? Do I know about the secret? Have I arranged for it to be revealed in the event of my death? You'll only find out if something happens to me. This case is closed.'

Sam walked briskly from the room, making sure it was locked behind him. He ignored the lift, taking the back staircase back down to the lobby, then strode casually from the hotel. He dropped the key on the floor as he left. *One of the cleaners will find it soon enough,* he told himself.

Outside, Sam stepped into the cool, fresh spring air, and headed towards the lake. A boat was leaving in a few minutes. *Step on to that, and I disappear for ever. And from now on, I work only for myself.*

EPILOGUE

Sam could tell within seconds that the man wasn't going to buy anything. It was written in the way he walked through the shop. He was thin, with greying hair, and skin that looked as if he showered in dishwater every morning. He was wearing a flimsy black suit and scuffed shoes. Yet in his hand there was an immaculate black leather holdall, with a polished brass lock: the kind of case that has something valuable inside it.

Mossad? thought Sam. No. It was more than a year now since he had left Rotanski that note in Geneva. He had not heard from his former employers since then. If they were sending him a message, it wouldn't be here, and it wouldn't be like this.

It would be an inch of hardened steel fired from the barrel of a gun.

Sam watched the man closely. He was trying to feign interest in some of the items, but making a poor show of it. It was six months now since Sam had reopened the shop. The five million reward for closing the Robertson File had never materialised: Dowler said there was no proof of what had happened to him, and Sam knew it was too risky to reveal the truth. He'd scraped together the money anyway, borrowing from everyone he knew, and had enough to retake the lease on the building and put some stock into it. It was tough, and since the start of 1991 the economy had hardly been in great shape, but he was starting to make a living. It was OK.

I'm out of the spying game, anyway. And I plan to stay out.

'Is your name Sam Wolfman?' said the man shuffling towards the desk.

Sam nodded.

'We need to talk.'

'What about?'

'I have something I might be able to sell you.'

Sam shrugged. It was in the case, he could tell that already. And he wasn't interested. He could tell that as well.

'Can we speak in private?'

Sam led him through to the back office. It was just after five in the afternoon. Upstairs, he could hear Elena giving the kids their supper. Samantha was refusing to eat her vegetables. Again. Sam smiled to himself and sat down beside the desk. The same stack of papers that was always there was towering in front of him. He felt a twitch of guilt as he caught sight of the VAT return that still hadn't been filled in. Later, he told himself. After I've dealt with this joker.

'What is it?' said Sam.

The man bent over, his back clearly causing him pain as he did so. He couldn't have been even fifty, but looked in bad shape. Unclasping the brass lock, he reached inside the bag, and pulled out an oval-shaped object, just bigger than his fist, and encrusted with gold, enamel and diamonds. Even in the dim light of the back office, it glimmered and sparkled, lighting up the room with its brilliance.

'You know much about Fabergé eggs?'

'Some,' said Sam quietly. 'Not enough to know whether it's real or a fake.'

The man nodded, putting the egg down on the desk. For a moment, Sam could not help but be captivated by its intricate craftsmanship and beauty. 'Between 1885 and 1916 the firm of Peter Carl Fabergé made eggs for all their wealthy clients in Russia,' he stated. 'They also made fifty

Imperial eggs for Tsar Alexander and his family. This is an Imperial egg.'

'How can I tell?'

'Under Imperial rules, any gold detail of more than two grams had to have its own separate assay mark. Then, Fabergé put his own assay of 56 on the gold, and next to it another mark with a sceptre and two anchors, the symbol of the city of St Petersburg, where the egg would have been made if it was authentic.' He paused, glancing up at Sam. 'Take a look. It's genuine all right.'

Sam shook his head. 'I'm not interested.'

A look of disappointment crossed the man's face. 'For a man who was willing to pay cash, not ask too many questions and mind his own business, this egg might be available at a very attractive price,' he said. 'The man who bought it would make himself a handsome profit.'

'I told you, I'm not interested,' said Sam flatly.

'There are lots of deals to be done in Russia,' said the man. He leaned forward, resting his elbows on the desk. His expression turned conspiratorial. 'The old order is collapsing over there. A few people are going to make a lot of money in the next few years. The clever ones. And the quick ones.'

Sam laughed. 'Well, I'm slow and stupid. And that's how I like it.'

The man's eyes narrowed. 'I think the Robertson family might think differently.'

A secret, thought Sam to himself. It doesn't matter how deeply you bury it, it always struggles back to the surface somehow. *Even the dead don't know how to keep their mouths shut.*

Sam stood up and escorted the man to the door. 'This shop is closing for the night,' he said firmly. 'You'll have to take your business elsewhere.'